J. Sadlier

The Poems of Thomas Dàrcy McGee

With Copious Note

J. Sadlier

The Poems of Thomas Dàrcy McGee
With Copious Note

ISBN/EAN: 9783741182341

Manufactured in Europe, USA, Canada, Australia, Japa

Cover: Foto ©Andreas Hilbeck / pixelio.de

Manufactured and distributed by brebook publishing software
(www.brebook.com)

J. Sadlier

The Poems of Thomas Dàrcy McGee

THE

POEMS

OF

THOMAS D'ARCY McGEE.

WITH COPIOUS NOTES.

Also an Introduction and Biographical Sketch,
By MRS. J. SADLIER.

I'd rather turn one simple verse
  True to the Gaelic ear,
Than classic odes I might rehearse
  With Senates list'ning near.
                              McGee.

Read from some humbler poet,
  Whose songs gush from the heart;
As rain from the clouds of summer,
  Or tears from the eyelids start;
Who, through long days of labor,
  And nights devoid of ease,
Still heard in his soul the music
  Of wonderful melodies.
                              Longfellow.

LONDON: NEW YORK: MONTREAL:
D. & J. SADLIER & CO., 31 BARCLAY STREET.
BOSTON:—P. H. BRADY, 149 TREMONT STREET.
MONTREAL:—COR. NOTRE DAME AND ST. FRANCIS XAVIER STREET.

Stereotyped by VINCENT DILL,
25 & 27 New Chambers St., N. Y.

PREFACE.

Tme poems which are now for the first time presented in a collective form to the public, were gathered together from various parts of the Old and the New World. Very many of them were written for the Dublin *Nation*, as well under Mr. Sullivan's as Mr. Duffy's editorial management. It seemed to be one of Mr. McGee's most lingering fancies, to keep up his connection all his life long with the far-famed journal in whose brilliant pages he had made his name as a poet. The several volumes of the journals he himself edited, namely, the New York *Nation*, the *American Celt*, and the *New Era*, Mrs. McGee supplied from his own library. Some of the poems appeared in Duffy's *Hibernian Magazine*, to which he was also an occasional contributor, and others in the *Boston Pilot*. Many of the best of his later poems were written for the *New York Tablet*, the last journal with which he was connected ; not a pecuniary connection, but simply one of friendship, and community of thought and feeling with its conductors, one of whom has the sad privilege of editing his poems. I am indebted to the Messrs. Sullivan, of the Dublin *Nation*, Mr. Donahoe, proprietor of the *Boston Pilot*, and several private friends of Mr. McGee's, for transcribed copies of poems ; also to Mr. Meehan, of the New York *Irish American*, for files of Duffy's *Nation*, without which I could not have completed my collection. By Major Maher, of New Haven, Ct., I was loaned the missing volume of the *American Celt* for 1852. Those written for the *Boston Pilot* were, of course, juvenile productions, lacking the grace and finish we find in those of his later years. These I have placed as a

poems are still wanting, as I observed on the author's lists of his poems the names of some that I could nowhere find—some, too, of the most valuable—such as "The Spoiling of Armorica," "St. Bridget and St. Flaine," "Earl Sigud and his Sons," "The Vale of Angels," "The Dog of Aughrim," "The Isle of St. Iberius," and other historical poems. Should any of these be found hereafter, they will be given in another edition.

In the arrangement of the poems, I have followed the actual course ot our poet's mind. I have placed the Patriotic poems first, the Legendary and Historical next, then the Poems of the Affections, the Occasional or Miscellaneous, and lastly, the Religious, which, happily for him, represented the last phase of his mind. The Historical Poems, it will be seen, I have arranged chronologically, following the course of the history of the Irish Celts, including their life in their new American home.

The Biographical Sketch being merely intended as a key to the poems, I would respectfully request the reader to read it first, then the Introduction, which will prepare the way for the poems themselves.

Some errors will be detected by critics in the *rhyme* of certain of the poems, none, however, in the *rhythm*, which, in all, is perfect. I have done what I legitimately could to correct errors, which the author himself would have done in a general revision, had he lived to prepare his works for publication. Some of the defects in rhyme I could not venture to correct without taking unwarrantable liberties with the author's thought.

The editing of these scattered remains of a genius all too soon extinguished in death, was truly a labor of love to one who knew the lamented author long and well, and from an intimate knowledge of his many noble qualities of head and heart, set a high value on his friendship. This collection of his poems is as complete as I could make it, and such as it is, I commend it to public favor as a volume of genuine poetry, springing from a heart that was deeply imbued with a love of the beautiful, tho good, the heroic.   M. A. S.

New York, November 18, 1869.

CONTENTS.

HISTORICAL AND LEGENDARY POEMS:

MISCELLANEOUS POEMS:

BIOGRAPHICAL SKETCH
OF THE AUTHOR.

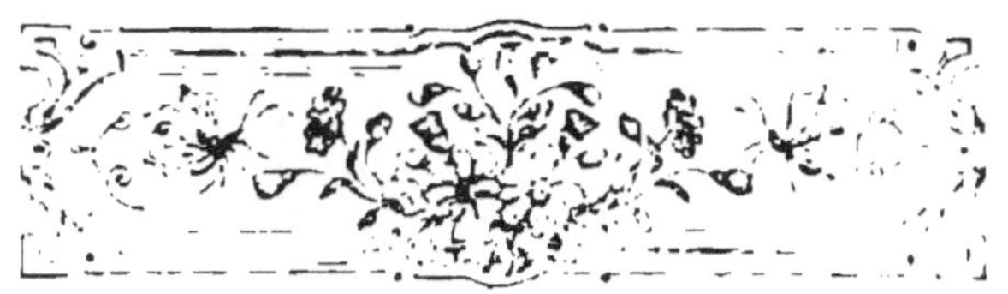

BIOGRAPHICAL SKETCH.

THOMAS D'ARCY McGEE, whose poems are now for the first time presented in a collective form to the public, was born at Carlingford, County Louth, Ireland, on the 13th day of April, 1825. His father, Mr. James McGee, then in the Coast Guard Service, had married Miss Dorcas Catherine Morgan, the highly-educated daughter of a Dublin bookseller, who had been imprisoned and financially ruined by his participation in the conspiracy of 1798.* Of this union, Thomas D'Arcy was the fifth child and second son. Born and nurtured amid the grand and lovely scenery of the Rosstrevor coast, his early childhood fleeted by in a region of wild, romantic beauty, which impressed itself forevermore on his heart and mind, and tended not a little, as we may well suppose, to foster, if not create, that poetic fancy which made the charm of his life, and infused itself into all he wrote and all he said. He was eight years old when the family removed to the historic town of Wexford, where the elder Mr. McGee had received a more lucrative appointment.

* " Both on the father and mother's side," says a biographer of Mr. McGee, " he was descended from families remarkable for their devotion to the cause of Ireland. With the exception of his father, all the men of the families on both sides were ' United Irishmen.' "—See " Short Sketch of the Life of Hon

Soon after their removal to Wexford, the McGee family sustained a heavy blow in the death of the accomplished and most exemplary wife and mother. The rare worth and the varied attainments of this lady may be estimated by the profound respect, the more than filial affection, so to say, with which her eminent son cherished her memory all the days of his life. Of his father he was wont to speak as an honest, upright, religious man ; but his mother he loved to describe as a woman of extraordinary elevation of mind, an enthusiastic lover of her country, its music, its legends, its wealth of ancient lore. Herself a good musician and a fine singer, it was to the songs of her ancient race she rocked her children's cradle, and from her dear voice her favorite son, the subject of our sketch, drank in the music—the sweet old Gaelic melody—that rings in all his poetical compositions, as a lingering echo from the past. His passionate and inextinguishable love for the land of his birth, her story and her song, may be traced, and was ever traced by himself, to the same source. Even the strong and vigorous, yet simple religious faith, which was one of the mother's characteristics, was no less discernible in her son—at every stage of his life manifesting itself in profound respect for religion and its ministers, and for everything that men should hold sacred here below ; while the fervent piety of the true Irish mother is happily found reflected in the truly religious tone of all his latest poems.

The loss of such a mother, it is needless to say, was keenly felt by such a son ; and through all the changeful years of his after-life, her gentle memory shone like a star through the clouds and mists that never fail to gather round the path of advancing life.

But the mother slept in her quiet grave in the old Cistercian Abbey, and years rolled over the head of our young genius developing itself year by year without other aids than a day-school in Wexford afforded, the higher advantages of education being as yet beyond the reach of the middle classes in Ireland, unless a religious vocation called their sons to Maynooth.　But the boyish years of the future statesman and historian were not passed in mean or frivolous pursuits.　His love for poetry and for old-world lore grew with his growth, and by the age of seventeen he had read all that had come within his reach relating to the history of his own and other lands.　He had read of Washington, and of the great country beyond the Atlantic where Freedom had established her throne, and where the oppressed of all nations found a welcome, a home, and equal laws for all.　He knew that many of his race had there found fame, and wealth, and honor; and seeing little prospect of advancement at home, he emigrated to America, with one of his sisters.　He was little over seventeen when, after a short visit to his aunt in Providence, R. I. (the only sister of his much-loved mother), he arrived in Boston, just at the time when the "Repeal movement" was in full strength amongst the Irish population of that city, warmly aided by some of the prominent public men of America of that day. It was in June, 1842, that our young Irish poet arrived in Boston.　When the 4th of July came round, the roar of artillery and the gladsome shouts of the multitude, the waving of flags, and the general jubilation of a people who had freed themselves, fired his youthful imagination.　It seemed to him that what he saw that day was but the foreshadowing of similar scenes in his own beloved land.

Thomas D'Arcy McGee addressed the people that day, and the eloquence of the boy-orator enchained the multitudes who heard him then, as the more finished speeches of his later years were wont

A day or two after, our young exile was offered, and accepted, a situation in connection with the *Boston Pilot*, of which widely-circulated Irish-American journal he became chief editor some two years later, just when the Native-American excitement was at its height, and the American people were about to witness the disgraceful riots in Philadelphia which resulted in the sacking and burning of two Catholic churches. It was a critical period in the history of the Irish race in America; they were proscribed and persecuted on American soil, and were once again, as of old in their own land, obliged to defend their lives, their property, their churches. Few were then their defenders in the press of America, but of those few stood foremost in the van Thomas D'Arcy McGee, a host in himself. With all the might of his precocious genius, and all the fire of his fervid eloquence, he advocated the cause of his countrymen and co-religionists, and so scathing were his fiery denunciations of the Native Americans, as the hostile party were styled, that all New England rang with their unwelcome echo. This outburst of fanaticism at length subsided and passed away, but the popularity which the young Irish editor and orator had gained during the struggle continued to grow and flourish. The Repeal agitation was then at its height both in Ireland and America, and again the *Boston Pilot* and T. D. McGee took a leading part. By his speeches at Repeal meetings, his lectures delivered all through New England, and his already powerful pen, our young "Wexford boy," as he was often called, rendered so good service to the cause he loved, that his fame crossed the Atlantic and reached O'Connell himself, who, at some of the public meetings of the day, referred to his splendid editorials as "the inspired writings of a young exiled Irish boy in America." So mightily had his fame increased, that he was

then as now one of the leading Irish journals—to become its editor. No offer could be more acceptable to Mr. McGee, as none could have been more flattering, or more in accordance with his heart's dearest wish, to do something for the advancement of his native land. But what a change in his fortunes! Three years before he had left his home by the Slaney side to better his fortune in the New World : he had left Ireland unnoticed and unknown ; he returned radiant with fame, his youthful brow already crowned with the laurels he had won in defence of his people at home and abroad, called to aid the greatest of patriots and his associates in the cause of Irish freedom.

So, at the age of twenty, our poet-journalist took his place in the front rank of the Irish press. But the *Freeman* was too moderate in its tone, too cautious, as it were, for the fervid young patriot ; and finding that he was not at liberty to change its character or its course, he gladly accepted the offer of his friend Charles Gavin Duffy to assist him in editing the *Nation*, in conjunction with Thomas Davis, John Mitchel, and Thomas Devin Reilly.

In such hands the *Nation* soon became the great organ of the National party, the mouth-piece of all the fervent aspirations of what was called "Young Ireland." Perhaps no journal was ever published in any country with such a galaxy of genius shining on its pages. Like a magnet, it drew to itself men and women of all their race the most brilliantly endowed with the gifts of mind. Their names became household words—words of pride and power— amongst the Irish people. The poetry of the *Nation*, even more than its prose, was read and quoted everywhere, and its voice stirred the people like a trumpet's sound. The immediate result was the secession of the War party, represented by the *Nation*, from the ranks of the National or Old

who had done much for his country, and would have done more, in all human probability, were it not for this fatal secession of the younger and more ardent spirits who had been wont to follow his banner.

But the end came, and a sad end it was. The great "Liberator" died, while on foreign travel, a broken-hearted man. Famine had stricken the land of Erin, and her people, made desperate by despair, were judged by the "Young Irelanders" ripe for rebellion. Mr. McGee, who was secretary of the Committee of the Confederation, was one of those deputed by his party to rouse the people to action; and after the delivery of a stirring address at Roundwood, in the county of Wicklow, he was arrested, but succeeded soon after in obtaining his release. Nothing daunted by this first mishap, he agreed to go to Scotland for the purpose of enlisting the active sympathies of the Irish in the manufacturing towns, and obtaining their co-operation in the contemplated insurrection.* He was in Scotland when the news reached him that the "rising" had been attempted in Ireland, and had signally failed—that some of the leaders had been arrested, and a reward offered for the apprehen-

---

* Amongst other accusations brought against Mr. McGee by his bitter and unscrupulous enemies, is that of having betrayed his trust, or, at least, sadly mismanaged his Scotch mission—"the Dumbarton affair," as they call it. Happily, we have on record the public testimony of Mr Duffy, by whom, amongst others, he was sent on that mission, that he had acquitted himself with honor and fidelity of the duties it imposed upon him. These are his words, well known indeed, but ever fresh, because so true:

"To forty political prisoners in Newgate, when the world seemed shut out to me forever, I estimated him" (meaning Mr. McGee) "as I do to-day. I said, 'If we were about to begin our work anew, I would rather have his help than any man's of all our confederates. I said he could do more things like a master than the best amongst us since Thomas Davis; that he had been sent, at the last hour, on a perilous mission, and performed it not only with unflinching courage, but with a success which had no parallel in that era; and, above all, that he has been systematically blackened by the Jacobins to an extent that would have blackened a saint of God. Since he has been in America, I have watched his career, and one thing it has never wanted—a fixed devotion to

sion of himself, and others who had effected their escape. These were sad tidings for our ardent young patriot—sadder all the more for that he had married less than a year before, and a fair young wife, to whom he was tenderly attached, anxiously awaited his return in their quiet, happy home, in a pleasant suburb of Dublin. A few short months before he had been a gay and happy bridegroom, spending the first bright days of married life with his young bride amid the romantic solitudes of Wicklow, dreaming proud dreams for Ireland, and fair ones for himself and her he loved. All that was past now. Ruin had already come on the national cause, and death or exile awaited himself. The dreams he had dreamed and the hopes he had cherished were all flown, it might be, forever. But something must be done, and that quickly. He succeeded in crossing in safety the narrow sea between Scotland and Ireland, and in the far North found a generous friend and host in the late ever-lamented Dr. Maginn, the gifted and patriotic Bishop of Derry. Protected and sheltered by that great and good prelate, Mr. McGee awaited the visit of his wife, whom he had contrived to make acquainted with his place of conceal-ment. He could not and would not leave Ireland without seeing and bidding her farewell. Sad indeed was their part-ing, for the young wife was soon to become a mother, and who might tell if she were ever to see her husband's face again? Yet with the unselfishness of true affection she urged him to hasten his departure for America, and he once again sailed, in the disguise of a priest, for what he fondly and proudly called the Land of Freedom. He landed in Philadelphia on the 10th of October, in that memorable year of '48, and on the 26th day of the same month appeared the first number of his *New York Nation*, the advent of which was hailed with enthusiasm by the great majority of the Irish in America. The *prestige* of the *Dublin Nation*, of which Mr. McGee was known to have been one of the editors, the *éclat* he had before gained as editor of the *Boston Pilot*, and, lastly, the great want the American Irish had of a powerful organ, all combined to make the first issue of the *New York Nation* an event most anxiously looked for.

As far as ability and power were concerned, the *Nation* fully realized the most sanguine expectations of Mr. McGee's friends, and it took, as it were by right, the place of the great Irish organ of America. But unfortunately for himself and the prospects of his paper, Mr. McGee—naturally feeling sore on account of the utter and most ignoble failure of his party in Ireland, and the imprisonment of his dearest friend, Gavin Duffy, and others of the leaders—in writing on the causes of the revolutionary collapse, threw the blame on the priesthood and hierarchy of Ireland, who had, he said, used their boundless influence in dissuading the people from joining the insurrection. As might be expected, the illustrious Bishop Hughes, then happily governing the diocese of New York, took up the defence of the Irish clergy, and triumphantly proved, through the columns of the press, that in acting as they had done, they saved their people from utter ruin by rushing into a rebellion for which no adequate preparation had been made. Mr. McGee stoutly maintained his own opinion, and many took sides with him ; but all the religious sympathies of the Irish people, and their profound reverence for their clergy, were arrayed against him, and he found, when too late, that he had lost ground considerably in the favor of the best portion of his countrymen in America. To do him justice, his own truly Irish respect for the clerical order speedily regained its paramount place in his mind and heart, and he not only desisted very soon from writing against the Bishop, but ever after deplored this controversy with him as one of the false steps of his life. What

quently expressed, both in public and in private, his un-qualified regret that he had so far given way to the irritation consequent on the soreness of defeat, as to raise his voice or wield his pen against a prelate whose greatness none knew better than he, or more fully acknowledged.

But the *New York Nation* never recovered the effect of this unwise controversy, and, yielding to the wishes of his numerous friends in Boston, Mr. McGee removed, with his wife and an infant daughter, to that city, and commenced, in the year 1850, the publication of the *American Celt.* During the first two years of the *Celt's* existence, it was characterized by the same, or nearly the same, revolutionary ardor ; but there came a time when the great strong mind and far-seeing intellect of its editor began to soar above the clouds of passion and prejudice into the regions of eternal truth. The cant of faction, the fiery denunciations that, after all, amounted to nothing, he began to see in their true colors ; and with his whole heart he then and ever after aspired to elevate the Irish people, not by impracticable Utopian schemes of revolution, but by teaching them to make the best of the hard fate that made them the subjects of a foreign power differing from them in race and in religion ; to cultivate among them the arts of peace, and to raise themselves, by the ways of peaceful industry and increasing enlightenment, to the level even of the more prosperous sister-island. Who will say that he was less a patriot, less a lover of Ireland after than before this remarkable change from out-and-out radicalism to that calm conservatism which was the result of no selfish motive, but simply of matured thought and the sage counsels of such profound Christian thinkers as the late most eminent Bishop Fitzpatrick of Boston? As this change in Mr. McGee's principles has been, and still is, grossly misrepresented by the revolutionary party, whose ranks he quitted then and forever, and as many even of those who most admired his genius and his poetry have accepted the views of his unscrupulous enemies, I think it my duty to dwell at more length on this particular point than the limit of this introductory sketch might seem to warrant. In justice to his memory, I will leave him to explain in his own terse and vigorous style the reasons, or rather the chain of argument, by which he arrived at the new set of principles which governed his whole remaining life. It was in the August of 1852 that he addressed, through the columns of the *Cell*, a "Letter to a Friend" on what he aptly styled "the recent Conspiracy against the Peace and Existence of Christendom." This friend, we have reason to think, was the late brilliantly-endowed Thomas F. Meagher.* The second paragraph of this remarkable letter reads as follows :

"Let me beg of you, in the sacred name of God, your Author and Redeemer, and in the dear name of Ireland, that you use this interval of exemption from a decided course to review the whole field of European politics, and to bring the proposals of the most conspicuous organs of power and agitators of change in our time to the only test of a Christian— the beam and scales in which St. John saw the angels weighing men, actions, and motives. This standard of right and wrong, a Protestant Christian might say, does not exist in this world ; but a Catholic knows better. You are a Catholic. For you there is an exact and infallible standard, to which nothing is too high and nothing too low—which will detect a grain wanting in a pennyweight, or a stone missing from a pyramid. The field of that standard is Christendom —Christ's kingdom—that is, his Church, and the angels of

* Few will have forgotten poor Meagher saying only a little before, that even if the altar stood in the way of Ireland's freedom, it must be overthrown. Happily even he lived to see his fatal error, and to admit, as he did in his far Australian exile, that if ever Ireland is to be liberated, she must first be

the standard are the bishops and doctors of the Church. Sir, you have been born in the kingdom, and enlisted as a soldier under the standard, and you are bound to bring all that concerns the one to be weighed and measured by the other."

After speaking then at some length of the investigation of the principles on which that choice ought to be made, the writer goes on to say :

" Permit me, as one who has been over the ground of this inquiry, to tell you what discoveries I made upon it. This I will do as candidly and plainly as if I were dictating a last will and testament, for in this case all plainness is demanded.

" I discovered, at the very outset of the inquiry, my own ignorance. This I discovered in a way which, I trust in God, you will never have to travel—by controversy and bitterness, and sorrow for lost time and wasted opportunities. Had we studied principles in Ireland as devoutly as we did an ideal nationality, I might not now be laboring double tides to recover a confidence which my own fault forfeited. But I will say it, for it is necessary to be said, that in Ireland the study of principles is at the lowest ebb. Our literature has been English—that is, Protestant ; our politics have been French, or implicit following of O'Connell ; and under all this rubbish, the half-forgotten Catechism was the only Christian element in our mental Constitution. Since Burke died, politics ceased to be a science in our island and in England. The cruel political economy of Adam Smith never had disciples among us ; the eloquence of Shiel is not bottomed upon any principle ; the *ipse dixit* of O'Connell could be no substitute to ardent and awakened intellect, for the satisfying fullness of a Balmes or a Brownson. . . . . .

" Having discovered, by close self-examination, that the reading chiefly of modern books, English and French, gave

very superficial and false views of political science, I cheerfully said to myself, 'My friend, you are on the wrong track.
You think you know something of human affairs, but you
do not. You are ignorant, very ignorant of the primary
principles that govern, and must govern, the world. You
can put sentences together, but what does that avail you,
when perhaps those sentences are but the husks and pods
of poisonous seeds? Beware! look to it! You have a soul!
What will all the fame of talents avail you, if you lose *that?*'
Thus I reasoned with myself, and then, setting my cherished
opinions before me, one by one, I tried, judged, and capitally
executed every one, save and except those which I found to
be compatible with the following doctrines:

"I. That there is a Christendom.

"II. That this Christendom exists by and for the Catholic Church.

"III. That there is, in our own age, one of the most dan-
gerous and general conspiracies against Christendom that
the world has yet seen.

"IV. That this conspiracy is aided, abetted, and tolerated
by many because of its stolen watchword—'Liberty.'

"V. That it is the highest duty of 'a Catholic man' to go
over cheerfully, heartily, and at once, to the side of Christendom—to the Catholic side, and to resist, with all his
might, the conspirators who, under the stolen name of
'Liberty,' make war upon all Christian institutions."

Such, then, were the motives which induced the subject
of this memoir to go over, as it were, from one camp to the
other—from the ranks of irreligion and universal revolution
to those whose standard was the Cross—whose motto was
and is, "Peace and good will amongst men"—whose end and
aim is the freedom wherewith God maketh free—not the
lawless liberty of doing evil. To this set of principles Mr.

governed his whole public life, and made him the conservative statesman he was in his more mature years.

After publishing the *American Cell* for some years in Boston, where he obtained a high place amongst the eminent literary men of the day, Mr. McGee transferred his publication office to Buffalo, at the urgent request of the late Bishop Timon, but was ultimately persuaded by his many friends in New York to remove thither, and here for some five years he held the first position in the Irish-American press. During the years from 1852 to 1857, the *American Cell* was regarded by friend and foe as the great champion and advocate of the Irish race in America, and was considered the best authority on all matters affecting Irish interests. But while editing the *Cell* with unequalled power and matchless skill, Mr. McGee continued to instruct and delight crowded audiences in the various cities and towns with his lectures on all manner of subjects—very many of them delivered for charitable and religious objects. His lectures on "The Catholic History of America," "The Reformation in Ireland," "The Jesuits," etc., can never be forgotten by those who heard them. Yet amid all his arduous and toilsome avocations, he found time to institute and inaugurate various associations and movements having the social and moral elevation of the Irish race for their object ; and it may truly be said, that to his undying love of his own race, and his yearning aspirations for their well-being, they owed some of the most valuable suggestions for their guidance as a people that have yet been made. It was his special object to keep them bound together by the memories of their common past, and to teach them that manly self-respect that would elevate them before their fellow-citizens, and keep them from political degradation. To make them good citizens of this their adopted country, lovers of the old "cradle-land"

Catholicity—these were the ends and aims visible on every page of the *American Celt.* But unfortunately for the pecuniary prospects of its editor, the *Celt* took sides with no political party here, and warned the Irish population not to trust implicitly in any. The consequence was, that it lost ground with "the politicians;" and the very reason that should have made it a power in the land—its steadfast adherence to principle, its lofty disregard of party interests or party intrigues—made it languish for want of support, and become a heavy burden on the over-taxed mind of its editor and proprietor. Yet who will say that the *American Celt* was not more honored in its high, unselfish mission than it would have been in the more remunerative sphere of party-politics? Who will say that its teachings died with it, or that the self-devoting labors of its editor have left no fruit behind them? The best and most intelligent of the Irish race even to-day in these countries are proud to acknowledge their debt of gratitude to the *American Celt* and "D'Arcy McGee."

Amongst other projects for the advancement of his own race, Mr. McGee had early conceived, and consistently advocated in the *Celt*, that of colonizing—spreading abroad and taking possession of the land—making homes on the broad prairies of the all-welcoming West, instead of herding together in the demoralizing "tenement-houses" of our great cities. To promote this most laudable end, Mr. McGee inaugurated what was called "the Buffalo Convention"—namely, a meeting or senate of one hundred Irish-American gentlemen, both lay and clerical, held in the border city above named, as being easy of access to delegates from both sides of the frontier line. In this Convention, composed of the most intelligent and distinguished amongst the men of their race in the several localities which they represented,

ganizer; yet his characteristic modesty made him keep rather in the background, while others were placed in the van, and made the apparent leaders of the movement. This might be called his *début* in that senatorial career in which he subsequently attained so great distinction. Well had it been for the Irish in America had the views and suggestions of the Buffalo Convention been more generally adopted.

That Convention was, however, an epoch in Mr. McGee's life. His eminent talents, his untiring assiduity, his indomitable perseverance, were so strikingly manifested then, that some of the Canadian delegates became impressed with the idea of inducing him to take up his abode in the Provinces, where his name and fame were already known as one of the great Irishmen of the day. He had lectured in the Canadian cities during the preceding years, and the spell of his genius and the might of his wondrous eloquence had, as usual, enchained those who heard him. He had made warm friends in Montreal and other cities, and they all united in urging him to take up his abode in Montreal, where the want of a ruling mind such as his was sensibly felt by the rapidly-increasing Irish population. It was represented to him that he had not met in the United States with that encouragement or that degree of appreciation which his great abilities and devotion to principle deserved; whereas in Canada his countrymen stood in need of his services, and had the power and the will to advance his interests.

After some negotiation on the subject, Mr. McGee at length consented to make Canada his home, sold his interest in the *American Cell*, and removed with his family to Montreal, where he at once commenced the publication of a journal called *The New Era*. This paper was not very successful, owing to the fact that its editor was as yet but

it were, to feel his way before he ventured to take his stand amongst the publicists of the Province. But the success or failure of the *New Era* was of small account, as it soon appeared. Before the end of his first year in Montreal, Mr. McGee's friends and countrymen, against all odds, returned him to the Canadian Parliament, as one of the three members for Montreal. This was undoubtedly a great triumph, for his election had been warmly contested, and it was only the united action and the honest enthusiasm of his own countrymen and co-religionists that carried the day.

The modesty which, as we have said, was one of Mr. McGee's characteristics as a public man, made him keep rather in the background for some time after he had entered on his senatorial duties. His position in the House of Assembly, too, was not what he could have wished, and was, in fact, somewhat anomalous, as he found himself, for the time being, identified with what was called the *Rouge* party, the Radicals of Canada, with whom he had little or nothing in common. But even though laboring under this disadvantage, and that other of being still comparatively a stranger, Mr. McGee failed not to make his mark in the legislative halls of his new country, and before the close of his first session, the Irish member for Montreal was recognized as one of the most popular men in Canada. Many of those who had been his enemies, and the enemies of his race, were already disarmed of their prejudices, and began to perceive that an Irish Catholic could rise to any level ; that, after all, something good could come out of the heart of Celtic Ireland. Considering the fierce opposition which Mr. McGee's first nomination and subsequent election met from the English and Scotch and Protestant Irish electors of Montreal, and the cold, indifferent, and merely accidental support of his fellow-Catholics, the French Canadians, to

of genius and of a noble nature has been seen in our times than his second, and third, and fourth elections for Montreal by acclamation, and without opposition. This "Irish adventurer," this "stranger from abroad," while elevating his own people, and defending his own faith, its laws and its institutions, as it never had been defended in a Canadian Parliament, while proving himself the great Catholic Irishman of Canada, made friends for himself and his co-religionists even amongst those who had been most prejudiced against everything Catholic and Irish, and stood forth, not by any assumption of his own, but by general consent, the rising star of British America, the life and light of the Canadian Legislature, already distinguished for eminent men and able statesmen. Yet, at times, his early connection with the revolutionary party was made the subject of biting sarcasm and ungenerous reproach by some political opponent. On one of these occasions, when twitted with having been a " rebel " in former years, he replied with that candor and that calm sense of rectitude that distinguished him in his parliamentary career :

"It is true, I was a rebel in Ireland in '48. I rebelled against the misgovernment of my country by Russell and his school. I rebelled because I saw my countrymen starving before my eyes, while my country had her trade and commerce stolen from her. I rebelled against the Church Establishment in Ireland; and there is not a Liberal man in this community who would not have done as I did, if he were placed in my position, and followed the dictates of humanity."

About the year 1865, Mr. McGee's countrymen in Montreal and other cities presented him with a substantial mark of their esteem and admiration—viz., a handsome residence, suitably furnished, in one of the best localities in the city he so ably represented.

In 1862 he accepted the office of President of the Executive Council (whence his title of *Honorable*), and while discharging the duties of that onerous position, he likewise acted for a time as Provincial Secretary, Hon. Mr. Dorion, who had held that office, having resigned. Who could believe that it was at this particular time, and amid all the multifarious avocations of his double office, that he completed his "History of Ireland," in two 12mo. volumes, confessedly one of the best, if not the very best, digest of Irish history yet written? Yet such was the fact.

In 1865, Mr. McGee visited his native land, in company with some friends, and, while staying with his father in Wexford, delivered in that city a speech on the condition of the Irish in America, which gave offence to his countrymen in the United States, inasmuch as he took pains to show that a larger proportion of them became demoralized and degraded in that country than in Canada. It was either during this visit, or a previous one in 1855, just ten years before, that he caused a tomb to be erected over the grave of the mother he had loved so well.*

In 1867, Mr. McGee was sent to Paris by the Canadian Government as one of the Commissioners from Canada to

---

* Speaking of this touching act of filial affection, the *Wexford Independent* of that date remarked:

"Some years ago a little poem was copied into the *Nation* and several of our contemporaries from an American paper; it was addressed 'To my Wishing-cap,' and bore the well-known poetical title of our townsman, Mr. Thomas D'Arcy McGee. Among the other wishes expressed was the following:

> 'Wishing-cap, Wishing-cap, let us away
> To walk in the cloisters, at close of day,
> Once trod by friars of orders gray,
> In Norman Selskar's renown'd abbaye,
>   And Carmen's ancient town;
> For I would kneel at my mother's grave,
> Where the plumy churchyard elms wave,
>   And the old war-walls look down.'

The poet lived to see his wish fulfilled, and, on his late visit to Wexford, caused a ~at tomb to be placed over that beloved grave."

the great Exposition held during that year in the French metropolis. From Paris he went to Rome as one of a deputation from the Irish inhabitants of Montreal on a question concerning the affairs of St. Patrick's congregation in that city. During his visit to Paris, Rome, and other cities of the European continent, he wrote for the *New York Tablet* a series of very interesting letters, entitled "Irish Episodes of Foreign Travel." In London he met, by previous appointment, some of his colleagues in the Canadian Cabinet, who had gone to England to lay before the Imperial Government the plan of the proposed union of the British Provinces. In the important deliberations which followed, Mr. McGee took a leading part, as he had a right to do, for this grand project, so much in accordance with his lofty genius, was, in fact, his own, and had been for years the object of his earnest endeavors. He was then Minister of Agriculture and Emigration, which office he continued to hold up to the time when, in the summer of 1867, the confederation was at last effected, and the three great maritime Provinces were politically united with the Canadas, under the general title of the "Dominion of Canada." Mr. McGee was offered a place in the new Cabinet, but with a disinterested patriotism and a high sense of honor, which the country failed not to appreciate, he declined accepting office, in order to make way in the Cabinet for Hon. Mr. Kenny, of Nova Scotia—like himself, an Irishman and a Catholic.

But with all his great and well-deserved popularity, and the high position he had attained amongst the statesmen of the Dominion, Mr. McGee had made for himself bitter enemies by his open and consistent opposition to the Fenian movement, in which his clear head and far-seeing mind saw no prospect of permanent good for Ireland, and much that was likely to demoralize and de-catholicize the people

of the great universal scheme of revolution which, like a net-work, overspreads, or rather underlies, every state and kingdom of the Old World—that very "conspiracy" against religion, law, and order, in relation to which he had warned, as already seen, one of his early associates in the "Young Ireland" movement on his landing in America, after escaping from penal servitude in Australia. But it was in regard to Canada, and their avowed intention of invading that country, his home and the home of his family, where he had been kindly welcomed and raised by his own countrymen and others, to honor and eminence, that Mr. McGee most severely denounced the Fenians. He rightly considered that it was a grievous wrong to invade a peaceful country like Canada, only nominally dependent on Great Britain, and where so many thousands of Irishmen were living happily and contentedly under just and equitable laws of the people's own making. And it is quite certain that the great body of the Irish in every part of Canada reprobated these projects of "Fenian" invasion as strongly as did Mr. McGee. But the whole vial of Fenian wrath was poured on his devoted head, and no means was left untried to damage his character, public and private. The vilest calumnies were set afloat concerning him, and the honest sympathies of the Irish people of Montreal and Canada for their native land were worked upon by artful and unprincipled persons, who represented him as a traitor to Ireland and her cause, and even to the Catholic faith, which is Ireland's best inheritance. Influenced more than they ought to have been by these mean and dastardly underhand proceedings of his enemies, a portion of his countrymen in Montreal, chiefly, if not all, of the lowest classes, were induced to accept another Irish Catholic, a prominent member of the Canadian bar, as *their* candidate, in opposition to Mr. McGee,

cessful, and on the 6th day of November, 1867, took his seat as member for Montreal West in the first Parliament of the Dominion. The victory, however, cost him dear, for the vile means that had been used to turn the Irish of Montreal against him for electioneering purposes were the immediate causes of his assassination a few months later. The evil passions of the basest and most degraded of his country-men had been excited against him, and he was thenceforth a doomed man, although he probably knew it not.

At the time of that ill-starred election, Mr. McGee was but recovering from illness, and the stormy scenes inciden-tal to so fierce a struggle, with the grief and mortification of seeing some of his own countrymen his bitterest oppo-nents, all combined to produce a reaction, which threw him again on a bed of sickness. During many tedious weeks of suffering, and the necessary seclusion from the world conse-quent thereon, he thought much on subjects affecting his soul's welfare; he reflected on the ingratitude of men, the emptiness of fame, the nothingness of earthly things, the grandeur and solidity of the imperishable goods of eternity. In the deep silence of his soul, shut in from the great tu-mult of the outer world, he pondered on the eternal truths and on the religious traditions of his race, and the strong faith that his Christian mother had implanted in his heart grew and flourished until it brought forth flowers of piety that would have shed a glory and a beauty on the altar of religion, had he been permitted to live to carry out his ex-alted and purified ideas. Strange to say, with all his brill-iant success as a public man, neither politics nor public life had ever been his choice; by the force of circumstances he was drifted on to those troubled waters, where rest and peace are things unknown. The calm pursuits of literature, the study of that old-time lore which, even in boyhood, he

which had so early developed itself in his wonderfully-gifted mind—these were his favorite occupations, and for himself he would have desired none other.   How often, when writing to his best-loved friends, has he spoken of some bright season of calm rest, when, far from the bustle of public affairs, he should be at liberty to devote himself to literary pursuits.   What plans he had projected! what dreams dreamed of what he was then to do for the advancement of Irish and Catholic literature!

Yet who that heard him in debate, even in the last months of his life, during that last session of Parliament, could have guessed that his hopes and wishes were far in the dim retreats of quiet life, with his books and his pen, and that harp whose chords were his own heart-strings! On the very night preceding his cruel murder he delivered one of the noblest speeches ever heard within the walls of a Canadian Parliament, and fully equal to the best of his own. The subject was the cementing of the lately-formed Union of the Provinces by bonds of mutual kindness and good-will. It was a glorious speech, they said who heard it ; but, alas! alas! the echoes of that all-potent voice had scarcely died on the air, when the great orator, the preacher of peace, the sagacious statesman, the gifted son of song, the loved of many hearts, had ceased to live!

He had reached the door of his temporary home, the fair moon of April shining down from the cold, clear depths of heaven,—silence reigned around, broken only by the distant roar of the cataract,* coming softened and subdued on the still air of night, his poet-soul drinking in the ethereal beauty of the hour,—when a lurking assassin stole from his place of concealment, and, coming close behind, shot him through the head, causing instantaneous death.   A few minutes later and all Ottawa was in commotion over "the

* The Chaudière Falls, near Ottawa City.

murder of Hon. T. D. McGee," and the sad news was flying on the telegraph's wings to the quiet home in Montreal where the wife of his youth and their two fair daughters were wrapped in sleep, dreaming, it might be, of the calm delights of the coming days which the husband and father was to spend with his family ; for it was the Tuesday morning in Holy Week, and the next evening he was to have reached home for the Easter recess. Over the sorrow of that household we cast a veil; it was too sacred for the public eye.

Secret and unseen by mortal eye was the death of the great Irish-Canadian ; grand and imposing, and of regal pomp, were his funeral rites, and lofty the honors that greeted his cold remains. His obsequies were solemnized first in the Cathedral of Ottawa; then in St. Patrick's Church and in the Church of Notre Dame, in Montreal; and again in the beautiful Cathedral of Halifax, N. S., on which latter occasion a noble funeral oration was delivered by his true and most appreciative friend, Archbishop Connolly. And the people of Canada mourned him many days, and still do mourn the great loss they sustained in his premature death. In their social *réunions*, in their national festivals, they speak of him, whose voice was wont to delight all hearts, whose subtle and bright, yet gentle humor shed light on all around, whose genial nature diffused a spirit of brotherly love and the best of good-fellowship wherever its influence reached.*

* In proof of this, I may mention that at the annual celebration of " Hallowe'en " by the St. Andrew's Society of Montreal, at which Mr. McGee was wont to speak, and where it is customary to read prize poems on that old Scotch and Irish festival, of forty-six poems sent in competition on the Hallowe'en following his death, *thirty-seven* contained some touching allusion to that sad event. From one of the poems to which prizes were awarded, we quote the following stanzas, in the ancient dialect to Scotia dear :

> " Ah! wad that he were here the nicht,
> Whase tongue was like a faerie lute !
> But vain the wish: McGee ! thy might
> Lies low in death—thy voice is mute.

His assassination took place on the morning of April 7th, and on the St. Patrick's Day previous, just three weeks before, he had been entertained at a public banquet in Ottawa City. His speech on that occasion was one of the noblest efforts of his marvellous eloquence. It was on the general interests of the Irish race, with the present condition and future prospects of Irish literature—shadowing forth, in no indistinct lines, his own abiding and all-enduring love of his race and country, and the work he had marked out for himself in the after years for the service of one and the other. He alluded to certain representations he had made while in London, during the previous year, to Lord Derby, then Premier of England, with regard to the misgovernment of Ireland, and the necessity of satisfying the just demands of the Irish people, remarking, at the same time, in his humorous way, that "even a *silent* Irishman might do something to serve his country." Following up the same train of thought, he wrote, only a few days before his death, that memorable letter to the Earl of Mayo, Chief Secretary of Ireland, earnestly recommending that some permanent measures should be taken to improve the condition of Ireland, and remove the disaffection of her people by a more just and equitable course of legislation than that hitherto pursued. The funeral vault had closed on the writer of that remarkable document—since quoted by Mr.

> He's gane, the noblest o' us a'—
> Aboon a' care o' warldly fame;
> An' wha sae proud as he to ca'
> Our Canada his hame?
>
> "The gentle maple weeps an' waves
> Aboon our patriot-statesman's heed;
> But if we prize the licht he gave,
> We'll bury feuds of race and creed.
> For this he wrocht, for this he died;
> An' for the luve we bear his name,
> Let's live as brithers, side by side,
> In Canada, our hame."

Gladstone in support of his just and statesman-like views in regard to the government of Ireland—before it reached America, after publication in England. "A prophetic voice from the dead coming from beyond the Atlantic," the English statesman aptly styled that letter of earnest pleading for Ireland. At the very time of his death, too, Mr. McGee was engaged writing, for the *Catholic World* of New York, an essay on "Oliver Plunket, Archbishop and Martyr." Thus, it may truly be said that he died, as he had lived, "loving and serving his mistress, IRELAND, as a true knight." His last writings were for Ireland—his last words for the peace and unity of his adopted country, the New Dominion of Canada.

The following touching tribute to his memory, from the pen of one of our very few remaining Irishmen of genius, will be read with interest :

"D'Arcy McGee!" wrote Henry Giles to the present writer, soon after the sad death of their common friend— "D'Arcy McGee! I knew him. well, and loved him greatly. He was but a boy when I first made his acquaintance, and even then he was engaged in writing brilliant articles in Mr. Donahoe's *Pilot*. He had, besides, published some of his literary efforts. As he advanced in years, so he did in power. . . . . Great in his eloquence, his reputation grew with the growth of that country" (meaning Canada) "which his energies helped to increasing force. All this had as yet but served to indicate his power, to put forth the branches of his deep-lying energy, when the assassin drew near, and, with his stealthy step, in darkness, crushed the growing and advancing strength."

But he is dead, "the noblest Roman of us all ;" lost to friends and country—lost to literature—lost to song.

"Far away," says one of his biographers, "from that glorious but unhappy isle where he dreamt away the bright fleeting hours of his childhood—far away from the home of his dearest hopes, of his highest aspirations—far away from the green churchyard where the ashes of his parents rest in the friendly embrace of the land of their birth—in the New World, far over the sea, in the land of his adoption, high up on the sunny side of beautiful 'Mount Royal,' which, sloping towards the far-famed St. Lawrence, laves its foot in the limpid waters of the majestic river, overlooking the fair city of Montreal, where for years his voice was the most potent, his smile the most friendly, his influence in all that was most noble, patriotic, and good, was most felt, sleeps the greatest poet, orator, statesman, historian, the best, the truest friend, counsellor, and guide of the Irish race in America. His grave is bedewed by a young nation's tears; his memory lives, and shall live, in that young nation's heart; his name and fame shall cast lustre on the pages of her history, and his life-labors stand forth as an example worthy of emulation to future millions." *

* "Short Sketch of the Life of the Hon. Thomas D'Arcy McGee," by Henry J. O'C. Clarke, Q. C., Montreal

INTRODUCTION TO THE POEMS.

Of all the poets of our time, Thomas D'Arcy McGee was, in many ways, the most remarkable. Unaided by collegiate education, thrown entirely on his own resources—even in boyhood an emigrant to the New World, where his supreme genius made him a brilliant editor and an effective orator long before the age when other men enter on the stage of ordinary life—a popular lecturer—a writer of acknowledged power, equal to the best of our time—a careful and reliable historian—an essayist of grace and skill—a legislator—a ruler—a projector of mighty plans for the government of nations—yet a singer of sweet songs, interweaving the wearing, wasting cares of daily life, and the lofty conceptions of the statesman's mind, with the glittering thread of poesy, the golden fringe of life's dull garment, giving brightness and beauty to the meanest things, the dryest pursuits, the weariest hours,—Poetry was his solace in the manifold troubles of his life. It cheered him in poverty; it enlivened his dreariest hours; it breathed a charm over the dry details and joyless struggles of political life; it illumined the editorial pages; it refreshed his overtaxed mind when Nature called for repose; it made love fonder and friendship dearer; and softened grief, and brightened joy, and made Thomas D'Arcy McGee the best-loved friend, the most genial companion, the most hospitable and cordial host, the best entertainer our modern society has seen in America, while lending to his speeches, to his public writings, as well as to his private correspondence, the ineffable charm that poetry, the offspring of mind and heart, alone can give.*

That this poetry of his nature was expressed in noble and most melodious verse, we have very high literary authority. Many years have passed away since Charles Gavin Duffy, himself a poet of no mean order, said of McGee's poetry, and of his devotion to "Irish interests :"

"Who has served them with such fascinating genius?

* Amongst other remarkable proofs of the charm that pervaded even the public discourses of Mr. McGee, I will cite the following : In 1862, he was invited to assist at the great "Popham Celebration" at Portland, Me. On that occasion he spoke on "Samuel de Champlain," and a few days after he received from Mrs. Lydia H. Sigourney the following graceful tribute,—she afterwards sent him a copy of her poems :

"HARTFORD, CONN., U. S. A., October 1st, 1862.
"Mrs. Sigourney was delighted with the perusal of the address of Mr. McGee at the celebration of the 155th anniversary of the settlement of Maine, as reported in our public prints, and regretted not having had the privilege of listening when it was delivered.

"She has long cherished an interest in the character and exploits of Sieur de Champlain, and felt that they had scarcely won due appreciation. Of the accompanying brief poem, which owes its existence to the eloquence of Mr. McGee, she requests his acceptance as a slight acknowledgement of the pleasure for which she is indebted.

"LE SIEUR DE CHAMPLAIN.

"Onward o'er waters which no keel had trod,
　No plummet sounded in their depths below,
No heaving anchor grappled to the sod
　Where flowers of Ocean in seclusion glow.
From isle to isle, from coast to coast he press'd
　With patient zeal, and chivalry sublime,
Folding o'er Terra Incognita's breast
　The lillied vassalage of Gallia's clime ;
Though Henry of Navarre's profound mistake
　Montcalm must expiate and France regret,
Yet yonder tranquil and heaven-mirror'd Lake,
　Like diamond in a marge of emerald set,
Bears on its freshening wave from shore to shore
The baptism of his name forevermore."

His poetry and his essay's touch are like the breath of spring, and revive the buoyancy and chivalry of youth. I plunge into them like a refreshing stream of 'Irish undefiled.' What other man has the subtle charm to invoke our past history and make it live before us? If *he* has not loved his mistress, 'Ireland,' with the fidelity of a true knight, I cannot name any one who has."

The Dublin *Nation*, of May 20th, 1857, speaking of "True Poetry, and how it has been appreciated," speaks as follows of Mr. McGee's poetry : "Perhaps, however, the poetic recreations of T. D. McGee, taking them as a whole, are the most intensely Irish verses which have, as yet, been contributed to our literature. No one, not even Davis, seems to have infused the spirit of Irish history so thoroughly into his mind and heart as McGee ; nor can any more melancholy proof of the decay of national spirit be given than the fact that these poems, the composition of which has been a labor of love to him—exile as he is from the Old Green Land— remain uncollected. We might search in vain, even through the numberless volumes of English poems and lyrics, for any that equal in their passion, fire, and beauty his verses entitled 'The War,' 'Sebastian Cabot to his Lady,' 'The Celt's Salutation,' and many others."

Since his lamented death, Henry Giles wrote, "All this" (meaning his outward life, his visible strength and power) "has beneath it an ever-abiding, underlying principle, a well-spring ever fresh and ever sweet of glorious poetry, with its softest melody, or, in passion, indignant and strong, with its wild and varied vehemence. How varied the poems were which he breathed forth upon the woes and wrongs of Ireland! How noble the strains in which he celebrates that beautiful land of much calamity and countless wrongs!"

And the London *Athenæum*, speaking of Canadian poetry, said, years ago, while Mr. McGee was still amongst the living : "They have one true poet within their borders—that is, Thomas D'Arcy McGee. In his younger·days the principle of rebellion inspired him with stately verse ; let us hope that the conservative principles of his more mature years will yield many a noble song in his new country."

It has also been said, and I think with truth, that McGee was, even more than Moore, entitled to be called "the Bard of Erin," for that his genius was more distinctively Irish, and his inspiration more directly and more exclusively from Ireland and her ancient race. His poetry bears all the characteristics of genuine Irish minstrelsy ; it is redolent with the purest Irish feeling ; the passionate love of country and of kin, the reverence for what is old and venerable, the strong religious faith, the high appreciation of the beautiful and the good—these underlie all his poems ; while over all are diffused the choicest graces of fancy, the most subtle humor, the most delicate beauty of thought and·expression. Like some strain from the bardic ages of old, comes to the ear and to the heart one of McGee's ballads. Whether he sings of love or friendship, of faith or charity, of war or peace, or chants some old-time legend, or a grand historic tale of other days, the under-tones are still the same, and the chords are swept with a master's hand. When he sings of

> "The green grave of my mother
> 'Neath Selskar's ruin'd wall,"

or of the young wife of his love, whom he was forced to leave in the first year of their marriage, now sighing—

> "Sad the parting scene was, Mary,
> By the yellow-flowing Foyle,"

now reminding her of the calm joys of their bridal days in lovely Wicklow—

> "Dost thou remember the dark lake, dearest,
> Where the sun never shines at noon ?"

and passionately cries—

> "My darling, in the land of dreams, of wonder, and delight,
> I see you, and sit by you, and woo you all the night;
> Under trees that glow like diamonds upon my aching sight,
> You are walking by my side in your wedding garments white"—

we hear his voice like the sighing of the breeze in summer boughs, and we think of the forgotten bards of the long-past ages, who left us "The Last Rose of Summer" and "Savourneen Dheelish." Anon, he sings of battle, as was his wont in the fiery days of youth, and his voice is a trumpet-call—

> "Gather together the nations! arouse and arm the men!"

How the martial spirit of the Celts of old rings in Cathal's "Farewell to the Rye :"

> "Farewell sickle! welcome sword!"

in the "Harvest Hymn," and "The Reaper's Song," and "The Summons of Ulster," and the "Song of the Sheiks!"

We read these warlike lays, and the "Pilgrims of Liberty," and many another patriot strain, and we feel our souls stirred within us, and we marvel that the calm, meditative mind of the statesman we knew in later days could ever have conceived such burning thoughts.

Again, and how often our poet sings of his native land, her woes, her beauties, the passionate love wherewith she inspired him from youth up, a love that no time or space could ever cool, ever diminish! As a boy leaving Ireland, he sang to home and country—to "Carmen's ancient town," "to Wexford in the distance ;" in exile, he chanted sweetly and mournfully the memories of his own land and his yearnings to behold it again. His "Parting from Ireland" is an agonizing wail of sorrow :

> "Oh, dread Lord of heaven and earth! hard and sad it is to go
> From the land I loved and cherish'd into outward gloom and woe ;
> Was it for this, Guardian Angel! when to manly years I came,
> Homeward, as a light, you led me—light that now is turn'd to flame !"

And whoever sang with fonder pride, or in more melodious verse, the romantic beauty of Ireland, her household virtues, her ever-abiding faith in things divine? How fondly he apostrophizes his

> "Ireland of the Holy Islands,
> Belted round with misty highlands!"

In "The Deserted Chapel" we have a most touching and graphic description of the desolating effects of emigration in the old land ; in "The Woful Winter," a mournful lament for the myriad victims of famine and pestilence in the dreary year of '47:

> "They are flying, flying, like northern birds, over the sea for fear;
> They cannot abide in their own green land, they seek a resting here
> Oh! wherefore are they flying—is it from the front of war,
> Or have they smelt the Asian plague the winds waft from afar?"

And again, in the noble poem entitled "Famine in the Land,"

> "Death reapeth in the field of life, and we cannot count the corpses!"

the same subject is pursued with sorrowful interest. It was indeed one that addressed itself to the tenderest sympathies of the poet's heart, and we find it touchingly prominent in several of the poems ; and this is natural, for "the Ancient Race," the "Celtic Race," was one of his favorite themes ; he loved more than all to sing its praise ; he loved it, he was proud of it ; then how could he fail to feel its woes, and the dark doom that made it subject to periodical famine and pestilence? Even in the land of his exile, we find his "Meditations" interwoven with sad reflections on the hard lot that makes so many of his countrymen wanderers on the face of the earth :

> "Alone in this mighty city, queen of the continent!
> I ponder on my people's fate in grief and discontent;
> Alas! that I have lived to see them wiled and cast away,
> And driven like soulless cattle from their native land a prey!"

strongest and most abiding instincts.   How grandly he sings of "Ossian's Celts," of the warlike Milesians! how fraternal and how noble his "Salutation to the Celts!"—

> "Hail to our Celtic brethren wherever they may be,
>   In the far woods of Oregon, or by the Atlantic sea!"

His love for Ireland inspired Mr. McGee beyond all doubt with some of the very best and sweetest of his poems. It was so a part of his nature that, like the theme of some noble piece of music, it runs through all his poetry, yielding ever the sweetest notes, charming us, while we read, like the matins of the lark, or the vesper-hymn of the bird of eve. His songs of Ireland come gushing from the innermost depths of his heart, warm, and fresh, and glowing,—

> "O Pilgrim, if you bring me from the far-off lands a sign,
>   Let it be some token still of the Green Old Land once mine;
>   A shell from the shores of Ireland would be dearer far to me
>   Than all the wines of the Rhine-land, or the art of Italie."

His "Wishes," his "Memories," his "Heart's Resting-place," all echo the same strain—

> "Where'er I turn'd, some emblem still
>   Roused consciousness upon my track;
> Some hill was like an Irish hill,
>   Some wild-bird's whistle call'd me back."

And how touching is the apology we find in more than one of the poems for his passionate devotion to Ireland and her literature! In one he sings—

> "Oh! blame me not if I love to dwell
>   On Erin's early glory;
> Oh! blame me not, if too oft I tell
>   The same inspiring story!"

In another we find the singularly characteristic lines—

> "I'd rather turn one simple verse
>   True to the Gaelic ear,
> Than classic odes I might rehearse
>   With senates list'ning near."

Now this is precisely what he did, and it makes the chief charm of his poetry. It was because he, more than any poet of our time, "turn'd" his verses "true to the Gaelic ear," that, whether grave or gay, tender or pathetic, or martial or religious, they ever reach the Gaelic heart, and mirror all its many-hued aspects.

The noblest of his poems are undoubtedly the historical. Indeed, it was one of the dreams of his life to complete, in some season of rest (which never came!) a ballad-history of Ireland : some broken links of that golden chain will delight many a reader of this volume, as they have delighted thousands in days gone by. "Amergin's Hymn on Seeing Innisfail," "Milesius, the Spaniard," "Ossian's Celts," "Ireland of the Druids," "The Coming of St. Patrick," and other poems on the life and death of that apostle ; "The Voyage of Eman Oge," "The Gobhan Saer," "St. Cormac, the Navigator," "St. Brendan and the Strife-Sower," "St. Columba to his Irish Dove," "St. Columbanus to St. Comgall," "The Testament of St. Arbogast," "The Pilgrimage of Sir Ulgarg," the two noble poems on "Margaret O'Carroll, of Offaly;" "Lady Gormley," "Flan Synan's Game of Chess," "Sir John De Courcy's Pilgrimage," "Good Friday, 1014," "Shawn na Gow's Guest," and other poems on King Brian Boromhe ; the fine, but unfinished poem on "The Death of Donnell More," "Cathal's Farewell to the Rye," "The Wisdom-Sellers before Charlemagne," "The Lament of the Irish Children in the Tower," "Earl Desmond's Apology," "Rory Dall's Lamentation," "Feagh McHugh," "Sir Cahir O'Dogherty's Message," "The Rapparees," "The Midnight Mass," "The Death of Art McMurrogh," "The River Boyne," "The Execution of Archbishop Plunket," "The Death of O'Carolan," the poems on the famine and pestilence in Ireland, and on the emigration and the Irish in America, are his-tle of Ayachucho," "Moylan's Dragoons," "The Sage of King Olaf Tregvyason," "The Death of King Magnus," "The Death of Hudson," the two musical ballads on "Jacques Cartier," "The Launch of the Griffin," "Sebastian Cabot to his Lady," "Hannibal's Vision of the Gods of Carthage," "Diephon," and various other poems on general historical subjects. With these may be classed "Iona," the wonderfully fine poems on "The Four Masters" and their chief, "Brother Michael," the "Prayer for Farrell O'Gara," their benefactor and employer, and "Sursum Corda" addressed to his friend, the venerable and most estimable Eugene O'Curry.

Another remarkable class of these poems is the obituary or commemorative. Of these, the loftiest and grandest are "The Dead Antiquary" (John O'Donovan), "Eugene O'Curry," and "Richard Dalton Williams; very fine too, and very solemn, is the "Monody on the Death of Gerald Griffin;" whilst "William Smith O'Brien," "John Banim," and other eminent Irishmen, are duly commemorated. The lament for Banim is not equal to any of the others, being a mere juvenile composition, written while Mr. McGee was editing the *Boston Pilot.* Some of the most graceful and effective, however, of his poetical efforts were his tributes to the memory of private friends long known and well esteemed, but of no historical importance. Chief amongst these are "The Prayer for the Soul of the Priest of Perth," and "Requiem Æternam," which last, written but one short month before his own sad death, applied so entirely to himself, that it almost seemed like the voice of presentiment, and as though he, like Mozart, were inspired to chant his own *requiem.* It was in these heart-piercing strains of sorrowing affection, as well as in the numerous poems addressed to his wife, and some few to his chosen friends, that the winning tenderness of our poet's nature made itself manifest.

In this connection may be mentioned the exquisite little poems "Consolation," "Mary's Heart," "God be Praised," and "To my Wishing-Cap." Amongst the poems expressive of friendship, one of the most beautiful is that "To a Friend in Australia," in which are found these exquisite lines :

> " Old friend ! the years wear on, and many cares
> And many sorrows both of us have known ;
> Time for us both a quiet conch prepares—
> A conch like Jacob's, pillow'd with a stone."

To the manifold trials, troubles, and heart-wearing struggles of his life, Mr. McGee gives unwonted expression in the musical and sorrowful little poem entitled "Ad Misericordiam," written during his darkest days, when publishing the *American Celt* in New York. No one, we would hope, can read without emotion the concluding lines :

> " Welcome, thrice welcome, to overtax'd nature,
> The darkness, the silence, the rest of the grave ;
> Oh ! dig it down deeply, kind fellow-creature,
> I am weary of living the life of a slave !"

It is quite remarkable, however, that, amongst the poetical remains of Thomas D'Arcy McGee, the religious element, the strong, lively, simple faith of his Celtic fathers is supremely evident. In every stage of his life, the most stirring, the most unfavorable to religious thought or feeling, we find his muse devoted to the Saints of God, especially those of his own race ; how he sang of "St. Patrick," "St. Brendan of the West," "St. Arbogast," "St. Kieran," "St. Columbanus," "St. Comgall," "St. Cormac, the Navigator," "St. Bride, of Kildare," and "St. Columba, of the Churches," this volume will bear witness. His poem on "Eternity" contains, within a short space, much sublime thought and the fulness of faith ; yet it was written many years ago, when life was young and warm, and its cares were many and heavy on the poet's heart. Even "The Rosary" received its tribute from

life long Mr. McGee cherished the special veneration which
his mother taught him in early infancy for the blessed Mother
of our Lord.   In his latest years, when the legislative halls
of his adopted country were wont to echo with his matchless
eloquence, and the multitudinous cares of statecraft weighed
upon his mind, and the tumult of party strife jarred harshly
on his finely-tuned ear and heart, we find his poetry chiefly
of a religious character.   It was then that he sang of
"Humility," of "First Communion," of "Sister Margaret
Bourgeois," of Montreal, and her wonderful life of sanctified labor ; it was then he penned these deathless lines—

> " Mighty our Holy Church's will
> To guard her parting souls from ill,
> Jealous of death, she guards them still—
> > *Miserere, Domine !*

> " The dearest friend will turn away,
> And leave the clay to keep the clay,
> Ever and ever *she* will stay—
> > *Miserere, Domine !*"

Had he lived longer, this religious aspect of his mind, this
fervent, ever-living faith would have been still more strikingly
manifested.   Amongst his papers was found a list of "Topics"
for poems, evidently written quite recently, all of them of a
most solemnly religious character.   These were the "Topics"
written in pencil in his own fair hand : "He came unto His
own, and His own received Him not," "The night cometh
in which no man can work," "I believe in the Communion
of Saints," "*Ergo expecto resurrectionem mortuorum,*" "It is
a holy and wholesome thought to pray for the dead."

The solemn significance of these scriptural texts, selected
as the subject of poems probably but a few weeks or a few
days before his untimely and most melancholy death, will be
noted with interest.   Indeed, we find in several of the poems
expressions that read like the voice of impending doom ;

> "So have bright spirits been eclipsed and lost,
>   Forever dark, if by Death's shadow cross'd;"

and again—still more like presentiment:

> "Oh, even thus Death strikes the gifted, then
>   Come the worms—inquests—and the award of men!"

The beautiful little poems, "*Stella! Stella!*" "I will go to the Altar of God," and the "Sunday Hymn at Sea," were written during Mr. McGee's last voyage from Europe, in 1867. They breathe the very spirit of faith, called into poetical expression by the abiding presence of the great waters, the boundless mirror of Creative Power. "The Christmas Prelude," "A Prayer for the Dead," "The Star of the Magi," "An Irish Christmas," "The First Communion," "Eternity," "The Pearl of Great Price," and others, are eminently religious.

Of the pathetic ballads, "The Death of the Homeward Bound," one of the best known of all Mr. McGee's ballads, will be read with most pleasure. It is wonderfully beautiful. "The Trip over the Mountain" is a capital specimen of the Irish popular ballad, showing with graphic fidelity the process of love-making amongst the peasantry, not only of Wexford, but of all the Irish counties.

The "dramatic sketch," as he called it, "King Dermid; or, The Normans in Ireland," although not so finished as it would have been had he written it some years later, still gives evidence of considerable power, and shows that the author might have shone as a dramatist had he followed up this first attempt. Take the poems for all in all, they are, to my thinking, the most truly Irish collection in our day given to the public. They are intensely, thoroughly Irish, in the sense of genius, of national idiosyncrasy—Irish in thought, in feeling, in expression. They are Irish in reverential love for what is old and venerable—witness the

Key : they are Irish in the depth and simplicity of religious faith ; they are Irish in passionate devotion to native land ; they are Irish in the warmth and sincerity of affection they breathe, whether in love or friendship ; Irish in the peculiar forms of expression, rich and racy of Irish idiom—hence most "true to the Gaelic ear;" and Irish, too, in the eloquent flow of words, adapting itself with ease to the musical intonation of the sweetest and most perfect melody.   Even those written for and of the Irish in America are as true to Irish thought and expression as any written in and for Ireland.   Of this class, the singularly graceful poem, "An Invitation Westward," is a fine example ; so, too, is "The Cross in the West," "St. Patrick's in the Woods," "The Irish Homes of Illinois," "Graves in the Forest," and various others.   "The Army of the West," "The Free Flag of America," "Hail to the Land," and some others, bear graceful homage to the country where he had, for the time, sought a home, the greatness of which none better than he appreciated.   The noble verses on "*Prima Vista*" (Newfoundland) and "Peace hath her Victories"—the latter written in Paris *apropos* to the great Exposition in that city—"St. Patrick's Dream," and "Iona to Erin," are amongst the last of his published poems.   It will be seen that some of the poems are unfinished, such as "The Death of Donnell More" (one of the best of his historical poems), "The Banshee and the Bride," "The Four Students," and "The Sinful Scholar."   The latter, a truly charming production even in its fragmentary state, he seems to have intended for larger proportions ; its great intrinsic beauty induced the editress to collect and arrange all she could find of it with special care.*

* " Another poem, called "The Emigrants," on which he was engaged, I found in so fragmentary a state, that I have not attempted to connect the scattered links.   The author appears to have intended it for a poem of some length, to form a volume in itself; the dedication which he had written for it will be found in this collection.   Many years ago, Mr. McGee had, I see,

One couplet of this poem is strikingly characteristic of the
author's peculiar delicacy of thought and expression :

> " The lone lake, like a lady, grieves,
>   *Saddest in the long autumn eves.*"

To ordinary readers nothing can be more simple than these
two lines, but to the cultivated poetical taste they will present a graceful thought, most happily rendered in musical
words.   Some other such exquisite snatches of song the
editress found here and there on scraps of paper, without
any apparent connection—broken links of thought, or rather
gushes of song welling forth from the fount of genius.   Here
is one of these :

> " Spell-bound or asleep, I was wand'ring all alone
>   Where, beneath monastic rocks old and gray,
>   The deep sea beats its breast with many a sigh and moan
>   For its stormy frantic passions, or the ships it cast away."

Another was as follows :

> " A moon that sheds a needless light
>   On soulless streets in the far-gone night."

On another scrap was found this stanza, which the author
evidently meant for the beginning of a poem to be named
"The War of the Holy Cross :"

> " Art thou brave, and lovest glory, then rise and follow me,
>   And thou shalt have for captain the Lord of land and sea ;
>   Where the mighty men of ages left foot-prints stamp'd in gore,
>   We will bear the sacred banner that our fathers bore of yore."

This poem, to judge from its opening lines, would have been
one of great vigor and of stately measure, conceived in that
religious spirit which marked exclusively the closing period
of our poet's life.   The following stanza is of strange, sweet

mapped out the plan of a grand epic on the Jewish exodus, which was to
have extended over twelve books. How thoroughly he mastered every subject on which he wrote may be judged from the following note appended to
the plan of this poem :

 " Read for *Exodus*, ' St. Jerome and the Fathers,' ' Divine Legation,' Histories of Egypt, Arabia, the Jews, etc., Natural History, Josephus, and the

melody; would that the poem so commenced had been ended!—

> "Oft through the gloaming,
> Like shadows coming,
> Around me roaming,
>   In scenes afar—
> Than the present nearer
> Come the old days dearer,
> Beaming brighter, clearer
>   Than the evening star."

The first lines of a historical poem called "King Nial's Expedition to Armoria" will give an idea of what it would have been if completed, as it may have been, since a poem of that name was found on one of Mr. McGee's lists of his poems:

> "King Nial hath gone with his chieftains all
> For a royal raid into Armoric Gaul;
> Right well do the island-warriors know
> That the Roman now is a yielding foe—
> Though, truth to tell, in its days of pride,
> They smote it often, south of Clyde;
> Yet much it rejoices the heart of the West
> To see the brave bird flying back to its nest."
>
> *   *   *   *   *   *   *

Other broken snatches of glorious song I have embodied in the poems, where there were even two consecutive verses. One of these commences thus—"I would not die with my work undone;" another, "A happy bird that hung on high." These detached verses I commend to the reader's special attention, for they are indeed of touching significance, when viewed in connection with the author's chequered life and sad, sad death.

> "I dream'd a dream when the woods were green,
> And my April heart made an April scene,
>   In the far, far distant land,
> That *even I might something do*
> That would keep my memory for the true,
>   And my name from the spoiler's hand!"

That even *he* might something do!—he who devoted all the years of life, from boyhood to the grave, to the hardest brain-toil for country, for literature, for religion!—he who delivered over *eleven hundred* lectures on every subject that could elevate and instruct the people!—he who wrote many books of rare value, and edited some fifteen volumes of news-papers!—he whose poetry, like his eloquence, has thrilled the hearts of tens of thousands! Ah! if *he* did not do work enough "to keep his name from the spoiler's hand," then no man or woman of our generation has a claim to lasting re-membrance.

As one of those who knew him best, and all he had done and meant to do for the real interests of society, especially those of his own race, which is also hers, and as one of his humble fellow-laborers in the field of Irish and Catholic lit-erature, the editress has done what in her power lay to "keep his memory for the true" and his "name from the spoiler's hand." The following beautiful poem from the pen of "Thomasine," one of the sweetest singers of the Dublin *Nation* in its palmiest days, appeared so late as 1860 in the columns of that paper. It is a response to Mr. McGee's heart-warm stanzas, "Am I remember'd in Erin?"

THE EXILE'S QUESTION, "AM I REMEMBER'D?"

I.

Well have the poets imaged forth
  The fear-cross'd hope of lovers true—
A needle turning towards the north,
  Constant, yet ever trembling too ;
And love the purest soonest feels
  This thrilling doubt arise,
As homeward memory sadly steals
  From exile's distant skies.
      Thou art remember'd !

II.

But doubt like this doth grievous wrong
  To Her round whom thy heart-strings twine?
And, Brother of the sweet-voiced Song !
  Never such fervent love as thine
Did Erié's grateful nature leave
  Unnoticed or forgot;
Still for thy absence doth she grieve,
  Still mourn thy exiled lot.
      Thou art remember'd !

III.

Nay, and though long the glorious roll
  Of gifted sons who loved her well,
Much were that tender mother's dole,
  If one forgotten fell.
E'en as the Church holds record proud
  Of every sainted name,
She counts for each in that bright crowd
  A son's especial claim—
          Thou art remember'd !

IV.

She sends this greeting fond by me,
  To bid thy heart rejoice ;
Eager from lands beyond the sea,
  She listens for thy voice.
By many a hearth her daughters sing
  Thy strains of Celtic lore,
While round their knees the children cling
  To learn the deeds of yore—
          And thou'rt remember'd !

V.

Oft, too, when themes of import grave
  Call men to council high,
Some voice recalls thy lessons brave,
  Faithful to live or die ;
And constant still—believe it, friend !—
  Before God's holy shrine,
Few names with her petitions blend
  More warmly loved than thine—
          Thou'rt *well* remember'd !

To this we append, selected from scores of poems written in America on Mr. McGee's death, the following musical and eloquent tribute to his memory from the pen of an accomplished Catholic priest of Pennsylvania :

" Dark is the house of our fathers, O brother,
  Fast fall the tears of its inmates for thee—
Grief-stricken man his emotions may smother,
But loud is the wail of the wife and the mother,
          Loved D'Arcy McGee !

" Sweetly the Muses thy loss are bewailing,
  Sighing in chorus the sad dirge—ah me !
Life's golden sunset in darkness is paling—

> "Lo! the great dead of the long-buried ages,
>   Thronging innumerous, moan over thee—
> Spirits of heroes, of saints, and of sages,
> Glowing with life in thy bright-pictured pages,
>   O gifted McGee!
>
> "Thousands, the wide world o'er, who with gladness,
>   Spell-bound, enraptured, erst listen'd to thee,
> Silver-tongued Orator! now, in deep sadness,
> Horror-struck, gaze on the dark deed of madness,
>   O martyr'd McGee!
>
> "Poet, Historian, the Forum's bright glory—
>   Light lie the sod, noble D'Arcy! on thee;
> Blest be thy name till the ages are hoary—
> Honor'd, oft utter'd in pray'r, song, and story,
>   O deathless McGee!"

With these echoes of his fame from either side the Atlantic, we close our introduction to the poems of Thomas D'Arcy McGee—poems which will, we think, justify me in saying that he himself, more than any of his race, struck "the harp of King Brian," and breathed over its strings the Celtic spirit of Ossian, whom he once addressed in this prophetic strain:

> "Oh, inspired giant! shall we c'er behold
>   In our own time
> One fit to speak your spirit on the wold,
>   Or seize your rhyme?
> One pupil of the past, as mighty soul'd
>   As in the prime
> Were the fond, fair, and beautiful, and bold—
>   They, of your song sublime!"

If Thomas D'Arcy McGee was not the one "fit to speak *that* spirit on the wold"—if he was not the "pupil of the past," the "mighty-soul'd," representing in our new age the great father of Celtic song—then is there none such among living men.

PATRIOTIC POEMS.

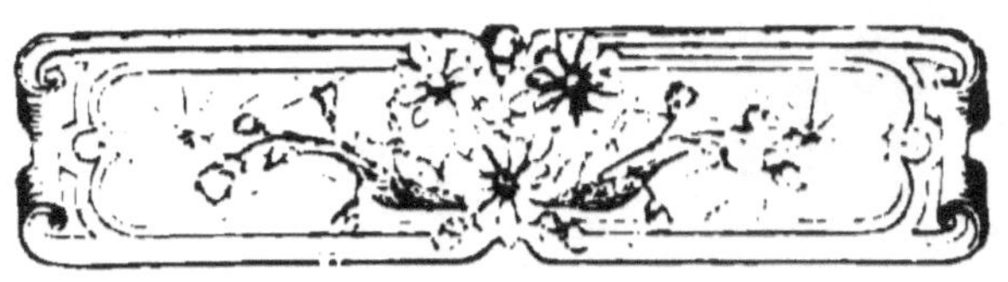

AN APOLOGY TO THE HARP.

I.

Harp of the land I love! forgive this hand
  That reverently lifts thee from the dust,
And scans thy strings with filial awe and love,
  Lest by neglect the chords of song should rust.

II.

Deep buried in tall grave-yard grass thou wert—
  The shadows of the dead thy sole defence—
The wild flowers twining round thee meekly fond,
  Fearing their very love might be offence.

III.

Seeing thee thus, I knew the bards were gone
  Who thrilled thee—and themselves thrilled to thy touch :
Mangan and Moore, I knew, were vanishèd ;
  I knelt and raised thee : did I dare too much ?

IV.

If Griffin, or if Davis lived, a night
  Had never fallen upon thee, lying there ;
Or if our living poets, loyal held
  To native themes so much, I dare not dare.

v.

But could I see thee, glorious instrumcnt !
   The first time in long ages silence-bound ?
Thou ! who wert nursed on ancient Ossian's knee—
   Thence sacredly through ages handed down.

VL

I ! who have heard thy echoes from my soul,
   A sickly boy, couched at my mother's knee :
I ! who have heard thy dirges, wild as winds,
   And thy deep tidal turns of prophecy !

VII.

I ! whom you tuned in sorrow day by day,
   For friend, adviser, solace, companie,
Could I pass by thee, prostrate, nor essay
   To bear thee on a stage—harp of my loved Erie ?

VIII.

Forgive me ! oh, forgive me, if too bold !
   I twine thy chords about my very heart,
And make with every pulse of life a vow,
   Swearing—nor years, nor death, shall us two part.

IX.

I have no hope to gather bays, on high
   Beneath the snows of ages, where they bloom,
As many votaries of thine desired,
   And the great favor'd few have haply done ;

x.

But if emblem o'er my dust should rise,
   Let it be this : Our Harp within a wreath
Of shamrocks twining round it lovingly,
   That so, O Harp ! our love shall know no death !

THE THREE MINSTRELS.

THREE Minstrels play within the Tower of Time,
 A weird and wondrous edifice it is:
One sings of war, the martial strain sublime,
 And strikes his lyre as 'twere a foe of his.
The sword upon his thigh is dripping red
 From a foe's heart in the mid-battle slain;
His plumèd casque is doff'd from his proud head,
 His flashing eye preludes the thundrous strain.

Apart, sequester'd in an alcove deep,
 Through which the pale moon looks propitious in,
Accompanied by sighs that seem to weep,
 The second minstrel sadly doth begin
To indite his mistress fair, but cruel, who
 Had trampled on the heart that was her own;
Or prays his harp to help him how to woo,
 And thrills with joy at each responsive tone.

Right in the porch, before which, fair and far,
 Plain, lake, and hamlet fill the musing eye,
Gazing toward the thoughtful evening star
 That seems transfixed upon the mountain high,
The third of Country and of Duty sings:
 Slow and triumphal is the solemn strain;
Like Death, he takes no heed of chiefs or kings,
 But over all he maketh Country reign.

Sad Dante. he, love-led from life, who found
 His way to Eden, and unhappy stood
Amid the angels—he, the cypress-crown'd,

Thoughts deeper and more solemn it inspires
    Than even his lofty spirit dare essay;
How then shall we, poor Emberers of old fires,
    Kindle the beacons of our country's way?

We all are audience in the Tower of Time;
    For us alone at this hour play the three,—
Choose which ye will—the martial song sublime,
    Or lover fond; but thou my Master be,
O Bard of Duty and of Country's cause!
    Thee will I choose and follow for my lord!
Thy theme my study and thy words my laws—
    Muse of the patriot lyre and guardian sword!

THE EMIGRANT AT HOME.

"I had a dream which was not all a dream."—*Byron.*

I.

A youth return'd from the far, far West
    Lay slumber-bound in his early home,
When a fairy vision beguiled his rest,
    And a voice of music fill'd the room.

II.

"What saw you in the Western land
    Beyond the sea, my Irish boy?"
"Oh! forests vast, and rivers grand,
    And a sun that shone, as if for joy."

III.

"What saw you else in the Western land
    That lures so many across the sea?"
"Oh! I saw men toiling on every hand,
    And right merry men they seem'd to be."

IV.

" When you were abroad in the Western land,
    Saw you any who ask'd for me?"
" Oh ! I met marching many a band,
    And the air they play'd was *Grammachree.*

V.

" And their order'd ranks you should have seen,
    In guarded camp, or festive hall,
When their manly limbs were clad in green,
    And a flag of green flew over all."

VI.

The spirit clapp'd her pearl-pale hands,
    Proudly her silvery wings she shook,
And the sleeping youth from the far-off lands
    Bless'd, as she pass'd, with a loving look.

THE PILGRIMS OF LIBERTY.

I.

BESIDE a river that I know, shrined in a laurel grove,
I see my idol—Liberty, that wears the smile of Love ;
Her face is toward the city, four paths are at her feet,
They bear her hymns from the four winds as rays converging
    meet.

II.

By the four paths I see approach my idol's votaries:
Those from the highlands of the West, from Northern valleys

From Shannon shore and Slaney's side, yon other pilgrims
    throng:
Oh! wild around my idol's shrine will surge their mingled
    song.

III.

And thither wends that wounded man, who bears the muf-
    fled sword
Once borne by the comrade true his kindred heart adored;
The sacred stains upon the blade are drops of tyrant blood:
He brings it now to Freedom's shrine, as loyal comrade
    should.

IV.

And thither wends the widow, with her fair son at her side,
The banneret, whose eye is wet, beneath his brow of pride;
The sable crape around the staff his father bore is roll'd—
The shining Sun across the Green flings many a ray of gold.

V.

The maiden with the funeral urn close gathered to her
    breast
Goes thither to give up the heart she loved on earth the
    best ;
She girt his sword and gave him for Ireland's holy fight—
And once again to Liberty, Love yields her equal right.

VI.

The Artist, with his battle piece—the Poet, with his song—
The Student, with his glowing heart, pour to the shrine along,
Where Liberty, my idol, sits on a shrine like snow,
By a gliding river that I love, near a city that I know.

VII.

Oh! long around my idol's throne may bloom the laurel trees,
The ever green and ever glad, they laugh at blight and
    breeze—

True children of our hardy clime, long may they there be
    seen—
Like our nation's banners folded, as deathless and as green.

VIII.

Oh! long may the four pathways join beneath my idol's
    feet,
And long may Ireland's mingled men before her altar meet;
Oh! long may man and maid and youth go votaries to the
    grove
Where reigns my idol, Liberty, that wears the smile of Love.

HAIL TO THE LAND.

I.

Hail to the land where Freedom first
Through all the feudal fetters burst,
And, planting men upon their feet,
Cried, Onward! never more retreat!
Be it yours to plant your starry flag
On royal roof and castle crag;
Be it yours to climb Earth's eastern slope
In championship of human hope,
Your war-cry, Truth! immortal word;
Your weapon, Justice! glorious sword;
Your fame far-traveled, as the levin,[1]
And lasting as the arch of heaven.
        Hail to the Happy Land!

II.

Hail to the land where Franklin lies
At peace beneath disarmèd skies,

Where Jefferson and Jackson rest,
Like valiant men, on Victory's breast,
Where, his benignant day-task done,
The clouds have closed round Washington—
The star amid the luminous host
Which guides mankind to Freedom's coast.
I feel my heart beat fast and high,
As to the coast our ship draws nigh ;
I burn the fresh foot-prints to see
Of the heroes of Humanity.
     Hail to the Happy Land !

III.

Hail to the land whose broad domain
Rejoices under Freedom's reign—
Where neither right nor race is bann'd,
Where more is done e'en than is plann'd—
Where a lie liveth not in stone,
Nor truth in Bible-leaves alone—
Where filial lives are monuments
To noble names and high intents—
Oh! where the living still can tread,
Unblushingly, amid the dead !
     Hail to that Happy Land !

IV.

What can I lay on Freedom's shrine
Meet-offering to the power divine ?
I have nor coronet nor crown,
Nor wealth nor fame can I lay down ;
But I have hated tyrants still,
And struggled with their wrathful will ;
And when through Europe's length they lied,

And oft, in better champion's stead,
In thy behoof I've striven and said,
" Ah, be the offering meet to thee,
My life, my all, dread Liberty!
        Hail to thy Happy Land!

v.

"The land is worthy of its place,
The vanguard of the human race ;
Its rivers still refresh the sea,
As Truth does Time, unceasingly ;
Its prairie plains as open lie
As a saint's soul before God's eye ;
Its broad-based mountains firmly stand
Like Faith and Hope in their own land.
Heaven keep this soil, and may it bear
New worth and wealth to every year ;
And may men never here bend knee
To any lord, O Lord, but Thee.
        Hail to the Happy Land!"

A MALEDICTION.

L

"My native land! how does it fare
    Since last I saw its shore?"
"Alas! alas! my exiled frère,
    It aileth more and more.
God curse the knaves who yearly steal
    The produce of its plains;
Who for the poor man never feel,

II.

" We both can well recall the time
    When Ireland yet was gay;
It needed then no wayside sign
    To show us where to stay.
A stranger sat by ev'ry hearth,
    At ev'ry board he fed;
It was a work of maiden mirth
    To make the wanderer's bed.

III.

" 'Tis altered times : at every turn
    A shiftless gang you meet;
The hutless peasants starve and mourn,
    Camp'd starkly in the street.
The warm old homes that we have known
    Went down like ships at sea;
The gateless pier, the cold hearth-stone,
    Their sole memorials be.

IV.

" We two are old in years and woes,
    And Age has powers to dread ;
And now, before our eyes we close,
    Our malison be said:
The curse of two gray-headed men
    Be on the cruel crew*
Who've made our land a wild-beast's den—
    And God's curse on them too."

* Meaning the " exterminating " landlords.

A SONG FOR THE SECTIONS.

I.

Ye, who still love our native land,
  Who doubt not, nor despair,
Come, let us make another stand,
  And never droop for care.
If she is poor, she needs the more
  The service of the true,
And laurels will be plenty yet,
  Though heroes may be few.

II.

What though we failed in 'Forty-eight
  To form th' embattled line,
The more our need to compensate
  Our friends in 'Forty-nine ;
What though ships bear to isles afar
  The foremost of our race—
For them and Ireland both we'll war,
  And their slavish bonds efface.

III.

All Europe shakes from shore to shore ;
  The Jews bid for her crowns ;
Democracy, with sullen roar,
  Affrights her feudal towns :
The kings are struggling for their lives
  Amid the angry waves,

IV.

Up! up! ye banish'd Irishmen,
    The soldier's art to learn ;
A time will come—Will ye be then
    Fit for the struggle stern ?
A time will come when Britain's flag
    From London Tower shall fall—
Will ye be ready then to strike
    For Ireland, once for all ?

V.

Oh ! by the memories of your youth,
    I conjure you prepare ;
By all your vows and words of truth,
    I ask you to prepare.
Oh, by the holy Christian Creed,
    Which makes us brothers, rise !
And staunch the kindred wounds that bleed,
    Ere yet our nation dies !

VI.

Ye who still hope in Fatherland,
    Your trial-time shall come,
When many a gallant exile band
    Can strike a blow for home !
For Ireland and for vengeance, then,
    Arise and be prepared,
And strike the tyrant to the heart
    The while his breast is bared.

VII.

No more of mercy—not a word
    Of scorning 'vantage ground—
No more of measuring sword and sword,
    Of being content to wound :—

But when the battle is begun,
    Cleave open crown and crest ;
Then only will your work be done,
    Then only can you rest.

"*THE ARMY OF THE WEST.*"

I.

WE fight upon a new-found plan, our Army of the West—
Our brave brigades, along the line, will leave the foe no rest—
Our battle-axes, bright and keen, with every day's swift
        sands,
Lay low the foes of Liberty, and then annex their lands;
On, onward through the Western woods our standard saileth
        ever
And shadows many a nameless peak and unbaptizèd river—
The Army of the Future we, the champions of the Unborn—
We pluck the primal forests up, and sow their sites with
        corn.

II.

That ruggèd standard beareth the royal arms of toil—
The axe, and pike, and ponderous sledge, and plough that
        frees the soil—
The field is made of stripes, and the stars the crest supplies,
And the living eagles hover round the flag-staffs where it
        flies.
And thus beneath our standard, right merrily we go,
The Future for our heritage, the tangled Waste our foe :
The Army of the Future we, the champions of the Unborn—
We pluck the primal forests up, and sow their sites with

III.

Down in yon glade the anvil rings beneath the arching oaks,
Behind yon hills our neighbors drive young oxen in the
    yokes,
Yon laughing boys now boating down the rapid river's tide,
Go to the learnèd man who keeps the log-house on its side—
Like suckers of the pine they grow, elastic, rugged, tall,
They will hit a swallow on the wing with a single rifle ball—
The cadets of our army they, from " the West-Point" of the
    unborn,
They too will pluck the forests up, and sow their sites with
    corn.

IV,

Oh ye who dwell in cities, in the self-conceited East,
Do you ever think how by our toils your comforts are
    increased?
When you walk upon your carpets, and sit on your easy
    chairs,
And read self-applauding stories, and give yourselves such
    airs—
Do you ever think upon us, Backwoodsmen of the West,
Who, from the Lakes to Texas, have given the foe no rest?
On the Army of the Future, and the champions of the
    Unborn,
Who pluck the primal forests up, and sow their sites with
    corn?

SONG OF THE SIKHS.

L

Allah! il allah! the rivers are red
With the blood and the plumes of the Infidel dead;
Allah! il allah! their far isle grows pale

II.

This morning, how proud was their muster and show,
As their squadrons swift wheel'd, and their columns came
  slow !
Wheel'd swift to their death by the spears of Lahore—
Came slow to feed Jhailum full with their gore.

III.

Allah ! il allah ! the Dost and his son *
Shall hear of the deeds on this bloody day done,
And a stream from the hills to our camp we shall see,
Like the Ganges, refreshing the shores of the sea!

IV.

Let your hearts shout aloud to the arch of the sky,
For thither the souls of our dead brothers fly;
Oh! sweet from the Houris their welcome will be,
As they tell how they fell 'neath the cool Tamboo tree.

V.

Allah ! il allah ! trust cannon and sabre !—
Rest not ! Paradise is the payment of labor !
Allah ! il allah ! another such day,
And, like spirits cast out, they will flee and away !

FREEDOM'S LAND.

I.

Where is Freedom's glorious land ?
  Is it where a lawless race

No! for man's wild passions still
   Heavier chains their tyrants forge,
And his own unbridled will
   Is itself the fiercest scourge,
And a land of anarchy
Never can be truly free.

II.

When her fetters Gallia broke
   And indignant cast away,
With the old and galling yoke,
   Every salutary sway,
Were not the destroyers then
   Tyrants worse to meaner slaves?
Freedom is miscall'd of men
   When her footsteps tread on graves—
Where unpunish'd crime goes free
Is no land of liberty.

III.

But where men like brethren stand,
   Each one his own spirit rules,
Serving best his own dear land,
   Turning from the anarch's schools,
Reverencing all lawful sway—
   Patient if it be unjust;
If the fabric should decay,
   Build, improve—not raze to dust;
Liberty and justice fair
Find their holiest altars there!

IV.

Such be thou oh land of mine!
   Still'd be every discord rude!
Erin, let thy sons combine

Prudent, temperate, firm, and strong—
  Loyalty our watchword be!
Truth our shield 'gainst taunt and wrong,
  And warm hearts our chivalry!
Loyal soul and stainless hand,
Make our country Freedom's land!

THE DESERTED CHAPEL.

I.

SUNDAY morning, calm and fair!
  Ah, how beautiful the scene is!
The blue hills shade the amber air,
  The Slaney flows, my home, between us!
Do you note the Sabbath sun,
  Burnish'd for the day's devotion?
Do you note the white ships on
  The distant, silent, silver ocean?

II.

"God be praised for Ireland's beauty!
  Such a mother as He gave us?
Did we only do our duty,
  Could the powers of hell enslave us?
E'en this river, did we heed it,
  Safety's lesson yet might teach us.
Far and weak the founts that feed it,
  But to what great end it reaches!"

III.

So I thought, my way across
  To that wayside chapel lowly,
Whose rude eves, festooned with moss,

(Thoughts that do not love the city!)
  Now, alas! all here was altered—
  Even the Mass-boy's accent falter'd ;
  The congregation, few and sad,
  Such a look of ruin had,
That I could not pray for pity!

IV.

  Signs of grief on every face,
  In the consecrated place ;
  At the altar I heard weeping,
  Tears the agèd priest's face steeping ;
  And a moan might rend a stone,
  Round the silent walls was creeping.
  The very carved Saint in his nook
  Had compassion in his look—
Chimed the sad winds through the steeple—
"Save, O Jesus! save thy People!"

V.

"Where," thought I, "is now the maiden
Who once knelt here, blossom-laden ?
Where the farmer, whose broad breast
Here its simple sins confess'd?
Some, perchance, beyond Lake Erie,
Toil as slaves in forests weary ;
Some are nearer home beside us,
In their cold graves, whence they chide us,
That we still let feuds divide us!"

VI.

Whoso has a human heart,
  Let him our old chapel see,
Note all round it, nor depàrt,

He has vowed his part to take
With us aye, for Ireland's sake,
And her feudal bonds to break.

A MERE IRISHMAN'S LAMENT.

I.

OH, ancient land! where are those lords
  Whose palace-gates to me
Seem'd rusted as their father's swords,
  Which won their share in thee!
Their avenues are all grass-grown,
  Their courts with moss are green,
Cold looks each tree, and tow'r, and stone,
  Where no master's face is seen.

II.

Yon swan that sails across the lake,
  How sad its state appears!
The raven's hoarse, dull echoes wake
  Among the oaks of years.
Neglected feeds the fav'rite steed
  Up to the very door ;
It whines : poor beast! thy lord, I rede,
  Will ne'er caress thee more.

III.

Far, far beyond the crumbling wall
  Which marks that wide domain,
Silence and sorrow over all

The stout yeoman hath lost his pride,
　The toilsman's strength hath past,
And lifeless homes, from every side,
　Stare us, like skulls, aghast.

IV.

Ah, ancient land! what tree could keep
　Its bearing high, or strength,
If the roots that in the soil were deep
　Fail'd, as its stay, at length?
And art thou not a rootless tree,
　Dear land! fair land?—ah! how
Should sap or firmness be in thee—
　What stay of strength hast thou?

V.

In foreign halls thy lords laugh loud,
　Are gayest 'mid the gay—
Their day of life has not a cloud,
　In the strange climes far away.
Free flows their wealth, and shines their worth,
　In France, Spain, Italy;
They've smiles and wealth for all the earth,
　And cold neglect for thee.

VI.

Not such our lords of ancient time,
　Whose ample roofs rose o'er
Aileach, Carmen, Tara sublime—
　They loved their natal shore;
Theirs were the homes that fill'd the land
　With light like lofty lamps—
Unlike this errant, night-born band,
　Chiefs of death-dews and damps!

VII.

But weak as froth such plaintive strain—
  Let us no more repine ;
Let them still from our soil remain,
  Still laugh at wrath divine.
The sterner and the louder call,
  Shall drag them o'er the sea—
"The lord that dwells not in his hall,
  No lord o'er us shall be !"

THE RECUSANT.*

I.

You swore me an oath when the grass was green,
  To win me a royal dower,
To take me hence to the altar, I ween,
  And thence beyond *their* power.

II.

By St. Berach's staff, and St. Ruadan's bell,
  And by all the oaths in heaven,
You swore to love me, when spring was green,
  While breath to your body was given.

III.

And your faith has flown ere the corn was ripe,
  And your love ere the leaves do fall—
I am not treated as queen or as wife,
  Or honor'd or dower'd at all.

IV.

Oh! false and fair and fickle of faith,
  Nor lover nor name need I,
I have had young lovers true to the death,
  And others who shall not die.

V.

I shall be woo'd when the spring is green,
  I shall win me a royal dower,
And my true lovers all, ere long, I ween,
  Shall save me from your power!

THE CELT'S CONSOLATION.

I.

If our island lies prostrate, why should we despair?
What race, for resistance, with ours can compare?
Some wiser, some richer, are found in the world,
But their souls are as red as the flags they unfurl'd!

II.

With swords by their sides some are harness'd to shame,
But the bronze of success cannot hide the black name;
Nor the diamonded brow shield the guilty abhorr'd,
When their pride topples down in the breath of the Lord.

III.

O'er the waters of Time, in the chronicler's bark,
As we sail by the Ages, some brilliant, some dark,
We behold how the empire of blood is o'erthrown,

IV.

If we may not be free, let us try to be frank,
Let us fight life's long battle with well-order'd rank
If we may not be great, let us try to be good,
And long for no laurels besprinkled with blood!

NO SURRENDER.

I.

HEARD amid the landlord's wassail,
In his tear-bemoated castle—
Heard by peer and heard by peasant,
As the prophet of the present—
Heard in Dublin's dimest alleys,
Heard in Connaught's saddest valleys—
In our night-time, from the North,
Came a voice to stir the earth,
    With its watchword, "No surrender!"

II.

"No surrender!" It is spoken—
Be the people's vow unbroken!
"No surrender!" Sons of toil,
Lineal heirs of Irish soil!
Holy lips have blessed the bans,
Wedding of the hostile clans—
"No surrender!" Men of God—
Ye shall break the tyrant's rod
    With your Gospel, "No surrender!"

III.

"No surrender!" Man of might,

Whose heart is fire, whose brain is light—
You shall lead and win the fight !
On Slieve Donard plant your banner,
Let the mountain breezes fan her.
Ireland feels its dawning splendor,
Hoping, chiding, guiding, tender,
      Shining on us, " No surrender !"

DEEDS DONE IN DAYS OF SHAME.

I.

A DEED ! a deed ! O God, vouchsafe,
  Which shall not die with me,
But which may bear my memory safe
  O'er time's wreck-spotted sea,—
A deed, upon whose brow shall stand
  Traced, large in lines of flame—
" This hath been done for Ireland,
  Done in the days of shame !"

II.

An age will come, when Fortune's sun
  Will beam in Ireland's sky,
And mobs of flatterers then will run
  To hail her majesty.
Amid that crowd I shall not be
  To join in the acclaim ;
But deeds will have their memory,
  Though done in days of shame.

III.

When six feet of a stranger soil
Shall press upon my heart,
And envy's self will pause awhile
To praise the manly part—
Oh ye who rise in Ireland, then,
To fight your way to fame,
Think of the deeds by mouldering men
Done in the days of shame!

THE GATHERING OF THE NATIONS.

I.

Gather together the nations! proclaim the war to all :
Armor and sword are girding in palace, tower, and hall ;
The kings of the earth are donning their feudal mail again—
Gather together the nations! arouse and arm the men.

II.

Who cometh out of the North?   'Tis Russia's mighty Czar ;
With giant hand he pointeth to a never-setting star ;
The Cossack springs from his couch—the Tartar leaves his
    den !—
Ho! herald souls of Europe, arouse and arm the men.

III.

What does the Frank at Rome, with the Russian at the
    Rhine ?
And Albion, pallid as her cliffs, shows neither soul nor sign ;
Pope Pius sickeneth daily, in the foul Sicilian fen—
Ho! wardens of the world's strongholds, arouse and arm the

IV.

The future circleth nearer on its grey portentious wings,
Pale are the cheeks of princes, and sore afraid are kings !—
Once faced by the furious nations, they'll flee in fear, and
    then,
By the right divine of the fittest, we shall have the reign of
    men !

ROCKS AND RIVERS.

AN IRISH FABLE.

I.

When the Rivers first were born,
  From the hill tops each surveyed,
Through the lifting haze of morn,
  Where his path through life was laid.

II.

Down they pour'd through heath and wood,
  Ploughing up each passing field ;
All gave way before the flood,
  The Rocks alone refused to yield.

III.

"Your pardon !" said the Waters bland,
  "Permit us to pass on our way ;
We're sent to fertilize the land—
  And will be chid for this delay."

IV.

" You sent !" the Rocks replied with scorn,
  "You muddy, ill-conditioned streams ;
Return and live, where ye were born,

V.

"You will not?" "No!" The Waters mild
  Called loudly on their kindred stock,
Wave upon wave their strength they piled ;
  And cleft in twain rock after rock.

VI.

They nurtured towns, they fed the land,
  They brought new life to fruits and flocks :
The Rivers are the People, and
  Our Irish Landlords are the Rocks.

NEW-YEAR'S THOUGHTS.

I.

A Spirit from the skies
  Came into our trodden land ;
It glow'd in roseate dyes,
  And around its brow a band
Was bound like a sun-stream in the west ;
    And as its accents broke
    O'er the land, our men awoke,
    And each felt the stranger's yoke
      On his breast!

II.

And first a flush of shame
  Spread along their manly brows,
And next, in God's dread name,
  They swore, and sealed their vows,
That Ireland a free state should be ;

And from the mountains then,
And from each glade and glen,
Gray spirits taught the men
    To be free.

III.

There was candor in the land,
  And loud voices in the air,
And the poet waved his wand,
  And the peasant's arm was bare,
And Religion smiled on Valor as her child ;
    But, alas! alas! a blight
    Came o'er us in a night,
    And now our stricken plight
       Drives me wild !

IV.

But wherefore should I weep,
  When work is to be done ?
Wherefore dreaming lie asleep
  In the quick'ning morning sun ?
Since yesterday is gone and pass'd away
    I will seek the holy road
    That our martyr saints have trod,
    And along it bear my load
       As I may !

V.

I will bear me as a man—
  As an Irish man, in sooth—
No barrier, wile, or ban,
  Shall stay me from the truth,
I will have it, or perish in the chace—

That I loved my own isle well
My bones at least shall tell,
And on what quest I fell
   In that place.

VI.

But if God grant me life
   To see this struggle out,
The end of inward strife
   And the fall of foes without,
I will die without a murmur or a tear ;—
   For in that holy hour,
   You'd not miss me from your dower
Of love, and hope, and power,
   Erin, dear !

CHANGE.

I.

How fair is the sun on Lough Gara !
   How bright on the land of the Gael !
For Summer has come with her verdure,
   To gladden the drooping and pale ;
And morn o'er the landscape is stealing,
   The meadows are joyous with May ;
All lightsome and brightsome the hours—
   Poor Erin was never so gay !

II.

How loud is the storm on Lough Gara !
   How dark on the land of the Gael !
The clouds they are split with red lightning,
   The blasts how they mutter and rail !

Oh, black is the evening around us,
　And gone are the smiles of the morn,
All gloomsome and dreary the hours—
　Poor Erin was never so lorn!

III.

Sweet mother! how like to our story!
　How like our own mournfullest doom—
Now bright with the prestige of glory—
　Now dashed into gloomiest gloom!
How late since our dear flag flew o'er us!
　How soon did our poor struggles fail!
And frail as the gladness of Gara
　Were the hopes in the heart of the Gael!

THE DAWNING OF THE DAY.

I.

In our darkness we find comfort,
　In our loneliness some joy,
When Hope, like the moon arises,
　Night's phantoms to destroy ;
The spectral fires that haunt us
　Before its light give way,
And the Unseen cannot daunt us
　At the dawning of the day.

II.

There are empty homes in Ireland,
　There are full ships on the sea ;
Sons and brothers are awaiting

Their eyes are on the ocean,
 And they cannot turn away,—
How sweet will be their meeting
 At the dawning of the day.

III.

I, too, am like a merchant
 Whose wealth is on the deep ;
The blast that blows unkindly
 Could almost make me weep ;
I think of the friend-freighted ship,
 That leaves my native bay—
May the saints be its protection
 Till the dawning of the day !

THE SEARCH FOR THE GAEL.

I.

I LEFT the highway—I left the street—
 In Albyn I sought them long ;
I follow'd the track of Kenneth's feet,
 And the sound of Ossian's song ;
By the Kymric Clyde, and in Galloway wild,
 I sought for the wreck of my race ;
But the clouds that the hills of Albyn hide
 Have pitied their forfeit place.

II.

I look'd for the Gael in the Cambrian glen,
 From the Cambrian mountains 'mid,
And I saw only mute, coal-mining men—

At Merlin's work in Caernarvon waste
  They knew not Merlin's name—
And the lines the hand of the master traced
  As the Devil's craft they claim.

III.

I look'd for the Gael in green Innisfail,
  And they showed me cowering there
Misshapen forms, cast down and pale,
  Thy disciplined host, despair!
But I noticed yet in their stony eyes
  A flash they could not veil,
And I said, "Will no brave man arise
  To strike on this flint with steel?"

IV.

I have found my race—I have found my race,
  But oh! so fallen and low,
That their very sires, if they look'd in their face,
  Their own sons would not know.
Still I've found my race—I've found my race,
  And to me this race is dear,
And I pray that Heaven may grant me grace
  To toil for them many a year.

IT IS EASY TO DIE.

I.

It is easy to die
  When one's work is done—
To pass from the earth
  Like a harvest day's sun,
After opening the flowers and ripening the grain

II.

It is easy to die
    When one's work is done—
Like Simeon, the priest,
    Who saw God's Son ;
In the fulness of years, and the fulness of faith,
It is easy to sleep on the clay couch of death.

III.

But 'tis hard to die
    While one's native land
Has scarce strength to cry
    'Neath the spoiler's hand ;
O merciful God ! vouchsafe that I
May see Ireland free,—then let me die.

ODE TO AN EMIGRANT SHIP.[1]

I.

LET us speak the ship that stands
Boldly out from sheltering lands :
Like a proud steed for the goal—
Like a space-defying soul ;
Comet bright, and swift that hath
Enter'd on her chosen path !

II.

By the color that thou wearest,
By the precious freight thou bearest,
By the forests where you grew,
In the land you steer unto—

III.

Tremble not beneath the weight
Of your anxious human freight ;
Freight beyond all cost or price,
Of gold, or pearls, or Indian spice ;
　　Steadily, oh steadily,
Through fickle winds and troubled sea
Bear the fallen to the free,
　　Tenderly, oh tenderly !

IV.

Munster's headlands fade away ;
Old Kinsale dons its *baraid* grey ; ⁴
No Channel light here shows the way—
It is no landlock'd boating bay
　　·Their vessel heads for now—
From the east unto the setting sun,
A watery field their eyes rest on,
　　Green is the soil they plough.
Here wave vaults wave in sportive speed,
Like schoolboys in·a summer mead ;
While the brave ship with lofty port,
Ambitious, spurns their idle sport,
And holds upon her way afar,
For higher prize and sterner war.

V.

Upon her deck a child I see,
A young adventurer on the sea ;
And ever hath its mother press'd
Her infant to her gentle breast ;
Now looking westward hopefully,
Now turning eastward mournfully—
The Past and Future—light and shade
Upon her brow a truce have made.

VI.

By the ocean fame thou'st won,
Gallant ship, sail fleetly on !
Proudly, safely, sail once more
To thine own paternal shore ;
Stars upon thy standard shine—
Never shame that flag of thine !

VII.

Pleasant harborage waiteth thee,
Off beyond this surging sea :
Where thy mighty anchors shall,
In the ooze, sleep where they fall ;
And thy brave, unbending masts
Creak no more to northern blasts ;
Quiet tides and welcoming cheer
Waiteth, good ship, for you here !

VIII.

Steadfast to one purpose still,
Hold on with unwavering will ;
Thus the hero wins renown—
Thus the martyr wins his crown :
Thus the poet—thus the sage
Find their port in history's page ;
Stars upon thy standard shine—
Never shame that flag of thine !

"*WHEN FIGHTING WAS THE FASHION.*"

I.

We've ships of steam, and we have wires,
   Thought travels like a flash on—
But much we've lost that was our sires',
   When fighting was the fashion.

II.

Oh gay and gentle was their blood—
  Who Danes and Dutch did dash on,
Who to the last all odds withstood,
  When fighting was the fashion.

III.

The grain that grew in Ireland then,
  Their own floors they did thrash on—
They lived and died like Christian men,
  When fighting was the fashion.

IV.

Then Milan mail, in many a field,
  Mountmellick swords did clash on,
And generals to our chiefs did yield,
  When fighting was the fashion.

V.

But now, oh shame! we lick the hand
  That daily lays the lash on—
Luck never can befall our land,
  Till fighting comes in fashion.

HOPE.

HIBERNIA.

I.

Tell me truly, pensive sage,
Seest thou signs on any page,
Know'st a volume yet to ope,

II.

Dare I seek it where the wave
Grieves above Leander's grave?
Must I follow forth my quest
In the wider, freer West?

III.

Shall I seek its sources still,
Delving under Aileach hill?
Must I wait for Cashel's fall
To build anew Temora's hall?

THE SAGE.

IV.

Genius, no! the destined morn
In the East shall ne'er be born;
Genius, no! thy ancient quest
May not be answer'd in the West.

V.

Not where the war-laden tide
Continents and camps divide,
Not where Russ and Moslem cope,
Shall break the morn of Erin's hope.

VI.

On Antrim's cliffs, on Cleena's strands,
Thou shalt marshal filial bands;
And deep Dunmore and dark Dunloe
Shall kindle in the sunburst's glow.

VII.

On native fields, by native strength,
Thy fetters shall be burst at length,
Then will and skill, not note and trope,

THE REAPER'S SONG.

Air—*The Jolly Shearers.*

I.

THE August sun is setting
  Like a fire behind the hills—
'Twill rise again to see us free
  Of life or of its ills ;
For what is life, but deadly strife
  That knows no truce or pause,
And what is death, but want of breath
  To curse their alien laws?

> Chorus—Then a-shearing let us go, my boys,
>   A-shearing let us go,
>   On our own soil 'twill be no toil
>   To lay the corn low.

II.

The harvest that is growing
  Was given us by God—
Praise be to Him, the sun and shower
  Work'd for us at his nod.
The lords of earth, in gold and mirth,
  Ride on their ancient way,
But could their smile have clothed the isle
  In such delight to-day ?
      Chorus.

III.

" How will you go a-shearing,
  Dear friends and neighbors all?"
" Oh, we will go with pike and gun,

We'll stack our arms and stack our corn
    Upon the same wide plain ;
We'll plant a guard in barn and yard,
    And give them grape for grain."
        Chorus.

IV.

God speed ye, gallant shearers,
    May your courage never fail,
May you thrash your foes, and send the chaff
    To England on the gale !
May you have a glorious harvest-home,
    Whether I'm alive or no ;
Your corn grows *here*, the foe comes *there*—
    Or *it* or *he* must go.

    Chorus—Then a-shearing let us go, my boys,
        A-shearing we will go,
        On our own soil 'twill be no toil
        To cut the corn low.

A HARVEST HYMN.

I.

God has been bountiful ! garlands of gladness
Grow by the waysides exorcising sadness,
Shedding their bloom on the pale cheek of slavery,
Holding out plumes for the helmets of bravery,
Birds in them singing this sanctified stave—
"God has been bountiful—Man must be brave !"

II.

Look on this harvest of plenty and promise—

See where the sun on the golden grain sparkles !
Lo ! where behind it the reaper's home darkles !
Hark ! the cry ringing out, " Save us—oh, save !
God has been bountiful—Man must be brave !"

III.

From the shores of the ocean, the farther and hither,
Where the victims of famine and pestilence wither,
Lustreless eyes stare the pitying heaven,
Arms, black, unburied, appeal to the levin—
Voices unceasing shout over each wave,
" God has been bountiful—Man must be brave !"

IV.

Would ye live happily, fear not nor falter—
Peace sits on the summit of Liberty's altar !
Would ye have honor—honor was ever
The prize of the hero-like, death-scorning liver !
Would ye have glory—she crowns not the slave—
God has been bountiful, you must be brave !

V.

Swear by the bright streams abundantly flowing,
Swear by the hearths where wet weeds are growing—
By the stars and the earth, and the four winds of heaven,
That the land shall be saved, and its tyrants outdriven,
Do it ! and blessings will shelter your grave—
God has been bountiful—will ye be brave ?

THE LIVING AND THE DEAD.

I.

Bright is the Spring-time, Erin, green and gay to see ;
But my heart is heavy, Erin, with thoughts of thy sons and
    thee ;
Thinking of your dead men lying as thick as grass new
    mown—
Thinking of your myriads dying, unnoted and unknown—
Thinking of your myriads flying beyond the abysmal waves—
Thinking of your magnates sighing, and stifling their
    thoughts like slaves !

II.

Oh ! for the time, dear Erin, the fierce time long ago,
When your men felt, dear Erin, and their hands could strike
    a blow !
When your Gaelic chiefs were ready to stand in the bloody
    breach—
Danger but made *them* steady; they struck and saved their
    speech !
But where are the men to head ye, and lead ye face to face,
To trample the powers that tread ye, men of the fallen race ?

III.

The yellow corn, dear Erin, waves plenteous o'er the plain ;
But where are the hands, dear Erin, to gather in the grain ?
The sinewy man is sleeping in the crowded churchyard near,
And his young wife is keeping him lonesome company there ;
His brother, shoreward creeping, has begged his way abroad,
And his sister—though, for weeping, she scarce could see

IV.

No other nation, Erin, but only you would bear
A yoke like yours, O Erin ! a month, not to say a year ; '
And will you bear it forever, writhing and sighing sore,
Nor learn—learn now or never—to dare, not to deplore—
Learn to join in one endeavor your creeds and people all—
'Tis only thus can you sever your tyrant's iron thrall.

V.

Then call your people, Erin ! call with a prophet's cry—
Bid them link in union, Erin ! and do like men or die—
Bid the hind from the loamy valley, the miller from the fall—
Bid the craftsman from his alley, the lord from his lordly
　　　hall—
Bid the old and the young man rally, and trust to work,
　　　not words,
And thenceforth ever shall ye be free as the forest birds.

DEATH OF THE HOMEWARD BOUND.

I.

PALER and thinner the morning moon grew,
Colder and sterner the rising wind blew—
The pole star had set in a forest of cloud,
And the icicles crackled on spar and on shroud,
When a voice from below we feebly heard cry,
"Let me see, let me see my own land ere I die.

II.

"Ah ! dear sailor, say ! have we sighted Cape Clear ?
Can you see any sign ?　Is the morning light near ?
You are young, my brave boy ! thanks, thanks for your hand,

Thank God, 'tis the sun that now reddens the sky,
I shall see, I shall see my own land ere I die.

III.

" Let me lean on your strength, I am feeble and old,
And one half of my heart is already stone-cold :
Forty years work a change ! when I first cross'd this sea,
There were few on the deck that could grapple with me ;
But my youth and my prime in Ohio went by,
And I'm come back to see the old spot ere I die."

IV.

'Twas a feeble old man, and he stood on the deck,
His arm round a kindly young mariner's neck—
His ghastly gaze fix'd on the tints of the east
As a starveling might stare at the sound of a feast ;
The morn quickly rose and reveal'd to his eye
The land he had pray'd to behold, and then die !

V.

Green, green was the shore, though the year was near done—
High and haughty the capes the white surf dash'd upon—
A gray ruin'd convent was down by the strand,
And the sheep fed afar, on the hills of the land !
" God be with you, dear Ireland !" he gasp'd with a sigh ;
" I have lived to behold you—I'm ready to die."

VI.

He sunk by the hour, and his pulse 'gan to fail,
As we swept by the headland of storied Kinsale ;
Off Ardigna Bay it came slower and slower,
And his corpse was clay-cold as we sighted Tramore ;
At Passage we waked him, and now he doth lie

THE THREE DREAMS.

I.

Borne on the wheel of night, I lay
  And dream'd as it softly sped—
Toward the shadowy hour that spans the way
  Whence spirits come, 'tis said :
And my dreams were three;—
  The first and worst
  Was of a land alive, yet 'cursed,
  That burn'd in bonds it couldn't burst—
And thou wert the land, Erie !

II.

A starless landscape came
  'Twixt that scene and my aching sight,
And anon two spires of flame
  Arose on my left and right ;
And a warrior throng
Were marching along,
Timing their tramp to a battle song,
And I felt my heart from their zeal take fire,
But, ah ! my dream fled as that host drew nigher !

III.

Next, methought I woke, and walk'd alone
On a causeway all with grass o'ergrown,
That led to ranks of ruins wan,
Where echo'd no voice or step of man ;
Deadly still was the heavy air,
Horrible silence was everywhere—
No human thing, no beast, no bird

Saint Patrick's image up in a nook
Held in its hand a Prophecy Book,
And its mystic lines were made plain to me,
And they spoke thy destiny, loved Erie !

IV.

"The skene and the sparthe,
The lament for the dearth,
The voice of all mirth
Shall be hush'd on thy hearth,
O Erie !
And your children want earth
When they bury !
Till Tanist and Kerne
Their past evils unlearn,
And in penitence turn
To their Father in heaven ;
Then shall wisdom and light,
Then manhood and might,
And their land and their right
To the sons of Milesius be given.
But never till then—
'Till they make themselves men—
Can the chains of their bondage be riven !"

THE EXILE'S MEDITATION.

I.

ALONE in this mighty city, queen of the continent !
I ponder on my people's fate in grief and discontent—
Alas ! that I have lived to see them wiled and cast away,
And driven like soulless cattle from their native land a

II.

These men, are they not our brethren, grown at our mother's
    breast?
Are they not come of the Celtic blood, in Europe held the
    best?
Are they not heirs of Brian, and children of Eoghan's race,
Who rose up like baited tigers and sprung in the foeman's
    face?

III.

And why should they seek another shore, to live in another
    land?
Had they not plenty at their feet, and sickles in their hand?
Did an earthquake march upon them, did Nature make them
    flee,
Or do they fly for fear, and to seek some ready-made Liberty?

IV.

I have read in ancient annals of a race of gallant men
Who fear'd neither Dane nor devil; but it is long since then—
And "cowardice is virtue," so runs the modern creed—
The starving suicide is praised and sainted for the deed!

THE PARTING FROM IRELAND.

I.

Oh! dread Lord of heaven and earth! hard and sad it is
    to go
From the land I loved and cherish'd into outward gloom
    and woe;
Was it for this, Guardian Angel! when to manly years I
    came,
Homeward, as a light, you led me—light that now is turn'd
    to flame?

II.

I am as a shipwreck'd sailor, by one wave flung on the shore,
By the next torn struggling seaward, without hope for-
     evermore ;
I am as a sinner toiling onward to the Redemption Hill—
By the rising sands environ'd, by siroccos baffled still.

III.

How I loved this nation ye know, gentle friends, who share
     my fate—
And you too, heroic comrades, loaded with the fetter's
     weight—
How I coveted all knowledge that might raise her name with
     men—
How I sought her secret beauties with an all-insatiate ken.

IV.

God! it is a maddening prospect thus to see this storied
     land
Like some wretched culprit writhing in a strong avenger's
     hand—
Kneeling, foaming, weeping, shrieking, woman-weak and
     woman-loud—
Better, better, Mother Ireland! we had laid you in your
     shroud !

V.

If an end were made, and nobly, of this old centennial feud—
If, in arms outnumbered, beaten, less, O Ireland! had I
     rued ;
For the scatter'd sparks of valor might relight thy dark-
     ness yet,
And thy long chain of Resistance to the Future had been
     knit.

VI.

Now *their* castle sits securely on its old accursèd hill,
And their motley pirate-standard taints the air in Ireland
    still ;
And their titled paupers clothe them with the labor of our
    hands,
And their Saxon greed is glutted from our plunder'd fathers'
    lands.

VII.

But our faith is all unshaken, though our present hope is
    gone ;
England's lease is *not* forever—Ireland's warfare is *not* done.
God in heaven, He is immortal—Justice is His sword and
    sign—
If Earth will not be our ally, we have One, who is Divine.

VIII.

Though my eyes no more may see thee, island of my early
    love !
Other eyes shall see thy Green Flag flying the tall hills
    above ;
Though my ears no more may listen to the rivers as they
    flow,
Other ears shall hear a Pæan closing thy long *caoine* of woe!

THE EXILE'S DEVOTION.

I.

If I forswear the art divine
  Which deifies the dead—
What comfort then can I call mine,
  What solace seek instead ?

For, from my birth, our country's fame
   Was life to me and love,
And for each loyal Irish name
   Some garland still I wove.

II.

I'd rather be the bird that sings
   Above the martyr's grave,
Than fold in fortune's cage my wings
   And feel my soul a slave ;
I'd rather turn one simple verse
   True to the Gaelic ear,
Than classic odes I might rehearse
   With senates list'ning near.

III.

Oh, native land ! dost ever mark
   When the world's din is drown'd,
Betwixt the daylight and the dark
   A wondering, solemn sound
That on the western wind is borne
   Across thy dewy breast ?
It is the voice of those who mourn
   For thee, far in the West ?

IV.

For them and theirs I oft essay
   Your ancient art of song,
And often sadly turn away
   Deeming my rashness wrong ;
For well I ween, a loving will
   Is all the art I own ;
Ah me ! could love suffice for skill,
   What triumphs I had known !

v.

My native land! my native land!
   Live in my memory still ;
Break on my brain, ye surges grand!
   Stand up! mist-cover'd hill.
Still in the mirror of the mind
   The scenes I love I see ;
Would I could fly on the western wind,
   My native land! to thee.

THE SAINT'S FAREWELL.

I.

Oh, Aran blest! oh, Aran blest!
Bright beacon of the wavy West!
Henceforth through life long seas must roll
Between thy cloisters and my soul.

II.

Farewell, farewell, thou holy shore,
Where angels walk with men, once more!
In Hy, my lonely hut shall ne'er
Receive such guests of earth or air.

III.

Thou Modan, Mersenge's pious son,
Sad is my heart, and slow my tongue
To say farewell to friend like thee!
May Christ, our Lord, your keeper be!

IV.

Far eastward, far too far, lies Hy,
Darkness is o'er its morning sky ;

The sun loves not his ancient East,
But hastens to the holier West.

v.

Aran ! thou sun of realms terrene,
Would that, lull'd by thy airs serene,
I slept the sleep that lasts till *day*,
Wrapp'd in thy consecrated clay.

vi.

Aran, thou sun ! no tongue may tell
How, haunted by each holy bell,
My love, call'd backward to your breast,
Longs for its evening in the West.

TO MY WISHING-CAP.

L

Wishing-cap, Wishing-cap, I would be
Far away, far away o'er the sea,
Where the red birch roots
Down the ribbed rock shoots,
  In Donegal the brave,
    And white-sail'd skiffs
    Speckle the cliffs,
  And the gannet drinks the wave.

II.

Wishing-cap, Wishing-cap, I would lie
On a Wicklow hill, and stare the sky,
Or count the human atoms that pass

Where once the clans of O'Byrne were ;
  Or talk to the breeze
  Under sycamore trees,
In Glenart's forests fair.

III.

Wishing-cap, Wishing-cap, let us away
To walk in the cloisters, at close of day,
Once trod by friars of orders gray,
In Norman Selskar's renown'd abbaye,
  And Carmen's ancient town ;
For I would kneel at my mother's grave,
Where the plumy churchyard elms wave,
  And the old war-walls look down.

THE SONG OF LABOR.

I.

To the tired toilers' ring,
  Brother, bring your song and tabor ;
Poets of all nations, sing
  To-day a hymn of praise to Labor.

    Chorus—"Viva Labor! long live Labor!
        Strongest sceptre! keenest sabre!
        Chant the hymn! strike on the tabor!
        Liegemen! sing the Song of Labor."

II.

GERMAN.

On the German Rhine-banks I
Have beheld his banners fly,
While the order'd ranks beneath
Struck a stroke with every breath—

Sledges on the anvils ringing,
Poets in their gardens singing—
      "Viva Labor! long live Labor!" etc.

III.

ITALIAN.

Where the Arno winding comes,
Under shade of Florence domes—
Where Genoa rises steep,
Crowning high the subject deep—
Where live Rome and dead Rome dwell,
Like corpse in crypt near sexton's cell—
Through Italia's storied length,
Skill and art, surpassing strength,
Daily toil and chant at even
The great human song to Heaven—
      "Viva Labor! long live Labor!" etc.

IV.

FRENCHMAN.

Ah! my France, thy dauntless spirit
Love of toil doth still inherit,
And no power but armèd wrong
Ever yet hath hush'd thy song!
In the province, in the street,
Troops of toilers you may meet—
Men who make as light of labor
As our minstrel of his tabor.
      "Viva Labor! long live Labor!" etc.

V.

IRISHMAN.

Ask not me for merry song,

By the noble Shannon river,
Wretched land-serfs moan and shiver—
Whining all day in the city
Are the partners Woe and Pity :
Lordlings think toil don't beseem them,
Though their own sweat might redeem them.
     "Viva Labor! long live Labor!" etc.

VI.

AMERICAN.

In the land where man is youngest,
On the soil where nature's strongest,
Come and see a greater glory
Than the old vine-bender's story!
Come and see the city's arms
Filling forests with alarms—
See before the breath of steam
Space and waste fly like a dream.
     "Viva Labor! long live Labor!" etc.

[Written for the Annual Festival of the St. Patrick's Literary Association of Montreal, of which the author was the founder and first president.]

PROLOGUE TO ST. PATRICK AT TARA.°

I.

THE stranger entering at yonder door,
Who never saw our *amateurs* before,
May ask, What have we here? an Irish play?
In Lenten times, and on St. Patrick's day?

II.

Our answer is, The very day inspires
With memories of the green land of our sires ;

The very day unfolds, from age to age,
The Christian drama of that island-stage—
The martyr, hero, scholar, warrior, bard,
The plot, the stake—virtue and its reward ;
The good man's grief, the heartless villain's gain,
The strong-arm'd tyrant righteously slain ;
The thousand memorable deeds which give
Zest to the Past, and make its actors live !

III.

This day, in every Irish heart and brain,
Calls up that Past, nor does it call in vain ;
Surrounds the mental theatre with all
The fond embellishments of Tara's hall ;
Seats on that Meathian mound the kings of old,
In flowing vest and twisted tongues of gold—
A warlike race, to whom repose was rust,
Mingled of good and ill, just and unjust :
Men much the same ruled all the pagan West—
Some gentler, wiser, greater than the rest ;
War was their game, and, eagle-like, they bore
Back to their cliffs the spoils of many a shore.

IV.

To Tara in its most auspicious day
We would transport you in the coming play ;
While yet " the Road of Chariots " round its slope,
To eyes far off, shone as the path of Hope ;
Ere yet its hospitable hearths were cold,
Or Ruin reign'd where mirth abode of old—
To Tara, as it rose upon the way
Of the apostle, on that eve of May
When first he kindled the forbidden fire

V.

Remote the time, and difficult the task
For which your kind indulgence here we ask ;
Yet what more meet for this our Irish play—
Saint Patrick's life upon Saint Patrick's Day ?

TO DUFFY IN PRISON.

I.

THROUGH the long hours of the garish day I toil with brain
    and hand,
In the silent watches of the night I walk the spirit-land ;
Our souls in their far journeyings want neither lamp nor
    guide,
They need no passports, wait no winds upon the ocean wide,
And, dreadful power of human will! they grub out of the
    earth
The crumbled bones of mighty men, and give them second
    birth ;
They travel with them on the paths which through the world
    they took,
And converse with them in the tongues which, when alive,
    they spoke.

II.

One night I stood with Sarsfield where his heart's blood was
    outpour'd,
On Landen's plain, in Limerick's name, he show'd it with
    his sword ;
Ere morn, upon the Pincian Hill, I heard Tir-Owen's tale
Of the combats, and the virtues, and the sorrows of the

Since then I've walk'd with Grattan's shade amid the gothic
    gloom
Of Westminster's monkless abbey, forecasting England's
    doom,
And in green Glassnevin I have been beside the tombs where
    rest—
There, Curran, here, O'Connell, on our mother-land's warm
    breast.

III.

'Twas but last night I traversed the Atlantic's furrow'd face—
The stars but thinly colonized the wilderness of space—
A white sail glinted here and there, and sometimes o'er the
    swell
Rung the seaman's song of labor, or the silvery night-watch
    bell ;
I dreamt I reach'd the Irish shore, and felt my heart re-
    bound
From wall to wall within my breast, as I trod that holy
    ground ;
I sat down by my own hearth-stone, beside my love again—
I met my friends and Him, the first of friends, and first of
    Irish men.

IV.

I saw once more the dome-like brow, the large and lustrous
    eyes—
I mark'd upon the sphinx-like face the clouds of thought
    arise—
I heard again that clear quick voice that, as a trumpet,
    thrill'd
The souls of men, and wielded them even as the speaker
    will'd—
I felt the cordial-clasping hand that never feign'd regard,
Nor ever dealt a muffled blow, nor nicely weigh'd reward.

My friend! my friend! oh! would to God that you were
    here with me,
A-watching in the starry West for Ireland's liberty!

V.

Oh, brothers! I can well declare, who read it like a scroll,
What Roman characters were stamp'd upon that Roman
    soul—
The courage, constancy, and love, the old-time faith and
    truth,
The wisdom of the sages, the sincerity of youth—
Like an oak upon our native hills, a host might camp there
    under,
Yet it bare the song-birds in its core, above the storm and
    thunder ;
It was the gentlest, firmest soul that ever, lamp-like, show'd
A young race seeking Freedom up her misty mountain road.

VI.

You grew too great, dear friend! to stand under a tyrant's
    arm,
His tall tow'rs trembling o'er your mines had fill'd him with
    alarm ;
He was the lord of hirèd hosts, of ill-got wealth well kept,
You led a generation, and inspired them while he slept :
He woke—ye met—and once again, O Earth and Heaven!
    ye see
Might's dagger at Right's throat, Right's heart beneath his
    · knee ;
Yea, once again in Ireland, as of old in Calvarie,
The truth is fear'd and crucified high on a felon tree.

VII.

Like a convoy from the flag-ship, our fleet is scatter'd far,
And you, the valiant admiral, chain'd and imprison'd are :

Like a royal galley's precious freight flung on sea-sunder'd
    strands,
The diamond wit and golden worth are far-cast on the
    lands—
And I, whom most you loved, am here, and I can but indite
My yearnings, and my heart hopes, and curse *them* while I
    write :
Alas! alas! ah! what are prayers, and what are moans or
    sighs,
When the heroes of the land are lost—of the land that will
    not RISE?

VIII.

But I swear to you, dear Charles, by my honor and my
    faith,
As I hope for stainless name and salvation after death,
By the green grave of my mother 'neath Selskar's ruin'd
    wall,
By the birth-land of my mind and love, of you, of M——,
    ——, all,
That my days are dedicated to the ruin of the power
That holds you fast and libels you in your defenceless hour ;
Like an Indian of the wild woods, I'll dog their track of
    slime,
And I'll shake the Gaza-pillars yet of their godless mammon
    shrine.

IX.

They will bring you in their manacles beneath their bloody
    rag—
They will chain you like the Conqueror to some sea-moated
    crag—
To their fiends it will be given your great spirit to annoy—
To fling falsehood in your cup, and to break your martyr-
    joy ;

But you will bear it nobly, like Regulus of eld—
The oak will be the oak, and honor'd e'en when fell'd :
Change is brooding over earth, it will find you 'mid the
    main,
And, throned beneath its wings, you'll reach your native
    land again.

TO DUFFY, FREE.

I.

THROUGH long sorrows and fears,
And past perilous years,
And darkness and distance,
And seas, where the mists dance,
    I see a new star!
Not a comet, or wild star,
But a radiant and mild star,
Still shining as Venus,
Still bright'ning like Sirius,
On a night in July,
Is the star I descry !
And though myriads of miles and of waves intervene,
Admonish'd, I worship the star I have seen.

II.

It beams from the far cloud, whose wild stormy heaving
Has fill'd all our souls with a fearful misgiving,
    On the storm-waters dark,
    Where, half-savage and stark,
    Men, with sinew and shout,
    Are seeking about
    For lost stanchion and spar ;

With its light and its smile,
Guides their task and their toil ;
And the seekers, anon,
Look that it shines on ;
And they bless still the good star, evening and morning,
For their guide and their comfort, their hope and their
    warning.

III.

'Tis thy star, oh, my friend,
That doth shine and ascend
    On the night of our race ;
Thou art the appointed,
By affliction anointed,
    As through grief cometh grace ;
Born heir of tho planet,
See now that you man it
With the heroes whose worth
Hath made this round earth
    A circular shrine ;
For the sun hath not shone
On such work as, when done,
    Will be thine.

IV.

'Tis given to you
That work to renew
Which the blood of past builders hath hallow'd in vain,
When their helpers bore sceptres in France and in Spain,
To try the sphinx-task of our kindred again ;
    Death waits in the way
    For defeat or a prey,
    And horrors hedge round

Where Ireland, dishonor'd, awaiteth the knight
Who shall conquer for her both renown and her right.
      And should none such appear
      In a day and a year,
      Her 'scutcheon, disgraced,
      Is forever displaced
From the midst of the ancient and noble,
Who, through time and through trouble,
In the cavalcade's rush, in the locking of shields,
Have still seen her banner abroad in their fields.

v.

      The fate of our land
      God hath placed in your hand ;
      He hath made you to know
      The heart of your foe,
      And the schemes he hath plann'd ;
      Think well what you are,
      Know your soul—and your star ;
      Persevere—dare—
      Be wise and beware—
      Seek not praise from to-day ;
      Be not wiled from your way
      By visions distracting ;
      Heed not the detracting
      Of souls imbecile
      Who your mastership feel,
Yet hate you, as pride hates the sky-piercing spire,
Because than its own gaudy dome it springs higher.

vi.

      Go forth, knight, to the altar
        With bold heart and holy,
      And fear not, nor falter,
        But ask, and ask solely

The might and the grace
  To redeem our fall'n nation
  From its deep desolation,
And lift up our race ;
  Let your vigil be long,
  For prayer maketh strong
The arm of the weakest,
And the will of the meekest,
  To wrestle with wrong ;
Born heir of the planet,
See now that you man it
With the heroes whose worth
Hath made this round earth
  A circular shrine ;
For the sun hath not shone
On such work as, when done,
  Will be thine!

A VOW AND PRAYER.*

I.

IRELAND of the Holy Islands,
Circled round by misty highlands—
Highlands of the valleys verdant,
Valleys of the torrents argent,
  If I ever cease to love thee,
  If I ever fail to serve thee,
May I fall, and foulness cover
All my hopes and homestead over ;
Die a dog's death, outcast, hurried !
Into earth as dogs are buried.

II.

Though in thee each day of sorrow,
Led unto more sad to-morrow—
Though each night fell darker, bleaker,
Round my couch, a careworn waker—
    If I ever cease to love thee,
    If I ever fail to serve thee,
May my children rise around me,
Like Acteon's brood, to hound me,
Over all life's future landscape
With a hate that nothing can 'scape.

III.

Since the trance of childhood bound me,
I have felt thy arms around me ;
More to me than any other
Hast thou been a nurse and mother ;
    Could I ever cease to love thee ?
    Could I ever fail to serve thee ?
Thou whose honied words forever
Flow before me like a river,
Vocal ever, ever telling
Of the source from whence they're welling ?

IV.

God look on thee, ancient nation !
God avert thy desolation !
Oh ! hold fast his dread evangels,
And he'll set his shining angels
    As a guard of glory keeping
    Watch about thee, waking, sleeping.
Tempt Him not, and all thy evils,
And the ulcer-giving devils
Who possess thee, shall be pow'rless,
And thy joys to come be hourless.

HOME SONNETS—ADDRESS TO IRELAND.

I.

MOTHER of soldiers! once there was a time
When your sons' swords won fame in many a clime;
When Europe press'd on France, they fought alone
For her, and served her better than their own!
Those were the days your exiles made their fame
By gallant deeds which put our age to shame—
Those were the days Cremona city, saved,
Stood to attest what Irish valor braved!
When England's chivalry, sore wounded, fled
Before the stormy charge O'Brien led— [5]
When travellers saw in Ypres' choir display'd
The trophies of your song-renown'd brigade!
Mother of soldiers! France was proud to see
Your shamrock then twined with the *fleur de lis!* [6]

II.

Mother of soldiers! in the cause of Spain
The Moors in Oran's trench by them were slain; [7]
For full an hundred years their fatal steel
Has charged beside the lances of Castile.
Carb'ry's, Tyrconnell's, Breffny's exiled lords
To Spain and glory gave their gallant swords; [8]
And Spain, of honor jealous, gave them place
Before her native sons in glory's race;
Her noblest laurels graced your soldiers' head,
Her dearest daughters shared your soldiers' bed;
In danger's hour she call'd them to the front,
And gave to them the praise who bore the brunt:
Mother of soldiers! Spain to-day will be

III.

Mother of soldiers ! on the Volga's banks
Your practised leaders form'd the Russian ranks ;
And fallen Limerick gave the chiefs to lead
The hosts who triumph'd o'er the famous Swede. [8]
That time even Austria gave them host on host,
The ruling *baton*, and the perilous post—
Buda, Belgrade, Prague, Deva—every trust
That man could earn, and found them bold as just.
Velettri, Zorndorff, Dantzic, still can tell
How Austria's Irish soldiers fought and fell,
And how the ruling skill that led them on
To conquer was supplied by your own son ! [10]
Mother of soldiers ! while these trophies last,
You're safe against the sland'rers of the past !

IV.

Mother of exiles ! from your soil to-day
New myriads are destroy'd or swept away ;
The crowded graveyards grow no longer green,
The daily dead have scanty space, I ween ;
The groaning ships, freighted with want and grief,
Entomb in every wave a fugitive ;
The sword no more an Irish weapon is—
The spirit of the land no longer lives ;
Mother ! 'twas kill'd before the famine came—
The stubble was prepared to meet the flame ;
All manly souls were from their bodies torn,
And what avails it if the bodies burn ?
Mother of soldiers ! may we hope to be
Yet fit to strike for vengeance and for thee !

THE HEART'S RESTING-PLACE.

I.

Twice have I sail'd the Atlantic o'er,
　Twice dwelt an exile in the West ;
Twice did kind nature's skill restore
　The quiet of my troubled breast—
As moss upon a rifted tree,
　So time its gentle cloaking did,
But though the wound no eye could see,
　Deep in my heart the barb was hid.

II.

I felt a weight where'er I went—
　I felt a void within my brain ;
My day-hopes and my dreams were blent
　With sable threads of mental pain ;
My eye delighted not to look
　On forest old or rapids grand ;
The stranger's joy I scarce could brook—
　My heart was in my own dear land.

III.

Where'er I turn'd, some emblem still
　Roused consciousness upon my track ;
Some hill was like an Irish hill,
　Some wild bird's whistle call'd me back ;
A sea-bound ship bore off my peace
　Between its white, cold wings of woe ;
Oh ! if I had but wings like these,

OH! BLAME ME NOT.

I.

Oh! blame me not if I love to dwell
  On Erin's early glory;
Oh! blame me not if too oft I tell
  The same inspiring story;
For sure 'tis much to know and feel
  That the Race now rated lowly
Once ruled as lords, with sceptre of steel,
  While our Island was yet the Holy.

II.

'Tis much to know that our sainted, then,
  To their cloisters the stranger drew,
And taught the Goth and Saxon men
  All of heaven the old earth knew—
When Alfred and Dagobert students were
  In the sacred "Angel's Vale,"
And harp heard harp through the midnight air
  Pealing forth the hymns of the Gael.

III.

'Tis much to know that in the West
  The Sun of our wisdom rose,
And the barbarous clouds that scarr'd its breast
  Were scatter'd like baffled foes—
To know that in our hearts there dwell
  Some seeds of the men of story:
Oh! blame me not if I love to tell
  Of Erin's ancient glory.

QUESTION AND ANSWER.

L

" Young Thinker of the pallid brow,
  What care weighs on your brain ?
What tangled problems solve you now
  Of glory or of gain ?
Is that you seek of heaven or hell ?
  Work you with charm or fire ?
What is your quest ? what is your spell ?
  And what your hope or hire ?"

II.

" Oh, brilliant is my quest," he said,
  " And eminent my hope,
As any star that yet hath shed
  Its light through heaven's cope ;
I seek to save mine ancient race—
  'Tis knowledge is my spell—
Their lines of life and fate I trace,
  To know and serve them well."

III.

" Their mission—say, what may it be
  That thus inspires your toil,
And holds you back to native earth
  Like saplings to the soil ?
Their mission—is't to rob and reign
  O'er half the sons of earth ?
Or is it not to hug the chain,
  And die of doubt and dearth ?"

IV.

"Oh, no! oh, no!" the Thinker said,
  "Their future far I see—
Their path through pleasantness is led,
  Their arms and minds are free ;
They walk the world like gods of old,
  Incensed, enshrined, obey'd ;
'Tis this I seek, for this I strive—
  My answer now is made!"

SONNET.*

Nor of the mighty! not of the world's friends
  Have I aspired to speak within these leaves ;
These best befit their joyful kindred pens—
  My path lies where a broken people grieves ;
By the Ohio, on the Yuba's banks,
  As night displays her standard to their eyes,
Alone, in tears, or gather'd in sad ranks,
  Stirring the brooding air with woful sighs,
I see them sit : I hear their mingled speech,
  Gaelic or Saxon, but all from the heart ;
"Home !" is the word that sways the soul of each—
  A word beyond the embellishments of art :
Yet of this theme I feebly seek to sing,
And to my banish'd kin a book of "Home" I bring.

* This appears to have been intended by the author for the dedication of an epic he was writing, called "The Emigrants."—ED.

A SALUTATION TO THE FREE FLAG OF AMERICA.

I.

Flag of the Free! I remember me well
　When your stars in our dark sky were shining—
'Twas the season when men like the cold rain fell,
　And pour'd into graves unrepining—
'Twas the season when darkness and death rode about
　In the eye of the day dim with sorrow,
And the mourner's son had scarce strength to moan out
　Ere he follow'd his sire on the morrow.

II.

Flag of the Free! I beheld you again,
　And I bless'd God who guarded me over—
And I found in your shade that the children of men
　Half the glory of Adam recover.
And they tell me, the knaves! thou dost typify sin,
　That thy folds fling infection around them,
That thy stars are but spots of the plague that's within,
　And which shortly will raging surround them.

III.

Not so! oh, not so! thou bright pioneer banner!
　Thou art not what factions miscall thee ;
Where Humanity is there must ever be Honor—
　Shame cannot stain let what else may befall thee :
Over Washington's march, o'er the Macedon's freight
　When flying, the angels ordain'd thee—
"The Flag of the Free, the belovèd of Fate,

THE ANCIENT RACE.

I.

WHAT shall become of the ancient race—
The noble Celtic island race?
Like cloud on cloud o'er the azure sky,
When winter storms are loud and high,
Their dark ships shadow the ocean's face—
What shall become of the Celtic race?

II.

What shall befall the ancient race—
The poor, unfriended, faithful race?
Where ploughman's song made the hamlet ring,
The village vulture flaps his wing ;
The village homes, oh, who can trace,—
God of our persecuted race?

III.

What shall befall the ancient race?
Is treason's stigma on their face?
Be they cowards or traitors?   Go
Ask the shade of England's foe ;
See the gems her crown that grace ;
They tell a tale of the ancient race.

IV.

They tell a tale of the ancient race—
Of matchless deeds in danger's face ;
They speak of Britain's glory fed
On blood of Celt right bravely shed ;
Of India's spoil and Frank's disgrace—
They tell a tale of the ancient race.

V.

Then why cast out the ancient race?
Grim want dwelt with the ancient race,
And hell-born laws, with prison jaws,
And greedy lords with tiger maws
Have swallow'd—swallow still apace—
The limbs and the blood of the ancient race.

VI.

Will no one shield the ancient race?
They fly their fathers' burial-place;
The proud lords with the heavy purse—
Their fathers' shame—their people's curse—
Demons in heart, nobles in face—
They dig a grave for the ancient race!

VII.

They dig a grave for the ancient race—
And grudge that grave to the ancient race—
On highway side full oft were seen
The wild dogs and the vultures keen
Tug for the limbs and gnaw the face
Of some starved child of the ancient race!

VIII.

What shall befall the ancient race?
Shall all forsake their dear birth-place,
Without one struggle strong to keep
The old soil where their fathers sleep?
The dearest land on earth's wide space—
Why leave it so, O ancient race?

IX.

What shall befall the ancient race?
Light up one hope for the ancient race?

O Priest of God—*Soggarth aroon!*
Lead but the way—we'll go full soon ;
Is there a danger we will not face
To keep old homes for the Irish race?

x.

They will not go, the ancient race !
They must not go, the ancient race !
Come, gallant Celts, and take your stand—
The League—the League—will save the land—
The land of faith, the land of grace,
The land of Erin's ancient race !

xi.

They will not go, the ancient race !
They *shall* not go, the ancient race !
The cry swells loud from shore to shore,
From em'rald vale to mountain hoar—
From altar high to market-place—
They shall not go, the ancient race !

THE EXILE'S REQUEST.

I.

Or, Pilgrim, if you bring me from the far-off lands a sign,
Let it be some token still of the green old land once mine ;
A shell from the shores of Ireland would be dearer far to me
Than all the wines of the Rhine land, or the art of Italie.

II.

For I was born in Ireland—I glory in the name—
I weep for all her sorrows, I remember well her fame !
And still my heart must hope that I may yet repose at rest

III.

Her beauteous face is furrow'd with sorrow's streaming rains,
Her lovely limbs are mangled with slavery's ancient chains,
Yet, Pilgrim, pass not over with heedless heart or eye
The island of the gifted, and of men who knew to die.

IV.

Like the crater of a fire-mount, all without is bleak and bare,
But the rigor of its lips still show what fire and force were
      there ;
Even now in the heaving craters, far from the gazer's ken,
The fiery steel is forging that will crush her foes again.

V.

Then, Pilgrim, if you bring me from the far-off lands a sign,
Let it be some token still of the green old land once mine ;
A shell from the shores of Ireland would be dearer far to me
Than all the wines of the Rhine land, or the art of Italie.

SALUTATION TO THE CELTS.

I.

Hail to our Celtic brethren wherever they may be,
In the far woods of Oregon, or o'er the Atlantic sea—
Whether they guard the banner of St. George in Indian
      vales,
Or spread beneath the nightless North experimental sails—
        One in·name and in fame
         Are the sea-divided Gaels.

II.

Though fallen the state of Erin, and changed the Scottish
      land—
Though small the power of Mona, though unwaked Lewel-
      lyn's band—

Though Ambrose Merlin's prophecies degenerate to tales,
And the cloisters of Iona are bemoan'd by northern gales—
      One in name and in fame
      Are the sea-divided Gaels.

III.

In Northern Spain and Brittany our brethren also dwell ;
Oh ! brave are the traditions of their fathers that they tell ;—
The eagle and the crescent in the dawn of history pales
Before their fire, that seldom flags, and never wholly fails :
      One in name and in fame
      Are the sea-divided Gaels.

IV.

A greeting and a promise unto them all we send ;
Their character our charter is, their glory is our end ;
Their friend shall be our friend, our foe whoe'er assails
The past or future honors of the far-dispersèd Gaels :
      One in name and in fame
      Are the sea-divided Gaels.*

BOSTON, August 30, 1850.

UNION IS STRENGTH.

L

A MAN whose corn was carried away
Before his eyes, and whose oats and hay
Were piled up into the landlord's cart,
Look'd toward his castle with sorrowful heart.

* This poem was published in the first number of the *American Celt.*

II.

"You seem," said he, "so strong and grand,
Like a giant you overlook the land ;
And a giant in stomach you sure must be,
That of all my crop can leave none to me."

III.

Quoth another—"Of such weak words what end ?
Have you any hope that the devil will mend,
Or the wolf let the kid escape his maw,
Or a landlord yield his rights at law ?

IV.

"Let us go over to Rackrent Hall
By twos and threes—it may befall,
As wisdom is found in the multitude,
Enough of us might do the cause some good."

V.

At first they went by twos and threes,
But Rackrent's lord they could not please ;
And next they went in number a score,
But the case was even the same as before.

VI.

By fifties and hundreds they gather'd then,
Resolute, patient, dogged men,—
And the landlord own'd that he thought there was
Some slight defects in the present laws.

VII.

A barony spoke—a country woke—
A nation struck at their feudal yoke—
'Twas found the Right could not be withstood,

A SALUTATION.

DAUNTLESS voyagers who venture out upon the wreck-paved
 deep,
Who can sail with hearts unfailing o'er the ages sunk in
 sleep ;
There is outlet—ye shall know it by the tide's deep conscious
 flow;
There is offing—may ye show it to the convoy following slow !

Gallant champions, whose long labors file away in vista'd
 space,
Lost the fitful hour of sabres—not the Archimedean place ;
In the future realm before ye down the vale of labor looms
Your new Athens, oh ! pine benders, rear'd above the rob-
 bers' tombs.

Be ye therefore calm in council, Patience is the heart of
 Hope—
Never wrangle with the brambles when with old oaks ye
 must cope ;
William, Walpole, Pitt, and Canning, ye shall smite and
 overthrow,
Not by practising with pygmies can ye giant warfare know.

Whoso ye find fittest, wisest, he your suzerain shall be,
Yield him following and affection, stand like sons around his
 knee ;
Make his name a word of honor, make him feel you as a

Brothers, ye have drain'd the chalice late replenish'd by
    defeat ;
Unto brethren bear no malice, put the past beneath your
    feet ;
For the love of God, whose creatures ye see daily crucified,
For your martyrs, for your teachers, shun the selfish paths
    of pride.

Then, by all our pure immortals, ye, true champions, shall
    be blest,
By St. Patrick and St Columb, by St. Brendan of the West,
By St. Molling and St. Bridget, and our myriad martyr
    bands,
And your land shall be delivered, yea! delivered by your
    hands.

SONNET—RETURN.

I HAVE a sea-going spirit haunts my sleep,
    Not a sad spirit wearisome to follow,
Less like a tenant of the mystic deep
    Than the good fairy of the hazel hollow ;
Full often at the midwatch of the night
    I see departing in his silver bark
This spirit, steering toward an Eastern light,
    Calling me to him from the Western dark.
"Spirit !" I ask, " say, whither bound away?"
    " Unto the old Hesperides !" he cries.
"Oh, Spirit, take me in thy bark, I pray."
    " For thee I came," he joyfully replies ;
"Exile ! no longer shalt thou absent mourn,

DREAM JOURNEYS.

I.

Signall'd by something in our dreams,
  The ship of night, swift-sided sleep,
Glides out from all these alien streams
  To waft us homeward o'er the deep.

II.

We lead two lives, estranged, apart,
  By day a life of toil and care,
Till darkness comes with magic art,
  And bears us through the enchanted air.

III.

How oft have I not heard the swell
  Of Ocean on the farther shore!
Heard Skellig-Michael's holy bell,
  Or Cleena's warning off Glandore!

IV.

Rising afar from Arva's lake
  Have I not heard the wild swan's call?
Or paused, a wayside vow to make,
  By Saint Dachonna's waterfall?

V.

Before the dawn, when no star shined,
  Have I not knelt on Tara hill,
And felt my bosom glad to find

VL.

The sacred strand our fathers' feet
  Have often trod, I nightly view,
The island of the Saint's retreat,
  Amid the mountains of Tirhugh.

VIL.

The field of fame, the minstrel's grave,
  Though sad, rejoicingly I trace ;
From Ara to the Iccian [19] wave,
  I gather relics of the race.

VIIL.

Thus borne on wings of woven dreams,
  The ship of night, swift-sided sleep,
Finds us along those alien streams,
  And wafts us homeward o'er the deep.

NATIVE HILLS.

I know, I know each storied steep
  Throughout the land—
Where winds enchanted, love-lock'd sleep,
  Where teem the torrents grand—
For them I pine, for them I weep,
  An outcast man, and bann'd.

I see th' assembled bards of old
  On those grand hills—
Their music o'er the upland fold
  Like dew distills,
Or flashes downward bright and bold,
  As cave-born rills.

Content, my soul! in vain you long
    To breathe that air
Sweet with the loving breath of song,
    Felt everywhere,—
For man is weak, and Fate is strong,
    Not there! not there!

TIME'S TEACHINGS.

I.

Time bears a scythe around the earth,
An hour-glass noting death and birth,
A pouch for proverbs by his side,
And scatters broadcast, far and wide,
Truths that in manly breasts should 'bide,
        To light and lead them—
Truths to the shepherd-kings once told—
Truths flowing from the hills of old,
And good for men to feel, though cold—
        And much *we* need them!

II.

Time singeth gayly night and morn,
"The longest lane must have a turn :"
And who knows lanes like Father Time—
A travelling man since Adam's prime,
In every age, through every clime,
        By moon and sun?
My brothers, lay this "must" to heart—
The goal, though distant from the start,
To struggle for is true man's part,
        Till all is won.

III.

Time chanteth gravely night and day,
"God never shuts, but He makes a way ;"
And Time is God's own messenger,
His herald and avenger here—
He files the chain and dries the tear—
    Rears tomb and shrine.
And, brethren, shall we doubt it—we!
That no road leads to Liberty
Save by dungeon vault, and gory tree,
    And battle line?

IV.

Time hath sung now, even as he pass'd,
"Reckoning delay'd will come at last ;"
And, as he sung this holy strain,
I saw the island once again
Expanded under seas of grain,
And saw it fall as thick as rain
    'Fore yeomen bold ;
And cities, girding round the land,
And merchants crowding all the strand,
And Peace at Plenty's full right hand
    Upon her throne.

ANOTHER YEAR.

I.

ANOTHER year for young and old,
  For East and West, is flown forever!
The tatter'd miner counts his gold
  Beside the yellow Yuba river ;

The senate of our nation bows
   Before a Tartar idol brazen ;
And lovers in their Christmas vows
   Declare contempt of time and season.

II.

Europe looms darkly into day,
   Save where one sudden gleam enlightens
And rolls from France the fogs away,
   And Order's horizon now brightens.
The Sultan in his sage divan
   Smiles at our clam'rous Western frenzy
That styles Kossuth " the coming man,"
   And glorifies the new Rienzi !

III.

The Vaderland is all a dream,
   And to our New Year nothing germane ;
The Scandinavian Bund—a scheme
   To stir the bile of Baltic mermen ;
The Danube rolls in headlong haste
   From Austria's arm'd, troubled border,
And moans along the Hungarian waste—
   A desert through the wreck of Order.

IV.

The Cossack trains his horse and lance,
   Smiled on by the approving Russian,
And, longing, asks the road to France,
   And counts the spoil of Pole and Russian ;
The Tuscan, proud of Dante's tongue,
   Yet thinks the Savoyard his foeman,
While mines by secret murder sprung,

V.

Our race—the Celtic race—remains—
  Limbs of a life once so gigantic!—
Proscribed upon their native plains,
  Far-parted by the deep Atlantic!
But heaven for us has stars and saints,
  And earth a creed, a need, a mission;
Then let us hush our weak complaints,
  And mend, like men, our own condition.

VI.

By Emmet's death, O'Connell's life,
  And Smith O'Brien's pure endeavor,
Let's quench the kindling stuff of strife,
  And stifle Faction's voice forever.
Sons of the brave! shall we descend
  To spend our souls in parish quarrels;
Have we no altars to defend,
  No breach to breast in search of laurels?

VII.

God in His goodness gives us strength,
  And time, and courage to recover;
Let us look forward now at length,
  And cease to live the poor past over.
Let us from shadowy griefs arise,
  Admit the sun—employ the season—
Now and forever let's be wise,
  And leal to God, and led by Reason.

New Year's Eve, 1851.

AN INVITATION WESTWARD.

L.

YE are weary, O my people, of your warfare and your woes,
In the island of your birthright every seed of sorrow grows ;
Hearken to me, come unto me, where your wearièd souls
　　may rest
And plume their wings in peace, in the forests of the West.

II.

This life—ah ! what avails it by which shore we may be led
To the mounds where lie entrench'd all the army of the
　　dead?
In the Valley of All Souls, when the Lord of judgment
　　comes,
The Cross shall be our banner, our country all the tombs.

III.

Is it wise to waste the present in a future of the brain ?
Is it wise to cling and wither under Mammon's deadly reign ?
If the spirit of the toiler is by daily hate oppress'd,
How shall he pray to Heaven, as we do in the West ?

IV.

It grieves my soul to say it—to say to you, Arise !
To follow where the evening star sings vespers down the
　　skies ;
It grieves my soul to call you from the land you love the
　　best—
But I love Freedom better. and her home is now the West.

V.

Then, children of Milesius, from your house of death arise,
And follow where the evening star sings vespers to the
    skies ;
Though it grieve your souls to part from the land you love
    the best,
Fair Freedom will console you in the forests of the West.

    On Lake Erie, September, 1852.

O'DONNELL OF SPAIN.

I.

Let it be told in Donegal,
   Above the waves on Swilly's shore,
To Assaroe's hush'd waterfall,
   To wreck'd Kilbarron's ruin hoar,
That in the Fatherland, Old Spain,
The race of Conal rules again.

II.

Bid those who doubt the force of blood,
   The mean philosophers of pride,
Account for how this hidden flood
   Rises their *dictum* to deride !
Show them where, spurning every chain,
The race of Conal rules again.

III.

Ten ages of the life of man
   Have pass'd o'er earth since that dark day
When, under James Fitz-James's ban,
   Tyrconnel's chieftains sail'd away.
That galley might, in after years,
Have sail'd in widow'd Erin's tears.

IV.

Ten ages ! but the heap'd up woes
   Of confiscation, exile—all
Could never quench the blood of those
   Whose sires were chiefs in Donegal.
Thy hatred, Albion, raged in vain—
The slain of Erin rise in Spain !

V.

Let it be told from Malin's waves
   To Lough Derg's penitential strand,
Whisper it o'er the ancient graves—
   O'Donnell rules his Fatherland !
Tell it till every trampled hind
Can hear Hope's voice in every wind.

VI.

And thou, Lucena ! fortune's son,
   Rest not too long upon thy blade,
The smaller victory is won,
   The greater may be yet essay'd !
An hour may come, shall come, if thou
Art worthy so to bind thy brow !

WISHES.

I.

Though there the damp from ocean's moat
   Hangs thick and gray o'er town and hill,
And sudden storms drive bark and boat
   Helpless before their furious will,
      Yet would I be
      To-day with thee,
        My own dear nati

II.

Though here the sky of freedom pours
  Its golden blaze incessant down,
And men wield their own sov'reign powers,
  Unawed by any monarch's frown,
        Yet would I be
        To-day with thee,
            My own dear native land !

III.

For what is wealth, when hearts are sad ?
  And what can exile's freedom be ?—
The freedom of the harmless mad,
  A pitied, poor inanity.
        Ah ! I would be
        To-day with thee,
            My own dear native land !

IV.

There is no home, the wide world o'er,
  Like Ireland to the Irishman ;
Absence, through all, we must deplore,
  And pine beneath the exile's ban.
        Ah ! I would be
        To-day with thee,
            My own dear native land !

SONG OF THE SURPLUS.

I.

THE oak-trees wave around the hall,
  The dock and thistle own the lea,
The hunter has his air-tight stall,

The rabbit burrows in the hill,
  The fox is scarce begrudged his den,
The cattle crop the pasture still,
  But our masters have " no room for men."

II.

Each thing that lives may live in peace—
  The browsing beast and bird of air ;
No torturers are train'd for these,
  While man's life is a long despair.
The Lady Laura's eyes are wet
  If her dog dies beneath her feet ;
It has its burial rites—and yet
  Our human griefs no mercy meet.

III.

Well may'st thou ask, O Preacher true,
  Of manly sense and fearless tongue—
Like Israel's prophet, well may you
  Exclaim, " How long, O Lord ! how long ?"
How long may Fraud, and Pride, and Power
  Conspire to slay the immortal soul ?
How long shall Ireland groan and cower
  Beneath this thrice-accursed control ?

IV.

When shall we see free homes abound,
  And meet by street, and bridge, and stile,
The freeman's lifted brow unbow'd,
  As free from guilt, as free from guile ?
The song of peace, the hum of toil
  Will flow along our rivers when ?
When none within our native isle

MIDSUMMER, 1851.

L

Why standeth the laborer in the way, with sunken eyes and
    dim?
Is there no work, is there no hope, is there no help for him?
Why rusteth the swift, bright sickle that swept down Saxon
    grain,
Stuck in a patch of ragged thatch that keepeth not out the
    rain?

II.

Why lieth the plough on the headland, with broken stilt and
    tusk?
Why gapeth the sun-dried furrow from gray dawn unto dusk?
Why cometh no singing sower, scattering song and seed,
Where the field-mouse rangeth fat and free amid his groves
    of weed?

III.

There was no earthquake in the land—the ocean swept not
    here—
Since we beheld the grateful soil enrich the waning year;
The kind clouds in the west are throng, and hither bring
    their rain—
Now, why is the laborer lost for work, and the land disrobed
    of grain?

IV.

Ask not the peasant nor the priest—ask not the papers
    why—
Why would you shame the manly cheek, or fill the feeling

But go to the gate of Windsor, and ask its lady gay
Why her Irish farm has gone to waste, and its farmers gone
    to clay.

V.

Ah! if the sceptre had a soul, if conscience topp'd the
    crown,
We soon would have the truth made plain in country and in
    town—
Plain as the ancient mountains—plain as the girdling sea—
That in the laws lie all the cause of Ireland's misery.

VI.

You, Irish farmers, whose thin ranks are broken and dis-
    may'd,
You know what spoil is made of toil, how all this woe is
    made ;
The Lady of Windsor little thinks how you have rack'd and
    wrought
Your bones and brains to foster all that thus has gone to
    nought.

VII.

Little she knows that round her stand a gang of thievish
    earls,
Whose founts are fed, whose wines are cool'd with tears of
    humble churls ;
Little she knows that to their gods of Rank and Fashion rise
Daily a litany of groans, and a human sacrifice !

VIII.

The plough will rot, the furrow gape, the worker wait in
    vain,
Till Law and Labor, side by side, shall grapple Pride again.

Oh, Lady of Windsor, think betimes that even the strongest
    throne
May not withstand the just demand of Labor for "his own."

IX.

We ask no shares of Indian wealth, no spoils of Eastern
    shores ;
Kaffir and Dyak still, for us, may heap and hide their stores ;
We ask not London's pride and pomp, nor Yorkshire's iron
    arms—
We ask the law to guard and judge the farmers on their
    farms.

X.

The robber knights are all around; from every castle-top
They stretch their necks, a-hungering after the poor man's
    crop :
We ask that Justice have her seat amid the upstack'd corn,
That all he sowed and nursed may not from Labor's grasp
    be torn.

XI.

Is this too much? Is this a crime? Let men and angels
    judge.
Hark to the lords' hired advocate, but hear us for the drudge;
Between our causes let the state in lawfulness preside,
And we will gladly take the share awarded to our side.

XII.

Hear us and judge, while yet on earth our fiery race remain;
"Too late" can never be unsaid, nor ever said in vain.
To the far West—to God's own court—already hosts are
    fled ;—
Oh hear and save the living left, ere again "too late" be

LORD GL—GALL'S DREAM.

" A dream which was not all a dream."

I.

Lord Gl—Gall slept in "the House" last night,
When a terrible vision oppress'd his sight ;
'Twas not of Incumbor'd Estates ('tis said),
Nor the Durham Bull, nor the hat so red—
But he dreamt that a balance he saw in air,
Above the broad Curragh of famed Kildare—
That God and the landlords both were there.

II.

He heard the recording angel call
The titled criminals one and all,
And the witnesses to testify—
And he heard the four far winds reply ;
And myriads heap'd on myriads throng
From unnumber'd graves to denounce the wrong,
And with their sins to confront the strong !

III.

His lordship scarce could tell for fear,
Of every name that met his ear ;
But he saw that the archangel took
Note of them all in his blackest book—
From Farney some, and from Skibbereen,
From West and East and the lands between,
Such a skeleton tryst has never been seen.

IV.

He heard how Sir George gave the widow's mite
As instalment to a sybarite—

He heard how Lord Dick his fox-hounds fed
With ten starved cottiers' daily bread—
Anon, he trembled to hear his own
Name, named in the angel's sternest tone,
And thereat, upstarted he with a groan.

v.

Sadly he paces his silent hall,
Still muttering over the name Gl—Gall—
And penitent thoughts depress his head,
But the grave will not give up its dead.
Far, far away from their native Suir
Are scatter'd the bones of the exiled poor,
But the angel has note of them all, be sure!

LONDON.

RISE AND GO.

I.

In the valleys of New England,
    Are you happy, we would know?
Are you welcome, are you trusted?
    Are you not?—Then, RISE AND GO!

II.

Ye are toiling, toiling ever,
    Toss'd like sea-waves to and fro;
Up at sunrise, up at sunset,
    Still detested—RISE AND GO.

III.

You are merry o'er your infants,
    Yet you tremble as they grow;
'Tis the land makes them your masters,

IV.

As ye act, or as ye falter,
  We will deem ye men or no ;
For the homestead, for the altar,
  Take advice—ARISE AND GO !

TRY AGAIN.

I.

WHEN the equinoctial blast
Tears the canvas from the mast,
Does the sailor stand aghast
        To complain ?
Nay ; rather through the storm
You can mark his manly form—
        Try again.

II.

When the night-clouds overtake
The hunter in the brake,
Where the wild wolf and snake
        Have domain,
Does he fling him down to weep,
Like a sluggard in his sleep,
Or, with fearless heart and leap,
        Try again ?

III.

If friends or fate should prove
An overmatch for love,
And we vainly try to move
        Their disdain,

Oh! who would then lie down,
Though friends or fate should frown—
Who would not, for his own,
       Try again?

IV.

And when our land we see
Still sighing to be free—
When we should teach her—we!
       How to gain
Her rights, and rise sublime
From the torture-bed of time,
Why not ring upon the chime—
       Try again?

V.

Try again, thou fallen land,
With united heart and hand—
Try with rifle and with brand,
       Though blood rain!
Try for the sacred sod
That valiant men once trod;
In the holy name of God,
       Try again! try again!

A PROFESSION.

I.

I've thought and toil'd from boyhood's days,
  Not for gain, nor rank, nor glory,
But to gather a few Hibernian bays,
  And to master our island story.

When friends grew cold, and the very sky
  Seem'd darkly to deny me,
I pray'd for aid, and, from on high,
  The patriot's star drew nigh me.

II.

All nought to me is pomp and wealth,
  And the multitude's hoarse praises—
Give me, O God! but life and health,
  And the lofty thought that raises ;
Give me the power to weave a wreath—
  An evergreen rustic garland,
Which, when my exile ends in death,
  May be kept for me in a far land.

III.

Or, if I ask what is denied
  Save to the elect immortal,
If I may not merit a niche inside,
  Let me lodge without in the portal ;
Let me be lay-brother to the bards,
  The Muse's life-apprentice—
I'll envy not their high awards
  While I am amanuensis.

IV.

I've thought and toil'd from boyhood's days,
  Not for gain, nor rank, nor glory,
But to gather a few Hibernian bays,
  And to master our island story.
When friends grew cold, and the very sky
  Seem'd darkly to deny me,
I pray'd for aid, and, from on high,
  The patriot star drew nigh me.

AM I REMEMBER'D.

L

Am I rememebr'd in Erin—
    I charge you, speak me true—
Has my name a sound, a meaning
    In the scenes my boyhood knew?
Does the heart of the Mother ever
    Recall her exile's name?
For to be forgot in Erin,
    And on earth, is all the same.

II.

O Mother! Mother Erin!
    Many sons your age hath seen—
Many gifted, constant lovers
    Since your mantle first was green.
Then how may I hope to cherish
    The dream that I could be
In your crowded memory number'd
    With that palm-crown'd companie?

III.

Yet faint and far, my Mother,
    As the hope shines on my sight,
I cannot choose but watch it
    Till my eyes have lost their light;
For never among your brightest,
    And never among your best,
Was heart more true to Erin
    Than beats within my breast.

A FRAGMENT.

I.

I WOULD not die with my work undone,
My quest unfound, my goal unwon,
  Though life were a load of lead ;
Ah ! rather I'd bear it, day on day,
Till bone and blood were worn away,
  And Hope in Faith's lap lay dead.

II.

I dream'd a dream when the woods were green,
And my April heart made an April scene,
  In the far, far distant land,
That even I might something do
That should keep my memory for the true,
  And my name from the spoiler's hand.

FREEDOM'S JOURNEY.

I.

FREEDOM ! a nursling of the North,
  Rock'd in the arms of stormy pines,
On fond adventure wander'd forth
  Where south the sun superbly shines ;
    The prospect shone so bright and fair,
    She dreamt her home was there, was there.

II.

She lodged 'neath many a gilded roof,
  They gave her praise in many a hall,

Their kindness check'd the free reproof,
  Her heart dictated to let fall ;
    She heard the Negro's helpless prayer,
    And felt her home could not be there.

III.

She sought through rich savannas green,
  And in the proud palmetto grove,
But where her altar should have been
  She found nor liberty nor love ;
    A cloud came o'er her forhead fair,
    She found no shrine to Freedom there.

IV.

Back to her native scenes she turn'd,
  Back to the hardy, kindly North,
Where bright aloft the pole-star burn'd,
  Where stood her shrine by every hearth ;
    "Back to the North I will repair,"
    The goddess cried ; "my home is there !"

ALONG THE LINE.
A. D. 1812.

I.

STEADY be your beacon's blaze
    Along the line ! along the line !
Freely sing dear Freedom's praise
    Along the line ! along the line !
Let the only sword you draw
Bear the legend of the law,
Wield it less to strike than awe

II.

Let them rail against the North*
      Beyond the line! beyond the line!
When it sends its heroes forth
      Along the line! along the line!
On the field or in the camp
They shall tremble at your tramp,
Men of the old Norman stamp,
      Along the line! along the line!

III.

Wealth and pride may rear their crests,
      Beyond the line! beyond the line!
They bring no terror to our breasts,
      Along the line! along the line!
We have never bought or sold
Afric's sons with Mexic's gold,
Conscience arms the free and bold,
      Along the line! along the line!

IV.

Steadfast stand, and sleepless ward,
      Along the line! along the line!
Great the treasures that you guard
      Along the line! along the line!
By the babes whose sons shall be
Crown'd in far futurity
With the laurels of the free,
      Stand your guard along the line!

* It is unnecessary to say that these verses were written after the removal to Canada.—ED.

ARM AND RISE!

I.

Arm and rise! no more repining.
See, the glorious sun is shining—
      What a world that sun beholds.
White ships glancing o'er the ocean,
All earth's tides, too, in swift motion,
      Pouring onward to their goals.

II.

'Tis no life for sighing, dreaming—
Read the riddle—full of meaning—
      Written on your own broad palm ;
For this needs no gipsy guesses,
Here the line that curses, blesses—
      Say, I shall be—say, I am !

III.

You have borne the parting trial—
Dare the rest ; let no denial
      Daunt your hope at Fortune's door ;
See, a new world waits your wooing,
Courage is the soul of sueing—
      All things yield the brave before.

IV.

One tear to the recollections
Of our happy young affections,
      One prayer for the ancestral dead,
Then right on ; the sun is shining,
No more doubting or repining,

V.

In the forest stands the castle,
Silent, gloomy, bell nor wassail
    Echoes through its sable halls ;
Night and Chaos guard its portals,
They shall bow even to us mortals—
    Strike ! and down their standard falls.

VI.

On the round Canadian cedars
Legends high await but readers—
    From the oaks charm'd shields depend ;
Strike ! thou true and only champion,
Lord of the first land you camp on !
    Strike ! and win your crown, my friend!

VII.

Crowns—ay, golden, jewel'd, glorious—
Hang in reach before and o'er us—
    Sovereign manhood's lawful prize ;
He who bears a founder's spirit
To the forest, shall inherit
    All its rights and royalties.

AN INTERNATIONAL SONG.

CHORUS.—Comrades ! awhile suspend your glee,
    And fill your glasses solemnly—
    I give the Brave Man's Memory.

I.

There is one Brotherhood on earth,
Whereto brave men belong by birth.

And he who will not honor one,
Wherever found, himself is none—
>   Comrades! awhile, etc.

II.

Where'er they fought, howe'er they fell,
The question is—Was't ill or well ;
Victors or vanquish'd, did they stand
True to the flag they had in hand ?
>   Comrades! awhile, etc.

III.

What! shall we, then, at Waterloo
Deny to either honor due ?
Belie the hero of the day,
Or grudge the fame of gallant Ney ?
>   Comrades! awhile, etc.

IV.

Who looks on Abram's storied plain
May honor most one hero's name ;
But we conjure to-night the three—
Here's Wolfe, Montcalm, Montgomery !
>   Comrades! awhile, etc.

IRISH
HISTORICAL AND LEGENDARY POEMS.

THE HARP OF KING BRIAN.

I.

Mute harp of King Brian, what bard of these days
  Shall give to thy cold chords the spirit of song?
Who shall win thee to gladness, or tune thee to praise,
  Or rouse thee to combat with faction and wrong?
Cold, cold is the hand of the master who first
  In the halls of Kinkora thy melody woke,
When the pæan of conquest triumphantly burst,
  As the soul of the land pass'd from under the yoke!

II.

He sat by the Shannon, well worthy to hear
  The strains he gave forth, swift and strong as its tide;
And his hand, long familiar with falchion and spear,
  Clung to thee in grief, and caress'd thee with pride!
Long, long will his clansmen remember the strain—
  Now sinking in sorrow, now madd'ning to rage—
He sang in the morning when Mahon was slain,
  And went forth the war of his vengeance to wage.

III.

Nor less dear to their hearts was the king when the cloud
  Of warfare had broken and melted away,
When, unarm'd and retired from the worshipping crowd,

In battle he bore thee aloft on his shield,
  In peace, too, the hosts of thy lovers he led ;
If his glory shone first on the war-cover'd field,
  Fame's mellow'd light on Kincora was shed !

IV.

Mute harp of King Brian ! Time's sceptre has pass'd
  O'er the high homes of Erin, and conquer'd them all;
Adare's royal oak has gone down in the blast,
  And the cattle are housed in Kinkora's old hall.
But the muse that hangs over thy time-stricken fame
  May console thee that yet there are left in the land
Bards as leal to thy lord, and as proud of his fame
  As any that ever took gifts from his hand !

V.

Yes ! the hero may sleep and his grave be unknown,
  And Armagh, the fallen, may blush at his praise—
No need hath King Brian of shrine or of stone
  To live in the hearts of the bards of these days.
Mute relic of ages ! if haply thy strains
  Still visit the master who first gave thee birth,
Say his name is revered with the holiest names
  That ever won honor and worship on earth !

AN INVOCATION.

I.

Soul of my race ! Soul eternal !
  That liveth through evil and time—
That twineth still laurels all vernal,

Oh hear me, oh cheer me, be near me,
  Oh guide me or chide me alway,
But do not fly from me or fear me—
  I'm all clay when thou, Soul, art away.

II.

My mother died young; I inherit
  For thee all her love and my own ;
Oft I heard in thy fields her dead spirit
  Sing thy songs with Eternity's tone.
Friends fled, years have sped, hopes are dead—
  Fruitless tasks, restless age leadeth on—
But thy smile, free of guile, hope can shed
  On the future, from years that are gone!

III.

Soul of my race! Soul eternal!
  Who passeth o'er ocean and earth—
With thy new woven garlands so vernal,
  To sit at thy true lover's hearth—
Oh hear me, oh cheer me, be near me,
  Oh guide me or chide me alway,
But do not fly from me or fear me—
  I'm all clay when thou, Soul, art away.

ADDRESS TO MILESIUS.

I.

"Father Milesius! in the world where dwell
  All spirits once of earth, each one in place,
If earthward gazing, can you trace or tell

II.

" Are we to pass or perish in this sea
   Of sorrow coldly compassing us round ?
Or are we still in bonds and woe to be
   Saddest of men on earth that may be found ?

III.

" Indian, Etruscan, Israelite are gone
   Out of the world like water down a steep ;
Man might deny them, but that sculptured stone
   And brazen chronicle the record keep.

IV.

" Lost science, unknown armor, massive piles,
   In which the dwarfish Present stands aghast—
Ruins of cities spread o'er mournful miles
   Tell of the heirless races of the Past.

V.

" Lost ! lost to earth ! it is the body's lot
   To be secreted in its kindred clay:
Father Milesius ! must we come to nought ?
   Must Innisfail be blotted out for aye ?"

MILEADH-ESPAGNE. [13]

I.

Spoke Milesius ere he died—
" Here, my children, do not 'bide ;
Right fruitful is the land of Spain,
 But here you may no more remain.
'Tis written that your home shall be

There sea-monsters freely feed,
There the eagles mate and breed;
There the sacred oak is born—
Thence it looketh forth with scorn
On the tempest-trodden waves,
Crouching in their shelter'd caves.
Where the pathless forests stand
Interlock'd around the land,
Where the ocean vapors thicken,
There your warlike seed shall quicken—
There shall be the abiding-place
Of your broad and branching race."

II.

Death has closed the Patriarch's eyes,
Closed his ears to Scotia's cries ;
Still the heart and cold the brain
Where thoughts grew thick as summer grain ;
Mute the lips whose eloquence
Mingled wit, and faith, and sense ;
Nerveless now the arm of might
That thunder'd through the stormy fight.
Well may there be bitter grief
For thy loss, O matchless chief !
Well may they in silence mourn
The man of men beyond the bourne ;
Well may flow fond woman's tears
For him who loved them all his years ;
Sad and dark the day they made
His grave in the Gallician shade.
Clanna-Mileadh may have many
Arms of oak and lips of honey,
But, until their last great man,

III.

Thick and dense the April rain
Falls upon the o'erclouded plain,
But the sun shines out anon,
And the sudden shower is gone;
Likewise passeth human grief,
Though the lost one be the chief!
Pass'd the sad Milesian shower
That fell around Betanzo's tower,
And in its halls, and in its ships,
The last words on the Patriarch's lips—
About a land far in the sea,
Destined their fertile home to be—
Was all that that adventurous host
Remember'd of the chief they lost.

AMERGIN'S ANTHEM ON DISCOVERING INNISFAIL.[14]

I.

BEHOLD! behold the prize
Which westward yonder lies!
Doth it not blind your eyes
    Like the sun?
By vigil through the night,
By valor in the fight,
By learning to unite
    'T may be won! 't may be won!
By learning to unite, 't may be won!

II.

Of this, in Scythian vales,
Seers told prophetic tales,
Until our Father's sails
    Quick uprose;

But the gods did him detain
In the generous land of Spain,
Where in peace his bones remain
      With his foes, with his foes—
Where in peace his bones remain with his foes.

III.

Sad Scotia! mother dear!
Ccase to shed the mournful tear—
Behold the hour draws near
      He foretold ;
And, ye men, with one accord,
Drop the oar and draw the sword,
For he only shall be lord
      Who is bold, who is bold—
He only shall be lord who is bold!

IV.

They may shroud it up in gloom
Like a spirit in the tomb,
But we hear the voice of doom
      As it cries ;
Let the cerements be burst,
And from thy bonds accursed,
Isle of isles, the fairest, first,
      Arise! arise!
Isle of isles, the fairest, first, arise!

V.

Couch the oar and strike the sail,
Ye warriors of the Gael!
Draw the sword for Innisfail!
      Dash ashore!

With such a prize to gain,
Who would sail the seas again!
Innisfail shall be our Spain
　　　Evermore! evermore!
Innisfail shall be our Spain evermore!

THE CELTS.

Long, long ago, beyond the misty space
　　Of twice a thousand years,
In Erin old there dwelt a mighty race,
　　Taller than Roman spears ;
Like oaks and towers, they had a giant grace,
　　Were fleet as deers,
With winds and wave they made their 'biding-place,
　　These Western shepherd-seers.

Their ocean-god was Mân-â-nân,[15] M'Lir,
　　Whose angry lips,
In their white foam, full often would inter
　　Whole fleets of ships ;
Cromah,[16] their day-god and their thunderer,
　　Made morning and eclipse ;
Bride[17] was their queen of song, and unto her
　　They pray'd with fire-touch'd lips.

Great were their deeds, their passions, and their sports ;
　　With clay and stone
They piled on strath and shore those mystic forts
　　Not yet o'erthrown ;
On cairn-crown'd hills they held their council-courts ;
　　While youths alone,
With giant dogs, explored the elk resorts,
　　And brought them down.

Of these was Finn, the father of the bard
    Whose ancient song
Over the clamor of all change is heard,
    Sweet-voiced and strong.
Finn once o'ertook Granu, the golden-hair'd,
    The fleet and young ;
From her the lovely, and from him the fear'd,
    The primal poet sprung.

Ossian ! two thousand years of mist and change
    Surround thy name—
Thy Finian heroes now no longer range
    The hills of fame.
The very name of Finn and Gaul sound strange—
    Yet thine the same—
By miscall'd lake and desecrated grange—
    Remains, and shall remain !

The Druid's altar and the Druid's creed
    We scarce can trace,
There is not left an undisputed deed
    Of all your race,
Save your majestic song, which hath their speed,
    And strength and grace ;
In that sole song they live, and love, and bleed—
    It bears them on through space.

Oh, inspired giant ! shall we e'er behold
    In our own time
One fit to speak your spirit on the wold,
    Or seize your rhyme ?
One pupil of the past, as mighty soul'd
    As in the prime,
Were the fond, fair, and beautiful, and bold—
    They, of your song sublime !

THE GOBHAN SAER.[16]

He stepp'd a man out of the ways of men,
  And no one knew his sept, or rank, or name—
Like a strong stream far issuing from a glen
  From some source unexplored, the master came ;
Gossips there were who, wondrous keen of ken,
  Surmised that he should be a child of shame !
Others declared him of the Druids—then
  Through Patrick's labors fall'n from power and fame.

He lived apart wrapp'd up in many plans—
  He woo'd not women, tasted not of wine—
He shunn'd the sports and councils of the clans—
  Nor ever knelt at a frequented shrine.
His orisons were old poetic ranns,
  Which the new Ollaves deem'd an evil sign ;
To most he seem'd one of those pagan Khans
  Whose mystic vigor knows no cold decline.

He was the builder of the wondrous towers,
  Which tall, and straight, and exquisitely round,
Rise monumental round the isle once ours,
  Index-like, marking spots of holy ground.
In gloaming glens, in leafy lowland bowers,
  On rivers' banks, these *Cloiteachs* old abound,
Where Art, enraptured, meditates long hours,
  And Science flutters like a bird spell-bound !

Lo ! wheresoe'er these pillar-towers aspire,
  Heroes and holy men repose below—
The bones of some glean'd from the pagan pyre,
  Others in armor lie, as for a foe :

It was the mighty Master's life-desire
  To chronicle his great ancestors so ;
What holier duty, what achievement higher
  Remains to us than this he thus doth show ?

Yet he, the builder, died an unknown death ;
  His labor done, no man beheld him more ;
'Twas thought his body faded like a breath,
  Or, like a sea-mist, floated off Life's shore.
Doubt overhangs his fate, and faith, and birth ;
  His works alone attest his life and lore ;
They are the only witnesses he hath—
  All else Egyptian darkness covers o'er.

Men call'd him Gobhan Saer, and many a tale
  Yet lingers in the by-ways of the land
Of how he cleft the rock, and down the vale
  Led the bright river, child-like, in his hand ;
Of how on giant ships he spread great sail,
  And many marvels else by him first plann'd :
But though these legends fade, in Innisfail
  His name and towers for centuries shall stand.

ORIGIN OF THE ISLE OF MAN.

Of all the Celtic gods, I envy most
    That son of Lir,
Who drove his harness'd dolphins round our coast
    The live-long year,
Follow'd by an uproarious, spouting host,
    Deafening to hear.

The gay gods [illegible]
    Beneath the [illegible]
Where [illegible]
    For [illegible]
From earl[illegible]
    A [illegible]

And, certes, this [illegible]
    E[illegible]
Here's to thee, Milesian, [illegible]
    No [illegible]
Around this board [illegible]
    Your [illegible]

IRELAND OF THE OLD [illegible]

I.

A thousand years [illegible]
    Of Erin [illegible]
Since the Milesian [illegible]
    From Spain [illegible] Vee
A thousand years [illegible]
    A brave [illegible]
And "Sons of Ireland" [illegible]
    Had conquer'd fame [illegible]
Wise laws by [illegible] framed
    And Ogma's letters spread as wide
As Scotia's blood, each [illegible]
    An homage then by [illegible]

II.

It was an island fair and bland
    Lying within its blue sea-wall,

Still belted round with forests grand,
  Braving the stormy ocean squall.
The trapper by the mountain rill
  Watch'd for his prey with eager eye ;"
The elk still walk'd his native hill
  In free and fearless majesty ;
The Asian arts as yet abode
  By river-ford and chief's domain ;
And Druids to their thundering god
  Gave thanks for seas of summer grain.

III.

"The Druids!" sad, mysterious word,
  Whence comes that meaning unexpress'd
Which every Celtic pulse hath stirr'd,
  Rousing old thoughts in brain and breast?
Dear was the name to our first sires—
  Dear every symbol of their line ;
Awe-struck, they saw their altar-fires,
  And deem'd their mystic chants divine.
O'er anger's heat the Druid's breath
  Pass'd like the healing southern breeze,
And warriors on the field of death
  Chanted their odes in ecstacies.
Their artful creed was woven round
  The changeful year—for every hour
A spirit and a sense they found,
  A cause of piety or power.
On every rock that drinks the sprey,
  On every hill, in every wood,
Unto great "Crom," the god of day,"
  The Druid's mighty altar stood.
The wrath of Crom spoke in the storm.

The cooling show'r, the sunshine warm
  Answer'd the Druid's plaintive cry.
The flocks, the flow'rs, the babes unborn,
  The warrior's courage—all obey'd
Those elements, whose love or scorn
  The Druid's prayer removed or made!
The crystal wells were spirit-springs,
  The mountain lakes were peopled under,
And in the grass the fairy rings
  Excited rustic awe and wonder.
Far down beneath the western sea
  Their Paradise of Youth was laid ; [23]
In every oak and hazel tree
  They saw a fair, immortal maid!
Such was the chain of hopes and fears
That bound our sires a thousand years.

IV.

'Twas past : a foreign rumor ran
  Along the peopled eastern shore—
A legend of a God and Man,
  And of a Crown and Cross he bore.
At first 'twas like a morning tale
  Told by a dreamer, to a few,
Till, year by year, among the Gael
  More wide the circling story grew.
A mingled web of false and true,
  'Twas pass'd about on every side ;
The when or where they scarcely knew,
  But all agreed He lived and died
  Far in the East, the Crucified.

V.

Travellers who had been long abroad,

To serve ('twas said) the Unknown God,
  With harp, and hymn, and harmless rite.
One, bolder than the rest, essay'd
  To spread his creed on Leinster's shore,
But, by a tumult sore dismay'd,
  He fled, and ventured back no more.
Palladius like a courier came,
  And spoke and went—or, like St. John,
To the broad desert breath'd the name
  Of the Expected, and was gone—
Leaving to every pagan seer
The future full of doubt and fear.

THE COMING OF ST. PATRICK.

I.

In Antrim's mountain solitude,
  Above the fabled northern sea,
The pagan plain and Druid's wood,
  The Shepherd-Saint I dimly see. [14]
Young and a slave! he tends the flocks
  Which spot the purpled heath around,
And, 'mid the misty topmost rocks,
  A secret shrine for prayer hath found.

II.

There, next to heaven, he rears his cross,
  And there at morn, at noon, and eve,
Kneeling upon the dripping moss,
  I see him pray and hear him grieve.
The exile mourns his far-off home,
  The Christian humbly prays for grace ;
And sometimes from his heart will come

III.

Seven years I watch'd him work and pray,
  Trusting that still he might be free,
Until, one bright auspicious day,
  I saw him seize his staff and flee.
To Sligo—to the Loire—through Gaul—
  I saw him pass, 'till that dread hour
When " Victor " came, charged with his call,
  And moved him with angelic power.
Along the umbrageous Appenine,
  To Rome, his tottering feet I trace ;
Lo ! there the pontiff, Celestine,
  Ordains the Apostle of our race. *

IV.

After this pilgrim-interval,
  Again the Shepherd-Teacher saw
His Antrim highlands soaring tall
  Above the flock-enamell'd shaw.
Landed on the familiar shore,
  He seeks to save his ancient lord,
But, rudely spurn'd from Milcho's door,*
  Turneth his footsteps Tara-ward,
  Still scattering, as he goes, " the Word."

THE CAPTIVITY OF ST. PATRICK.

I.

Gather'd and perch'd the multitude on Howth's romantic
  rock,
As thick as o'er the fish-strewn strand the craving sea-birds

On lofty peak, on jutting pier, on sea-wash'd shelving cliff,
On anchor'd mast, and weedy wreck, and cautious coasting
    skiff.
Fast beat their hearts as, from the east, advancing one by
    one,
Each well-known prince's galley swims, gilded by the sun;
And in their midst King Nial's prow, a head above its peers,
Arises, crown'd with captives, and glittering with spears—
The captives of Armorica, the spears that smote the foe
Where the swift Loire rolls back before the ocean's steadfast
    flow.

II.

Cheer upon cheer, with endless peal, they send across the sea—
The sailor's hail, the goat-herd's horn, the voice of boyish glee;
And beauty's banner, flung abroad, streams downward to
    the wave,
To welcome home the well-beloved, the fortunate, the brave.
Alas! no shout responds that fleet, no thrilling trumpets
    clang—
The echoes only answer'd to the welcome as it rang.
Slow, silent, as in sorrow, the galleys landward come,
And every cheek has whiten'd, and every voice is dumb;
Slow, silent, as in sorrow, the victors reach the shore,
And then they raise the shriek of grief—"King Nial is no
    more!"

III.

Oh! what were all the conquests to Erie when she lost
The hero of her heart beloved, her guardian and her boast.
Sadly she left ungather'd spoils on Howth's forsaken strand,
And, weeping, bore the body to Tara, through the land.
The very captives of the sword forgot their bitter grief
In this wild public sorrow for a father and a chief,
And oft, with unused accents, repeated o'er and o'er
The wild words heard on every side—"King Nial is no more!"

IV.

Nay, there was one who stood a stone amid the fall of tears—
Dark Milcho, lord of Dalriad, grown old in sins and years,
Whose love of war was meted by the treasures of the field,
Who counted that alone well won which gave a golden yield.
Unmoved he stood ; then gave command unto his order'd
    men,
And sought his hoarded treasures in Sliemish guarded glen.
With him go many captives, fair daughters of the Rhine,
Whose feet shall ne'er be red again with juice of Alsace vine;
And one, a Christian youth, there is, the saddest of the train,
Who grieves to think he ne'er shall see the shores of France
    again.

V.

The captive is a keeper of sheep on Antrim's hills;
The captive is a weeper by Antrim's icy rills ;
The captive is a mourner in the midhours of the night;
The captive is a watcher for the coming of the light;—
A watcher for *His* coming who is the light of men,
A mourner for the darkness that shadows Sliemish Glen—
A weeper for the sins of youth, aforetime unconfess'd,
A keeper of the passions that rush through boyhood's breast;
The captive is a Shepherd, but his future flock shall be
All the countless generations of that Garden of the Sea.

ST. PATRICK'S DREAM.[VI]

I.

Poor is the pallet he dreams upon,
   In the holy city, Saint Martin's of Tours ;
Is it a beam of the morning sun
   Flushes that face so pale and pure ?

Is it the ray of a cloister lamp?
 Is it some chalice jewel bright?
No! night and the cell are dim and damp—
 Here is nor earthly nor astral light!

II

Oh, such a dream! From Foclut wood,
 Near the sounding sea of an earlier day,
Ten thousand voices, well understood,
 Spoke! and the sleeper heard them say :
"Hear the Unborn! by the hand
 Of the angel Victor—swift is he!
Oh, Patrick, far in thy Christian land,
 Erin's unborn we send to thee!"

III.

And then he dreamt that Saint Victor stood
 By his pallet in that cell at Tours—
And the cries were hush'd in Foclut wood;
 But the heavenly messenger, swift and sure,
Presents the scroll that bore their prayer,
 In the speech of his exile fairly writ—
And waking, the Saint beheld it there—
 And these were the words he read from it :

"Come! holy one, long preordain'd,
 For thee the swans of Lir are singing ;
Come! from the morning, Orient-stain'd,
 Thy Mass-bell through our valleys ringing!

"Man of the hooded hosts, arise !
 Physician, lo! our souls lie dying—
Hear o'er the seas our piteous cries,
 On thee and on our God relving !

"Come, powerful youth of Sliemish hill!
  Come, in the name and might of Rome!
Come with the psalm that charms from ill—
  Cross-bearer! Christ-preparer! come."

IV.

The sleeper read! still doubts arose—
  Till to Aurora's torches red
He held the scroll—repeating those
  Wild suppliant words the Unborn said!
He look'd where late the angel pass'd,
  Many the big drops on his brow;
His robe he girt, his staff he grasp'd,
  He only said, "In God's name, Now!"

MONTREAL, February, 1868.

ST. PATRICK'S FIRST CONVERTS.*

I.

MORN on the hills of Innisfail!
The anchor'd mists make sudden sail,
The sun has kiss'd the mountain gray,
For ancient friends and fond are they!

II.

In the deep vale, where osiers verge
The clear Lough Sheeling's gentle surge,
Two royal sisters doff their dresses,
And, binding up their night-black tresses,
Fair as the spirits of the streams,
Or Dian's nymphs in poets' dreams,

' The legend here versified, almost literally, is one of the oldest episodes in

They bathe them in the limpid lake,
And mock the mimic storm they make !

III.

Scarce had their sandals clasp'd their feet,
Scarce had they left their still retreat,
Scarce had they turn'd their footsteps, when
Strange psalmody pervades the glen ;
And full before them in the way
There stood an ancient man and gray,
Chanting with fervent voice a prayer
That trembled through the morning air.

IV.

He was no Druid of the wood,
Arm'd for the sacrifice of blood ;
He was no poet, vague and vain,
Chanting to chiefs a fulsome strain ;
His reverent years and thoughtful face
Gave to his form the Patriarch's grace ;
His sacred song declared that he
Shared in no gross idolatry !

V.

" Where dwells your God ?" the sisters said ;
" Where is His couch at evening spread ?
Sinks he with Crom into the sea,
And rises from his bath as we
Have done ?　Is it his voice we hear
Thundering above the buried year ?
Or doth your God in spirit dwell
Deep in the crystal, living well ?
Or are the winds the steeds which bear
His unseen chariot everywhere ?"

VI.

The Saint replied, "Oh, nobly born !
Haply encounter'd here this morn ;
You ask the only truth to know
That Adam's children need below ;
Your quest is God, like them of old
Who found the gravestone backward roll'd
From where they left the Saviour cold."

VII.

Mildly to tell, the holy man
The story of our faith began—
Of Eve, of Christ, of Calvary,
The baleful and the healing tree ;
Of God's omnipotence and love,
Of sons of earth, now saints above ;
Of Peter and the Twelve, of Paul,
And of his own predestined call.

VIII.

"Not on the sea, not on the shore,
In solemn woods or tempest roar,
Dwelleth the God that we adore.
No! wheresoe'er His cross is raised,
And wheresoe'er His name is praised ;
The pure life is His present sign,
The holy heart His favorite shrine ;
The old, the poor, the sorrowful,
To them He is most bountiful ;
Palace or hovel, land or sea,
God with His servants still will be !"

*　　*　　*　　*　　*　　*　　*

IX.

Leogaire, the last of our pagan kings,

For he had dreamt his daughters fair
Pillars of fire on Tara were,
And that the burning light thence streaming
Melted the idols in his dreaming—
And the dream of Leogaire, our annals say,
Was fulfill'd in the land in an after day.

A LEGEND OF ST. PATRICK.

Seven weary years in bondage the young Saint Patrick pass'd,
Till the sudden hope came to him to break his bonds at last;
On the Antrim hills reposing, with the north star overhead,
As the gray dawn was disclosing, "I trust in God," he said—
"My sheep will find a shepherd, and my master find a slave,
But my mother has no other hope but me this side the
 grave."

Then girding close his mantle, and grasping fast his wand,
He sought the open ocean through the by-ways of the land;
The berries from the hedges on his solitary way,
And the cresses from the waters, were his only food by day;
The cold stone was his pillow, and the hard heath was his
 bed,
Till, looking from Benbulben, he saw the sea outspread.

He saw that ancient ocean, unfathom'd and unbound,
That breaks on Erin's beaches with so sorrowful a sound;
There lay a ship at Sligo bound up the Median sea —
"God save you, master mariner, will you give berth to me?
I have no gold to pay thee, but Christ will pay thee yet."
Loud laugh'd that foolish mariner, "Nay, nay, *He* might
 forget!"

Forget !   Oh, not a favor done to the humblest one
f all His human kindred can 'scape th' Eternal Son !"
ı vain the Christian pleaded, the willing sail was spread,
ïis voice no more was heeded than the sea-birds overhead ;
nd as the vision faded of that ship against the sky,
ʼn the briny rocks the captive pray'd to God to let him die.

ʒut God, whose ear is open to catch the sparrow's fall,
ıt the sobbing of His servant frown'd along the waters all ;
Ґhe billows rose in wonder and smote the churlish crew,
Аnd around the ship the thunder like battle-arrows flew ;
Ґhe screaming sea-fowl's clangor in Kish-corran's inner
        caves
Was hush'd before the anger of the tempest-trodden waves.

Like an eagle-hunted gannet, the ship drove back amain
To where the Christian captive sat in solitude and pain—
"Come in," they cried; "O Christian ! we need your com-
        pany,
For it was sure your angry God that met us out at sea."
Then smiled the gentle heavens, and doff'd their sable veil,
Then sunk to rest the breakers and died away the gale.

So, sitting by the pilot, the happy captive kept
On his rosary a reck'ning, while the seamen sung or slept.
Before the winds propitious past Achill, south by Ara,
The good ship gliding left behind Hiar-Connaught like an
        arrow—
From the southern bow of Erin they shoot the shore of Gaul,
And in holy Tours, Saint Patrick findeth freedom, friends,
        and all.

In holy Tours he findeth home and altars, friends and all ;

There's no lord to make him tremble, no magician to endure,
Nor need he to dissemble in the pious streets of Tours;
But ever, as he rises with the morning's early light,
And still erewhile he sleepeth, when the north star shines
    at night,
When he sees the angry Ocean by the tyrant Tempest trod,
He murmurs in devotion, "Fear nothing! trust in God!"

THREE SONNETS FOR ST. PATRICK'S DAY.

I.

Nor yet had dawn'd the day-star of the soul
On that dark isle beyond which land was not;
Far in the East it blazed, and in the South,
And high above the Alpine summits stood,
Shooting its rays along the vales of Gaul;
Albion's cold cliffs had felt the cheering beam,
Though soon eclipsed and lost.   Like sinful Eve,
Hidden amid the thickest Eden grove,
Our island-mother knew not of her hope!
Enfolded by the melancholy main,
A sea of foliage fill'd the eagle's eye—
A sea within a sea—one wave-wash'd wood,
Save where some breezy mountain, bare and brown,
Rose 'mid the verdant desert to the skies!

II.

Swarming with life, these woods gave forth a race
Of huntsmen and of warriors, whose delight
Was spoil and havoc; o'er the Roman wall
They leap'd like wolves upon their British prey;
Far flash'd their oars upon the Gallic tide;
And in the Alpine valleys rose the shout
Of "Farrah!" to the onset upon Rome!

And still, where'er they dwelt, or sail'd, or camp'd,
In native woods, in ships, or on strange shores,
Moved the dread Druid, with his bloody knife,
And rites obscene of Bel and of Astarte—
The fearful brood of that corrupted will
Which brought imperial Tyre down to the dust,
Which conquer'd Carthage more than Scipio's sword,
And left them heirless in the world's esteem!

III.

Into that land where he, wet with his tears,
Had seven years eaten of the bitter bread
Of slavery and exile, came the Saint
Whose day we celebrate throughout the earth!
Before his mighty words false gods fell down,
And prostrate pagans, rising from the plain,
Knew the true God, and, knowing, were baptized.
Praise to his name, the ransom'd Slave who broke
All other chains, and set the bondsman free!
Praise to his name, the Husbandman who sow'd
The good seed over all that fertile isle!
Praise to the Herdsman who into the fold
Of the One Shepherd led our Father's flock,
Whose voice still calls us wheresoe'er we hide!
Montreal, March 12, 1862.

THE LEGEND OF CROAGH PATRICK.

Ask you why we repair
  Every Lent as pilgrims lowly
To Croagh Patrick, and make there
  Vows to God, and all the Holy
    Now in glory?

True and plainly I will tell
What in ancient days befell,
And sanctified this place
To th' Apostle of our race—
Thus the story :

I.

When Patrick came to Cruachan Eigle first
  (Steep the side is of that mountain in Mayo),
'Twas girt about with woods where the accursed
  Plotting Druids still flitted to and fro—
With fasting and with prayer upon the summit,
  He sought his ardent soul to assoil,
Kneeling over chasms wall'd as by a plummet,
  Treading stony paths with patient toil.

II.

The gray mists hid the earth as day was ended,
  The sea as with another sea was cover'd,
When, with loud shrieking cries, a host of birds descended,
  And over his anointed head dark hover'd ;
Some breathed an obscene odor which appall'd him,
  Some utter'd cries that shook his soul with fear,
Some with blasphemies distracted and miscall'd him,
  Some hiss'd like springing serpents at his ear.

III.

The tempted one went praying fast and faster,
  His knees seem'd to freeze unto the stone ;
At length he cried aloud—"O Lord and Master,
  I am wrestling with a hell-host all alone !"
Seizing, then, the holy bell that lay before him
  ('Twas a gift from the good Pope Celestine),
Thrice ringing it, he speedily, full o'er him,
  Saw the Lenten moon's fair face shine.

IV.

Then a choir of cherubs round the mountain winging,
  Lauds and vespers for tho holy Saint began,
And he, though soul-entranced by the divinest singing,
  Still trembling felt the feebleness of man.
And he pray'd three prayers to God that blessèd even',
  That Slieve Eigle to no stranger might belong,
That an Irish death-bed shrift might lead to heaven ;
  And once more he pray'd, fervently and long—

V.

That, before the final Judgment-morn had risen,
  Ere the angel of the trumpet cleft the air,
Ere Christ's coming should loose Death from his long prison,
  Ere the pale horse for his rider should prepare—
That, through the woful scenes Apocalyptic,
  Innisfail, ten thousand thousand fathoms deep,
Among old Ocean's caverns labyrinthic,
  The destruction of the world might outsleep.

————

Of Patrick this was the prayer
  For our fathers and their kindred ;
Hence, as pilgrims we repair
  Every Lent to Cruachan Eigle.
But no more as such 'tis known
  (Croagh Patrick is its name)—
Time will wear the very stone—
Ireland's eagles all have flown ;
Of things old, her Faith alone
  Stands unconquer'd and the same!

ST. PATRICK'S DEATH.

[From the ancient rhyme called St. Fiech's Hymn.]

I.

To his own Armagh the Saint's feet turn'd,
As the lamp of his life obscurely burn'd,
And he bade them make his dying bed
In that holy city, the Church's head!

II.

Midway, an angel, at midnight deep,
Came by the couch and soothed his sleep;
It was Victor, the guardian of his life,
Who had led him safe through storm and strife.

III.

To the eyes of the sleeper that angel seem'd
The same as when first of his call he dream'd;
By a belt of fire he was girt around,
And he sang with a strangely solemn sound :

IV.

"Thy Armagh shall rule in Erie forever,
Praise be to Christ, the primacy-giver!
Your prayer was heard, your soul I call,
Prepare for the end in the cell at Saul!"

V.

At Saul, to the people, St. Tassach said :
"We shall see him no more—our Father is dead!
People of Erie, lament not nor mourn—
A mortal has died, but a Saint is born!"

VI.

From far and near, from isle and glen,
Came mourning priests and sorrowing men,
And with hymns repeated, the sleepless throng
Waked him with solemn psalter and song.

VII.

Torches like stars burn'd thick and bright
Round his tomb for many a day and night ;
As the Sun of Ajalon steadfast stood,
So blazed the Church for the Chief of the Rood.

VIII.

Our Father, who lived without stain or pride,
Now dwells in his mansion beatified,
With Jesus and Mary in perpetual morn—
The mortal has died, the Saint is born.

ST. BRENDAN AND THE STRIFE-SOWER.

WHAT time Saint Brendan on the sea
   At night was sailing,
A spirit-voice from the ship's lee
   Rose, wildly wailing,
Crying, "Blessèd Brendan ! pray for me
   A prayer availing ;

"For I have been, O Saint, through life,
   A sinner ever ;
With murmurings my course was rife
   As any river ;
I never ceased from sowing strife,

"Within our convent's peaceful wall
    Was song and prime ;
But I loved never music's call,
    Nor voice of chime ;
The Host that holiest hearts appal
    Awed never mine.

"In chancel, choir, in lonely cell,
    On the sea-shore,
The love of strife, as a strong spell,
    Was evermore
Upon me—'till sore sick I fell,
    And was given o'er.

"Then, in the brief hours of my pain,
    To God I cried
And mourned—nor, Father, mourned in vain—
    My strifes and pride—
My soul departed—rent in twain—
    Half justified.

"'Twixt heaven and hell, in doubt I am,
    O holy Saint !
Oh ! supplicate the bleeding Lamb
    To hear my 'plaint—
Oh ! bless me with thy words of balm—
    I faint—I faint—"

Saint Brendan seized his rosary,
    And knelt him low
And pray'd, whoso the soul might be
    That pass'd him fro,
That God and Christ His Son would free
    It from its woe.

And never any night at sea,
    In his long sailing,
Heard the Saint after from the lee
    The Spirit's wailing—
He deem'd it with the Just to be,
    Through prayer availing.

THE VOYAGE OF EMAN OGE.[30]

In the Western Ocean's waters, where the sinking sun is lost,
Rises many a holy *cloiteach* high o'er many an island coast,
Bearing bells rung by the tempest when the spray to heaven
    is toss'd :

Bearing bells and holy crosses, that to Arran men afar
Twinkle through the dawn and twilight, like the mist-
    environ'd star
Hung in heaven for their guidance, as, in sooth, such symbols
    are.

Tis a rosary of islands in the Ocean's hollow palm—
Sites of faith unchanged by storms, all unchanging in the
    calm,
There the world-betray'd may hide them, and the weary
    heart find balm.

Wayward as a hill-stream chafing in a sad fir-forest glen,
Lived the silent student, Eman, among Arran's holy men,
Sighing still for far Hy-Brasil—sight of fear to human ken.

Born a chieftain, and predestin'd by his sponsors for a sage,
Eman Oge[31] had track'd the sages over many an ancient page,
Drain'd their old scholastic vials, nor did these his thirst
    assuage.

       * *Eman Oge* means Young Edward.

Thinking thenceforth, and deploring, sat he nightly on the
　　strand,
Ever watching, ever sighing, for the fabled fairy land;
For this earth he held it hateful, and its sons a soulless
　　band.

'Twas midsummer midnight, silence on the isles and ocean
　　lay,
Fleets of sea-birds rode at anchor on the waveless moon-
　　bright bay,
To the moon, across the waters, stretch'd a shining silver
　　way—

When, *O Christa!* in the offing, like a ship upon the sight,
Loom'd a land of dazzling verdure, cross'd with streams
　　that flash'd like light,
Under emerald groves whose lustre glorified the solemn
　　night.

As the hunter dashes onward when the missing prey he
　　spies,
As to a gracious mistress the forgiven lover flies,
So, across the sleeping ocean Eman in his currach hies.

Nay, he never noted any of the holy island's signs—
Saint Mac Duach's tall cathedral, or Saint Brecan's ivyed
　　shrines,
Or the old Cyclopean dwellings—for a rarer scene he pines.

Now he nears it—now he touches the gold-glittering precious
　　sand—
Lir of Ocean[35] is no miser when such treasures slip his
　　hand—
But whence come these antique galleys crowding the deserted
　　strand?

Tyrian galleys, with white benches, sails of purple, prows of
    gold;
Triremes, such as carried Cæsar to the British coast of old;
Serpents that had borne Vikings southward on adventures
    bold;

Gondolas, with glorious jewels sparkling on their necks of
    pride;
Bucentaurs, that brought the Doges to their Adriatic bride;
Frisian hulk and Spanish pinnace lay reposing side by side;

Carracks, currachs—all the vessels that the ocean yet had
    borne,
By no envious foemen captured, by no tempests toss'd or
    torn,
Lay upon that stormless sea-beach all untarnish'd and unworn.

But within them, or beside them, crew or captain saw he
    none—
" Have mankind forever languish'd for the land I now have
    won ?"
So said Eman, as he landed, by his angel tempted on.

Where it led him—what befell him—what he suffer'd—who
    shall say ?
One long year was pass'd and over—a midsummer's night
    and day;
Morning found him pallid, pulseless, stretch'd upon the
    island bay.

Dead he lay: his brow was calcined like a green leaf scorch'd
    in June,
Hollow was his cheek and haggard, gone his beaming smile
    and bloom—
Dead he lay, as if his spirit had already faced its doom.

Who shall wake him? who shall care him? wayward Eman,
　　stark and still—
Who will nerve anew his footsteps to ascend life's craggy
　　hill?
Who will ease his anguish'd bosom? who restore him thought
　　and will?

Hark! how softly tolls the matin from the top of yonder
　　tower—
How it moves the stark man! Lo, you! hath a sound such
　　magic power?
Lo, you! lo, you! Up he rises, waked and saved! Ah,
　　blessèd hour!

Now he feels his brow—now gazes on that shore, and sky,
　　and sea—
Now upon himself—and lo, you! now he bends to earth his
　　knee;
God and angels hear him praying on the sea-shore fervently.

THE PRAYER OF EMAN OGE.

God of this Irish isle!
　　Blessèd and old,
Wrapp'd in the morning's smile
　　In the sea's fold—
Here, where Thy saints have trod—
　　Here, where they pray'd—
Hear me, O saving God!
　　May I be saved?

God of the circling sea!
　　Far-rolling and deep—
Its caves are unshut to Thee,
　　Its bounds Thou dost keep—

Here, from this strand,
  Whence saints have gone forth—
Father! I own Thy hand,
  Humbled to earth.

God of this blessèd light
  Over me shining!
On the wide way of right
  I go, unrepining.
No more despising
  My lot or my race,
But toiling, uprising,
  To Thee through Thy grace.

THE "WISDOM-SELLERS" BEFORE CHARLEMAGNE.

MONACHUS SAN-GALLENSIS *loquitur:*

"Grandson of Charlemagne! to tell
  Of exiled Learning's late return,
A task more grateful never fell
  To one still drinking at her urn ;
    Of Force, O King!
    Too many sing,
Lauding mere sanguinary strength ;
    But Wisdom's praise
    Our favor'd days
Have ask'd to hear at length.
When he whose sword and name you bear
  Reign'd unopposed throughout the West,
And none would dream, or, dreaming, dare
  Reject his high behest—
He found no peace nor near nor far,
  No spell to stay his swaying mind ;

For Glory, like the sailor's star,
   Still left her votary far behind.
The wreck of Roman art remain'd,
   Casting dark lines of destiny ;
The very roads they went proclaim'd
   The modern man's degeneracy ;
Our Charles wept like Philip's son,
For that Time's noblest wreaths were won.

"One morn upon his throne of state
   Crown'd and sad the conqueror sate.
 'What stirs without, my chiefs?' said he,
 'Do all things rest on land and sea ?
Has France slept late, or has she lost
The love of being tempest-toss'd ?'
Spake an old soldier of his wars,
   One who had fought in Lombardy,
Whose breast, besides, bore Saxon scars—
   The soldier-emperor's friend was he:
 'O Carl ! strange news your steward bears,
   Of merchants in the mart, who tell,
Standing amidst the mingled wares,
   That they bring *Wisdom* here to sell ;
Tall men, though strange, they seem to be,
And somewhere from ayont the sea.'
Quoth Charles—' 'Twere rare merchandise
That, purchased, could make Paris wise.
Fetch me those wisdom-sellers hither—
We fain would know their whence and whither.'

"Of air erect and full of grace,
   With bearded lip and arrowy eye,
And signs no presence could efface
   Of Learning's meek nobility,

The men appear'd.   Carl's iron front
  Was lifted as each bow'd his head ;
With words more gentle than his wont,
  To the two strangers thus he said :
' Merchants, what is the tale I hear,
  That in the market-place you offer
Wisdom for sale ?   Is wisdom dear ?
  Is't in the compass of our coffer ?'

" In accents such as seldom broke
  The silence there, Albinus spoke :
' O Carl ! illustrious emperor !
We are but strangers on your shore :
From Erin's isle, where every glen
  Is crowded with the sons of song,
And every port with learnèd men,
  We, venturing without the throng
(And longing, not the least, to see
The person of your majesty,
Whose fame has reach'd the ends of ocean),
Forsook our native isle, to bear
The lamps of wisdom everywhere,
Our heavenly Master's work to do—
And first we came, O King ! to you :
In His dread name, the Eternal King,
Clemens and I, His errand bring—
Whose soldier is the sandall'd priest,
Whose empire neither West nor East—
Whose word knows neither South nor North,
Whose footstool is the subject Earth—
Who holds to-day as yesterday,
O'er age and space, his sovereign sway—
Whose wisdom in our books enroll'd
  Unto your majesty we offer—

Neither for guerdon nor for gold
  Within the compass of your coffer.
On Carnac's *cromleach* you have gazed,
  And seen the proud strength of the past ;
You saw the piles the Cæsars raised—
  Saw Art his empire-cause outlast.
All scenes of war, all pomps of peace,
  Armies and harvests in array—
Your longing soul from sights like these
  To Time and Art oft turns away.
Great hosts are bristling over earth
  Like grain in harvest, till anon
A wintry campaign, or a dearth
  Of valor, and your hosts are gone.
The soldier's pride is for a season,
  His day leads to a silent night ;
But sov'reign power, inspired by reason,
  Creates a world of life and light.
We've rifled the departed ages,
  And bring their grave-gifts here to-day ;
We sell the secrets of the sages—
  The code of Calvary and Sinai.
To wisdom, King! we set no measure ;
  For wisdom's price, there is but one—
To value it above all treasure,
  And spend it freely when 'tis won.
By every peaceful Gaelic river
  The Bookmen have a free abode ;
They celebrate each princely giver,
  And teach the arts of man and God.
All that we ask for all we bring
  Is eager pupils round our cell,
And your protection, mighty King!
  While in the realms of France we dwell.'

"Bow'd the great king his lofty head—
 'Be welcome, men of God!' he said;
 'Choose ye a home, it shall be given,
 And held in seignory of heaven.'

"Grandson of Carl! I need no more;
  The rest throughout the earth is known—
How learning, lost to us before,
  Spread like a sun around his throne,
Till now, in Saxon forests dim,
New neophytes their lore-lights trim—
How even my own Alpine heights
Are luminous through studious nights—
How Pavia's learnèd half regain
The glory of the Roman name—
How mind with mind, and soul with soul,
Press onward to the ancient goal—
How Faith herself smiles on the chase
Of Chimera and Reason's race—
How 'wisdom-sellers' one may meet
In every ship and every street—
Of how our Irish masters rest
In graves watch'd by the grateful West—
How more than war or sanguine strength
    Of Wisdom's praise
    Our favor'd days
Have ask'd to hear at length."

FLAN SYNAN'S GAME OF CHESS.

I.

FLAN SYNAN from the south had come, with tributes in his train
From the Desmond men and Thomond men by fear or force
   he'd ta'en;

A thousand harness'd horses, with bells to their harness
    triced,
Seven chariots piled with silver cups and robes kings only
    priced ;
And boastfully, on captured harps, bards sung the battle
    rann,
And all agreed there ne'er had lived a conqueror like Flan.

II.

That was the night in Tara ! such singing and such wine ;
The morning sun shone in on them, but they said, "Let it
    shine;"
A Thomond hostage play'd at chess against the royal host,
Who vauntingly to the southern chief thus foolishly made
    boast—
That he "to Thurles' Green would bring his board, and not
    a man
In all the south, in open day, durst spoil the game of Flan."

III.

Bright shines the sun along the Suir, and warm on Thurles'
    Green ;
Strange is the sight and singular that there this day is seen:
A king and court, in merry sport, like boys on holiday,
Have sat them down to tables laid, round which they laugh
    and play.
"Did I not say, Dalcassian ! that here there was no man
Who dare essay, in open day, to spoil the game of Flan ?"

IV.

Smiled gayly the Dalcassian, "Kings have been check'd ere
    now."
"What mean you?" quoth the monarch, with anger on his

"Here come some who can answer!" cried the other; and
    amain
A thousand arm'd Thomond-men defiled into the plain.
" 'Tis our turn now," exclaim'd the chief, as here and there
    they ran;
"You've lost your game on Thurles' Green, O boastful
    monarch Flan!"

LADY GORMLEY.[34]

A GAELIC BALLAD.

I.

She wanders wildly through the night,
    Unhappy Lady Gormley!
And hides her head at morning light,
    Unhappy Lady Gormley!
No home has she, no kindly kin,
But darkness reigneth all within,
For sorrow is the child of sin,
    With hapless Lady Gormley!

II.

What time she sate on Tara's throne,
    Unhappy Lady Gormley!
Bright jewels sparkled on her zone,
    Unhappy Lady Gormley!
But her fair seeming could not hide
The wayward will, the heart of pride,
The wit still ready to deride,

III.

The daughter of a kingly race
    Was lovely Lady Gormley!
A monarch's bride, the first in place,
    Was noble Lady Gormley!
The fairest hand she had, the skill
The lute to touch, the harp to thrill,
Melting and moving men at will,
    The peerless Lady Gormley!

IV.

Nor was it courtly art to call
    The splendid Lady Gormley!
The first of minstrels in the hall,
    All-gifted Lady Gormley!
Song flow'd from out her snowy throat
As from the thrush, and every note
Taught men to dream, and bards to dote
    On lovely Lady Gormley!

V.

But arm'd as is the honey-bee
    Was fickle Lady Gormley!
And hollow as the alder-tree
    Was smiling Lady Gormley!
And cold and haughty as the swan
That glancing sideward saileth on,
That loves the moon and hates the dawn,
    Was heartless Lady Gormley!

VI.

God's poor had never known her care—
    The lofty Lady Gormley!
She had no smile for nun or frere,
    The worldly Lady Gormley!

She fed her heart on human praise,
Forgot her soul in prosp'rous days,
Was studious but how to amaze,
    The haughty Lady Gormley!

VII.

At last she fell from her great height,
    Unhappy Lady Gormley!
Her lord had perish'd in the fight,
    Unhappy Lady Gormley!
And now she has nor house nor home,
Destined from rath to rath to roam,
Too proud to make amend or moan,
    Unhappy Lady Gormley!

VIII.

Behold her on her lonely way,
    The wretched Lady Gormley,
And mark the moral of my lay,
    The lay of Lady Gormley!
When Fortune smiles, make God your friend,
On His love more than man's depend,
So may you never in the end
    Share the woe of Lady Gormley!

BRYAN, THE TANIST.

I.

Bryan, the son of the Tanist, grew
Stately and strong, and brave and true,
The heart of his house and the pride of his name,
Till Torna, the poet, his guest became,
And lit his blood with words of flame,
And soil'd his breast with schemes of shame.

II.

Torna hated Sil-Murray, branch and root,
And he swore to spoil the tree of its fruit;
And Torna, steadfast as any hill,
Had a fiend's soul with a minstrel's skill,
And Bryan he used as his ladder until
He reach'd his mark and wrought his will.

III.

Through fear, and fire, and settling gloom,
I hear a fray, and I see a tomb,
From a rifled bed, through a rifted wall,
I see the son of the Tanist fall,
And like the exulting eagle's call,
The poet's voice is over all!

IV.

Oh human passion! oh human strife!
How do you taint the springs of life!
A thousand souls are black to-day
From the smoke of this fratricidal fray,
And peace from our sept has pass'd away,
And the end of the guilty—who shall say?

HOW ST. KIERAN PROTECTED CLONMACNOISE.

I.

There is an ancient legend,
  By the Donegal Masters told,
How St. Kieran kept his churchos,
  As a shepherd keeps his fold.

II.

Ages had lain in their ashes,
  Crowns had outworn their kings,
Change had come over Clonmacnoise,
  As it comes o'er all earthly things.

III.

Long gone was the wooded desert,
  Where he broke the Druid's reign—
Long gone was the cruel bondage
  Of the proud usurping Dane.

IV.

And calm as a river of heaven
  The Shannon flow'd along,
By the towers and churches seven,
  From morn till even' song.

V.

With sounds of pious duty,
  By day it was all alive
With the low sweet voice of study—
  The hum of a holy hive.

VI.

In the street the youth uncover'd,
  In the meadow the mower knelt,
When the call to prayer, far or near,
  Was heard or only felt.

VII.

The Spenser left his store-house,
  The Ostrarus left his load,
And sage and lector silent,
  Bow'd to the call of God.

VIII.

Now Night, the priest of labor,
    Had spread his cope afar,
And brightly on his bosom
    Glitter'd the morning star.

IX.

Even as that sole star glitter'd
    On high in its guardian light,
So the lamp alone keeps vigil
    At St. Kieran's shrine to-night.

X.

The lamp alone keeps vigil,
    While a shape flits to the shore,
And a shallop down the river
    Has shot with muffled oar.

XI.

As at the stir of the latchet
    Flieth the beast of prey,
So swiftly into the darkness
    The shallop glides away.

XII.

No sound broke o'er the landscape
    As the guilty boatman sped
Through the ghastly gray of daybreak,
    Like the ferryman of the dead.

XIII.

But sounds of wail and wonder
    Ere noon, on every side,
Were heard by that peaceful river
    Down which he darkly hied.

XIV.

For the rifled shrine of St. Kieran
   Had been found on the river shore,
And an eager host surrounded
   The high-priest's open door.

XV.

And some were prompt to counsel,
   While many shook with fear—
For sure, they said, such sacrilege
   Foretold disaster near.

XVI.

At the door outspake the high-priest—
   "Let every one begone
To his daily task, to his chosen work,
   The saints will guard their own."

XVII.

And so the ancient legend
   Relates how oft in vain
The bold shrine-thief took shipping
   To pass beyond the main.

XVIII.

No ship wherein he enter'd
   Could ever find a breeze;
Her masts stood fast in their tackle
   As in the soil the trees.

XIX.

While right and left all freely
   Swept past the outward bound;
The ship that held the shrine-thief
   Seem'd hard and fast aground.

XX.

The sailors at the rowlocks
  Toil'd till their hearts grew faint;
Where they felt only the current,
  He felt the avenging Saint.

XXI.

At length remorse and anguish
  O'ertook the caitiff bold,
And stricken with mortal terror,
  His fearful tale he told.

XXII.

And now a glad procession
  Of galleys, with banner fine,
Has left Athlone with the gold and gems
  Of St. Kieran's plunder'd shrine.

XXIII.

A day of great rejoicing
  Is this for the land around;
The Saint has been exalted—
  That which was lost is found.

XXIV.

On the morrow spoke the high-priest—
  "Let every one begone
To his daily task, to his chosen work,
  The saints will guard their own."

IONA.[38]

I.

WOULD you visit the home St. Columbcille chose?
You must sail to the north when the west wind blows—
To the art where grows not flowers or trees,
On the soil of the sea-spent Hebrides;
There, over against the steep Ross shore,
In hearing of Coryvrekan's roar,
You will find the dwarfish holly growing,
And see the brave sea-bugles blowing
Around the roots of the belladonna,
On the shore of the island—holy Iona!

II.

In that lovely isle the north star shines
On crownless kings and saints *sans* shrines;
There, the small sheep crop the grass that springs
Lineally up from the loins of kings;
There, Jarls from Orkney and Heligoland,
And Thanes from York and from Cumberland,
And Maormars of Moray, and Lennox, and Levin,
Cruel in life, lie hoping for heaven;
There, Magnus of Norway, and stern Macbeth,
Are stretch'd at the feet of the democrat, Death;
And chieftains of Ulster, and lords of Lorn,
There wait for the trump of All-Soul's morn.

III.

"Here lived Saint Columb," the ferrymen say,
"He kept his boats in this shingly bay;
He fenced this glebe, he set up this stone
(The kirk it belong'd to was overthrown)
Upon this mound, at close of day;

Thousands of blessings he gave to the Gael—
'Tis pity they were not of more avail!"

IV.

Saint of the seas! who first explored
The haunts of the hyperborean horde—
Who spread God's name, and rear'd his cross
From Westra wild to the cliffs of Ross—
Whose sail was seen, whose voice was known
By dwellers without the Vikings zone—
Whose days were pass'd in the teacher's toil—
Whose evening song still fill'd the aisle—
Whose poet-heart fed the wild bird's brood—
Whose fervent arm upbore the rood—
Whose sacred song is scarce less sublime
Than the visions that typified all time—
Still, from thy roofless rock so gray,
Thou preachest to all who pass that way.

V.

I hear thy voice, O holy Saint!
Of to-day, and its men make dire complaint;
Thou speakest to us of that spell of power,
Thy rocky Iona's royal dower—
Of the light of love and love of light
Which made it shine out like a star in the night;
Thou pointest my eyes to the deep, deep waves—
Thou callest my ken to the mute, mute graves—
Thou wooeth young Life, and her lover, Faith,
As victors to enter the Castle of Death,
And to leave their beacons of being to warn
The weak and wild and the far unborn
Off perilous straits and fair-false shoals,
Where myriads have lost their adventured souls.

VI.

Saint of the seas! when the winds are out—
When, like dogs at fault, they quest about—
When I wake on ocean's rocky brink,
While the billows pause and seem to think,
My soul from its earthly mooring slips
And glides away through the midnight ships—
And all unheeding the face of Fear
That darkles down on the marineer,
It rushes through wind, and space, and spray,
And through the birds that embank the bay,
And over the holly and belladonna,
To chant its lauds in thy holy Iona!

IONA TO ERIN![*]

WHAT ST. COLUMBA SAID TO THE BIRD FLOWN OVER FROM IRELAND TO IONA.[37]

I.

Cling to my breast, my Irish bird,
　Poor storm-toss'd stranger, sore afraid!
How sadly is thy beauty blurr'd—
The wing whose hue was as the curd,
　Rough as the sea-gull's pinion made!

II.

Lay close thy head, my Irish bird,
　Upon this bosom, human still!
Nor fear the heart that still has stirr'd
To every tale of pity heard
　From every shape of earthly ill.

* This beautiful poem acquires additional interest from the fact that it was
one of the last the author wrote, having appeared in print only a few days

III.

For you and I are exiles both—
   Rest you, wanderer, rest you here!
Soon fair winds shall waft you forth
Back to our own belovèd North—
   Would God I could go with you, dear!

IV.

Were I as you, then would they say,
   Hermits and all in choir who join—
"Behold two doves upon their way,
The pilgrims of the air are they—
   Birds from the Liffey or the Boyne!"

V.

But you will see what I am bann'd
   No more, for my youth's sins, to see,
My Derry's oaks in council stand
By Roseapenna's silver strand—
   Or by Raphoe your course may be.

VI.

The shrines of Meath are fair and far—
   White-wing'd one, not too far for thee—
Emania, shining like a star,
(Bright brooch on Erin's breast you are!) [20]
   That I am never more to see.

VII.

You'll see the homes of holy men,
   Far west upon the shoreless main—
In shelter'd vale, on cloudy ben, [30]
Where saints still pray, and scribes still pen

VIII.

Above the crofts of virgin saints,
  There pause, my dove, and rest thy wing,
But tell them not our sad complaints,
For if they dreamt our spirit faints,
  There would be fruitless sorrowing.

IX.

Perch, as you pass, amid their trees,
  At noon or eve, my travell'd dove,
And blend with voices of their bees,
In croft, or school, or on their knees—
  They'll bind you with their hymns of love!

X.

Be thou to them, O dove! where'er
  The men or women saints are found,
My hyssop flying through the air ;
My seven-fold benedictions bear
  To them, and all on Irish ground.

XI.

Thou wilt return, my Irish bird—
  I, Columb, do foretell it thee ;
Would thou could'st speak as thou hast heard
To all I love—O happy bird !
  At home in Erie soon to be !

CATHAL'S FAREWELL TO THE RYE.

I.

Shining sickle ! lie thou there ;
  Another harvest needs my hand,
Another sickle I must bear
  Back to the fields of my own land.

II.

A crop waves red on Connaught's plain,
  Of bearded men and banners gay,
But we will beat them down like rain,
  And sweep them like the storm away.
        Farewell, sickle! welcome, sword!

III.

Peaceful sickle! lie thou there,
  Deep buried in the vanquish'd rye;
May this that in thy stead I bear
  Above as thick a reaping lie!
        Farewell, sickle! welcome, sword!

IV.

Welcome, sword! out from your sheath,
  And look upon the glowing sun ;
Sharp-shearer of the field of death,
  Your time of rust and rest is gone.
        Welcome, welcome, trusty sword!

V.

Welcome, sword! no more repose
  For Cathal Crov-drerg or for thee,
Until we walk o'er Erin's foes,
  Or they walk over you and me,
        My lightning, banner-cleaving sword!

VI.

Welcome, sword! thou magic wand,
  Which raises kings and casts them down ;
Thou sceptre to the fearless hand,
  Thou fetter-key for limbs long bound—
        Welcome, wonder-working sword!

VII.

Welcome, sword! no more with love
  Will Cathal look on land or main,
Till with thine aid, my sword! I prove
  What race shall reap and king shall reign.
              Farewell, sickle! welcome, sword!

VIII.

Shining sickle! lie thou there;
  Another harvest needs my hand,
Another sickle I must bear
  Back to the fields of my own land.
              Farewell, sickle! welcome, sword!

THE DEATH OF DONNELL MORE.[43]

A FRAGMENT.

*   *   *   *   *

V.

On they came to Thurles—better
  For their wives, if such men wed,
They had never left their mud-walls—
  On that wild adventure led
By Donnell More and the Sil-Murray—
  Seventeen hundred of them bled!

VI.

On the plain of Thurles rises
  High a memorable pile,
Rear'd to God by the great victor,
  Visible for many a mile:
Well may his majestic spirit

VII.

Piety becomes the valiant,
    As the garland does the bride—
All the saints lean down with favor
    To the man that hath been tried;
In the battle, their protection
    Is as armor to his side.

VIII.

Who avenged the saints like Donnell,
    When Prince John drove down his stake
On Ard-Finian, and in 'Tipraid,
    Sacred for Saint Factna's sake?
Who but he drove back the braggart,
    And his stone entrenchments brake?

IX.

Still they came—as their own armor,
    Brazen and unbroken—back;
And the clans of Munster wither'd
    In the havoc and the sack—
Came, but fled like thieving foxes,
    With the dun-dogs on their track!

X.

On Kilfeakle and Knockgraffon
    Waves no more their lawless flag—
Limerick owns no Saxon warder,
    None tops Saint Finian's crag;
Let them tell their tales of conquest,
    So the baffled always brag.

XI.

In his pride, the blue-stream'd Shannon,
    Roll'd between unfetter'd banks,

With meek joy, the gentle Suir,
  Maiden-like, but murmur'd thanks—
And the gray hills smiled upon him,
  Riding in his conquering ranks.

XII.

But there came a time, and Donnell
  With his kingly fathers slept ;
Other chieftains rose in Thomond,
  None that such strict guardship kept—
Other warriors rose, but never
  One like him for whom she wept.

XIII.

'Twas not that his blood was Brian's,
  'Twas not that his heart was great,
'Twas not that he took from no man,
  But gave worthy of his state—
He was born the land's defender,
  The fond foster-son of Fate !

XIV.

He was served, not for his bounty,
  Nor his favor, nor his name—
Not that Fame still bore his banner,
  And success was page to Fame—
But he was through all heroic,
  Hence his far-spread following came !

XV.

When the Saxons came like snow-flakes,
  Covering Banba's sacred strand,
He arose—the nation's chieftain,
  Warfare-wise, and strong of hand—
And his name became a spell-word

THE CAOINE OF DONNELL MORE.[a]

I.

HE is dead, and to the earth
We bear our shield and sparthe,
Thomond's prince and Ireland's promise,
In God's anger taken from us ;
And the bells he gave are pealing,
And the hosts he led are kneeling,
And the mourning priesthood falters
At his marble-builded altars—
    Chant slower, sisters, slower,
    'Tis the *Caoine* for Donnell More!

II.

Thomond's grief will not be hurried,
Royal deeds cannot be buried,
Men cannot cast a dungeon
O'er the stars, and he's among them,—
He, of his the liberal spender,
Of ours the stern defender—
The pillar of our power,
Snapp'd in our trial's hour—
    Chant slower, sisters, slower,
    'Tis the *Caoine* of Donnell More!

III.

Raise your voices, keener, shriller,
Till they reach the upland tiller,
And the seaward farthest man on
The blue-stream'd, splendid Shannon,
And the eagle, from the quarry,
Shall fly back to his high eyrie,

And the deer on *Slieve an Iron*
Flee as when the dogs environ,
And the eremitic heron
Shall fly o'er fen and fern—
 Walk slower, sisters, slower,
  'Tis the corpse of Donnell More!

IV.

To the bards of Erin he was
As to the harp the *Ceis ;* [a]
As o'er yon town the spire,
So he stood o'er others higher ;
As the fearless ocean ranger,
Laugh'd he in the hour of danger ;
As the rover on the land,
Was he free of mind and hand—
 Walk slower, sisters, slower,
  'Tis the corpse of Donnell More!

V.

When the Galls fell thick as hail
On the roof-trees of the Gael,

 * * * * * *

ST. CORMAC, THE NAVIGATOR. [44]

A LEGEND OF THE ISLAND OF LEWIS.

FIRST ISLANDER.

"Look out! look out! on the waves so dark,
And tell me dost thou see a bark
 Riding the tempest through ?
It bears a cross on its slender spar,
And a lamp that glances like a star,

SECOND ISLANDER.

"I see a bark far off at sea,
  With cross and lamp and crew of three,
    But sooth it labors sore ;
I see it rise, I see it fall,
Now the angry ocean swallows all,
    And I see the bark no more.

FIRST ISLANDER.

"'Tis he! 'tis he! I know his sail—
  'Tis the holy man of the distant Gael,
    True to his plighted word—
'Be't storm or calm, or foul or fair,'
He said, 'I will be surely there
    On the birthday of our Lord!'

"He is the saint whose hymn soars loud
  O'er shifting sail and crackling shroud,
    Who resteth on his oar
In the summer midnight's silent hour,
May haply hear that voice of power
    O'er Coryvrekan's roar.

"He knoweth how to steer aright,
  By the yard, and plough, and northern light,
    Through the battling Shetland Seas—
Knoweth of every port the sign
From Westra to Saint Columb's shrine
    In the southern Hebrides.

"A host will throng to cape and bay
  To meet him each appointed day,
    Be it festival or fast,
And if his bark comes not in sight
They deem they have not reckon'd right,
    Or that the day is past.

" His psalm hath waken'd Osmunwall,
And from the cavern of Fingall
Hath shaken down the spar;
The fishers on the midnight waves,
And the otter-hunters from their caves
Salute his cross and star."

SECOND ISLANDER.

" I see, I see through the night-fall dark
Saint Cormac sitting in his bark,
And now he draweth near!
Dear Father of the island men,
Welcome to Wallis' Isle again,
And to our Christmas cheer!"

SAINT COLUMBANUS IN ITALY TO SAINT COMGALL IN IRELAND.[45]

I.

HEALTH to my friend and Father! far beyond
Sliabh Colpa's snows!   My heart impels my pen—
My heart, however far, of thee still fond—
Thou first of Ireland's wise and holy men!

II.

Know, holy Comgall, since you saw our sail
Melt in the horizon of the Irish Sea,
God hath vouchsafed new conquests to the Gael
Through Gaul, and Allemain, and Italy—
Conquests, my Father, unlike those of old
Which our benighted chieftains undertook,
When Dathi by the thunderbolt was fell'd,
And Crimthan half the thrones Cis-Alpine shook.

III.

On other fields we win far other fame,
  With other foes we wage our mortal fight—
Our watchword now is Christ, our Saviour's name,
  Our forays far into the realms of night ;
Like exhalations from a fen, the powers
  Of darkness to the conflict thick ascend,
But the Eternal Charter still is ours—
  "Lo ! I am with you always, to the end !"

IV.

In Burgundy, a she-wolf broke our fold—
  A wolf in wiliness and craft and wrath—
A queen in infamy and beauty bold,
  Who raised a million barriers in our path ;
But God on Brunchant did judgment dread—
  By her own pride her funeral pyre was rear'd,
And on that pile I saw her haughty head
  Lopp'd by the axe, and by the lightning scarr'd.

V.

In bleak Helvetia, Gall and I essay'd,
  Not fruitlessly, the blessèd cross to raise—
And, though the powers of hell were all array'd
  Against us, we had courage, God have praise !
Idols of wood and bronze we overthrew
  At Arbona, Tucconia, Brigantium—
Where we found false gods we've left the true ;
  Now, Zurich, Constance, shrine their idols dumb.

VI.

My brother Gall, amid the Alps abides—
  I preach the Gospel through the Lombard plain—
The harvest ripens round me on all sides,
  But few there are to gather in the grain.

Send forth some laborers, as pure and keen
  As the steel'd sickle, to your scholar's aid—
The time is not yet come when weaklings glean
  Where Arius draws on Christ his rebel blade.

VII.

King Agilulph, the Ard-Righ of this land,
  God hath inspired him for my constant friend—
He clears my path with his strong sceptred hand,
  And doth himself my daily steps attend ;
And it has been my lot to intercede
  With Peter's *Coarbh*⁴⁶ for him happily—
And now we all are one in word and deed
  From the far Alps to the Tyrhenian Sea.

VIII.

Comgall, farewell!   May all the angels guard
  Banchor,* our mother, and her holy men,
And our dear island, isle of God's regard ;
  Be all our blessings on you all !   Amen.

THE TESTAMENT OF ST. ARBOGAST.

I.

St. Arbogast, the bishop, lay
  On his bed of death in Strasburg Palace—
And, just at the dawn of his dying day,
  Into his own hands took the chalice ;
And, praying devoutly, he received
  The blessèd Host, and thus address'd
His Chapter, who around him grieved,
  And, sobbing, heard his last request.

* A famous monastery in the province of Ulster, of which St. Comgall was Abbot.—Ed.

II.

Quoth he—"The sinful man you see
Was born beyond the Western sea,
In Ireland, whence, ordain'd, he came,
In Alsace, to preach, in Jesus' name.
There, in my cell at Haguenean,
Many unto the One I drew ;
There fared King Dagobert one day,
With all his forestrie array,
Chasing out wolves and beasts unclean,
As I did errors from God's domain ;
The king approached our cell, and he
Esteem'd our assiduity ;
And, when the bless'd St. Amand died,
He call'd us to his seat, and sighed,
And charged us watch and ward to keep
In Strasburg o'er our Master's sheep.

III.

"Mitre of gold we never sought—
Cope of silver to us was nought—
Jewel'd crook and painted book
We disregarded, but, perforce, took.
Ah! oft in Strasburg's cathedral
We sighed for one rude cell so small,
And often from the bishop's throne
To the forest's depths we would have flown,
But that one duty to Him who made us
His shepherd in this see, forbade us.

IV.

"And now—"   St. Arbogast spoke slow,
But his words were firm, though his voice was low—
"God doth require His servant hence,
And our hope is His omnipotence.

But bury me not, dear brethren, with
The pomp of torches or music, sith
Such idle and unholy state
Should ne'er on a Christian bishop wait;
Leave cope of silver and painted book,
Mitre of gold, and jewel'd crook,
Apart in the vestry's darkest nook;
But in Mount Michael bury me,
Beneath the felon's penal tree—
So Christ our Lord lay at Calvary.
This do, as ye my blessing prize,
And God keep you pure and wise!"
These were the words—they were the last—
Of the blessèd Bishop Arbogast.[47]

THE COMING OF THE DANES.[48]

I.

THE night is holy—'tis blessèd Saint Bride's—[49]
  The hour may be almost one :
Lord Murrough late on the rath-top bides,
  Gazing the new moon on.
The moon, he had dreamt, that night would throw
O'er his lands a sign of warning or woe.

II.

The night is holy—the visible sea
  Spreads like a dinted silver plain,
And Lord Murrough's oaks look shadowingly
  Across the vista meeting again.
The watch-dog sleeps, and though prayers are said,

III.

The watch-dog sleeps—enough are awake ;
  Chapel and cloister are wakeful all—
Long after the final prayer they make,
  Lord Murrough walks still on the shining wall,
Gazing the pale mute moon in the face—
By his feet lies his well-worn battle mace.

IV.

His battle mace!   What does it there ?
  Why are his greaves and armlets on ?
Has he thrown his guage to the fiends of air
  That his visor is barr'd in the moonlight wan ?
He awaiteth the sign he is to see—
If for war, he will hie forth instantly.

V.

The night is wearing of blessèd Saint Bride,
  The hour may be nigh to three,
Lord Murrough casts his glance aside
  From the moon out to the sea.
What sable shade from the zenith fell ?
Lord Murrough shuddered, yet could not tell.

VI.

He look'd aloft—a wing—a bill—
  Another—two ravens grim
O'erspread the moon, wrapt castle and hill,
  And the sea to the horizon's rim.
The birds of Odin in the spirit-sphere
Ne'er shed from their wings such darksome fear.

VII.

Lord Murrough mutter'd his longest prayer,
  With a few added words at the end :

And he held by his mace in the lightless air,
  With the grasp of a trusting friend ;
And full an hour it might have been
Till land, sky, and sea were again serene.

VIII.

Then looking seaward the sad lord saw
  A fisherman drawing his net,
And the sea was as bright as a summer shaw,
  Though the shore was like rocks of jet—
And the sea-bird croak'd, and the coming oar
Sent its dreary echoes to haunt the shore.

IX.

Lord Murrough knew that the days of rest
  For his native land were fled—
And he pray'd to God and St. Bride the blest
  To arm her—heart and head ;
Then he tenderly kiss'd, and lay down by his mace—
And he died—the last free lord of his race !

THE DEATH OF KING MAGNUS BAREFOOT.[40]

I.

On the eve of Saint Bartholomew in Ulfrek's-fiord we lay
  (Thus the importuned Scald began his tale of woe),
And faintly round our fleet fell the August evening gray,
  And the sad sunset winds began to blow.

II.

I stood beside our monarch then—deep care was on his
  brow—

Why tarry still my errand-men?—'tis time they were here
　　now,
　And that for some less guarded land we bore."

III.

Into the valley'd West these errand-men had gone—
　To Muirkeartach, the ally of our king
(Whose daughter late was wed to Earl Sigurd, his son),
　The gift-herd from Connacia to bring.

IV.

'Twas midnight in the firmament, ten thousand stars were
　　there,
　And from the darksome sea look'd up other ten—
I lay beside our monarch, he was sleepless, and the care
　On his brow had grown gloomier then.

V.

When morning dawning gray in lightsome circles spread,
　From his couch rose the king slowly up,
" Elldiarn, what! thou awake! I must landward go," he
　　said,
　" And with thee or with the saints I shall sup."

VI.

Then when the red sun rose, in his galley through the fleet
　Our noble Magnus went; and the earls all awoke,
And each prepared for land—the late errand-men to meet,
　Or to free them from the Irish yoke.

VII.

It was a noble army ascending the green hills
　As ever kingly master led ;
The memory of their marching my mournful bosom thrills,
　And I still hear the echo of their tread.

VIII.

Ere two hours had pass'd away, as I wander'd on the strand,
    Battle-cries from afar reach'd my ear ;
I climb'd the seaward mountain and look'd upon the land,
    And, in sooth, I saw a sight of fear.

IX.

As winter rocks all jagged with the leafless arms of pines,
    Stood the Irish host of spears on their path—
As the winter streams down dash through the terrible
    ravines,
    So our men pour'd along, white with wrath.

X.

The arrow flights, at intervals, were thicker o'er the field
    Than the sea-birds o'er Jura's rocks,
While the ravens[61] in the darkness were lost—shield on shield
    Within it clash'd in thunderous shocks.

XI.

At last one hoarse " *Farrah !*" broke from the battle-cloud
    Like the roar of a billow in a cave,
And the darkness was uplifted like a plague-city's shroud—
    And there lifeless lay our monarch brave.

XII.

And dead beside the king lay Earl Erling's son,
    And Erving and Ulf, the free ;
And loud the Irish cried to see what they had done,
    But they could not cry as loud as we.

XIII.

Oh, Norway! oh, Norway! when wilt thou behold
    A king like thy last in worth,

Whose heart fear'd not the world, whose hand was full of
        gold
For the numberless Scalds of the North.

XIV.

Ah! well do I remember how he swept the Western seas
    Like the wind in its wintry mood—
How he reared young Sigurd's throne upon the Orcades,
    And the isles of the South subdued.

XV.

In his galley o'er Cantire, how we bore him from the main—
    How Mona in a week he won,
By him, how Chester's earl in Anglesea was slain—
    Oh, Norway! that his course is run!

THE SAGA OF KING OLAF, OF NORWAY, AND HIS DOG.[1]

I.
[Of the early reign of Olaf, surnamed Tryggvesson.]

KING OLAF, Harold Haarfager's heir, at last hath reach'd the
        throne,
Though his mother bore him in the wilds by a mountain lake-
        let lone;
Through many a land and danger to his right the king hath
        pass'd,
Outliving still the low'ring storms, as pines outlive the blast;
Yet now, when Peace smiled on his throne, he cast his
        thoughts afar,
And sail'd from out the Baltic Sea in search of Western war.
His galley was that " Sea-Serpent" renown'd in sagas old,
His banner bore two ravens grim, his green mail gleam'd
        with gold—
The king's ship and the king himself were glorious to behold.

II.
[The success of King Olaf's cruise to the West.]

O'er the broad sea the Serpent leaves a train of foam behind,
The pillaged people of the isles the darker record find;
For the godly royal pirate, whene'er he took a town,
Sent all its souls to Odin's court, its treasures to his own.
His Scalds of prophet ear, oft heard—it lives still in their
     lays—
All the voices of Valhalla in chorus sing his praise;
But Tryggvesson was a fighting king, who loved his wolf-
     dog more,
His stalwart ship and faithful crew and shining golden store,
Than all the rhyming chroniclers gray Iceland ever bore.

III.
[How King Olaf made a descent on Antrim, and carried off the herds thereof.]

Where Antrim's rock-begirdled shore withstands the north-
     ern deep,
O'er Red Bay's broad and buoyant breast, cold, dark breezes
     creep—
The moon is hidden in her height, the night winds ye may see
Flitting like ocean owlets from the cavern'd shore set free—
The full tide slumbers by the cliffs a-weary of its toil,
The goat-herds and their flocks repose upon the upland soil—
The Sea-King slowly walks the shore, unto his instincts true
While up and down the valley'd land climbeth his corsair crew,
Noiseless as morning mist ascends, or falls the evening dew.

IV.
[The king is addressed by a clown having a marvellous cunning dog in his
company.]

Now looking to land and now to sea, the king walk'd on
     his way,
Until the faint face of the morn gleam'd on the darksome
     bay;

A noble herd of captured kine rank round its ebb-dried
    beach—
The galleys fast receive them in, when, lo! with eager speech,
A clown comes headlong from the hills, begging his oxen
    three,
And two white-footed heifers, from the Monarch of the Sea.
The hurried prayer the king allowed as soon as it he heard.
The wolf-dog of the peasant, obedient to his word,
Counts out and drives apart the five from the many-headed
    herd.

V.

[King Olaf offereth to purchase the peasant's dog, who bestows it on him with
a condition.]

" By Odin, king of men !" marvelling, the monarch spoke,
" I'll give thee, peasant, for thy dog, ten steers of better
    yoke
Than thine own five."   The hearty peasant said:
" King of the ships! the dog is thine; yet, if I must be paid,
Vow, by your raven banner, never again to sack
Our valleys in the hours of night—we dread no day attack."
More wonder'd the fierce pagan still to hear a clown so say,
And mused he for a moment, as was his kingly way,
If that he should not carry both the man and dog away.

VI.

King Olaf taketh the vow, and saileth with the dog away.]

The Sea-King to the clown made vow, and on his finger placed
An olden ring the sceptre-hand of his great sire had graced,
And round his neck a chain he flung of gold pure from the
    mine,
Which, ere another moon, was laid upon St. Columb's shrine;
Then with his dog he left the shore—his sails swell to the
    blast ;
Poor "Vig" hath howl'd a mournful cry to the bright shores
    as they pass'd.

Now brighter beam'd the sunrise, and wider spread the tide;
Away, away to the Scottish shore the Danish galleys hied—
There, revelling with their kindred, three days they did
    abide.

VII.
[Of the Sea-King's manner of life.]

King Olaf was a rover true—his home was in his bark,
The blue sea was his royal bath, stars gemm'd his curtains
    dark;
The red sun woke him in the morn, and sail'd he e'er so far,
The untired courier of his way was the ancient Polar star.
It seem'd as though the vèry winds, the clouds, the tides,
    and waves,
Like the sea-side smiths and Vikings, were his lieges and his
    slaves;
His premier was a pilot old, of bronzed cheek and falcon eye,
A man, albeit, who well loved life, yet fear'd he not to die,
Who little knew of crowns or courts, and less to crouch or lie.

VIII.
[The treason of the Jomsburg Vikings calleth home the king.]

Strange news have come from Norway—the Vikings have
    rebell'd;
Homeward, homeward fast as fate, his galley's sails are
    swell'd,—
Off Heligoland, Jarl Thover, and Rand the Witch they
    meet,
But a mystic wind bears the evil one, unharm'd, far from
    the fleet.
Jarl Thover to the land retreats—the fierce king follows on,
Slaying the traitors' compeers, who far from them doth run.
After him flung King Olaf his never-missing spear,
But Thover (he was named Hiort,* and swifter than the

IX.

[Thover Hiort treacherously killeth the king's dog]

The wolf-dog then the monarch loosed—the traitor trembled
    sore;
Vig holds him on the forest's verge—the king speeds from
    the shore.
Trembled yet more the caitiff to think what he should do—
He drew his glaive, and with a blow pierced his captor
    through.
And when the king came to the place, his noble dog lay
    dead,
His red mouth foaming white, and his white breast crimson
    red.
" God's curse upon you, Thover !"—'twas from the heart, I
    ween,
Of the grieved king this ban burst out beside the forest
    green.
The traitor vanish'd into the woods, and never again was
    seen.

X.

[How King Olaf and his dog were buried nigh unto one another by the sea.)

Two cairns rise by Drontheim-fiord, with two gray stones
    hard by,
Sculptured with Runic characters, plain to the lore-read
    eye,
And there the king, and here his dog, from all their toils
    repose,
And o'er their cairns the salt-sea wind, night and day, it
    blows;
And close to these they point you the ribs of a galley's
    wreck,
With a fork'd tongue in the curling crest, and half of a scaly
    neck;

And some late-sailing Scalds have told, that along the shore-
    side gray,
They have often heard a kingly voice and a huge hound's
    echoing bay—
And some have seen the traitor to the pine woods running
    away.

KING MALACHY AND THE POET M'COISI.[44]

I.

King Malachy, shorn of crown and renown,
With nothing left but his mensal board,
Hung in the troopless hall his sword,
Cared his own horse in the stable,
And daily sank deeper in joys of the table ;
For Brian the King by force and art,
By might of brain and hope of heart,
Conquer'd the sceptre and won the crown,
Leaving to Malachy little renown.

II.

In Tara's hall was room to spare,
For few were the chiefs and courtiers there ;
Of all who stood well in the monarch's graces,
But three retain'd their ancient places,
And two of the three had follow'd Brian,
Had the conqueror thought them worth his buyin',
The third, the Poet M'Coisi, alone
Stood true to the empty, discrown'd throne.

III.

And many a tale the poet told

Of Erin's wonderful builders three,
Of Troylane, the builder of Rath-na-ree,
And Unadh, who built the banquet-hall,
And the Gobhan Saer, the master of all ;
Of the Miller of Nith, and the Miller of Fore,
And many a hundred marvels more ;
Of the Well of Galloon that, like sudden sorrow,
Turns the hair to gray to-morrow ;
Of the Well of Slieve-bloom, which, who profanes
On the land around, draws down plagues and rains ;
Of the human wolves that howl and prey
Through Ossory's Woods from dark till day ;
Of speaking babes and potent boys,
And the wonderful man of Clonmacnoise,
Who lived seven years without a head,
And the edifying life he led ;
Of ships and armies seen in the air,
And the wonders wrought by St. Patrick's prayer.

*   *   *   *   *   *   *

KING BRIAN'S AMBITION.[34]

I.

KING BRIAN by the Shannon shore
  Stood musing on his power,
For now it had the torrent's roar,
  Swoll'n by the wint'ry shower—
But when the cold grave held him fast,
Where would it be, or would it last ?

II.

By him 'twas gather'd slowly as

And now the force and freight it has
    The depth, the spread, the length,—
The very greatness so long sought
Dark shadows from the future caught ;

III.

The cold distrust of meaner souls,
    The hatred of the vile,
That pride which nothing long controls—
    Worst evil of our isle—
All these like rocky barriers lay
In the Clan-Dalgais' onward way.

IV.

"Care crowns a monarch with his crown,
    And he who cannot bear it
Had better lay the burden down
    Nor vainly seek to share it ;
Wealth, honor, justice he may share,
But all his own is kingly care."

V.

So spoke the heart within the breast
    Of that brave king whose story
Burns redly in the Gaelic West,
    Its setting sun of glory.
When night his house of darkness bars,
There riseth after him but stars.

VI.

Dark shadows on the Shannon fell,
    The day was spent and gone,
Long in the unfrequented dell
    The monarch mused alone—
Well may you deem what was the prayer

KING BRIAN'S LAMENT FOR HIS BROTHER MAHON.[*]

A FRAGMENT.

I.

Ah! what is the news I hear,
My brother dear! my brother dear!
But yesterday we sent you forth
In hope and health, in joy and mirth,
But yesterday—and yet to-day
We lay you in your house of clay!

II.

O Mahon, of the curling locks,
With teeth like foam on ocean rocks,
With heart that breasted battle's wave,
Are mine the hands to make your grave—
These hands that first you taught to hold

*　　*　　*　　*　　*　　*　　*　　*

KING BRIAN'S ANSWER.

I.

"Go not forth to the battle," they said,
  "But abide with your councillors sage ;
A helmet would weigh down the head
  That already is weigh'd down with age.
There are warriors many a one
  In their prime, all impatient to go ;
Let the host be led on by your son,
  He will bring you the spoils of the foe."

[*] Treacherously slain by a Munster chieftain named O'Donovan.

II.

But the agèd king rose in his place,
    And his eye had the fire of long-past years,
And his hand grasp'd the keen-pointed mace,
    And silence came over his peers.
" 'Tis true I am old,"—and he smiled—
    " And the grave lies not far on my road,
But in arms I was nursed as a child,
    And in arms I will go to my God !

III.

" For this is no battle for spoil,
    No struggle with rivals for power ;
The gentile is camp'd on our soil,
    Where he must not exult for an hour.
'Tis true I am old,"—and he smiled—
    " And the grave lies not far on my road,
But in arms I was nursed as a child,
    And in arms I will go to my God."

THE BATTLE OF CLONTARF.

Good Friday, 1014.

I.

As the world's Redeemer hung
    On a tree this day to save,
In His love, each tribe and tongue
    From the thraldom of the grave,
We vow—attest, ye heavens !—by His gore
    To snap the damning chain
    Of this Christ-blaspheming Dane
    Who defiles each holy fane

II.

But—death to Erin's pride—
    Amid Sitric's host behold
Malmordha's squadron ride,
    Who betray, for Danish gold,
Their country, virtue, fame, and their souls.
    "False traitors, by the rood,
        Ye shall weep such waves of blood
        As in winter's spring-tide flood
                        Ocean rolls!"

III.

Thus spoke our wrathful king
    As he drew Kincora's sword,
And abroad he bade them fling
    The emblazonry adored,
The mystic sun arising on the gale ;
    And a roar of joy arose
    As they bent a wood of bows
On thy godless robber foes,
                        Innisfail !

IV.

The fierce Vikinger now
    On the dreadful Odin call,
And the gods of battle bow
    From Valhalla's cloudy hall,
And bend them o'er the dim "feast of shells,"
    But, like drops of tempest-rain,
    The innumerable slain
Of the traitor and the Dane
                        Strew the dells.

V.

Clontarf ! a sea of blood

And the billow's rising flood
Is repell'd by waves of gore,
That fling a sanguine blush o'er the tide,—
We have drawn the sacred sword
Of green Erie and the Lord,
And have crush'd the Sea-King's horde
　　　In their pride.

VI.

Rise! Ruler of the North!
Terrific Odin, rise!
Let thy stormy laughter forth
Burst in thunder from the skies.
Prepare for heroes slain, harp and shell!
For we crowd thy feast to-night
With the flow'er of Ocean's might,
Who, in Freedom's burning sight,
　　　Blasted, fell!

VII.

There lie the trampled Dane,
And the traitor prince's band,
Who could brook a foreign chain
On the green Milesian land,
Where immortal beauty reigns evermore;
And the surf is bloody red
Where the proud barbarian bled,
Or with terror wingèd fled
　　　From our shore.

VIII.

Such ever be the doom
Of the tyrant and the slave—
Be their dark unhonor'd tomb

Who, fired with Freedom's soul, clasp the brand—
O goddess thrice divine!
Be our isle again thy shrine,
And renew the soul of Bri'n
                    Through the land!

THE SINFUL SCHOLAR.

"O FATHER ABBOT!" the pale friar said,
"Awake! arise! our scholar's dead!"
"Dead! and so soon?"—"Ay! even now
His heart hath ceased."—"Yet tell me how?"
"Thus 'twas : As Clarence, Hugh, and I
Watch'd by his pallet prayerfully,
The gray dawn broke; up from the bed
Suddenly rose that mighty head—
'Oh! bring me forth into the light,'
He cried—'I would have one last sight
Of the fair morning as it breaks
Upon the antlers of the Reeks!' *
We bore him forth.   Clarence and Hugh
Turn'd and wept.   He drank the view
Into his very soul, and sigh'd
As if content.   I by his side
Then heard him breathe, in accents faint,
Some name—perchance his patron saint ;
He clasp'd my hand—I felt it quiver,
And the swift soul was fled forever!
Think me not crazed if now I tell
What instant on his death befel :
Beside the bed, become a bier,
We, kneeling, heard a rustling near—

* Celebrated mountains in Kerry.

Then dropp'd, like blossoms from a tree,
Three doves, as lilies fair to see—
Think me not void of mind or sense—
Three lighted there, but *four* flew hence—
Four doves, if ever I said a prayer,
Soar'd skyward through the lucid air—
Clarence and Hugh, as well as I,
That they were four, can testify!"

*   *   *   *   *   *

Close by Killarney's gentle wave
They made the scholar's simple grave—
The blue lake, like a lady, grieves
Saddest in the long autumn eves—
The stern hills, like a warrior host,
Look down upon their loved and lost—
The genius of the place *he* sleeps
Beneath the heights, above the deeps—
Who fed on sunshine, drank the dew,
Who mortal weakness never knew.

*   *   *   *   *   *

No stone spoke o'er him—rose alone
A wooden cross—long, long since gone—
But far and near, through many an age,
He lived in chronicles a sage—
One of the marvels of his race,
Whose lightest word 'twere joy to trace;
And so the unreal shape became
The heritor of all his fame—
And the true story slept as deep
As this world's memory can sleep.

Of gentle blood and generous birth,

Of careful sire and mother holy,
Our scholar was.   This, and this solely
He ever told.   No more was known,
Even when his fame afar had flown
On the four winds.   His after course
Obscured the interest of his source.
One, only one, in secret cell,
The whole of that strange life could tell—
All that the scholar had reveal'd
Could tell, but that his lips were seal'd
By solemn vows, which never yet
Did the worst-fallen priest forget ;
Yet, by the edict of the dead,
Some passages were register'd
Amid the abbey's psalter, where,
In Gaelic letters round and fair,
An after age's curious eye
Alighting, clear'd the mystery.

Hear, then, the tale, not idly told—
A story new as well as old—
A song of suffering and of fame,
Of false and true, of pride and shame.

*   *   *   *   *   *   *   *

Here ends the author's MS. and Part I. in the first rough draft. The plan of
this noble poem he had mapped out as follows: "Part II.—Glen-Manna; the
eve of victory ; the morning after the battle; Brian's apparition in the tent of
Maelsuthain; advises him to retire from the world ; the scholar departs from
the camp of the victorious king in search of Penance and Peace.

"Part III —His life at Irrelagh ; his literary work ; his school and scholars ; the
three Donalds; the strange lady ; the three Donalds wanted; they depart, beg
his blessing, and leave to visit the Land of our Redemption.

"Part IV.—Apparition of the three doves ; their message and warning ; Maelsuthain's resolution, repentance, and death."

Had the author lived to complete it, the "Sinful Scholar" would have been
one of the finest poems in Irish literature.—Ed.

THE LANDING OF THE NORMANS.

I.

"Alas! for this day,
  The accursed of all years!
In Banna's broad bay
  The invader appears;
The pennant of Cardigan
  Threatens the land,
And the sword of Fitzstephen
  Burns red in his hand.

> Sleep no more! sleep no more!
>   Up, Lagenians, from sleep!
> While you dream on the shore
>   They march o'er the deep!

II.

Wake, Cymri and Ostman!
  Wake, Cahirians! and gather
Your strength on the plain,
  Arm, brother! arm, father!
For our homes, for our lives,
  For the fair fields of Carmen,
For the love of our wives,
  Down, down on the Norman!

> Sleep no more! sleep no more! etc.

III.

Now, when Cardigan's chief
  And his penniless peers
Look doubtfully forth

l of the races!

ed,

of the races!

rs;

ht,
l of the races!

In the very first hour,
  Ere a camp they inclose,
Go, shatter the power
  Of our insolent foes!
      Sleep no more! sleep no more! etc.

EPITHALAMIUM.

THE BRIDAL OF EVA M'MURROGH.

I.

" Go forth into the fields,
  Bid the flow'rs to our feasts,
With the broad leaves which, as shields,
  Guard the noon-heat from their breasts ;
Bid the nobly-born rose,
  And the lily of the valley,
And the primrose of the sheep-walk,
  And the violet from the valley—
Where the order'd trees in ranks
Rise up from the river's banks,
  Bid them all—one and all—
  To our garland-hidden hall—
To the wedding of the worthy, to the bridal of the races—
Bid the humble and the noble, the virtues and the graces.

II.

" Go forth unto the shrines,
  Lift up your voices there ;
Lay your off'rings, more than mines,
  And the prince of off'rings, prayer ;
Beg our Lady of the Isle,

From her holy height to smile
  On this rare and noble bridal.
From St. Brendan's to St. Bees',
All along the Irish seas,
    Shore of shrines, pray a prayer
    For the valiant and fair,
For the wedding of the worthy, the bridal of the races!

III.

"Seek out the sons of song;
  Let them know who hath been wed,
That, amid the festive throng,
  Their seats are at the head;
Bid them come with harp and lay,
  And mellow mighty horn,
To charm the night away
  And to 'gratulate the morn.
    For the Lady Eva's sake,
    Royal largess they must take,
At the wedding of the worthy, the bridal of the races!

IV.

"They are come! they are here!
  The music and the flowers,
The blessings far and near,
  Have a sound of summer showers;
Here Beauty's conscious eyes
  Flash with emulous desire;
Ah! how many a gallant dies
  In this mortal arrowy fire!
    What lessons by this light
    May young lovers read to-night,
In the wedding of the worthy, the bridal of the races!

DE COURCY'S PILGRIMAGE.[M]

"I'm weary of your elegies, your keenings and complaints,
We've heard no strain this blessèd night but histories of
          saints ;
Sing us some deed of daring—of the living or the dead !"
So Earl Gerald, in Maynooth, to the Bard Neelan said.

Answer'd the Bard Neelan—"Oh, Earl, I will obey ;
And I will show you that you have no cause for what you
          say ;
A warrior may be valiant, and love holiness also,
As did the Norman Courcy, in this country long ago."

Few men could match De Courcy on saddle or on sward,
The ponderous mace he valued more than any Spanish
          sword ;
On many a field of slaughter scores of men lay smash'd and
          stark,
And the victors, as they saw them, said—"Lo! John De
          Courcy's mark !"

De Lacy was his deadly foe, through envy of his fame ;
He laid foul ambush for his life, and stigmatized his name ;
But the gallant John De Courcy kept still his mace at hand,
And rode, unfearing feint or force, across his rival's land.

He'd made a vow, for some past sins, a pilgrimage to pay
At Patrick's tomb, and there to bide a fortnight and a day ;
And now amid the cloisters the disarmèd giant walks,
And with the brown beads in his hand, from cross to cross

News came to Hugo Lacy of the penance of the knight,
And he rose and sent his murderers from Durrogh forth by
      night ;
A score of mighty Meathian men, proof guarded for the strife,
And he has sworn them, man by man, to take De Courcy's
      life.

'Twas twilight in Downpatrick town, the pilgrim in the porch
Sat, faint with fasting and with prayer, before the darken'd
      church—
When suddenly he heard a sound upon the stony street—
A sound, familiar to his ears, of battle-horses' feet.

He stepp'd forth to a hillock, where an oaken cross it stood,
And looking forth, he lean'd upon the monumental wood.
"'Tis he! 'tis he !" the foremost cried : " 'tis well you came
      to shrive,
For another sun, De Courcy, you shall never see alive !"

Then roused the soften'd heart within the pilgrim's sober
      weeds—
He thought upon his high renown, and all his knightly deeds;
He felt the spirit swell within his undefended breast,
And his courage rose the faster that his sins had been con-
      fess'd.

"I am no dog to perish thus! no deer to couch at bay !
Assassins ! ware* the life you seek, and stand not in my
      way !"
He pluck'd the tall cross from its root, and waving it around,
He dash'd the master-murderer stark—lifeless to the ground.

As row on row they press'd within the deadly ring he made,
Twelve of the score in their own gore within his reach he
      laid;

The rest in panic terror ran to horse and fled away,
And left the Knight De Courcy at the bloody cross to pray.

" And now," quoth Neelan to the Earl, " I did your will obey;
Have I not shown you had no cause for what I heard you
    say ?
" Faith, Neelan," answer'd Gerald, " your holy man, Sir John,
Did bear his cross right manfully, so much we have to own."

THE PILGRIMAGE OF SIR ULGARG.[37]

No supple ash in Cavan Wood
   Was fairer to the eye—
Not clearer on Lough Oughter's flood
   Was pictured the blue sky,
Than in the form and in the breast
Of Ulgarg, God and grace had rest.

In warlike camp, beneath the lead
   Of Breffni's potent flag—
In festal hall or sportive shade,
   On stormy sea or crag,
'Fore Ulgarg, none of all his race
Could win by worth the 'vantage-place.

One hope he held from boyhood's dawn
   Till manhood's rounded prime—
That he might live to look upon
   The fields of Palestine—
That he his swimming eyes might set

In vain the fairest of the land,
  Where beauty ever reigns,
Wove for his youth love's rosy band
  To bind him to their plains ;
In vain of glory sung his bards,
His footsteps yearn'd to trace our Lord's.

Free to command his after fate,
  He rose, and left behind
Glory and beauty, place and state,
  For only sea and wind—
For palmer's staff, and mourner's weed,
And desert thirst, and feet that bleed.

What years he spent in Palestine
  It may not now be known,
But all its hills and caves divine
  He knew them as his own—
Christ's route he traversed everywhere,
From the manger to the sepulchre.

Bound home, at last—'twas eventide,
  The sun was in the West,
When calmly by the Jordan's side
  He sat him down to rest ;
And looking toward the crimson sky,
A patriot tear suffused his eye.

He pray'd—he slept—the midnight moon
  Beheld him where he lay;
The night winds seized his mutter'd breath,
  And flew with it away;
Morn rose sublime on Jordan's tide,
Sir Ulgarg still lay by its side.

Another moon, and night, and morn
    Pass'd on, but never more
Arose that palmer, travel-worn—
    His pilgrimage was o'er.
By a chance-passing Christian hand,
His grave was made in Holy Land.

THE PENITENCE OF DON DIEGO RIAS.

A LEGEND OF LOUGH DERG.[16]

I.

THERE was a knight of Spain—Diego Rias,
    Noble by four descents, vain, rich, and young,
Much woe he wrought, or the tradition lie is,
    Which lived of old the Castilians among ;
His horses bore the palm the kingdom over,
    His plume was tallest, costliest his sword,
The proudest maidens wish'd him as a lover,
    The *caballeros* all revered his word.

II.

But ere his day's meridian came, his spirit
    Fell sick, grew palsied in his breast, and pined,—
He fear'd Christ's kingdom he could ne'er inherit,
    The causes wherefore too well he divined ;
Where'er he turns his sins are always near him,
    Conscience still holds her mirror to his eyes,
Till those who long had envied came to fear him,
    To mock his clouded brow and wint'ry sighs.

III.

Alas ! the sins of youth are as a chain
    Of iron, swiftly let down to the deep,

How far we feel not—till when, we'd raise 't again
  We pause amid the weary work and weep.
Ah, it is sad a-down Life's stream to see
  So many agèd toilers so distress'd,
And near the source—a thousand forms of glee
  Fitting the shackle to Youth's glowing breast!

IV.

He sought Peace in the city where she dwells not,
  He wooed her amid woodlands all in vain,
He searches through the valleys, but he tells not
  The secret of his quest to priest or swain,
Until, despairing evermore of pleasure,
  He leaves his land, and sails to far Peru,
There, stands uncharm'd in caverns of treasure,
  And weeps on mountains heavenly high and blue.

V.

Incessant in his ear rang this plain warning—
  " Diego, as thy soul, thy sorrow lives ;"
He hears the untired voice, night, noon, and morning,
  Yet understanding not, unresting grieves.
One eve, a purer vision seized him, then he
  Vow'd to Lough Derg, an humble pilgrimage—
The virtues of that shrine were known to many,
  And saving held even in that skeptic age.

VI.

With one sole follower, an Esquire trustful,
  He pass'd the southern cape which sailors fear,
And eastward held, meanwhile his vain and lustful
  Past works more loathsome to his soul appear,
Through the night-watches, at all hours o' day,
  He still was wakeful as the pilot, and

For grace, his vow to keep, doth always pray,
　And for his death to lie in the saints' land.

VII.

But ere his eyes beheld the Irish shore,
　Diego died.　Much gold he did ordain
To God and Santiago—furthermore,
　His Esquire plighted, ere he went to Spain,
To journey to the Refuge of the Lake,
　Before Saint Patrick's solitary shrine,
A nine days' vigil for his rest to make,
　Living on bitter bread and penitential wine."

VIII.

The vassal vow'd ; but, ah ! how seldom pledges
　Given to the dying, to the dead, are held !
The Esquire reach'd the shore, where sand and sedge is
　O'er melancholy hills, by paths of eld ;
Treeless and houseless was the prospect round,
　Rock-strewn and boisterous the lake before ;
A Charon-shape sat in a skiff a-ground—
　The pilgrim turn'd, and left the sacred shore.

IX.

That night he lay a-bed hard by the Erne,—
　The island-spangled lake—but could not sleep—
When lo ! beside him, pale, and sad, and stern,
　Stood his dead master risen from the deep.
" Arise," he said, " and come."　From the hostelrie
　And over the bleak hills he led the sleeper,
And when they reach'd Derg's shore, " Get in with me,"
　He cried,—" nor sink my soul in torments deeper."

X.

The dead man row'd the boat, the living steer'd,
  Each in his pallor sinister, until
The Isle of Pilgrimage they duly near'd—
  " Now hie thee forth, and work thy master's will!"
So spoke the dead, and vanish'd o'er the lake,
  The Squire pursued his course, and gain'd the shrine,
There, nine days' vigil duly he did make,
  Living on bitter bread and penitential wine.

XI.

The tenth eve shone in solemn, starry beauty,
  As he, rejoicing, o'er the old paths came,
Light was his heart from its accomplished duty,
  All was forgotten, even the latest shame—
When these brief words, some disembodied voice
  Spoke near him, " Oh, keep sacred, evermore,
Word, pledge, and vow, so may you still rejoice,
  And live among the Just when Time is o'er !"

A LEGEND OF DUNLUCE CASTLE.

THE northern winds howl'd through the sky,
  Above Dunluce's Tower,
And the raven with a bitter cry
  Wing'd away from her spray-wet bower ;
And the white foam, as it trickled back
  To the sea, in a stream of light
Appear'd, as the first ray of the morn
  Stealing through the clouds of night.

And though without the storm raged high,

Fair dames and chiefs held revelry
　That sea-beat pile within ;
And if they heard the tempest roar,
　They little reck'd, I ween—
It told them to enjoy the more
　Their own bright festive scene.

But there was one within that pile
　Whose heart was far from light,
For well she knew from Rathlin's Isle
　Her lover came that night.
She left the heartless revelry
　Unnoticed and unknown,
And from the lonely watch-tower high
　She gazed upon the gloom.

Fierce howl'd the blast on the rocky shore,
　And shook the cavern'd cliff,
And Ella's soul all hope gave o'er—
　Oh! could it spare his skiff?
The sea-sprites groan'd and the fortress moan'd,
　As the roaring north winds pass'd,
And the watch-towers shook like a reed by the brook
　In December's piercing blast.

And beneath the tower, from every cave,
　Such sounds came bursting forth
As the Sea-King sends from his frozen grave
　In the gulfs of the sunless North,—
When, lo! on the wave crest sparkling white
　A little boat she spied,
And her heart's blood warmèd with delight—
　"My bride! great heavens! my bride!"

The wild winds raged more furious still—
  Swept the watch-tower from the rock—
The waves dash'd high above the hill—
  His boat sank in the shock ;
He rose again, and through the gloom
  He saw his long-loved maid,
And though the tempest was in its noon,
  Still was he not dismay'd.

He clasp'd her close, and through the foam
  He cleft with a hero's stroke ;
He whisper'd hope, but the billows' moan
  Swept away the words he spoke.
The sea had nursed his infant years,
  Had given his boyhood joy,
The tempest to him had sport, not fears,
  And he hush'd his Ella's sigh.

A wave arose, and on its crest
  It bore them to the shore,
And it flung them far, where some falcon's nest
  Had been in days of yore.
The chief clung fast unto the rock—
  " We're safe, my bonnie bride !"
Then, wearied and worn by the struggle's shock,
  He fainted by her side.

DEATH OF ART M‘MURROUGH.[21]

I.

FROM the king's home rose a hum
  Like the rising of a swarm,
  And it spread round Ross, and grew

And from the many-gatèd town pass'd Easchlaghs[60] in affright,
Pale as the morning hours when rushing forth from night,
And north, east, south, and westward, as they spread,
They cried, "The king is dead! the king is dead!"

II.

As the mountain echoes mimic
    The *mort* of the bugle horn,
So far and farther o'er the land
    The deadly tale is borne ;
Echo answers echo from wood, and rath, and stream—
Easchlagh follows easchlagh, like horrors in a dream ;
And when entreated to repose, they only said,
In accents woe-begone and brief, "The king is dead!"

III.

The news was brought to Offaly,
    To the Calvach in his hall ;[63]
He said, " Still'd be the harp and flute—
    We now are orphans all."
The news was brought to O'Tuathal, in Imayle ;
He said, "We have lost the bulwark of the Gael ;"
And his chosen men a-south to the royal wake he led—
Sighing, "The king is dead! the king is dead!"

IV.

To O'Brin in Ballincor,
    To O'Nolan in Forth it came,
To MacDavid in Riavach,[64]
    And all mourn'd the same ;
They said, "We have lost the chief champion of our land,
The king of the stoutest heart and strongest hand ;"
The hills of the four counties that night for joy were red,
    ̄d boastfully their Dublin bells chimed out, "The king is
        dead !"

V.

It was told in Kilkenny,
   And the Ormond flag flew out,
That had hid among the cobwebs
   Since the earl's Callan rout ;
But the friars of Irishtown they grieved for him full sore,
And Innistioge and Jerpoint may long his loss deplore.
From Clones south to Bannow the holy bells they toll,
And every monk is praying for his benefactor's soul.

VI.

For ages in the eastward
   Such a wake was never seen;
Since Brian's death, in Erin
   Such mourning had not been ;
And as the clans to St. Mullins bore the fleshly part
That was earthy and had perished of King Art—
The crying of the keeners was heard by the last man,
Though he was three miles off when the burial rite began.

VII.

" Mourn, mourn," they said, " ye chieftains,
   From Riavach and from Forth ;[45]
Mourn, ye dynasts of the lowlands,
   And ye Tanists of the North ;
The noblest man that was left us here to-day,
In the churchyard of his fathers we make his bed of clay—
Unlucky is this year above all years—
His life was more to us than ten thousand tested spears.

VIII.

" No ash-tree in Shillelah
   Was more comely to the eye—
And, like the heavens above us,

The taker of rich tributes, the queller of our strife,
The open-handed giver, his life to us was life.
O Art! why did you leave us?   Oh! even from the grave,
Could you not return to live for us you would have died to
      save?

XI.

" When we think on your actions—
    How against you, all in vain,
The king's son, and the king himself
    Of London, cross'd the main—
When we think of the battle of Athcro and the day
When Roger Mortimer, at Kells, fell in the fiery fray,
They chant the *De Profundis*, and we cannot help but cry—
' Defender of your nation! oh, why did you die?'

X.

" If death would have hostages,
    A million such as we,
To bring you back to Erin,
    Oh! a cheap exchange 'twould be ;
But silent as the midnight, and white as your own hair,
With its sixty years of snow, O king! you lie there—
Your lip at last is pale—at last is closed your eye—
O terror of the Saxons! Art, why did you die?"

XI.

Thus by the gaping grave
    They mourn'd about his bier,
Challenging with clamorous grief
    The dead that could not hear ;
Then slowly and sadly they laid him down to rest,
His sword beside him laid, and his cross on his breast.
And each took his own way with drooping heart and head,
Sighing, " The king is dead! the king is dead!"

AVRAN.

His grave is in St. Mullins,
But to pilgrim eyes unknown—
Unmark'd by mournful yew,
Unchronicled in stone ;
His bones are with his people's, his clay with common clay,
His memory in the night that lies behind the hills of day,
Where hundreds of our gallant dead await
The long-foretold, redeem'd, and honor'd fate."

A BALLAD OF BANNOW.

I.

STRETCH'D recumbent by the sea-side, in the bright midsummer tide,
With the volume of Our Poets lying open at my side,
From the full urn of remembrance pressing on my heart—I
sigh'd.

II.

'Twas the storied shore of Carmen*; here, beneath our very
feet,
Bannow's buried city slumber'd in its sandy winding-sheet—
Yonder ripple of the sea-surf marks the once o'er-crowded
street.

III.

Heath, with blossom on the mountain, and the squat, un-
sightly thorn,
Will put forth its stainless blossom, perfuming the breath of
morn—
But for this long-buried city, spring can nevermore return.

IV.

On this coast, when winter thunders, woe unto the ship that
     drives—
One huge billow combing over, might engulf ten thousand
     lives;
Vain, oh! vain as dreams of madmen, is the mortal strength
     that strives.

V.

Yet is not the buried city saddest of these thoughts to me,
Nor the stranded, crewless vessel, torn and toss'd up from
     the sea;
There are heavier griefs to mourn—deem ye not what they
     may be?

VI.

Yonder, on that breezy sand-bar, where the thin bent scarce
     can grow,
First on soil or strand of Erin, stood the Anglo-Norman foe,
And my mind is with their landing, ages, ages, long ago.

VII.

High and dry the Flemish bottoms of Fitzstephen here
     were drawn:
Off to Ferns—to false King Dermod—their ambassador has
     gone;
Shore and sea alike deserted, all for days they look'd upon.

VIII.

Who could dream from such a vanguard such a following
     should come?
Veterans of France and England, bless'd in Palestine and
     Rome—
Who would dream the night that slumbers under yonder
     streak of foam?

IX.

Peace be with our fearless fathers! never let the breath of
    fame
Lightly pass your lips, to darken of their gallant deeds the
    fame;
Dimly now we see the actors in their fierce imperial game.

X.

Here no Battle Abbey rises—here no Falaise Pillar stands—
For, as ebbs the waves of ocean o'er these historic strands,
So the surge of battle waver'd o'er our ancestral lands.

XI.

If our fathers felt the prowess of the steel-clad Norman host,
Little had the valiant stranger in the after war to boast;
'Twixt the tides and 'twixt the races, leave we the disputed
    coast.

XII.

Three things stand: Throughout our borders, still the Gaelic
    race is found;
Manly stem and lovely blossom flourish on the ancient
    ground;
And the dear faith of our fathers—rooted deep as Danaan
    mound.

XIII.

Near the tomb of buried Bannow, with the Poets at my side,
Such the changing thoughts that found me in the bright
    midsummer tide—
Past and present, hope and solace, patriot grief and patriot
    pride.

THE PRAISE OF MARGARET O'CARROLL OF OFFALLY.[67]

L

Tae myriad shafts of the morning sun had routed the wood-
    land fays,
And in the forest's green saloons danced the victorious rays;
Birds, like Brendans in the promised land, chanted matins
    to the morn,
And the larks sprung up with their chorus broods from the
    yellow fields of corn.
In cloth of gold, like a queen new-come out of the royal
    wood,
On the round-proud-white-walled rath Margaret O'Carroll
    stood.
That day came guests to Rath Imayn[68] from afar, from
    beyond the sea—
Bards and Brehons of Albyn and Erin—to feast in Offally.

II.

With the Lady Margaret are her maidens, comely to the
    sight—
Ah! how their eyes will thrill the harps and hearts of men
    to-night!
And in their midst, like a pillar old in a garden of roses,
    stands
Gilla-n-noamh M'Egan, the Brehon of Offally's lands;
His sallow brow like a vellum book with mystic lines is
    traced,
But his eye is as an arrow, and his form as a bow unbraced,
And he holds in his hand a book wherein he writes each
    learnèd name,
And these were the men of lore who to this feast at Rath
    Imayn came.

III.

First, Mælyn O'Mulconry comes, Arch-Brehon of the West,
Who gives dominion to O'Connor on Carnfraoich's crest;
And with Mælyn comes M'Firbiss, from Tyrawley's hills afar,
Whose learning shines, in Erris glens, like a lamp or a lofty
     star;
And O'Daly, from Finvarra, renown'd in Dan,[68] appears,
Whose fame, like the circling oak, grows wider with his
     years;
And with them is O'Clery, from Kilbarron's castled steep,
Whose hearthstone covers the sea-bird's nest above the
     foamy deep.

IV.

And lo! where comes M'Curtin, sweet singer of the South,
And O'Bruadin, with keen thoughts that swarm out of a
     honied mouth,
And O'Doran, Leinster's upright judge, and MacNeogh of
     the lays,
Whose tales can make December nights gayer than July days,
And Nial Dal O'Higgin, whose words of power can drain
The life out of the heart he hates, and the reason from the
     brain,[70]
And Cymric bards from Cymric vales to the poet tryst have
     come,
And many a Scottish rhymer from his Caledonian home.

V.

The Calvagh at the outer gate, he bids them welcome all,
The Brehon meets them at the door, and leads them up the
     hall,
The lady on the dais sits, amid her rich awards,
Goblets, and golden harps, and ancient books for studious
     bards.

For them in the green meadow-lands a thousand horses feed,
And a golden bit and a gilded rein hangs in stall for every
    steed,
And the glorious eyes of Irish girls are glancing round her,
    too—
Guerdons, for which the poet-soul its noblest deeds can do.

VI.

Over the fields of Erin, war horns may blow to-day,
Many a man in tower and town may don his war array,
The mountain tops of Erin red alarm-fires may light,
But no foot shall leave that hall of peace for the track of
    blood to-night.
To-morrow as to-day shall rise in melody and peace,
The Mass be said, the cup be fill'd, nor the evening revels
    cease—
For Margaret, like Our Lady's self, unto the troubled land,
Brings quiet in her holy smile, and healing in her hand.

VII.

It is not that her father is renown'd through Innisfail,
It is not that her lord is hail'd the sentinel of the Gael,
It is not that her daughter is the wife of the O'Neil,
It is not that her first-born's name strikes terror through
    the pale,
It is not all her riches, but her virtues that I praise;
She made the bardic spirit strong to face the evil days,
To the princes of a feudal age she taught the might of love,
And her name, though woman's, shall be scroll'd their war-
    rior names above.

VIII.

Low lie the oaks of Offally—Rath Imayn is a wreck;
Fallen are the chiefs of Offally—Death's yoke on every neck;

Da Sinchel's[71] feast no more is held for holy in the land,
No queen-like Margaret welcomes now the drooping bardic
    band,
No nights of minstrelsy are now like the Irish nights of old,
No septs of singers such as then M'Egan's book enroll'd;
But the name of Margaret O'Carroll, who taught the might
    of love,
Shall shine in Ireland's annals even minstrel name above.

MARGARET O'CARROLL.[72]

I.

Of bards and beadsmen far and near, hers was the name of
    names—
The lady fair of Offally—the flower of Leinster dames,
And she has join'd the pilgrim host for the citie of Saint
    James.

II.

It was Calvagh, Lord of Offally, walk'd wretchedly apart,
Within his moated garden, with sorrow at his heart,
And now he vow'd to heav'n, and now he cursed his fate—
That he had not forbidden that far journey ere too late.

III.

" Why did I not remember "—'twas thus he wish'd in vain—
" The many waves that roll between Momonia's cliffs and
    Spain ?
Why did I not remember, how, fill'd with bitter hate,
To waylay Christian pilgrims the Moorish pirates wait ?"

IV.

He thought of Lady Margaret, so fair, so fond, so pure,
A captive in the galley of some Christ-denying Moor ;

He thought of all that might befal, until his sole intent
Was to gallop to the southward and take the way she went.

V.

The noon was dark, the bitter blast went sighingly along,
The sky hung low, and chill'd to death the warder's snatch
     of song ;
The lymph flag round the flagstaff lay folded close and furl'd,
And all was gloom and solitude upon the outer world.

VI.

A rush as of a javelin cast, the startled chieftain heard,
A glance—upon the castle-wall a carrier-dove appear'd !
A moment, and the courier had flutter'd to his breast,
And panting lay against his heart, low cooing and caress'd.

VII.

There lay a little billet beneath the stranger's wing—
Bound deftly to his body with a perfumed silken string—
By night and day, o'er sea and shore, the carrier had flown,
For of God's ways so manifold each creature knows its own.

VIII.

He press'd the billet to his lips, he bless'd it on his knees—
" To my dear lord and husband : From Compostella these—
We have arrived in health and peace, thank God and good
     Saint James "—
And underneath the simple lines, the lady's name of names.

IX.

"Now blessings on thee, carrier-dove !" the joyful Calva'
     cried ;
" In such a flight both heart and wing were surely sorely
     tried ;
True image of thy mistress dear, in mercy's errand bold,
Thy cage shall hang in her own bower, all barr'd with good
     red gold.

X.

"And ever on thee, while thine eyes shall open to the sun,
White-handed girls shall wait and tend—my own undaunted
　　　one!
And when thou diest, no hand but hers shall lay thee in the
　　　grave!
Brave heart! that bore her errand well across the stormy
　　　wave."

RANDALL M'DONALD.

A LEGEND OF ANTRIM.

SHOWING HOW RANDALL M'DONALD OF LORN WON THE LANDS OF ANTRIM AND THEIR LADY.

The Lady of Antrim rose with the morn,
　　And doun'd her grandest gear;
And her heart beat fast, when a sounding horn
　　Announced a suitor near;
Hers was a heart so full of pride,
　　That love had little room,
Good faith, I would not wish me such bride,
　　For all her beautiful bloom.

One suitor there came from the Scottish shore,
　　Long, and lithe, and grim;
And a younger one from Dunluce hoar,
　　And the lady inclined to him.
"But harken ye, nobles both," she said,
　　As soon as they sat to dine—
"The hand must prove its chieftainry
　　That putteth a ring on mine.

"But not in the lists with armèd hands,
  Must this devoir be done,
Yet he who wins my broad, broad lands
  Their lady may count as won.
Ye both were born upon the shore,—
  Were bred upon the sea,
Now let me see you ply the oar,
  For the land you love—and me!

"The chief that first can reach the strand,
  May mount at morn and ride,
And his long day's ride shall bound his land,
  And I will be his bride!"
M'Quillan felt hope in every vein,
  As the bold, bright lady spoke—
And M'Donald glanced over his rival again,
  And bow'd with a bargeman's stroke.

'Tis summer upon the Antrim shore—
  The shore of shores it is—
Where the white old rocks deep caves arch o'er,
  Unfathom'd by man I wis—
Where the basalt breast of our isle flings back
  The Scandinavian surge,
To howl through its native Scaggerack,
  Chanting the Viking's dirge.

'Tis summer—the long white lines of foam
  Roll lazily to the beach,
And man and maid from every home
  Their eyes o'er the waters stretch.
On Glenarm's lofty battlements
  Sitteth the lady fair,
And the warm west wind blows softly
  Through the links of her golden hair.

The boats in the distant offing,
  Are marshall'd prow to prow;
The boatmen cease their scoffing,
  And bend to the rowlocks now;
Like glory-guided steeds they start—
  Away o'er the waves they bound ;
Each rower can hear the beating heart
  Of his brother boatman sound.

Nearer! nearer! on they come—
  Row, M'Donald, row!
For Antrim's princely castle home,
  Its lands, and its lady, row!
The chief that first can grasp the strand
  May mount at morn and ride,
And his long day's ride shall bound his land,
  And she shall be his bride!

He saw his rival gain apace,
  He felt the spray in his wake—
He thought of her who watch'd the race
  Most dear for her dowry sake!
Then he drew his skein from out its sheath,
  And lopt off his left hand,
And pale and fierce, as a chief in death,
  He hurl'd it to the strand!

"The chief that first can grasp the strand,
  May mount at morn and ride ;"
Oh, fleet is the steed which the bloody hand
  Through Antrim's glens doth guide!
And legends tell that the proud ladye
  Would fain have been unbann'd,
For the chieftain who proved his chieftainry
  Lorded both wife and land.

THE IRISH WIFE.

EARL DESMOND'S APOLOGY.[D]

I WOULD not give my Irish wife
  For all the dames of the Saxon land—
I would not give my Irish wife
  For the Queen of France's hand;
For she to me is dearer
  Than castles strong, or lands, or life—
An outlaw—so I'm near her
  To love till death my Irish wife.

Oh, what would be this home of mine—
  A ruin'd, hermit-haunted place,
But for the light that nightly shines
  Upon its walls from Kathleen's face?
What comfort in a mine of gold—
  What pleasure in a royal life,
If the heart within lay dead and cold,
  If I could not wed my Irish wife?

I knew the law forbade the banns—
  I knew my king abhorr'd her race—
Who never bent before their clans,
  Must bow before their ladies' grace.
Take all my forfeited domain,
  I cannot wage with kinsmen strife—
Take knightly gear and noble name,
  And I will keep my Irish wife.

My Irish wife has clear blue eyes,

And, twin-like, truth and fondness lie
  Within her swelling bosom white.
My Irish wife has golden hair—
  Apollo's harp had once such strings—
Apollo's self might pause to hear
  Her bird-like carol when she sings.

I would not give my Irish wife
  For all the dames of the Saxon land—
I would not give my Irish wife
  For the Queen of France's hand ;
For she to me is dearer
  Than castles strong, or lands, or life—
In death I would lie near her,
  And rise beside my Irish wife.

KILDARE'S BARD ON TOURNAMENTS.

L

Sing not to me of Normandie,
  Its armor'd knights and bloodless sports,
Its sawdust battle-fields, to me,
  Are odious as its canting courts ;
But sing to me of hunting far
  The antler'd elk in Erris' vales,
Of flying 'neath the crackling spar,
  Off Arran, through Atlantic gales.

II.

Raymond was brave, De Courcy bold,
  And Hugo Lacy bred to rule—
But I am of the race of old,

Sing not to me of Guisnes field,
  Or how Earl Gerald match'd with kings —
I'd rather see him on his shield
  Than tilting in their wrestler rings.

'TWAS SOMETHING THEN TO BE A BARD.

I.

In long gone days when he who bore
  The potent harp from hall to hall,
His courier running on before,
  His castlo where he chose to call;
When youthful nobles watch'd for him,
  And ladies fair, with fond regard,
Fill'd the bright wine-cup to the brim,
  'Twas something then to be a bard.

II.

When seated by the chieftain's chair,
  The minstrel told his pictured tale,
Of whence they came and who they were,
  The ancient stock of Innisfail—
When the gray steward of the house
  Laid at his feet the rich reward,
Gay monarch of the long carouse,
  'Twas something then to be a bard.

III.

'Twas glorious then when banners waved,
  And chargers neigh'd, and lances gleam'd,
When all was to be borne or braved

'Twas glorious in mid-host to ride
  A king's gift graceful as the 'pard,
With famous captains by his side,
  Proud of the presence of the bard.

IV.

'Twas glorious, too, ere age had power
  To dim the eye or chill the blood,
To fly to Beauty's evening bower,
  And lift from Beauty's brow the hood;
To feel that Heaven's own sacred flame
  Can melt a heart however hard,
To gather love by right of fame—
  'Twas glorious then to be a bard.

THE BANSHEE AND THE BRIDE.

A FRAGMENT.

I.

On the landscape night and darkness,
  Sheep and shepherd sleeping lay—
Somewhere far the old moon wander'd,
  Scarce a star vouchsafed its ray;
While the cold breeze from the northward
  Stirr'd the anchor'd pleasure-boat,
And thrill'd the long reeds, making music
  All along the castle-moat.

II.

But the sadder sound was vanquish'd
  By the gazer from within,
As upon the unlighted landscape

For to-night Rath Imayn's chieftain
  Has brought home his lovely bride,
And her kinsmen and his clansmen
  Seven days at Rath Imayn abide.

III.

"Hark!" he said, "what voice of sorrow
  Is it thus I chance to hear,
Could they not await the morrow,
  Nor disturb our marriage cheer?
Bid them enter, though untimely,
  Never was it truly said
That we turn'd away the stranger,
  Or denied him board and bed!"

*   *   *   *   *

THE LOVE CHARM.

I.

"ANCIENT crones that shun the highways,
  In dark woods to weave your spells—
Holy dwellers in the byways,
  Erenachs of blessèd wells;
House and lands to whoso finds me
  Where the cure for Connor dwells!"

II.

One went out by night to gather
  Vervain by the summer star;
Hosts of Leeches sought the father
  In his hall of Castlebar;
Blessèd water came in vials
  From the wells of ancient saints;
Vain their knowledge—vain their trials—

III.

" Nearer, nearer, Sister Margaret—
    (Lest the baffled Leeches hear)—
Listen to me, sister dearest,
    'Tis of Love that I lie here.
In Athenree there is a blossom
    More than all their charms could do;
There is healing in her bosom,
    All my vigor to renew.

IV.

" But our father hates her father—
    Deadly feud between them reigns—
Peace may come when I am sleeping
Where the lank laburnum's weeping,
And the cold green ivy creeping
    O'er the grave where nothing pains !

V.

" Tell her *then*—". " Nay, brother, brother,
    Live and hope and trust to me;
In a guise none can discover,
I will be your lady's lover,
Woo her here to thee, my brother,
    Ere the new moon faded be !"

VI.

Clad in boyish guise sits Margaret,
    With a harp upon her knee,
Harping to the lovely mistress
    Of the castled Athenree—
Chanting how, in days departed,
All the world was truer-hearted—
How death only could have parted

VII.

Sighèd the lady—" Gentle minstrel,
  If such lovers e'en lived now,
Ladies might be found as faithful,
  But few such there are, I trow."
Quoth the singer, also sighing,
" Nay, I know where one is lying
For thy sake—know where he's dying—
  Tell me, shall he live or no ?"

VIII.

Through the green woods, blossom-laden,
Ride the minstrel and the maiden,
O'er the Robe's bright waters gushing—
He exhorting and she blushing—
Athenree behind them far,
Riding till the sun of even',
Lingering late upon Ben Nephin,
  Saw them enter Castlebar.

IX.

Sat the sick heir in his chamber,
  Sore besieged by early death,
Life and death's alternate banners
  Waver'd in his feeble breath;
All the Leeches had departed,
While the sad sire, broken-hearted,
Gazes from his turret lonely,
Thinking of his sick heir only—
  O'er his heirless lands beneath.

X.

" Connor! Connor! here's your blossom,
  Take her—take her to your bosom:

Said I not to trust to me?
And this reverend man will wive you—
Albeit he comes to shrive you—
    And the bridesmaid I shall be!"

XI.

On the turret wept the father,
    (While the son beneath was wed)—
Came the priest reluctant to him—
    "Ah! I know," he cried, "*he's dead!*"
" Nay, not so, my noble master,
    Young Lord Connor's come to life!"
" Say 't again, again—speak faster—"
    " Yea, my lord—and here's his wife!"

QUEEN MARY'S MERCY.

RESPECTFULLY DEDICATED TO MRS. JAMES SADLIER.

PART I.

I.

CALL her not " Bloody Mary "—she
Who loved to set the prisoner free,[76]
    And dry misfortune's tear—
Or, ere the ancient fraud prevail,
Attend unto a simple tale,
    As true as we sit here.

II

Long years in London's dismal Towers
O'Connor told the heavy hours,
    Unpitied and unknown;
The serf who brought the prison bread
Shook ominous his shagged head,

Within his ken, no living thing
Save some bat clinging to the wing,
  To the wet wall he saw—
While daily fainter grew his hope,
That that dread gate would ever ope—
  Such then was Saxon law.

III.

His manly locks were wither'd now,
Sorrow had trenched his joyous brow,
Quaver'd the voice at whose clear call
The tumult hush'd in camp and hall,
And trembled sore the limbs that once
Was tireless in the chase and dance,
And heavier than the chain he wore,
The heart that in his breast he bore!
Six years had pass'd since unaware,
He fell into the Saxons' snare;
False Francis Bryan's guest betray'd—[77]
From banquet-hall in chains convey'd!
And well he knows what strife for power
Rent Offally from that rash hour;
Three kinsmen, haughty, fierce, and vain,
Contending, rend his dear domain;
A fourth, a youth of milder mood,
In Mellifont draws close his hood,
And, shuddering o'er their evil deeds,
Seeks solace in his book and beads.

IV.

Ah! sad must fare the chieftain's child,
Left parentless in scene so wild!
No father's sway, no mother's art

With none to help her helplessness,
With none to cheer her loneliness,
Drifted at mercy of the storm—
What may befall this fragile form?
What eye keep guard? what accents plead?
What arm defend in hour of need?
The fearful father turn'd to heaven—
By its dread Lord her life was given;
Albeit, in his propitious day,
It cost him little time to pray;
Now all his soul went up in sighs
To the good angels in the skies,
To supplicate their guardian aid
In warden of his orphan'd maid.

v.

Would that the pining captive knew,
Sweet Marg'ret, how beloved you grew?
How lovely was the mould of grace
That charm'd the rustics of thy race ;
How lovelier far the pious mind
Thy beauty so devoutly shrined ;
Seldom was camp or fortress sway'd
By wiser head, or more obey'd ;
Seldom were laws of kings or earls
More potent than this orphan girl's ;
For early care gives shape and course
To minds that have the torrent's force,
Which else with wasteful want exhaust,
And quickly in life's sands are lost!
Fair Marg'ret's soul had all the fire
That mark'd in youth her captive sire,
With all the tenderness beside

And who need ask what load of care
For love, such bosoms will not bear?

VI.

Saint Bridget's holy sisterhood,
Restored to their time-hallow'd wood,
Watch'd o'er her youth with zeal as true
As mortal maiden ever knew,
And worthily she lived to pay
Their priceless care in after-day.
Of all the lore they knew to teach,
She most pursued the English speech,
Unthreading meaning's mazy round
Until the undoubted sense was found.
Soon all familiar and by rote
Was Surrey's lay and Chaucer's note;
With many a tear she ponder'd o'er
The story of Sir Thomas More,
And frequent flash'd her eye of jet
At thought of his true Margaret.
Not for its rythmic melody,
Nor for its aspirations high,
    She prized the stranger's tongue;
A higher hope, a better aim
Than pride of lore or love of fame
    From her fond fancy sprung.
Her sire in Saxon prison lay—
This speech alone could win her way!
It might—God grant that it might—be
A guide, a passport, and a key
To win that dear sire's liberty!

PART II.

I.

The western wind, with friendly zeal,
Eastward impell'd the willing keel ;
A cloudless morrow's sunrise shed
Its saffron shower on Holyhead ;
It seem'd the smiling Heaven bless'd
Her dauntless heart and filial quest,
As, lighted by a faithful hand,
She lightly leap'd on Cambria's strand.[60]
Instinct with hope, she sprung with speed
Upon a rough Carnarvon steed—
A colt untrain'd to silken rein
Or ambling in a lady's train—
Of foot unerring, skill'd to cross
The wildest ridge of Penman-ross.
High noon beheld the cavalcade
At Bangor Ferry, close array'd;
With Bangor's monks an hour they stay'd;
Then onward sped the impatient maid
Past Penman Mawr; at eve they stood
By Aberconway's rapid flood;
Another day, another night,
Gave Chester's war-walls to their sight;
By the third moon their course was bent
Along the eddying tide of Trent—
O'er Stoke's sad field, enrich'd and red
With ashes of the Irish dead,[61]
In Simnel's spurious cause misled.
They paused not Litchfield's tow'rs to see;
Snatch'd brief repose at Coventry;
O'er Dunsmore Heath at dawn they swept,
And, ere the midwatch, wearied, slept
Beneath the blessèd calm and shade
Saint Alban's ransom'd abbey made.[62]

II.

To royal Richmond's nuptial court
Our trembling suitor must resort:
There reigns Queen Mary; by her side
King Philip sits in silent pride;
Around, his glittering escort shine,
A living, moving, Mexic mine,
Mingling, like morning in the east,
The light and shade, grandee and priest;
From lip to lip pass'd many a name
Still living on the lips of fame;
Swart Alva and Medina's duke
Reflect their master's cheerful look;
The banish'd cardinal is there,
Grown gray with early woe and care;
Elizabeth, whose gay attire,
Like Etna's vines, hides heart of fire;
Repentant Gardiner stands a-near,
And many a high and puissant peer,
And many a lady fine or fair,
And many a jocund, hopeful heir.

III.

As when among the feather'd race,
Assembled in their wonted place,
Borne from its home by adverse blast,
Some fate a foreign bird may cast,
Whose plumage, rich with tropic dyes,
Startles the native warbler's eyes—
Such wonder seized the courtiers all,
As, trembling, up the audience-hall,
Came the bright maiden of the West,
In mourning weeds untimely dress'd—
Her cheek made pale by carking care,
No jewel in her turban'd hair—

Upon her troubled breast there lay
A starry cross, her only stay—
Through the long lash her eye that hid
The big tear swell'd beneath the lid—
The suppliant scroll that told her woe
Sore shaking in her hand of snow.

IV.

Before the throne she flung her down,
'Spite gallant's smirk and usher's frown—
" Mercy !" she cried, in accents wild,
" Behold, my Queen, O'Connor's child !
The hand my orphan youth caress'd,
The hand that night and morning bless'd—
The teaching voice, the loving face,
We miss them in his native place !
There is no music now, nor mirth
About Offally's hostless hearth—
Offally's fields lie bare and brown,
Offally's flowers all torn and strown—
Offally's desolate domain
Echoes its absent master's name ;
The peasant mourns, God's poor bemoan
His woes, which truly are their own ;
Contending Tanists rive and rend
The lordship of their fetter'd friend ;
O potent lady, by the name
Of Mercy, under which you reign,
(By Mary, Mother of our Lord,
Captive to treason and the sword),
By her who knew what 'twas to shed
Maternal tears o'er Jesus dead—
Be merciful to mine and me.

v.

Troubled with thought, Queen Mary's brow
Is turn'd to royal Philip now ;
Elizabeth has clench'd her hand,
As if it held a seering brand;
And moved her rigid lips, but hush'd
The stormy words that upwards rush'd.
The suppliant caught the sovereign's look,
And guidance from its meaning took :
"Oh, aid me, gracious Prince of Spain,"
She cried in piteous piercing strain;
"The same high blood your heart inspires
Still animates my captive sire's ;
By your own knightly vows, I crave
My father from his living grave—
By that dear faith we both revere,
My poor petition deign to hear ;
To you I turn, who still have stood
The champion of Christ's holy rood :
True to his faith my father fell,
By it, shall he not rise as well ?"
King Philip bow'd his lofty head,
And something to his consort said,
Who, smiling, spoke, "Fair maiden, well
Your father's woes you've learn'd to tell.
Arise ! the king agrees with me ;
Your prayer is heard ! your sire is free !"

VI.

Joy ! joy ! on Barrow's bowery side,
Joy throughout Erin far and wide ;
Rath Imayn rings with jubilee—
Its noble chief is safe and free.

Nor does he come alone,
Kildare's young lord, and Ossory,
Their fathers' halls have lived to see
And hold them as their own!

FEAGH M'HUGH.[1]

FEAGH M'HUGH of the mountain—
  Feagh M'Hugh of the glen—
Who has not heard of the Glenmalur chief,
  And the feats of his hard-riding men?
Came you the sea-side from Carmen—
  Cross'd you the plains from the West—
No rhymer you met but could tell you,
  Of Leinster men who is the best.

Or seek you the Liffey or Dodder—
  Ask in the bawns of the Pale—
Ask them whose cattle they fodder,
  Who drinks without fee of their ale.
From Ardamine north to Kilmainham,
  He rules, like a king, of few words,
And the Marchmen of seven score castles
  Keep watch for the sheen of his swords.

The vales of Kilmantan are spacious—
  The hills of Kilmantan are high—
But the horn of the Chieftain finds echoes
  From the waterside up to the sky.
The lakes of Kilmantan are gloomy,
  Yet bright rivers stream from them all—
So dark is our Chieftain in battle.

The plains of Clan Saxon are fertile,
    Their Chiefs and their Tanists are brave,
But the first step they take o'er the border,
    Just measures the length of a grave ;
Thirty score of them foray'd to Arklow,
    Southampton and Essex their van—
Our Chief cross'd their way, and he left of
    Each score of them, living, a man.

Oh, many the tales that they cherish,
    In the glens of Kilmantan to-day,
And though church, rath, and native speech perish,
    His glory's untouch'd by decay.
Feagh M'Hugh of the mountain—
    Feagh M'Hugh of the glen—
Who has not heard of the Glenmalur Chief,
    And the feats of his hard-riding men ?

LAMENT OF THE IRISH CHILDREN IMPRISONED IN THE TOWER.[68]

I.

For deep-valley'd Desmond we sigh and we weep,
The Funcheon and Maigue flow on through our sleep,
And our eyes wax dim as the red clouds rest
Like an advanced guard o'er our destined West.

II.

Oh ! who will break us these walls of stone ?
Oh ! who will list to our hapless moan ?
Oh ! who will bear us forever, far
From London Tower toward yonder star ?

III.

Children of Chieftains, we pine in chains,
Sighing in vain for our flower-strewn plains;
The ill wind that swept us so far away,
Flung us on stones, not on kindred clay.

IV.

We look through these loops on the Saxon swine
Carousing abroad over ale and wine,
And their speech is familiar to us as to theirs,
While our own sounds strange in our Gaelic ears.

V.

Oh! land without love! oh! halls without song!
How luckless the weak race who find you strong!
Chivalry grows not on English ground,
Nor can Mercy about its throne be found.

VI.

The day shall come men will doubt the tale
Of the captive children of Innisfail—
They will doubt that false England made a prey
Of orphans lured from their homes away.

VII.

Our mothers' eyes may grow dim with tears,
Our fathers may barb their blunted spears,
But this tower our charnel-house shall be,
Ere our lost we gain, or our land we see.

VIII.

Oh! Blessed Virgin, who saw thy Son
In a hostile city worse set upon,
Be Thou unto us brother, mother, and priest,

IX.

Farewell to Desmond! farewell Loch Lene!
To Adare's rich feast, and to Thurles Green!
Farewell to old scenes, and friends, and songs—
Death chains us forever to the land of our wrongs!

THE POET'S PROPHECY. [1]

I.

By the Druid's stone I slept,
While my dog his vigil kept,
And there on the mountain lone,
By that old weird-rising stone,
Visions wrapt me round, and voices
Spoke the word my soul rejoices.

II.

"Bard! the stranger's roof shall fall—
Grass shall grow in Norman hall—
Mileadh's race shall rise again,
Lords of mountain and of glen;
Nial's blood and Brian's seed,
Known for kingly word and deed—
Ollamh's skill and Ogma's lore,
Time to Banbha will restore.

III.

"Destiny has doom'd it so!
Through pass of death and waves of woe,
Banbha's sons shall come and go;
Twelve score years a foreign brood
Shall warm them in the native blood—
Shall lord it in the fields of Eri,

IV.

"When the long-wrong'd men of Eri
Of their very lives are weary—
In that hour, from cave and rath,
Mighty souls shall find a path—
They who won in Gaul dominion;
They who cut the eagle's pinion;
They of the prophetic race;[8]
They of the fierce blood of Thrace;[9]
They who Man and Mona lorded,[10]
Shall regain the land and guard it."

V.

So, upon that mountain lone,
By the gray, weird-rising stone,
Visions wrapt me round, and voices
Spoke the word my soul rejoices.

THE SUMMONS OF ULSTER.[91]

Arm! arm! ye men of Ulster, for battle to the death!
Arm to defend your fathers' fields, and shield your fathers'
    faith!
They are coming! they are coming! the foe is gathering
    near!
Arm for your rich inheritance, and for your altars dear!
They have sworn to rase from out Tyr-Owen the old Hy-Nial
    line;
They have sworn to spare no sacred thing, nor sex, nor holy
    shrine;
They have sworn to make the Brehons as elks rare on our
    hills;
They have vow'd to God to perish here, or work their evil

They say the Queen of England is the Queen of Innishowen—
That Hugh O'Neil must be her earl, or else be overthrown—
That Hugh Roe, our own, must kneel to her, and Tyrconnel
    be no more,
And an unbelieving bishop sit where Saint Patrick sat of
    yore.
And they will have us beard ourselves in their own boyish
    trim,
And put loyal-fashion'd garments on every Irish limb—
And our island-harps be broken, and our bards be turn'd
    away—
For the minstrel true must follow still the fortunes of his
    lay !

Now swear we by our fathers' graves, and by the wives we've
    wed,
And by the true-begotten heirs of each honest marriage-bed,
And by our bless'd Apostle, they shall perish one and all,
Ere they lord it thus o'er broad Tyr-Owen, Armagh, and
    Donegal !
Unfold our standards on the hills, and bid the heralds forth,
Let them blow their challenges abroad through all the
    valley'd North—
Let them summon every spearsman from Lough Ramor to
    Lough Foyle,
From Dundalk's bay of battles to the far-off Tory's Isle !

And if they ask for Hugh O'Neil and the O'Donnell Roe,
Bid them meet their trusted princes by the falls of Assaroë—
Let the *curraghs* of Fermanagh rot on fair Lough Erne's
    shore—
Let the fishers of Lough Swilly fling aside the peaceful
    oar—
Let the men of Ardnarigh leave their dogs upon the track,

And the pilgrim from Saint Patrick's Isle to the trysting
    hurry back ;
And, as over the deep-valley'd North the challenge thus they
    blow,
Bid them meet their trusted Princes by the Falls of Assaroe.

SONG OF O'DONNELL IN SPAIN.

CORUNNA, WINTER OF 1603.

I.

On, wild and wintry is the night, and lonely is the hour,
But I wish I were far off at sea, in spite of storm and shower,
So that the dawn might see me cast upon the Irish coast—
So that I had regain'd my land, whatever might be lost!
       No headland gray, so far away
         From house or place could be,
       But the voice of kin would bid me in,
         And welcome back from sea.

II.

Full pleasant is the land of Spain, and kind my lord the King,
And sweetly to the willing ear the Spanish minstrels sing;
But in my ear the song of love sounds idle and profane,
Until I clasp my only one—my native land again.
       No headland gray, so far away
         From house or place could be,
       But the voice of kin would bid me in,
         And welcome back from sea.

III.

Oh, happy is the beaten bird, that from the billowy West,
At fall of eve can still return in Erin to her nest;
Oh, happy is the fond sea wave, that, when the storms cease,

> No headland gray, so far away
>   From house or place could be,
> But the voice of kin would bid me in,
>   And welcome back from sea.

IV.

Blow, blow, ye winds, and fly ye clouds, let day and night be
    sped,
God speed the hour, and haste the help, by Spain long prom-
    ised;
But help who may, God speed the day, and send His strong
    wind forth,
To bear O'Donnell's flag again to combat in the North.
> No headland gray, so far away
>   From house or place could be,
> But the voice of kin would bid me in,
>   And welcome back from sea.

LOST, LOST ARMADA.

I.

One by one men die on shore,
  Falling as the brown leaves fall;
Daily some one doth deplore
  A sleeper in a sable pall.
Slowly single coffins pass
To cold crypts beneath the grass;
But on sea—oh, misery!
Death is frantic—death is free;
So they found who sailed with thee,

II.

What an Oriental show
  Thine was on the Biscayan tide;
Well might Philip's bosom glow
  When his power you glorified;
Indian wealth and Flemish skill,
Spanish pride and Roman will,
Borne on every carvel's prow;
Where are all your splendors now?
Fallen like gems from Philip's brow,
          Lost, lost Armada!

III.

Water-demons beat the deep—
  Lir, the sea-god, waked in rage—
Sped his couriers forth from sleep—
  None his anger durst assuage;
Then the god-demented seas
Whitened round the Hebrides,
On Albyn's rocks, on Erin's sands,
Banshees wrung their briny hands,
Keening for your perished bands,
          Lost, lost Armada!

IV.

Fifteen hundred men of Spain
  Sunk in sight of Knocknarea;
Twice a thousand strove in vain
  To reach your harbors, Tyrawley!
Oh! they·have not even a grave
In the land they came to save;
Only penitent Ocean moans
O'er their white, far-drifting bones,
Blends with it Erin's groans.

LAY OF THE LAST MONK OF MUCRUSS.

I.

If I forget thee,
      Irrelagh! Irrelagh![*]
If I forget thee,
      Irrelagh!
May the tongue ungrateful cleave
To my mute mouth's eave,
And the hand of my body wither—
      Irrelagh!

II.

Woe, woe to the hand,
      Irrelagh! Irrelagh!
Woe to the guilty hand,
      Irrelagh!
The hand the godless spoiler laid
On prayer-worn cell and sacred shade,
And thy lustrous altars—
      Irrelagh!

III.

An ever-shining lamp,
      Irrelagh! Irrelagh!
An ever-shining lamp,
      Irrelagh!
Wert thou o'er valley and o'er wave,
Taking only what you gave—
The oil of Aaron—

IV.

I am worn and gray,
  Irrelagh! Irrelagh!
I am worn and gray,
  Irrelagh!
Night and silence brooding o'er me,
Death upon the road before me,
While I kneel to bless thee—
  Irrelagh!

V.

May the myriad blessings,
  Irrelagh! Irrelagh!
May the myriad blessings,
  Irrelagh!
Of all the saints in heaven,
Through all time to come be given,
To him who builds thee up—
  Irrelagh!

VI.

For rebuilt thou shalt be,
  Irrelagh! Irrelagh!
Rebuilt thou shalt be,
  Irrelagh!
At new altars like the old,
Shining bright with gems and gold,
Ancient rites shall be renewed—
  Irrelagh!

THE OUTLAWED EARL.[23]

I.

Down through Desmond sailing,
Come the sea-flocks wailing,

Deep the snows that cover
All the landscape over,
Nor Rapparee nor rover
    Far to-night will be.

IL

Yet, ah! yet, remember,
In this wild November,
Who, without an ember,
    Ray, or rushlight, bides—
Who, in all the nation,
Fill'd the highest station—
Who, in desolation,
    Hunted, homeless, hides!

IIL

Some highland herds concealing
In his wretched shieling,
The Lord for whose revealing
    Golden snares are spread,—
All merciless the victor
Of our noble Hector,
May God be his protector,
    The God for whom he bled!

IV.

This shall be Desmond's glory,
Unknown in Norman story,
That the cross he bore, he
    Bore for Christ's dear sake.
Brother after brother,
Another and another,
Fell so, yet no other

V.

Death can but deliver
From man's worst endeavor,
Then will Christ forever
    Make His own of thee ;
For lost realm and palace—
For man's deadly malice—
His all-saving chalice
    Shall your banquet be !

VI.

Down through Desmond sailing
Come the sea-flocks wailing,
Storms without prevailing
    On the wintry sea ;
The hour may now be nearing,
When you, Death's challenge hearing,
Answer, all unfearing,
    " Master, I follow Thee !"

SIR CAHIR O'DOGHERTY'S MESSAGE.[M]

SHALL the children of Ulster despair?
  Shall Aileach but echo to groans?
Shall the line of Conn tamely repair
  To the charnel, and leave it their bones?
Sleeps the soul of O'Neill in Tyrone?
  Glance no axes around by Lough Erne?
Has Clan Randall the heart of a stone?
  Does O'Boyle hide his head in the fern?

Go, tell them O'Dogherty waits—
  Waits harness'd and mounted and all,
That his pikestaves are made by the gates—

Say, he turneth his back on the sea,
    Though the sail flaps to bear him afar !
Say, he never will falter or flee,
    While ten men are found willing for war !

Bid them mark his death-day in their books,
    And hide for the future the tale;
But insult not his corpse with cold looks,
    Nor remember him over their ale.
If they come not in arms and in rage,
    Let them stay, he can battle alone—
For one flag, in this fetter-worn age,
    Is still flying in free Innishowen !

If the children of Chieftains you see,
    Oh, pause and repeat to them then,
That Cahir, who lives by the sea,
    Bids them think of him, when they are men;
Bids them watch for new Chiefs to arise,
    And be ready to come at their call—
Bids them mourn not for him if he dies,
    But like him live to conquer or fall !

THE RAPPAREES.

I.

When the hand of the Tyrant was heavy and strong
On our island, and hush'd was the psalm and the song;
When hourly the blood of the unarm'd was spilt;
When the worship of God was deem'd treason and guilt;
When slaves' hearts were as callous as live hearts could be,
Who requited the wronger ?—the fierce Rapparee!

II.

Nay, smile as you will, they were real heroes then;
O'er a quagmire of terror, they, only, tower'd men!
The Hessian was lord of the plain, but the hill
Was a fortress unwon from the free native still,—
He shelter'd the poor, set the law's victim free,
In his high court of judgment—the proud Rapparee!

III.

The wild was his house, and the heather his bed,
And the cold stone the pillow that held up his head;
But the Hessian that lay in his treble-strong keep
Would have given his eyes for so dreamless a sleep.
His soul from all foul stains he ever kept free;
" I want only my own! "—said the stout Rapparee.

IV.

Nor was his life joyless, for oft in the shade
Of the summer woods sombre his banquet he made;
And, like " the good people," whoever pass'd by,
He charm'd to the ring of his wild revelry;
Oft, too, he adventur'd the wall'd towns to see,
And mask'd in their markets—the rash Rapparee!

V.

At evening his music was heard from the rath,
And the sprite-fearing herd turn'd aside from his path;
When the lowland deer-hunters the long chase gave o'er,
He follow'd, and homeward its broad honors bore;
And the salmon, for him, seem'd to swim from the sea,
And the mountain-birds bred for the stout Rapparee!

VI.

Oh! name them not slightingly, mete them no scorn,
Nor Bravoes, nor Thugs they, nor men basely born—

O'Connors and Kavanaghs, heirs of the East,
O'Dowds and O'Flaherties, old in the West;
O'Carroll, O'Kelly, O'Reilly, Mac Nee—
Are all names that were borne by the brave Rapparee.

VII.

Oh! name them not slightingly, mete them no scorn,
Was not Redmond true heir to the vales of the Mourne
Was not Cahir, who hunted the soft Harrow's side,
An O'Dempsey as true as e'er ruled it in pride?
Was not Donald O'Keeffe, of the old Desmond tree,
With the crown at its root—a renown'd Rapparee?

VIII.

Oh! call them not brigands, those chiefs in decay,
And weigh not their deeds in the scales of to-day;
Let sick children and gossips turn pale at the name,
But just men to brave men give fairness and fame.
Let us try them, and test them, and shame to us be
If we still blame the name of the wrong'd Rapparee!

AFTER THE FLIGHT.[*]
SEPTEMBER, 1607.

I.

FAR on the sea, to-night, ye are—ye noble
  Princes and captains brave, and ladies lorn,
And ship-pent children, happy in your trouble—
  Who know not to what trials you are born.

II.

Far on the sea—no gleam from any offing,
  No star in the mirk sky to guide you on,

* This poem was, I think, the last written by Mr. McGee for the Dublin
Nation; it appeared in that paper on the 14th of March, 1868, less than a

While here, your foes exultingly are scoffing
   At all your clansmen—now that you are gone.

III.

No port in sight—no nobly lighted mansion
   To greet ye in, lords of the open hand!
Cleaving I see you by the sea-wash'd stanchion,
   Praying for any but your native land.

IV.

For any land where God's name stirs devotion—
   For there some Christian prince would bid you hail—
For any star to light safe through this ocean
   To any shore, the Chieftains of the Gael.

V.

Gone from your land, you once made so resplendent
   With your achievements; darkness shrouds us o'er;
On you our hopes and prayers have gone attendant
   To serve their season on another shore.

VI.

For God in heaven will not permit forever
   This exile of our greatest and our best,
Who, for the Faith, in life-long leal endeavor
   Upheld the holy Crusade of the West.

VII.

They will return!   O God, the joy and glory
   Of that proud day to all the race of Conn—
They will return, and in their after story
   Find solace for the woes they've undergone.

RORY DALL'S LAMENTATION.[1]

Air—"*Ma Coleen dhas cruithe na bo.*"

I.

Ah, where is the noble one vanish'd ?
  I look through the day and the night ;
The sun and the north-star are steadfast,
  But my Eri is fled from my sight !
The mountainous Albyn I clamber,
  And Mona of winds I can see,
Wild Wallia still frowns on the ocean,
  But my Eri is hidden from me.

II.

Who passeth, all shrouded in sable,
  Moaning low like a wandering wind ?
What voice is this wailing ?   I fear me
  'Tis one that should madden my mind.
O Eri ! my saint and my lady—
  Oh ! musical, beautiful, brave ;
Why, why do you pass like a shadow
  That smiles on the sleep of a slave ?

III.

If these dark eyes were bright as the falcon's,
  If my soul would fly with me away,
And give me to-morrow with Eri,
  Death might have me for asking next day.
For what is my life without Eri ?
  A harp with the base of it gone ;
And glory ? a bright golden goblet,
  When the wine that should fill it is done !

IV.

Oh ! had I my foot on your heather,
  With my harp and my hound in my ken,
No door but would play on its hinges
  To have Rory Dall coming again.
Ah, potent the spell that would sever
  My Eri and me evermore—
The angel of judgment might part us,
  We could not be parted before!

THE LAST O'SULLIVAN BEARE.*

ALL alone, all alone, where the gladsome vine is growing,
All alone by the waves of the Tagus darkly flowing,
No morning brings a hope for him, nor any evening cheer
To O'Sullivan Beare, through the seasons of the year.

He is thinking, ever thinking, of the hour he left Dunbuie,
His father's staff fell from his hand, his mother wept wildly ;
His brave young brother hid his face, his lovely sisters twain,
How they wrung their maiden hands to see him sail away
    for Spain.

They were Helen bright and Norah staid, who in their
    father's hall,
Like sun and shadow, frolick'd round the grave armorial
    wall.
In Compostella's cloisters he found many a pictured saint,
But the spirits boyhood canonized no human hand can
    paint.

All alone, all alone, where the gladsome vine is growing,

No morning brings a hope for him, nor any evening cheer
To O'Sullivan Beare, through the seasons of the year.

Oh ! sure he ought to take a ship and sail back to Dunbuie—
He ought to sail back, back again, to that castle o'er the sea;
His father, mother, brother, his lovely sisters twain,
'Tis they would raise the roof with joy to see him back from
      Spain.

Hush ! hush ! I cannot tell it—the tale will make me wild—
He left it, that gray castle, in age almost a child ;
Seven long years with Saint James's friars he conn'd the page
      of might,
Seven long years for his father's roof was sighing every
      night.

Then came a caravel from the North, deep freighted, full of
      woe,
His houseless family it held, their castle it lay low;
Saint James's shrine, through ages famed as pilgrim haunt
      of yore,
Saw never wanderers so wronged upon its scallop'd shore.

Yet it was sweet, their first grief past, to watch those two
      sweet girls
Sit by the sea, as mermaiden hold watch o'er hidden pearls—
To see them sit and try to sing for that sire and mother old,
O'er whose heads five score winters their thickening snows
      had roll'd.

To hear them sing and pray in song for *them* in deadly
      work,
Their gallant brothers battling for Spain against the Turk.
Corunna's port at length they reach, and seaward ever stare,
Wondering what belates the ship their brothers home should

Joy! joy! it comes—their Philip lives!—ah! Donald is no
    more;
Like half a hope one son kneels down the exiled two before;
They spoke no requiem for the dead nor blessing for the
    living;
The tearless heart of parentage has broken with its grieving.

Two pillars of a ruin'd pile—two old trees of the land—
Two voyagers on a sea of grief, long sufferers hand in hand;
Thus, at the woful tidings told, left life and all its tears,
So died the wife of many a spring, the chief of an hundred
    years.

One sister is a black-veil'd nun of Saint Ursula, in Spain,
And one sleeps coldly far beneath the troubled Irish main;
'Tis Helen bright who ventured to the arms of her true lover,
But Cleena's stormy tides now roll the radiant girl over.

All alone, all alone, where the gladsome vine is growing,
All alone by the wave of the Tagus darkly flowing,
No morning brings a hope for him, nor any evening cheer
To O'Sullivan Beare, through the seasons of the year.

BROTHER MICHAEL.

When the wreck of noble houses
Strew'd the land, as the Armada
Strew'd the iron beach of Erris—
In those days when faith and science
Shared the fate of ancient lineage,
And the holy men—the planets
On this earthly side of heaven—
Faded from the blank horizon;
Then, when no man could determine

Show'd most darkly, came a stranger
From a distant shore, to gather
And to save the old memorials
Of the noble and the holy,
Of the chiefs of ancient lineage,
Of the saints of wondrous virtues;
Of the Ollamhs, and the Brehons,
Of the Bards and of the Betaghs,
That they might not die forever;
How he came, and how he labor'd,
What he suffer'd, what adventured,
That he might preserve the story
Of the dear ancestral Island,
That should never be forgotten!

Not a stranger, yet a stranger
Was the patient pale explorer;
Born the heir of bardic honors,
Where Kilbarron, like a topsail,
Soars above the North Atlantic—
Better days in green Tyrconnell,
High beside its chiefs had found him
Seated at the festal table;
Now, poor brother of Saint Francis,
Less than priest and more than layman,
On the threshold of the chancel
He is well content to hover;
So that, fare and garb provided,
Time to pray, and time to labor
In the work his soul delighted,
It might prosper—let him perish!

Looking northward from the city
By the Egyptian call'd Eblana,

We can trace the careful stages
Of the constant Brother Michael!
We can trace him where the Slaney
Spreads its waves around Beg-Erin,
Holy isle of Saint Iberius!
Where the gables of Dunbrody
Stand the proof of Hervey's penance,[120]
By the junction of the rivers;
Where the golden vale of Cashel
Leads the pilgrim to the altar—
To the tabernacles glorious,
Shining from that rocky altar;
Where, in beauteous desolation,
Like Saint Mary in the desert,
Quin's fair abbey pleads with heaven.

Looking northward from the city
By the Egyptian call'd Eblana,
We can trace the careful stages
Of the constant Brother Michael,
Where the Boyne, historic river,
Dear to Cormac and Cuchullin,
Stretches seaward, sad and solemn,
Loth to leave the plain of Tara;
Where the lakes and knolls of Cavan
Echo to the sound of harping;
From the yet unconquer'd forests,
Where Lough Erne's arbor islands
Waft their fragrance to the mountains;
Thence to the ancestral region
Turns the constant Brother Michael—
With the gleanings of his travel,
With the spoils of many ruins,

With the trophies of his Order,
With the title-deeds of races,
With the acts of Saints and Prophets;
Never into green Tyrconnell
Came such spoil as Brother Michael
Bore before him on his palfrey!
By the fireside in the winter,
By the sea-side in the summer,
When your children are around you,
And the theme is love of country;
When you speak of heroes dying
In the charge, or in the trenches;
When you tell of Sarsfield's daring,
Owen's genius, Brian's wisdom,
Emmet's early grave, or Grattan's
Life-long epic of devotion;
Fail not, then, my friend, I charge you,
To recall the no less noble
Name and works of Brother Michael,
Worthy chief of the Four Masters,
Saviors of our country's annals!

THE FOUR MASTERS.

Many altars are in Banba,
  Many chancels hung in white,
Many schools, and many abbeys,
  Glorious in our father's sight;
Yet whene'er I go a pilgrim,
  Back, dear Holy Isle, to thee,
May my filial footsteps bear me
  To that Abbey by the Sea,—
    To that Abbey roofless, doorless,

These are days of swift upbuilding,
   All to pride and triumph tends;
Art is liegeman to Religion,
   Genius speaks, and Song ascends.
As the day-beam to the sailor,
   Lighting up the wreckers' shore,
So the present lustre shineth
   On the barrenness before,—
      But no gleam rests on that Abbey,
      Silent by Tyrconnel's shore.

Yet I hear them in my musings,
   And I see them as I gaze,
Four meek men around the cresset,
   With the scrolls of other days;
Four unwearied scribes who treasure
   Every word and every line,
Saving every ancient sentence
   As if writ by hands divine.

On their calm, down-bended foreheads,
   Tell me what is it you read ?
Is there malice or ambition,
   In the will, or in the deed ?
Oh, no ! no ! the Angel Duty
   Calmly lights the dusky walls,
And their four worn right hands follow
   Where the Angel's radiance falls.

Not of Fame, and not of Fortune,
   Do these eager pensmen dream;
Darkness shrouds the hills of Banba,
   Sorrow sits by every stream;
One by one the lights that led her,

Hour by hour were quench'd in gloom ;
But the patient, sad, Four Masters,
  Toil on in their lonely room—
  Duty thus defying Doom.

As the breathing of the west wind
  Over bound and bearded sheaves,
As the murmur in the bee-hives,
  Softly heard on summer eves,
So the rustle of the vellum,
  So the anxious voices sound,
So the deep expectant silence
  Seems to listen all around.

Brightly on the Abbey gable
  Shines the full moon thro' the night,
While far to the northward glances
  All the bay in waves of light.
Tufted isle, and splinter'd headland,
  Smile and soften in her ray,
Yet within their dusky chamber,
  The meek Masters toil assay,
  Finding all too short the day.

Now they kneel! attend the accents
  From the souls of mourners wrung;
Hear the soaring aspirations,
  Barb'd with the ancestral tongue;
For the houseless sons of Chieftains,
  For their brethren afar,
For the mourning Mother Island,
  These their aspirations are.

And they said, before uprising,
  " Father, grant one other prayer—

Bless the lord of Moy-O'Gara,
  Bless his lady, and his heir;
Send the gen'rous chief, whose bounty
  Cheers, sustains us in our task,
Health, success, renown, salvation—
  Father! this is all we ask."

Oh! that we who now inherit
  All their trust, with half their toil,
Were but fit to trace their footsteps
  Through the Annals of the Isle;
Oh! that the bright Angel, Duty,
  Guardian of our tasks might be,
Teach us as she taught our Masters,
  In that Abbey by the Sea,
  Faithful, grateful, just, to be!

A PRAYER FOR FEARGAL O'GARA.

WRITTEN ON A BLANK LEAF OF O'DONOVAN'S "FOUR MASTERS."

A PRAYER for Feargal! Lord of Leyney—
He for whom this book was written,
By the life-devoted Masters—
Brother Michael and his helpers!

May the generous soul of Feargal,
In the mansions of the bless'd,
By the learnèd, gifted elders,
All whose love had elsewise perish'd—
By the countless saints of Erin,
By the pilgrims to the Jordan,
By the noble chiefs victorious,
Over all life's sinful combats—

Dwell forever, still surrounded;
As he gather'd up their actions,
As he drew their names around him
In these pages may he find them,
Still around him and about him,
In beatitude forever!

Oh! forever and forever,
Benedictions shower upon him,
Brighter glories shine around him,
And the million prayers of Erin,
Rise like incense up to heavan,
Still for Feargal, Lord of Leyney!

SONNET—TO KILBARRON CASTLE.[161]

BROAD, blue, and deep, the Bay of Donegal
  Spreads north and south and far a-west before
The beetling cliffs sublime, and shatter'd wall
  Where the O'Clery's name is known no more.
Kilbarron, many castle names are sung
  In deathless verse they less deserved than thee,—
The Rhine-tow'rs still endure in German tongue;
  Gray Scotland's keeps in Scottish poesy;
In chronicles of Spain, and songs of France,
  Full many a grim *chateau* and fortress stands;
And Albion's genius, strong as Uther's lance,
  Guards her old mansions 'mid their alter'd lands;
Home of an hundred annalists, round thy hearths, alas!
The churlish thistles thrive, and the dull graveyard grass.

ASHANGE, July, 1846.

"*IN-FELIX FELIX.*"[108]

WHY is his name unsung, oh minstrel host ?
Why do you pass his memory like a ghost ?
Why is no rose, no laurel, on his grave ?
Was he not constant, vigilant, and brave ?
Why, when that hero-age you deify,
Why do you pass "*In-felix Felix!*" by ?

He rose the first—he looms the morning star
Of the long, glorious, unsuccessful war;
England abhors him ! has she not abhorr'd
All who for Ireland ventured life or word ?
What memory would she not have cast away,
That Ireland hugs in her heart's heart to-day ?

He rose in wrath to free his fetter'd land—
"There's blood, there's Saxon blood, upon his hand."
Ay, so they say !—three thousand, less or more,
He sent untimely to the Stygian shore,—
They were the keepers of the prison-gate—
He slew them, his whole race to liberate.

O clear-eyed poets ! ye who can descry
Through vulgar heaps of dead where heroes lie—
Ye to whose glance the primal mist is clear—
Behold there lies a trampled noble here !
Shall we not leave a mark ? shall we not do
Justice to one so hated and so true ?

If ev'n his hand and hilt were so distain'd,—

His death redeem'd his life—he chose to die
Rather than get his freedom with a lie.
Plant o'er his gallant heart a laurel tree,
So may his head within the shadow be.

I mourn for thee, O hero of the North—
God judge thee gentler than we do on earth!
I mourn for thee, and for our land, because
She dare not own the martyrs in our cause;
But they, our poets, they who justify—
They will not let thy memory rot or die!

THE CONNAUGHT CHIEF'S FAREWELL.

[Scene—Galway Bay after sunset. A Connaught Chief and his daughter on
the deck of a departing ship. Time—1652. A few days after the surrender
of Galway city to the Parliamentarians.]

" My DAUGHTER! 'tis a deadly fate that turns us out to sea,
    Leaving our hearts behind us, where our hopes no more
            can be;
    The fate that lifts our anchor, and swells our sail so wide,
    Will have us far from sight of land ere morning's on the
            tide.

" Why does the darkness lower so deep upon the Galway
            shore?
    Will no kind beam of moon or star shine on the cliffs of
            Moher?
    My child, you need not banish so the heart's dew from
            your eye,
    We cannot catch an utmost glimpse of Arran sailing by.

" Thus all that was worth fighting for, for ever pass'd away,
    The true hearts all were given to death, the living turn'd
            to clay;

No wonder, then, the shamefaced shore should veil itself
    in night,
When slaves sleep thickly on the land, why should the
    sky be bright?

"Yes, thus their light should vanish, as vanish'd first their
    cause,
  Its hills should perish from our sight, as sunk its native
    laws,
  Its valleys from our souls be shut like chalices defiled,
  Nought have I now to love or serve, but God and you, my
    child."

"My father dear—my father, what makes you talk so wild?
  To God place next your country, and after her, your child;
  Though the land be dark behind us, and the sea all dim
    before,
  A morrow and a glory yet shall dawn on Connaught's
    shore.

"What though foul Fortune has her will, and stern Fate
    fills our sail,
  The slaves that sleep must waken up, nor can the wrong
    prevail;
  What though they broke our altars down, and roll'd our
    Saints in dust,
  They could not pluck them from that Heaven in which they
    had their trust."

"May God and his Saints protect you, my own girl, wise
    as fair,
  An angel wrestling with my will, indeed you ever were;
  Oh, sure, when young hearts hold such hope, and young
    heads hold such thought,
  Defeat can ne'er be destiny, nor the ancient fight unfought!

" Good land—green land—dear Ireland, though I cannot
    see you, still
May God's dew brighten all your vales, His sun kiss every
    hill;
And though henceforth our nights and days in strange
    lands must be pass'd,
Our hearts and hopes for your uprise shall keep watch till
    the last !"

EXECUTION OF ARCHBISHOP PLUNKETT.

LONDON, JULY, 1681.

I.

ANOTHER scaffold looms up through the night,
    Another Irish martyr's hour draws near,
The cruel crowd are gathering for the sight,
    The July day dawns innocently clear ;
There is no hue of blood along the sky,
Where the meek martyr waits for light to die !

II.

Which is the culprit in the car of death?
    He of the open brow and folded hands !
The turbid crowd court every easy breath,
    There is no need on him of gyves or bands;
Pale, with long bonds and vigils, yet benign,
He bears upon his breast salvation's sign.

III.

What was his crime ?   Did he essay to shake
    The pillar of the state, or undermine
The laws which vow a worthy vengeance,
    And punish treason with a death condign ?

Look in that holy face, and there behold
The secret of the sufferer's life all told.

IV.

Enough! he was of Irish birth and blood,
   He fill'd Saint Patrick's place in stormy days,
He lived, discharging duty, doing good,
   Dead to the world, and the world's idle praise,—
The faithless saw his faith with evil eyes,
They doom'd him without stain, and here he dies.

"CAROLAN THE BLIND."

I.

To the cross of Glenfad the Blind Bard came,
 And at the four roads he drew his rein,
And stopp'd his steed, and raised his hand
To learn from the currents the lie of the land ;
And spoke he aloud, unconscious that near
His words were caught up by a listening ear.

II.

" The sun's in the south, the noon must be past,
And cold on my right comes the northeast blast ;
What ho ! old friend, we 'll face to the west,
For Connaught 's the quarter the Bard loves best ;
'T is the heart of the land, and the stronghold of song,
So now for our Connaught friends march we along !

III.

" In Connaught," he humm'd, as on he rode,
" The heart and the house and the cup overflow'd ;

In Connaught alone does music find
The answering feet and the echoing mind ;
'Tis the soul of the soil and the fortress of song,
So now for our Connaught friends march we along !"

TO THE RIVER BOYNE.

I.

Banks of Lough Ramor, gently seaward stealing,
In thy placid depths hast thou no feeling
  Of the stormy gusts of other days ?
Does thy heart, O gentle, nun-faced river,
Passing Schomberg's obelisk, not quiver,
  While the shadow on thy bosom weighs ?

II.

Thou hast heard the sounds of martial clangor,
Seen fraternal forces clash in anger,
  In thy Sabbath valley, River Boyne !
Here have ancient Ulster's hardy forces
Dress'd their ranks and fed their travell'd horses,
  Tara's hosting as they rode to join.

III.

Forgettest thou that silent summer morning
When William's bugles sounded sudden warning,
  And James's answer'd, chivalrously clear;
When rank to rank gave the death-signal duly,
And volley answer'd volley quick and truly,
  And shouted mandates met the eager ear ?

IV.

The thrush and linnet fled beyond the mountains ;
The fish in Inver Colpa sought their fountains:

The unchased deer ran through Tredagh's* gates;
St. Mary's bells in their high places trembled,
And made a mournful music, which resembled
 A hopeless prayer to the unpitying fates.

Ah ! well for Ireland had the battle ended
When James forsook what William well defended,
 Crown, friends, and kingly cause ;
Well, if the peace thy bosom did recover
Had breathed its benediction broadly over
 Our race, and rites, and laws.

VI.

Not in thy depths, not in thy fount, Lough Ramor,
Were brew'd the bitter strife and cruel clamor
 Our wisest long have mourn'd ;
Foul faction falsely made thy gentle current
To Christian ears a stream and name abhorrent,
 And all its sweetness into poison turn'd.

VII.

But, as of old, God's prophet sweeten'd Mara,
Even so, blue bound of Ulster and of Tara,
 Thy waters to our exodus give life;
Thrice holy hands thy lineal foes have wedded,
And healing olives in thy breast imbedded,
 And banish'd far the bitterness of strife.[104]

VIII.

Before thee we have made a solemn *fœdus*,
And for chief witness called on Him who made us,
 Quenching, before his eyes, the brand of hate;
Our pact is made for brotherhood and union,
For equal laws to class and to communion,
 Our wounds to staunch, our land to liberate.

* Tredagh—now Drogheda.

IX.

Our trust is not in musket or in sabre—
Our faith is in the fruitfulness of labor,
  The soil-stirred, willing soil;
In homes and granaries by justice guarded,
In fields from blighting winds and agents warded,
  In franchised skill and manumitted toil.

X.

Grant us, oh God, the soil, and sun, and seasons!
Avert despair, the worst of moral treasons,
  Make vaunting words be vile;
Grant us, we pray, but wisdom, peace, and patience,
And we will yet re-lift among the nations
  Our fair, and fallen, and unforsaken isle!

THE WILD GEESE.

I.

" What is the cry so wildly heard,
    Oh, mother dear, across the lake?"
" My child, 't is but the northern bird
    Alighted in the reedy brake."

II.

" Why cries the northern bird so wild?
    Its wail is like our baby's voice."
" 'T is far from its own home, my child,
    And would you have it, then, rejoice?"

III.

" And why does not the wild bird fly
    Straight homeward through the open air?
I see no barriers in the sky—

IV.

" My child, the laws of life and death
　　Are written in four living books;
The wild bird reads them in the breath
　　Of winter, freezing up the brooks—

V.

" Reads and obeys—more wise than man—
　　And meekly steers for other climes,
Obeys the providential plan,
　　And humbly waits for happier times.

VI.

" The spring, that makes the poets sing,
　　Will whisper in the wild bird's ear,
And swiftly back, on willing wing,
　　The wild bird to the north will steer."

VII.

" Will *they* come back, of whom that song
　　Last night was sung, that made you weep?"
" Oh! God is good, and hope is strong;—
　　My son, let's pray, and then to sleep."

THE DEATH OF O'CAROLAN.[106]

THERE is an empty seat by many a board,
　　A guest is missed in hostelry and hall,
There is a harp hung up in Alderford
　　That was in Ireland sweetest harp of all.
The hand that made it speak, woe's me, is cold,
　　The darken'd eyeballs roll inspired no more;
The lips—the potent lips—gape like a mould,

In vain the watchman looks from Mayo's towers
  For him whose presence filled all hearts with mirth;
In vain the gathered guests outsit the hours—
  The honored chair is vacant by the hearth.
From Castle-Archdall, Moneyglass, and Trim,
  The courteous messages go forth in vain,
Kind words no longer have a joy for him
. Whose lowly lodge is in Death's dark demesne.

Kilronan Abbey is his castle now,
  And there till doomsday peacefully he'll stay;
In vain they weave new garlands for his brow,
  In vain they go to meet him by the way;
In kindred company he does not tire,
  The native dead, and noble, lie around,
His life-long song has ceased, his wood and wire
  Rest, a sweet harp unstrung, in holy ground.

Last of our ancient minstrels! thou who lent
  A buoyant motive to a foundering race—
Whose saving song, into their being blent,
  Sustained them by its passion and its grace—
God rest you! May your judgment dues be light,
  Dear Turlogh! and the purgatorial days
Be few and short, till, clothed in holy white,
  Your soul may come before the Throne of rays!

THE CROPPIES' GRAVE.[101]

I.

PEACE be round the Croppies' grave,
Let none approach but pilgrims brave;
This sacred hillside even yet

II.

Peace to their souls, whose bodies here
Met martyr's death and rebel's bier,
Who sleep in more than holy ground,
In death unparted and unbound.

III.

Fearless men of every time,
In Christian land and pagan clime,
Have sunk to rest by plain or hill,
O'erwatched by cairn and citadel.

IV.

The roving sea-kings' tumuli
Stand firm by northern strait and sea;
The Pharaoh hath his pyramid,
Whose gate and date the sands have hid.

V.

The Indian lies beside his lake,
Waiting the final voyage to take,
The good Manetto's passport given
To the green hunting-grounds of heaven.

VI.

The Roman vault, the Grecian shrine,
Are sacred haunts of all the "*Nine,*"
Who there unweave the shrouds of death,
And breathe around creative breath.

VII.

But vault, or shrine, or forest grave,
Or sea-kings' cairn beside the wave,
Or Egypt's proudest pyramid,

VIII.

What though of these none wore a crown,
None crouched beneath a monarch's frown;
What though none spoke the speech of Greece,
Spartans were not more brave than these.

IX.

Though pompous line and pillar'd stone
May never make their lost names known,
They sleep wrapp'd by the noble sod,
Ten thousand Irish chiefs have trod.

X.

Peace be round the Croppies' grave;
Peace to your souls, ye buried brave;
Tara's Hill, when crowned and free,
Had never nobler guests than ye!

SONG OF "MOYLAN'S DRAGOONS." [108]

[Supposed to be sung after the surrender of Lord Cornwallis at Yorktown, 1781.]

I.

Furl up the banner of the brave,
    And bear it gently home,
Through stormy scenes no more 't will wave,
    For now the calm has come;
Through showering grape, and drifting death,
    It floated ever true,
And by the signs upon its path,

II.

Yon flag first flew o'er Boston free,
    When Graves's fleet groped out ;
On Stony Point reconquered, we
    Unfurl'd it with a shout;
At Trenton, Monmouth, Germantown,
    Our sabres were not slack,
Like lightning, next, to Charlestown
    We scourged the British back.

II.

And here at Yorktown now they yield,
    And our career is o'er,
No more thou 'lt flutter on the field,
    Flag of the brave! no more;
The Redcoats yield up to "the Line,"
    Both sides have changed their tunes;
To peace our Congress doth incline,
    And so do we, Dragoons.

IV.

Furl up the banner of the brave,
    And bear it gently home,
No more o'er Moylan's march to wave,
    Lodge it in Moylan's home.
There Butler, Hand, and Wayne, perchance,
    May tell of battles o'er,
And the old flag, on its splinter'd lance,
    Unfurl for joy once more.

V.

Hurrah ! then, for the Schuylkill side,
    Its pleasant woody dells;
Old Ulster [109] well may warm with pride,

Comrades, farewell! may Heaven bestow
  On you its richest boons;
So let us drink before we go,
  To Moylan's brave Dragoons!

CHARITY AND SCIENCE.[110]

I.

THE city gates are bound and barr'd—whence comes the foe?
Sentinels move along the walls, speechlessly and slow;
The banner over the castle droops down despondingly—
New graves and fireless hearths are all the Castellan can see.

II.

The priest was at the altar, chanting a solem mass;
Fearlessly through the crowded nave we saw the Leaguer
    pass—
He slew the clerk at the *Agnus Dei*—he struck the priest to
    death—
He spill'd the consecrated cup—life wither'd at his breath.

III.

Then rose a cry to Heaven, "Who will stay this shape of
    fear—
This bodiless avenger? God! is no succor near?"
Street after street sent up the cry to the warders on the wall,
And the childless Castellan echo'd it from his heirless inner
    hall.

IV.

Now forth into the market-place there stepp'd two maidens
    young,

...nder the brow of one there lay the leeches' healing lore—
  was fair Science, led by Charity—they pass'd from door to
    door.

V.

...n days of peace, no two so fond of silence or repose,
...nt as the hearts of men sunk down, their spirits higher
    rose;
...Wealth had fled—its steeds fell dead—nor could its treasure
    bring
...A cool breath from the sultry heaven—a pure drop from the
    spring.

VI.

These maidens gave, for Jesus' sake, what treasures could
    not buy;
The air grew pure as they approach'd, the darkness left the
    sky;
The sentry at the eastern gate felt the foe hurrying out,
And the citizen and the Castellan raised a wildly joyful
    shout.

VII.

The people sang *Te Deum*, and, at eve, this other song—
" May Charity and Science in our island flourish long;
And wheresoe'er they turn their steps, let manhood bend
    the knee,
Let our fairest and our sagest their votaries still be!"

THE FAMINE IN THE LAND.

I.

DEATH reapeth in the fields of life, and we cannot count the
    corpses;
Black and fast before our eyes march the biers and hearses;

And daily unto Heaven their living kin are crying—
"Must the slave die for the tyrant, the sufferer for the sin—
And a wide inhuman desert be where Ireland has been;
Must the billows of oblivion over all our hills be roll'd,
And our land be blotted out, like the accursed lands of old?"

II.

Oh! hear it, friends of France! hear it, our kindred Spain!
Hear it, our kindly kith and kin across the western main—
Hear it, ye sons of Italy—let Turk and Russian hear it—
Hear Ireland's sentence register'd, and see how ye can
      bear it!
Our speech must be unspoken, our rights must be forgot;
Our land must be forsaken, submission is our lot—
We are beggars, we are cravens, and vengeful England feels
Us at her feet, and tramples us with both her iron heels.

III.

These the brethren of Gonsalvo! these the cousins of the
      Cid!
They are Spaniels and not Spaniards, born but to be *bid*—
They of the Celtic war-race who made that storied rally
Against the Teuton lances in the lists of Roncesvalles!
They, kindred to the mariner whose soul's sublime devotion
Led his caravel like a star to a new world through the
      ocean!
No! no! they were begotten by fathers in their chains,
Whose valiant blood refused to flow along the vassal veins.

IV.

Ho! ho! the devils are merry in the farthest vaults of night,
This England so out-Lucifers the prime arch-hypocrite;
Friend of Peace and friend of Freedom—yea, divine Religion's
      friend,
She is feeding on our hearts like a sateless nether fiend!

Ho! ho! for the vultures are black on the four winds;
No purveyor like England that foul camp-following finds;
Do you not mark them flitting between you and the sun?
They are come to reap the booty, for the battle has been
    won.

V.

Lo! what other shape is this, self-poised in upper air,
With wings like trailing comets, and face darker than despair?
See! see! the bright sun sickens into saffron in its shade,
And the poles are shaken at their ends, infected and afraid—
'Tis the Spirit of the Plague, and round and round the shore
It circles on its course, shedding bane for evermore;
And the slave falls for the tyrant and the sufferer for the
    sin,
And a wild inhuman desert *is* where Ireland has been.

VI.

'Twas a vision—'tis a fable—I did but tell my dream—
Yet twice, yea thrice, I saw it, and still it seem'd the same;
Ah! my soul is with this darkness nightly, daily overcast,
And I fear me, God permitting, it may fall out true at last;
God permitting, man decreeing! What, and shall man so
    will,
And our unseal'd lips be silent and our unbound hands be
    still?
Shall we look upon our fathers, and our daughters, and our
    wives,
Slain, ravish'd, in our sight, and be paltering for our lives?

VII.

Oh! countrymen and kindred, make yet another stand—
Plant your flag upon the common soil—be your motto Life

From the charnel shore of Cleena to the sea-bridge of the
    Giant,
Let the sleeping souls awake, the supine rise self-reliant;
And rouse thee up, oh! city, that sits furrow'd and in weeds,
Like the old Egyptian ruins amid the sad Nile's reeds.
Up, Mononia, land of heroes, and bounteous mother of
    song,
And Connaught, like thy rivers, come unto us swift and
    strong;
Oh! countrymen and kindred, make yet another stand—
Plant your flag upon the common soil—be your motto Life
    Land.

THE FLYING SHIPS.

AS SEEN FROM THE COAST OF IRELAND IN 1847.

I.

Where are the swift ships flying
    Far to the West away?
Why are the women crying,
    Far to the West away?
Is our dear land infected,
That thus o'er her bays neglected,
The skiff steals along dejected,
    While the ships fly far away?

II.

Skiff! can I blame your stealing
    Over the mournful bay?
Ships flee, but they have no feeling,
    Bent on their order'd way:

'Tis you, oh ! you lords of castles,
Keeping your godless wassails,
And banishing far your vassals,
  'Tis you I curse this day !

III.

Sad is the sight that daunts me,
  Far to the West away,
But a homeward hope still haunts me,
  Far to the West away;
I see a fair fleet returning,
I see bright beacons burning,
And gladness in place of mourning,
  As the ships to the shore make way,

THE WOFUL WINTER.

SUGGESTED BY ACCOUNTS OF IRELAND, IN DECEMBER, 1848.

I.

THEY are flying, flying, like northern birds over the sea for
  fear,
They cannot abide in their own green land, they seek a resting here;
Oh ! wherefore are they flying, is it from the front of war,
Or have they smelt the Asian plague the winds waft from
  afar?

II.

No ! they are flying, flying, from a land where men are sheep,
Where sworded shepherds herd and slay the silly crew they
  keep;
Where so much iron hath pass'd into the souls of the long
  enslaved,
That none was found by fort or field, or in Champion's right

III.

Yea! they are flying hither, breathless and pale with fear,
And it not the sailing time for ships, but the winter, dark
    and drear;
They had rather face the waters, dark as the frown of God,
Than make a stand for race and land on their own elastic sod.

IV.

Oh, blood of Brian, forgive them! oh, bones of Owen, rest!
Oh, spirits of our brave fathers, turn away your eyes from
    the West;
Look back on the track of the galleys that with the soldier
    came—
Look! look to the ships of Tyre, moor'd in the ports of
    Spain.

V.

But look not on, dread Fathers! look not upon the shore
Where valor's spear and victory's horn were sacred signs
    of yore;
Look not toward the hill of Tara, or Iveagh, or Ailech high!
Look toward the East and blind your sight, for they fly at
    last, they fly!

VI.

And ye who met the Romans behind the double wall,
And ye who smote the Saxons as mallet striketh ball,
And ye who shelter'd Harold and Bruce [111]—fittest hosts for
    the brave—
Why do you not join your spirit-strength, and bury her in
    the wave?

VII.

Alas! alas! for Ireland, so many tears were shed,

They are flying, flying from her, the holy and the old,
Oh, the land has alter'd little, but the men are cowed and
    cold.

VIII.

Yea! they are flying hither, breathless and pale with fear,
And it not the sailing-time for ships, but the winter, dark
    and drear;
They had rather face the waters, dark as the frown of God,
Than make a stand for race and land, on their own elastic
    sod.

SHAWN NA GOW'S GUEST.*

A FABLE FOR THE POETS OF THE NATION, IN 1848.

I.

A KILLALOE Gow wrought in his forge at night,
With a merry heart, in a glowing light;
His arm of strength and head of sense,
Brought the good heart due recompense.

II.

'Twas a red ploughshare on his anvil lay.
Thought the Gow—"Before a year and a day
Many a sod of valley and lea
Thy master will turn, clean colter, with thee."

III.

This Gow was a lonely bachelor man,
And lived, like a tree, where his life began;
His only love was that glorious river
Which flows by Killaloe over and ever.

* *Shawn na Gow* —John, the Smith.

IV.

He loved the trees and the men that rose
On its sides, for the sake of the river that flows,
And oft, though wearied, he lay awake,
To hear the rapids their clamors make.

V.

In through the smiddy door there came,
And stood full in the forge's flame,
A form most royal, and comely, and bold,
Crown'd like a King of Kinkora old.

VI.

There was regal power in every look,
And lineage plain as a herald's book,
As sitting down at the Gow's request,
Out spoke the unexpected guest:

VII.

" Shawn Gow, of Killaloe, I find
Your craft has left my lore behind—
These chains are not for the vanquish'd in battle,
But fetters, methinks, for pasture cattle."

VIII.

Answer'd the Gow: "My Khan and guest,
The sun and the sunburst have set in the West;
The conqueror lives in the heart of the land—
He alone hath fetters for foot and hand."

IX.

" And tell me, truly, my stalwart Gow,
Do you forge no swords in Banba now ?
I have temper'd a blade of old, and fain
Would see the brave art flourish again."

X.

" Khan, *Sliabh an Iron*, still retains
   The martial ore in its giant veins;
   But the men of Erin are thrown and bound,
   Without a wrestle, without a wound."

XI.

" Ha !" said the guest, " ill news is this—
   The slaves in spirit are slaves, I wis,
   That all the swords of Adam's race
   Can never uplift to freedom's place.

XII.

" But, Gow, where are the bards, whose words
   Struck late on my ears 'like the clash of swords ?'
   Hath the spirit of poesy stoop'd its pinion
   To laud the tyrant's dread dominion ?"

XIII.

" The bards," said the Gow, " as many as be,
   Still sigh that Erin is else than free;
   But of late they have only sigh'd and wept,
   And few the prophetic vigil hath kept."

XIV.

" Worse news than ill," replied the Khan,
" For never since Banba first began,
   Lack'd there of bards when trial was near,
   To shout their warnings in her ear.

XV.

" Throughout the age-long Danish fight,
   In camp and court, by day and night,
   The poet's brain and poet's hand

XVI.

"I must be gone! do thou go forth,
  Say Brian came from his grave in the north;
  Bid *clairseachs* sound and hearts be strung—
  Give freedom first to mind and tongue!

XVII.

"The land is old—the land lies low—
  They must not drown her soul with woe;
  The land's in sleep—but not death's sleep—
  'T is time to work, but not to weep."

XVIII.

Out through the smiddy door there pass'd
  The Ard-righ's fetch, nor turn'd, nor cast
  A backward look, in deeper night
  His form was blended from the sight.

THE IRISH HOMES OF ILLINOIS.

      CHORUS—The Irish homes of Illinois,
             The happy homes of Illinois;
             No landlord there
             Can cause despair,
             Nor blight our fields in Illinois.

I.

  'T is ten good years since Ellen *bawn*
    Adventured with her Irish boy
  Across the sea, and settled on
    A prairie farm in Illinois.
        The Irish homes of Illinois, etc.

II.

Sweet waves the sea of summer flowers
  Around our wayside cot so coy,
Where Ellen sings away the hours
  That light my task in Illinois.
        The Irish homes of Illinois, etc.

III.

Another Ellen 's at her knee,
  And in her arms a laughing boy;
And I bless God to see them free
  From want and care in Illinois.
        The Irish homes of Illinois, etc.

IV.

And yet some shadows often steal
  Upon our hours of purest joy;
When happiest we most must feel
  " If Ireland were like Illinois !"
        The Irish homes of Illinois, etc.

THE SHANTY.

I.

THIS is our castle ! enter in,
  Sit down and be at home, sir ;
Your city friend will do, I hope,
  As travellers do in Rome, sir !
'T is plain the roof is somewhat low,
  The sleeping-room but scanty,
Yet to the Settler's eye, you know,
  His castle is—his Shanty!

II.

The Famine fear we saw of old,
  Is, like a nightmare, over ;
That wolf will never break our fold,
  Nor round the doorway hover.
Our swine in droves tread down the brake,
  Our sheep-bells carol canty,
Last night yon salmon swam the lake,
  That now adorns our Shanty.

III.

That bread we break, it is our own,
  It grew around my feet, sir,
It pays no tax to Squire or Crown,
  Which makes it doubly sweet, sir !
A woodman leads a toilsome life,
  And a lonely one, I grant ye,
Still, with his children, friend, and wife,
  How happy is his Shanty !

IV.

No feudal lord o'erawes us here,
  Save the Ever-bless'd Eternal ;
To Him is due the fruitful year,
  Both autumnal and vernal;
We 've rear'd to Him, down in the dell,
  A temple, neat, though scanty,
And we can hear its blessed bell
  On Sunday, in our Shanty.

V.

This is our castle! enter in,
  Sit down, and be at home, sir ;
Your city friend will do, I hope,
  As travellers do in Rome, sir !

'T is plain the roof is somewhat low,
The sleeping-room but scanty,
Yet to the Settler's eye, you know,
His castle is—his Shanty!

ST. PATRICK'S OF THE WOODS.

I.

" SIR, my guest, it is Sunday morning,
And we are ready to mass to go,
For the sexton sent us word of warning
That the priest would be in the glen below."

II.

Quickly I rose, in mind delighted
To find the old faith held so fast,
That even in western wilds benighted
My people still to the cross were clasp'd.

III.

We trod the forest's broken byway,
We burst through bush, and forded floods,
Until we came to the valley's highway,
Where stood St. Patrick's of the Woods.

IV.

A simple shed it was, but spacious,
With ample entrance open wide;
Where forest veterans, green and gracious,
Stood sentinels at either side.

V.

And there, old friends with friends were meeting,
And the last new-comer told his tale;
And kindred kindred there were greeting,
In the loving speech of the island Gael.

VI.

And here a group of anxious faces
  Were drawn around a bowering tree,
While one, a reader, with sage grimaces
  Read from a record spread on his knee.

VII.

Betimes I heard loud bursts of laughter
  At O'Connell's wit, from the eager throng,
And then deep sighs would follow after
  Some verse of Moore's melodious song.

VIII.

Till at length the bell of the lowly altar
  Summon'd to prayer the scatter'd flock,
And they moved with steps that would not falter
  If that summons led to the martyr's block.

IX.

I've knelt in churches, new and ancient,
  In grand cathedrals betimes I've stood,
But never felt my soul such transport
  As in thine—St. Patrick's of the Woods.

THE BATTLE OF AYACHUCHO.[119]

I.

Earth's famous fields, how lost, how won,
From first Time saw the unchanging sun
    O'er hostile ranks preside,
The poet's voice hath given to fame—
But Ayachucho's glorious name
    Still sleeps on Andes' side.

II.

Where Condorkanki's battlement
With the steep tropic sky is blent,
    The tide of war had roll'd.
The Spanish tents along its base
Look'd down upon a kindred race,
    By many wrongs made bold.

III.

La Serna from his tent, at morn
Counted the Chilian host with scorn—
    Scorn 't were not wise to show;
As condors close their wings, his flanks
Drew up their far-distended ranks
    And swoop'd upon the foe.

IV.

Strange sight on Ayachucho's plain,
Spain smiting down the sons of Spain,
    The nurslings of her breast!
Untaught by Britain's past defeat
How Freedom guards her last retreat
    In the unfetter'd West!

V.

The Andes, with their crowns of snow,
Crowns crested with the fiery glow
    Of the volcanic flood;
The condor, sailing stiffly by,
The oak trees struggling to the sky
    Beyond the palm-tree wood—

VI.

These, Chili, were thy witnesses!
Long may 't be till scenes like this

But if, beneath the glowing Line,
Such warfare must again be thine,
    God send thee more such men!

VII.

As bend and break before the shower
The loaded wheat and scarlet flower,
    So broke the Spanish host!
As strikes the sail before the squall,
I see the Viceroy's standard fall—
    The day is won and lost!

VIII.

A day is won that dates anew
Thy story, Chili! thine, Peru!
    And, vast Pacific, thine!
By native skill and foreign aid
Young Freedom hath securely made
    A lodgment at the Line!

IX.

Of Sucre's skill, O'Connor's aid,
Cordova's flashing, ruddy blade,
    The Chilian muse will boast;
And seldom can the muse essay
The story of a nobler day
    Than that La Serna lost.

X.

The Andean echoes yet shall take
The burden from De Sangre's lake
    Of the heroic lay—
And Conkorkanki's passes drear
Age after age the tale shall hear

THE HAUNTED CASTLE.[113]

" How beautiful! how beautiful!" cried out the children all,
As the golden harvest evening's moon beamed down on
      Donegal;
And its yellow light that danced along the Esker to the
      Bay,
There tinged the roofless abbey's walls, here gilt the castle
      gray.
" How beautiful! how beautiful! let us go hide and seek."
Some run along the river's edge, some crouch beside the
      creek;
While two, more dauntless than the rest, climb o'er the Cas-
      tle wall,
And without note on horn or trump, parade the princely
      hall.

Brave little boys, as bright as stars, beneath the porch they
      pass'd,
And paused just where along the hall the keep its shadow
      cast;
And, Heaven protect us! there they saw a fire burning away,
And, sitting in the ingle-nook, an ancient man and gray;
He sat upon his stony seat like to another stone,
And ever from his breast there broke a melancholy moan;
But the little boys they feared him not, for they were two to
      one,
And the man was stoop'd and aged, and sad to look upon.

And he who was the eldest—his mother called him Hugh—
Said, " Why for, sir, do you make moan, and wherefore do

Are you one of the old-time kings lang syne exiled to
    Spain,
Like a linnet to its last year's nest, that here returns again ?"
And the shape stood up and smiled, as the tiny voice he
    heard,
And the tear that hung upon his cheek fell to his snowy
    beard.
"My boys," he said, "come sit ye here beside me, until I
Tell you why I haunt this hearth, and what so makes me
    sigh.

"I am the Father of their Race—the Cinnel-Connell's sire—
And therefore thus I watch their home, and kindle still their
    fire;
For the mystic heat would perish amid a land of slaves,
If it were not tended nightly by the spirits from their graves;
And here I still must keep my stand until the living are
Deem'd meet to track the men of might along the fields of
    war;
And, ah! my little men," he said, "my watch is very long,
Unpromised of an early end, uncheer'd by friend or song.

"And the present is embitter'd by the memories of old—
The bards and their delights, and the tales the gossips told;
I remember me the ringing laughs and minstrelsio divine,
That echoed here for Nial Garv and Thorlogh of the Wine;
I remember how brave Manus—an early grave he met—
Traced the story here of Columb-cille, a tale surviving yet;
And, oh! I weep like Jacob, when of Joseph's death he heard,
When I think upon you, young Hugh Roe, Tirconnell's staff
    and sword!

"My boys, he was not thirty years of age, although his name

Entrapp'd, imprison'd, frozen on Wicklow's wintry hills,
He rose, he fought, he died afar, crowning our country's ills.
Alas! I cannot help but cry—and you! what, crying, too?
Indeed, it might melt iron hearts to think upon my Hugh.
My boys, go home, remember him, and hasten to be men,
That you may act, on Irish soil, his gallant part again."

" How beautiful! how beautiful!" cried out the children all,
As the two boys clamber'd over the ancient castle wall;
" Run here—run there—take care—take care;" but silently
　　and slow
To their humble homes, the little friends, hand in hand
　　they go;
And from that night they daily read, in all the quiet nooks
About their homes, old Irish songs, and new-made Irish
　　books;
And many a walk, and many a talk, they had down by the
　　Bay,
Of the Spirit of the Castle Hall, and the words they heard
　　him say.

THE ABBEY BY LOUGH KEY. [114]

I.

PLEASANT it is in the summer time
　　To sail upon Lough Key,
Alone, or with a soul belov'd—
　　'T is a lonely lough to see;
But ah! the ancient charm is fled,
　　That charm'd that lough for me!

II.

Fair are the woods of Rockingham,

And fair McDermot's castle is,
  Though nodding to its fall;
But the ancient charm is fled away,
  Ah, me! beyond recall.

III.

Of old, o'er Nature's fairest holds
  God's holy standard stood,
The loveliest mirrors smiled to catch
  The image of the Rood;
Then, many a cross-crown'd turret rose
  Around this spreading flood.

IV.

Then, many a cot was saved with prayer,
  And hail'd with holy cheer,
And many a high-born penitent
  Was fain to labor here;
For holy names and holy deeds
  Then calendar'd the year.

V.

Full many a year sweet peace abode
  Beside the placid lake,
And whoso claim'd the stranger's place
  For God's all-glorious sake,
Was welcome still to stay his stay,
  And take what he would take.

VI.

Then on the evening traveller's ear
  Arose sweet chaunt of psalm,
Which all the forest list'ning to,
  Stood hush'd in cloistral calm,
And the only airs that stirr'd abroad
  Whisper'd the dread "I Am."

VII.

Ah! well-a-day! the charm is fled—
  No more across this flood,
Shall traveller catch the solemn song
  Of Norbert's brotherhood;
The pious peasant scarce can tell
  Where once their convent stood!

VIII.

Yet though the years be fled in flocks,
  Six hundred years and more,
I fancy yonder tree a tower,
  And there, along the shore,
I see the Abbot Clarus pass,
  With white-robed monks a score.

IX.

A prayer for Abbot Clarus,
  Whose holy house stood here—
One of God's strongholds for the land,
  For many and many a year;
For still Saint Norbert's brotherhood
  To Gael and Gaul were dear!

X.

A prayer for Abbot Clarus
  McMailen, he who plann'd
The house of the Blessed Trinity,
  Upon Lough Key to stand—
Who here as guardian of the lake,
  Gave peace unto the land!

SAINT BEES.

I.

Bright shone the joyful summer sun
  On Cumberland's dark shore,
The wind had fail'd the fishermen
  And put them to the oar;
The flippant swallow swept the shaw,
  The brown nuts bent the trees,
When, from the neighboring hill, I saw
  The village of Saint Bees.

II.

" Who was Saint Bees ?" I asked of one
    Who drove a lazy yoke.
"Saint Bees," quoth he, " is that place yon:
    You 'll find 'em stiffish folk."
" Who was Saint Bees ?" I asked again
    A squire in scarlet dress'd.
" *Who ?*" echoed he—" North Countrie men
    But little like a jest."

III.

I stood within the fontless porch,
  I paced the empty nave,
The very verger of the church
  A false tradition gave.
Hard by, a staring pile of brick
  (Or college, if you please)
Had played the Saint the scurviest trick—
  Had called itself—Saint Bees.

IV.

A well-fed pedant in a train
 Of stuff (not train of thought),
Who, like a great goose, strode before
 The gosling flock he taught,
Said, stroking down his neckcloth white,
 That he, " In times like these,
Must say that, being no Puseyite,
 He knew nought of Saint Bees."

V.

Was it for this, oh, virgin band,
 Your Irish home you left,
And set, for heathen Cumberland,
 The life-spring in this cleft?
Was it for this your vesper chant
 Charm'd all these savage seas?
Where is the fruit you strove to plant
 Along this shore, Saint Bees?

VI.

I could have borne the callous clown,
 The squire's chagrin amused,
But the dullard in his cap and gown
 I from my heart abused.
I wish'd that I had been *his* Pope,
 To put him on his knees,
And make his fine pedantic gown
 An offering to Saint Bees.

POEMS ON GENERAL HISTORY.

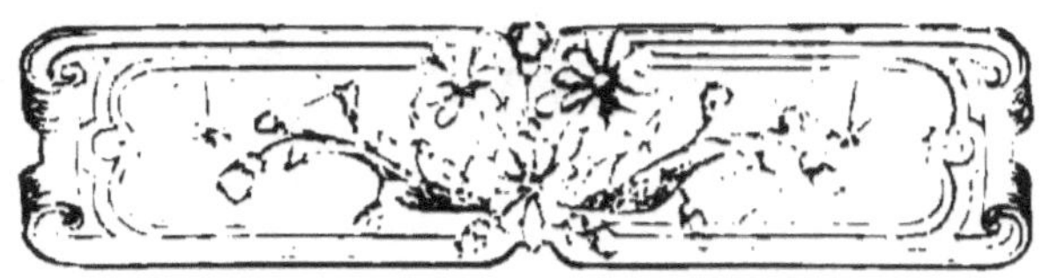

For King Celeus in Eleusis, the evening board was spread,
The monarch, with his youthful queen, sits at the table
    head ;
The fairest fields of Attica for him their harvest bore,
And generous was his royal heart and bountiful his store.
A tiller of the land by day, a teacher by the hearth,
When sunset seal'd his glorious book, the widespread,
    beauteous earth;
No tangling purple trail'd behind his active limbs, no rod
Of kingly show ere mock'd his hand; no mimicry of God;
His name through all Ionia was held in reverence meet,
And blessings circled round his head, and prayers enthroned
    his feet.
Metanira and her royal spouse sat at the table head,
And the household and the guests are there for whom the
    board was spread;
The wild boar, and the antler'd deer lie shorn of speed and
    strength,
Along that royal banquet board stretched in their ample
    length;
And the roof with ivy interlaced, and latticed with the
    vine,
Hangs its clustering grapes above their heads, over their

And the thick-set pillars, either hand, are cover'd down with
 flowers,
Which, on Ceplusus' bank late lured the wood-nymphs from
 their bowers.
But where are the two royal sons of Metanira's womb?
Their vacant seats affront their sire—why come the youths
 not home?
Triptolemus and Diephon were not wont to miss the feast;
Gloom deepen's on the mother's brow as the evening shades
 increased.
Lo! they enter that long banquet-hall leading in a stranger-
 guest,
A weary matron whom they found by the wayside taking
 rest;
Then smiled the queenly mother her two kind boys to see,
And the hospitable Celeus placed a son on either knee;
And the weary matron by the queen is placed with honor moet,
And maidens bear her water to cool her traveil'd feet;
And Diephon from his father's hand gave the ripe fruit of
 the vine;
And Triptolemus flung his arms round a beaker fill'd with
 wine,
And, in their artless, childish speech, which age can ne'er
 translate,
They press'd them on their matron friend, who bless'd them
 as she ate.
King Celeus bade his guests farewell, the lady alone sits still,
When, lo! what sudden glory the silent hall doth fill?
Aurora o'er the mountains ne'er loosed such golden flood
As pour'd around the spot where the guest a goddess stood—
"Nay, Celeus," cried her silvery voice, "stoop not your head
 in fear!
Nor thou, O happy mother, Metanira! but draw near—

Come to your guest, nor tremble at the halo on her brow,
For blessèd shall this household be, and blessèd every one—
Thou, monarch! and thou, mother! Triptolemus, Diephon!
Beside the way I languish'd, ah me! how wearily!
The fear of Pluto's darksome realm on my heart lay heavily;
They found me as a woman, their kindness hath restored
All the Immortal to my soul—Metanira, hear my word:
I will nurse thy boys until they grow of men the lordliest—
      best,
And their thirst for greatness shall be fed from Ceres' child-
      less breast;
They shall draw the pap's elixir that once fed Proserpine,
And never yet had Attica such sons as these of thine!"
Full thankful were the monarch and the mother for their
      sons,
Through whose veins the immortal ichor already plenteous
      runs—
Their tow'ring forms and glowing eyes bespeak their fos-
      terage rare,
And fills their father's heart with hope, their mother's with
      new care;
For beings cannot tenant Earth, if for Earth framed too
      finely,
Nor this world's limits satisfy souls that aspire divinely—
And sadder Metanira grew, as, every day apace,
Her sons walk'd godlier in thought, and heavenlier in grace;
And she watch'd with stealthy constancy the goddess' every
      move,
Lest she should bear away for aye the children of her love.
Each evening at the twilight hour Ceres retired apart
With the youths she loved, to work for them a rite's mys-
      terious art;
She sooth'd them to deep slumber, then spread a couch of

There she nightly laid them till they less and less of earth
  became.
Such is the art which still survives, such is the penal pain
Through which the sons of earth to a spirit-life attain;
But Metanira, on an eve, this ordeal chanced to spy,
It roused the human mother's fear, she raised a fearful cry—
The spell was broke, Diephon woke to perish in the fire,
And Triptolemus scarce escaped for death more quick and
  dire;
And Ceres, moaning piteously, forever passed away,
And Celeus never saw her more, though he sought her many
  a day.
Even yet Diephon's destiny tunes many an Attic lyre,
How he perish'd earth-waked on the couch of purifying fire!

HANNIBAL'S VISION OF THE GODS OF CARTHAGE.[116]

I.

I swear to thee, Silenus, 't was not an idle dream,
When the gods of Carthage call'd me by the Ebro's rushing
  stream,
When I stood amid the council of the deities of Tyre—
And I felt a spirit on me, the spirit of my sire.

II.

You know if I am fearful, yet I quiver'd when I saw
The mighty form of Kronos, full of majesty and awe—
His glance was far and lifted, like one looking into space,
When he turn'd it full upon me abash'd I hid my face.

III.

I heard the thrones communing in a language strange and
  high,
Words of earth and words of heaven, in opinion and reply:

Names and actions all familiar, cherish'd secrets all untold,
Were mingled in their councils with the unknown and the
      old.

IV.

The prayer I pray'd at Gades, the boyish oath I swore—
The slaughter at Saguntum which slaked the thirsty shore,
The tribes we smote at Tagus, all the actions of my youth
Pass'd bodily before me, till I trembled at their truth.

V.

Then a deity descended and touch'd me with his hand,
And I saw, outspread before me, the fair Italian land;
Its interwoven valleys, where the vine and olive grow
And the god who touch'd me, speaking, said gently, "Rise
      and go!"

VI.

But I knelt and gazed, as gazing I would have aye remain'd,
This was the destined labor—this was the task ordain'd—
As like a dragon breathing fire, I was loosed to overrun
These gardens of all flowers, these cities of the Sun.

VII.

Where on snow-fed Eridanus the sacred poplars grieve,
Where the artists of Etruria their spells and garments
      weave;
By a lake amid the mountains, by a gliding southern stream,
Hosts and consuls fell before me—I swear 't was not a dream.

VIII.

We smote them with the sling, we smote them with the bow,
Libyan and Numidian, and Iberian footmen slow;
And the elephants of Ind, and the lances of the Gaul,

IX.

I heard the voice of wailing, I heard the voice of Rome,
Then I knew my day was waning, I knew my hour was come,
For to me a bound is given by the gods whom I obey,
And the wail of Rome must usher in the evening of my
      day.

X.

But I swear to thee, Silenus, since the vision of that night,
When all the Tyrian deities were given to my sight,
I cast no look behind me, I nurse no weak desires
For the lovely one I quitted, for the palace of my sires.

XI.

The daughter of Caluso, whose beauty thou hast seen,
The ample halls of Barca, are as visions that have been;
The belov'd ancestral city, with its temples and its walls,
Has no message which my spirit from its destiny recalls.

XII.

Beyond those peaks of crystal, my path lies on and on,
Where the gods have drawn the channel there must the
      river run;
For me, a tomb or triumph, exile or welcome home—
But the dragon of the vision must work its work at Rome!

THE ANSWER OF SIMONIDES.

I.

"What say'st thou?"   Unto Simonides
  King Hiero spake: "O thou wise!
Who yieldeth yonder orb its rays—

Who stirreth up this wondrous sea
  That waiteth here in Syracuse ?
If thou hast read this mystery,
  I pray thee do not thy friend refuse !"
" Of nights and days I ask for seven,
  O King ! for this secret lies in heaven."

II.

Seven nights were pass'd and seven days,
  When thus again King Hiero said—
" I pray thee, wise Simonides,
  Hast thou our last week's riddle read ?
I know thou art not rash to speak,
  Nor dost thou fear what may befall,
That light will from thy darkness break—
  Now who is God and Lord of all ?"
But he answer'd : " Grant me another seven
Days, for this secret bides in heaven !"

III.

Seven days more were overpast,
  And Hiero sought the sage's cell,
Assured the hour was come at last,
  The secret of the skies to tell;
But he found the prophet worn and wan
  With travail, and vigil, and lonely thought;
" It is not given to mortal man
  To find," he said, " that which I sought:
Wherefore, if all life's days were given,
O King, I still should ask for seven !"

THE JEWS IN BABYLON.

[Psalm cxxxvi., verse i., "Upon the rivers of Babylon, there we sat and
wept, and we remembered Sion; v. ii. On the willows in the midst thereof we
hung up our instruments; v. iii. For there they, that led us into captivity,
required of us the words of song. And they that carried us away said: 'Sing
ye to us a hymn of the songs of Sion;' v. iv. How shall we sing the songs of the
Lord in a strange land?"]

I.

THE sun dwelt on the royal domes
   Of Babylon the great—
The captives sat upon the stones
   Without the water gate;
The river through the willows rush'd,
   Where they their harps have hung,
For sorrow all their songs had hush'd
   And all their harps unstrung.

II.

Forth came a thoughtless city throng,
   And round the mourners drew—
"Come, sing to us a Sion song,
   And string your harps anew?"
"Ah no, not so!" the captives said,
   "Not in a stranger land—
Song from our hearts is banishèd,
   And skill from every hand.

III.

"Jerusalem! dear Jerusalem,
   Could thy sons sing or play,
And thou that art all earth to them

O, Sion ! may the tongue or hand
    That first forgets thee, rot—
If thou art fallen, our native land,
    Thou art not quite forgot."

IV.

The Babylonian troop are gone
    In thoughtful mood, away—
The rivers and their tears flow on,
    And none their grief gainsay:
Their sad harps on the willows swing,
    Their lips in secret pray—
That yet in Sion they may sing
    Their native Sion lay.

AN EASTERN LEGEND.

I.

ONCE there was a Persian monarch,
    (So the Persian poets sing,)
Agèd, honor'd, great, religious,
    Every inch a man and king;
Night and Morning were his subjects,
    North and South bow'd down the head,
All went well within his palace,
    Till his only son fell dead.

II.

Then his grief broke out in frenzy,
    On the floor he dash'd his crown,
Tore his gray beard in his madness,

Till at length a Sage of sages,
  Who the Past and Future read,
By command was brought before him,
  Order'd to restore the Dead!

III.

And the Sage but stipulated
  This condition with the King,
That three men who never suffer'd
  Sorrow, first they there should bring;
Then the mighty monarch's servants
  Sought the three afar and long,
But the happiest had known sorrow,
  Disappointment, loss, or wrong!

IV.

Then the mighty Persian monarch,
  (So the Persian poets sing,)
Seeing sorrow universal,
  Felt himself again a king;
Calmly for the path of duty
  Girded he his armor on,
And perform'd his royal labors,
  Till, in time, he found his son.

CALEB AND JOSHUA.

[In the 13th and 14th chapters of the Book of Numbers, the reader will find the
history herein paraphrased.]

I.

Wᴴᴇɴ Moses led the doubting host
From Pharoah's power and Egypt's coast,
God was his ally and his guide

Though years were spent and young men bent—
Famine in field, and feud in tent,
The valiant Prophet and his band
Believed and sought the Promised Land.

II.

Now when in Pharan's sands they lay,
Twelve were sent forth to seek the way,
Which through the thick of foemen lay;
And ten returning, pale with dread,
Show'd figs and grapes, but trembling said,
‘ A giant race of Enac's brood
Possess'd the soil, where cities stood
Mid brazen walls and towers so high,
That whoso sought to take must die."

III.

But two—apart from all the rest—
Loudly the trembling tribes address'd:
" The walls," they said, " and towers are high,
But do not nearly reach the sky—
The men are men of mighty make;
But, if we brethren courage take
And trust in God and our own strength,
We'll win the Promised Land at length."

IV.

Above the camp there came a cloud,
And forth from it, as thunder loud,
A voice of power which swore, of men
Alive, and in the desert then,
The faithful two alone should tread

V.

Men have perish'd, years have flown,
The faithful two survive alone,
God's hostages to humau sense,
That faith is its own recompense.
Caleb! Joshua! when will men
Put trust in God, as ye did then?

New York, 1849.

THE MACCABEES.

["——And every man said to his neigbor, ' If we shall all do as our brethreu have done, and not fight against the heathen for our lives and our justifications, they will now quickly root us out of the earth.'

" And they determined in that day, saying—" Whosoever shall come up against us to fight on the Sabbath, we will fight against him, and we will *not* all die, as our brethren that were slain in the secret places."—*Maccabees*, chap. II., v. 40, 41.

I.

Darkness o 'ershadow'd Israel all,
    Woe, aud death, and lamentation;
The Heathen walk'd on Sion's wall,
    The Temple all was desolation;
A dumb demoniac shape of stone
    Was raised upon God's holy altar,
Where children of the Faith kneel down,
    And fearful priests through false-rites falter.

II.

Buried the Book of God, the spirit
    Of Moses and of David gone—
Lost the traditions they inherit,

Meek recusants, with bent necks bare,
  Besought swift death from fire and sword,
Of all deliverance in despair,
  Died, rather than deny the Lord.

III.

But other men of hardier mood
  In Modin's mountains wander'd free,
Their temple the o'erarching wood,
  The cave their solemn sanctuary;
Men who had sworn they would not die
  Like shambles-sheep a willing prey,
Had sworn to meet the enemy
  Though he should come on Sabbath-day.

IV.

Their chiefs were Judas—Israel's shield,
  Her buckler, sword, and morning star;
The first in every arduous field
  To bear the burden of the war;
And Simon sage, the man of lore,
  Whose downcast eyes read coming signs;
Who, from afar, could foes explore,
  And counteract their dark designs.

V.

Oh, valiant Assidean chiefs,
  How well your fathers' will ye wrought,
How lifted Israel from her griefs,
  And bore her on your shields aloft;
"She shall not perish!" so ye swore—
  They shall not root us out of earth;
Our fathers' God we dare adore,

VI.

Oh ! noble pair ! with awful odds
    Seron, Lysias, Nicanor, come !
Their trust is in their Syrian gods,
    Your firmer faith is in your own !
How valiantly, year after year,
    Ye gird your loins for warfare grand !
How proud at last your flag ye rear
    O'er your regenerated land !

VII.

O God ! I know an ancient race
    As sore oppress'd as Israel once,
Fierce foes from earth would fain erase
    Our faithful fathers' filial sons;
Wilt Thou not grant us shield and sword
    For this last Maccabean war ?
A Simon and a Judas, Lord !
    Thy outlaw'd faithful to restore ?

THE STAR OF THE MAGI AND OF BETHLEHEM.

I.

" Whence is the star that shineth so brightly ?
'Tis not of those that arise for us nightly—
Pale in its presence appearing all others,
It looms like a first-born over its brothers."

II.

The herds of Arabia lay gather'd and sleeping,
The sons of the shepherds their watches were keeping,
When the star of our faith all lustrous and tender,
Fill'd the desert of grass with the sheen of its splendor

III.

Then, in wonder and terror they ran to their seers,
Wisest of men, in those primitive years,
Ishmael's priests, the renown'd of Saboo,
Who grew pale in the light that arose o'er Judea.

IV.

To their eyes, star-reveal'd, an angelical choir
Fill'd the heavens with timbrel, and anthem, and lyre,
And they heard through the calm of that marvellous morn,
That the king, that the lion of Judah was born.

V.

Then the magi and lords of the desert arose,
And gath'ring the myrrh in the Orient that grows,
And the incense of Saba, in censer and coffer,
And the virginal ore from the far mines of Ophir!

VI.

By Jordan they sought the Messiah in Zion,
The desert-born look'd for the trace of " the Lion "—
Dark, dark as Sinai enshrouded in thunder,
Grew Herod, the king, at their tidings of wonder.

VII.

Again rose the star of the Orient, to guide them
To the ox and the ass, and earth's Saviour beside them,
Where, child-like and weak, the Master of Ages
Took tribute from Araby's princes and sages.

VIII.

So may God grant to us, amid all our demerit,
The faith, love, and hope of the men of the desert,
For us, as for them, dawns the marvellous morn,
And the angels are singing—"Lo! Jesus is born."

VIII.

RE-CONQUEST OF THE SPANISH LAND.

I.

MANY a day in summer time Ramiro, from the North,
On the fair fields of the South impatiently look'd forth;
And in winter, when the torrents came like bandits leaping
    down
From their high Asturian homes, he avoided tower and
    town,
And, scowling from some pathless pass, he spent the fruitless
    day
Counting the Moorish castles far beneath him as they lay.

II.

By the altar of Saint Jago upon Christmas Eve he stood;
Hoarsely thunder'd past the stream; wildly waved the naked
    wood.
In the little mountain chapel King Ramiro knelt alone,
When Saint Jago thus bespoke him, from his effigy of stone:
" Ramiro, King Ramiro! thou who wouldst re-conquer Spain,
You have allies in the winter, in the darkness, and the rain—
Strike when your foe is weakest, and you shall not strike
    in vain!"

III.

On the banks of the Douro there is darkness—there is rain;
On the banks of the Douro there is striking—not in vain!
The eagles of the North, from their high Asturian nests,
Are fasten'd on the Moslems, like falcons in their crests.
On the domes of Compostello there is darkness—there is
    rain,

THE VIRGIN MARY'S KNIGHT.[110]

A BALLAD OF THE CRUSADES.

BENEATH the stars in Palestine seven knights discoursing
    stood,
But not of warlike work to come, nor former fields of blood,
Nor of the joy the pilgrims feel; prostrated far, who see
The hill where Christ's atoning blood pour'd down the penal
    tree;
Their theme was old, their theme was new, 'twas sweet and
    yet 'twas bitter,
Of noble ladies left behind spoke cavalier and ritter,
And eyes grew bright, and sighs arose from every iron breast,
For a dear wife, or plighted maid, far in the widowed West.

Toward the knights came Constantine, thrice noble by his
    birth,
And ten times nobler than his blood, his high out-shining
    worth,
His step was slow, his lips were moved, though not a word
    he spoke,
Till a gallant lord of Lombardy his spell of silence broke.
" What aileth thee, O Constantine, that solitude you seek ?
If counsel or if aid you need, we pray thee do but speak;
Or dost thou mourn, like other *frères*, thy lady-love afar,
Whose image shineth nightly through yon European star ?"

Then answer'd courteous Constantine, " Good Sir, in simple
    truth,
I chose a gracious lady in the heydey of my youth,
I wear her image on my heart, and when that heart is cold,

For her I love and worship well by light of morn or even,
I ne'er shall see my mistress dear, until we meet in heaven,
But this believe, brave cavaliers, there never was but one
Such lady as my holy love, beneath the blessèd sun."

He ceased, and pass'd with solemn step on to an olive grove,
And kneeling there he prayed a prayer to the lady of his
    love,
And many a cavalier whose lance had still maintained his
    own
Beloved to reign without a peer, all earth's unequall'd one,
Look'd tenderly on Constantine in camp and in the fight;
With wonder and with generous pride they mark'd the light-
    ning light
Of his fearless sword careering through the unbelievers'
    ranks,
As angry Rhone sweeps off the vines that thicken on his
    banks.

"He fears not death come when it will, he longeth for his
    love,
And fain would find some sudden path to where she dwells
    above.
How should he fear for dying when his mistress dear is
    dead?"
Thus often of Sir Constantine his watchful comrades said;
Until it chanced from Sion wall the fatal arrow flew,
That pierced the outworn armor of his faithful bosom
    through;
And never was such mourning made for knight in Palestine
As thy loyal comrades made for thee, belovèd Constantine!

Beneath the royal tent the bier was guarded night and day,
Where with a halo round his head the Christian champion
    lay;

That talisman upon his breast—what may that marvel be
Which kept his ardent soul through life from every error
    free ?
Approach! behold! nay, worship there the image of his
    love,
The heavenly queen who reigneth all the sacred hosts above
Nor wonder that around his bier there lingers such a light,
For the spotless one that sleepeth, was *the Blessèd Virgin's*
    Knight!

    Written on Lady-day, 1853.

COLUMBUS.

A FRAGMENT.

I.

Star of the Sea, to whom, age after age,
    The maiden kneels whose lover sails the sea—
Star, that the drowning death-pang can assuage,
    And shape the soul's course to eternity—
Mother of God, in Bethlehem's crib confined,
    Mother of God, to Egypt's realm exiled—
Thee do I ask to aid my anxious mind,
    And make this book find favor with thy child!

II.

Of one who lived and labor'd in thy ray,
    I would rehearse the striving and success—
Through the dense past I ne'er shall find my way
    Unless thou helpest, holy Comfortress!
A world of doubt and darkness to evade,
    An ocean all unknown to Christian kind—
Another world by nature's self array'd,

III.

From Jesus death the fifteenth century's close
  Was near at hand for all the elder world,
When sharp and ominous the Crescent rose
  On shores from which the Holy Cross was hurl'd—
Constantine's city saw its banner torn,
  Its shrines all down, its people flying far—
Saw, year by year, the Moslem hosts return
  With some fresh trophies of the Christian war.

IV.

No more the Red Cross in the West inflamed
  The valiant to the ancient enterprise—
No more Jerusalem, all pale and maim'd,
  Bled, like its Lord, before the nation's eyes!
Godfrey and Richard in their armor slept,
  The sword of Tancred rusted, sheath'd in clay—
Europe still wept, but for herself she wept,
  And her grief wore not, in Time's course, away!

V.

Rome trembled, like Jerusalem of old,
  The Tiber shrank at every eastern breeze;
None in all Christendom was found so bold
  To seek the Sultan in his new-won seas;
The Adriatic sky by day was dark,
  Italian galleys crept more close to shore;
Venice, beneath the Lion of Saint Mark,
  Paid the Turk tribute, thankful 'twas not more!

VI.

France gather'd in her limbs, like one benumb'd
  Beneath an icy and destructive sky,
And once before the Crescent she succumb'd,
  And begg'd the peace she could not force or buy;

Albion, as yet disjointed and unbound,
　Slumber'd securely in the watery West,
One only champion Europe yet had found,
　One only arm to guard her naked breast.

VII.

Among the troubled Powers swart Spain arose,
　Arm'd and inspired, the battle's brunt to bear—
God's foes were hers, but even for heathen foes
　Her chivalry would open a career;
Gentle, but faithful, constant to her creed,
　Buoyant amid the banners of the field,
Grave in the council at the hour of need,
　Europe's true champion and Religion's shield.

VIII.

Two wedded sovereigns govern'd in Spain,
　He, from the North, as cautious and as cold—
She, from the South, of the more generous strain,
　Less bound in love of acres or of gold;
Isabel, bright and generous as the spring
　That plants the primrose in the peasant's path,
And Ferdinand, the sage but callous king,
　Whose muffled hand ne'er left the sign of wrath.

*　　*　　*　　*　　*　　*　　*

SEBASTIAN CABOT TO HIS LADY. [117]

Dear, my Lady, you will understand
By these presents coming to your hand,
Written in the Hyperborean seas,
(Where my love for you doth never freeze,)
Underneath a sky obscured with light,

That my thoughts are not of lands unknown,
Or buried gold beneath the southern zone,
But of a treasure dearer far to me,
In a far isle of the sail-shadow'd sea.

I ask'd the Sun but lately as he set,
If my dear Lady in his course he met—
That she was matronly and passing tall,
That her young brow cover'd deep thought withal,
That her full eye was purer azure far
Than his own sky, and brighter than a star;
That her kind hands were whiter than the snow
That melted in the tepid tide below,
That her light step was stately as her mind,
Steadfast as Faith, and soft as summer wind;
Whether her cheek was pale, her eye was wet,
And where and when my Lady dear he met?

And the Sun spoke not: next I ask'd the Wind
Which lately left my native shores behind,
If he had seen my Love the groves among,
That round our home their guardian shelter flung,
If he had heard the voice of song arise
From that dear roof beneath the eastern skies,
If he had borne a prayer to heaven from thee
For a lone ship and thy lone Lord at sea?
And the Wind answer'd not, but fled amain,
As if he fear'd my questioning again.

Anon the Moon, the meek-faced minion rose,
But nothing of my love could she disclose,—
Then my soul, moved by its strong will, trod back
The shimmering vestige of our vessel's track,
And I beheld you, darling, by our hearth.

And Care's too early print was on the brow,
Where I have seen the sunshine shamed ere now;
And as unto your widow'd bed you pass'd,
I saw no more—tears blinded me at last.

But mourn not, Mary, let no dismal dream
Darken the current of Hope's flowing stream;
Trust Him who sets his stars on high to guide
Us sinful sailors through the pathless tide,
The God who feeds the myriads of the deep,
And spreads the oozy couches where they sleep;
The God who gave even me a perfect wife,
The star, the lamp, the compass of my life,
Who will replace me on a tranquil shore,
To live with Love and you for evermore.

The watch is set, the tired sailors sleep,
The star-eyed sky o'erhangs the dreamy deep—
No more, no more: I can no further write;
Vain are my sighs, and weak my words this night;
But kneeling here, amid the seething sea,
I pray to God, my best beloved, for thee;
And if that prayer be heard, as well it may,
Our parting night shall have a glorious day.

JACQUES CARTIER.

I.

In the seaport of Saint Malo, 'twas a smiling morn, in May,
When the Commodore Jacques Cartier to the westward
    sail'd away;
In the crowded old cathedral all the town were on their
    knees,

And every autumn blast that swept o'er pinnacle and pier,
Fill'd manly hearts with sorrow and gentle hearts with fear.

II.

A year pass'd o'er Saint Malo—again came round the day
When the Commodore Jacques Cartier to the westward
     sail'd away;
But no tidings from the absent had come the way they went,
And tearful were the vigils that many a maiden spent;
And manly hearts were fill'd with gloom, and gentle hearts
     with fear,
When no tidings came from Cartier at the closing of the
     year.

III.

But the Earth is as the Future, it hath its hidden side,
And the Captain of Saint Malo was rejoicing, in his pride,
In the forests of the North—while his townsmen mourn'd
     his loss
He was rearing on Mount Royal the *fleur-de-lis* and cross;
And when two months were over and added to the year,
Saint Malo hail'd him home again, cheer answering to cheer.

IV.

He told them of a region, hard, iron-bound and cold,
Nor seas of pearl abounded, nor mines of shining gold,
Where the wind from Thulé freezes the word upon the lip,
And the ice in spring comes sailing athwart the early ship;
He told them of the frozen scene until they thrill'd with fear,
And piled fresh fuel on the hearth to make him better cheer.

V.

But when he changed the strain—he told how soon is cast

How the winter causeway, broken, is drifted out to sea,
And the rills and rivers sing with pride the anthem of the
    free;
How the magic wand of summer clad the landscape, to his
    eyes,
Like the dry bones of the just, when they wake in Paradise.

VI.

He told them of the Algonquin braves—the hunters of the
    wild,
Of how the Indian mother in the forest rocks her child;
Of how, poor souls! they fancy, in every living thing
A spirit good or evil, that claims their worshipping;
Of how they brought their sick and maim'd for him to
    breathe upon,
And of the wonders wrought for them through the Gospel
    of St. John."[118]

VII.

He told them of the river whose mighty current gave
Its freshness, for a hundred leagues, to Ocean's briny wave;
He told them of the glorious scene presented to his sight,
What time he rear'd the cross and crown on Hochelaga's
    height,
And of the fortress cliff that keeps of Canada the key,
And they welcomed back Jacques Cartier from his perils
    over sea.

JACQUES CARTIER AND THE CHILD.

I.

When Jacques Cartier return'd from his voyage to the west-
    ward,
All was uproar in Saint Malo and shouting of welcome—
Dear to his heart were the hail and the grasp of his towns-

And dear to his pride the favor and thanks of King Francis.
But of all who drew nigh—such was the cast of his nature—
A god-child beloved, he most delighted to answer
On all the surmises that fill the fancy of children.

II.

"Tell me," she said, " what you found far away in the wood-
  lands;
Say how you felt when you saw the savages standing
Arm'd on the shore, and heard the first sound of their war-
  cry?
Were you afraid then?" Quietly smiled the brave sailor—
"Nay, little daughter," he said, "I was not afraid of the
  red men;
But when I saw them, I sighed, alas! for the bondage,
The darkness that hangs over all the lost children of Adam.
As I in the depths of their forests might wander and wander
Deeper and deeper, and finding no outlet forever—
So they, in the old desolation of folly and error,
Are lost to their kindred divine in mansions eternal.

III.

"And then, daughter dearest, I bless'd God in truth and in
  secret,
That he had not suffer'd my lot to be with the heathen,
But cast it in France—among a people so Christian;
And then I bethought me, peradventure to me it is given
To lead the vanguard of Truth to the inmost recesses
Of this lost region of souls who know not the Gospel.
And these were the thoughts I had far away in the wood-
  lands,
When I saw the savages arm'd, and heard the roar of their
  war-cry,"

VERSES IN HONOR OF MARGARET BOURGEOYS.[119]

Dark is the light of Prophecy—no heavenly dews distill
On Sion's rock, on Jordan's vale, or Hermon's holy hill—
" *Save us, O Lord!* " the Psalmist cries, pouring his soul's
    complaint;
Save us, O Lord! in these our days, for Israel has no Saint.
Not half so dark the sky of night, her starry hosts without,
As the night-time of the nations when God's living lamps go
    out.

But wondrous is the love of God! who sends his shining
    host,
From age to age, from race to race, from utmost coast to
    coast;
And wondrous 'twas in our own land—e'en on the spot we
    tread—
Ere yet the forest monarchs to the axe had bow'd the head,
That in our very hour of dawn, a light for us was set,
Here on the royal mountain's side, whose lustre guides us
    yet.

'Tis pleasant in the gay greenwood—so all the poets sing—
To breathe the very breath of flowers, and hear the sweet
    birds sing,
'Tis pleasant to shut out the world—behind their curtain
    green,
And live and laugh, or muse and pray, forgotten and unseen;
But men or angels seldom saw a sight to heaven more dear,
Than Sister Margaret and her flock, upon our hillside here.

From morn till eve, a hum arose, above the maple trees,

Egyptian hue and speech uncouth, grew fair and sweet, when
    won
To sing the song of Mary, and to serve her Saviour Son;
The courier halted on his path, the sentry on his round,
And bare-head bless'd the holy nun who made it holy ground.

There came a day of tempest, where all was peace before—
The Huron war-cry rang dismay on Hochelaga's shore—
Then in that day all men confess'd, with all man's humbled
    pride,
How brave a heart, till God's good time, a convent serge may
    hide.
The savage triumph'd o'er the saint—a tiger in the fold—
But the mountain mission stands to-day! the Huron's tale is
    told!

Glory to God who sends his saints to all the ends of earth,
Wherever Adam's erring race have being or have birth,
Glory to God who sheds his saints, our sunshine and our
    dew,
Through all the realms and nations of the Old World and the
    New,
Who perfumes the Pacific with his lily and his rose,
Who sent his holy ones tob less and bloom amid our snows!

Dear Mother of our mountain home! loved foundress of our
    school—
Pray for thy children that they keep thy every sacred rule,
Beseech thy glorious Patron—our Lady full of grace—
To guide and guard thy sisterhood—and her who fills thy
    place,
Thy other self—to whom we know all glad obedience given
As rendered to thyself will be repaid tenfold in heaven!

For thee, my Country! many are the gifts God gives to thee,
And glorious is thine aspect, from the sunset to the sea;

And many a cross is in thy midst, and many an altar fair,
And many a place where men may lay the burden that they
    bear.
Ah! may it be thy crowning gift, the last as 'twas the first,
To see thy children at the knee of Margaret Bourgeoys
    nursed.

MONTREAL, October, 1865.

"*OUR LADYE OF THE SNOW!*"

IF, Pilgrim, chance thy steps should lead
Where, emblem of our holy creed,
    Canadian crosses glow—
There you may hear what here you read,
And seek, in witness of the deed,
    Our Ladye of the Snow![120]

I.

In the old times when France held sway
From the Balize to Hudson's Bay
    O'er all the forest free,
A noble Breton cavalier
Had made his home for may a year
    Beside the Rivers Three.

II.

To tempest and to trouble proof,
Rose in the wild his glitt'ring roof
    To every trav'ler dear;
The Breton song, the Breton dance,
The very atmosphere of France,

III.

Strange sight that on those fields of snow
The genial vine of Gaul should grow
    Despite the frigid sky!
Strange power of man's all-conqu'ring will,
That here the hearty Frank can still
    A Frenchman live and die!

IV.

The Seigneur's hair was ashen gray,
But his good heart held holiday,
    As when, in youthful pride,
He bared his shining blade before
De Tracey's regiment on the shore
    Which France has glorified.

V.

Gay in the field, glad in the hall,
The first at danger's frontier call,
    The humblest devotee—
Of God and of St. Catherine dear
Was the stout Breton cavalier
    Beside the Rivers Three.

VI.

When bleak December's chilly blast
Fetter'd the flowing waters fast,
    And swept the frozen plain—
When, with a frighten'd cry, half heard,
Far southward fled the Arctic bird,
    Proclaiming winter's reign—

VII.

His custom was, come foul, come fair,
For Christmas duties to repair
    Unto the *Ville Marie*,

The city of the mount, which north
Of the great River looketh forth,
    Across its sylvan sea.

VIII.

Fast fell the snow, and soft as sleep
The hillocks look'd like frozen sheep,
    Like giants gray the hills—
The sailing pine seem'd canvas-spread
With its white burden overhead,
    And marble hard the rills.

IX.

A thick dull light where ray was none
Of moon, or star, or cheerful sun,
    Obscurely show'd the way—
While merrily upon the blast
The jingling horse-bells, pattering fast,
    'Timed the glad roundelay.

X.

Swift eve came on, and faster fell
The winnow'd storm on ridge and dell,
    Effacing shape and sign—
Until the scene grew blank at last,
As when some seamen from the mast
    Looks o'er the shoreless brine.

XI.

Nor marvel aught to find ere long
In such a scene the death of song
    Upon the bravest lips—
The empty only could be loud
When Nature fronts us in her shroud
    Beneath the sky's eclipse.

XII.

Nor marvel more to find the steed,
Though famed for spirit and for speed,
     Drag on a painful pace—
With drooping crest, and faltering foot,
And painful whine, the weary brute
     Seems conscious of disgrace.

XIII.

Until he paused with mortal fear,
Then plaintive sank upon the mere
     Stiff as a steed of stone—
In vain the master winds his horn,
None, save the howling wolves forlorn
     Attend the dying roan.

XIV.

Sad was the heart and sore the plight
Of the benumb'd, bewilder'd knight
     Now scrambling through the storm.
At every step he sank apace—
The death-dew freezing on his face—
     In vain each loud alarm!

XV.

The torpid echoes of the rock
Answer'd with one unearthly mock
     Of danger round about!
Then muffled in their snowy robes,
Retiring sought their bleak abodes,
     And gave no second shout.

XVI.

Down on his knees himself he cast,
Deeming that hour to be his last,
     Yet mindful of his faith—

He pray'd St. Catherine and St. John,
And our dear Ladye call'd upon
      For grace of happy death.

XVII.

When lo! a light beneath the trees,
Which clank their brilliants in the breeze—
      And lo! a phantom fair,
As God's in heaven! by that bless'd light
Our Lady's self rose to his sight
      In robes that spirits wear!

XVIII.

Oh! lovelier, lovelier far than pen,
Or tongue, or art, or fancy's ken
      Can picture, was her face—
Gone was the sorrow of the sword,
And the last passion of our Lord
      Had left no living trace!

XIX.

As when the moon across the moor
Points the lost peasant to his door,
      And glistens on his pane—
Or when along her trail of light
Belated boatmen steer at night,
      A harbor to regain—

XX.

So the warm radiance from her hands
Unbind for him Death's icy bands,
      And nerve the sinking heart—
Her presence makes a perfect path.
Ah! he who such a helper hath
      May anywhere depart.

XXI.

All trembling, as she onward smiled,
Follow'd that Knight our mother mild,
    Vowing a grateful vow—
Until far down the mountain gorge
She led him to the antique forge,
      Where her own shrine stands now.

XXII.

If, Pilgrim, chance thy steps should lead
Where, emblem of our holy creed,
    Canadian crosses glow—
There you may hear what here you read,
And seek, in witness of the deed,
    Our Ladye of the Snow!

THE DEATH OF HUDSON.

The slayer *Death* is everywhere, and many a mask hath he,
Many and awful are the shapes in which he sways the sea;
Sometimes within a rocky aisle he lights his candle dim,
And sits half-sheeted in the foam, chanting a funeral hymn;
Full oft amid the roar of winds we hear his awful cry,
Guiding the lightning to its prey through the beclouded sky;
Sometimes he hides 'neath Tropic waves, and, as the ship
    sails o'er,
He holds her fast to the fiery sun, till the crew can breathe
    no more.

There is no land so far away but he meeteth mankind there—
He liveth at the icy pole with the 'berg and the shaggy bear,
He smileth from the southron capes like a May queen in her
    flowers,
He falleth o'er the Indian seas, dissolved in summer showers:

But of all the sea-shapes he hath worn, may mariners never
    know
Such fate as Heinrich Hudson found, in the labyrinths of
    snow—[121]
The cold north seas' Columbus, whose bones lie far interr'd
Under those frigid waters where no song was ever heard.

'Twas when he sail'd from Amsterdam, in the adventurous
    quest
Of an ice-shored strait, through which to reach the far and
    fabled West;
His dastard crew—their thin blood chill'd beneath the Arctic
    sky—
Combined against him in the night; his hands and feet they
    tie,
And bind him in a helmless boat, on that dread sea to sail—
Ah, me! an oarless, shadowy skiff, as a schoolboy's vessel
    frail.
Seven sick men, and his only son, his comrades were to be,
But ere they left the Crescent's side, the chief spoke, daunt-
    lessly:

"Ho, mutineers! I ask no act of kindness at your hands—
My fate I feel must steer me to Death's still-silent lands;
But there is one man in my ship who sail'd with me of yore,
By many a bay and headland of the New World's eastern
    shore;
From India's heats to Greenland's snows he dared to follow
    me,
And is HE turn'd traitor too, is HE in league with ye?"
Uprose a voice from the mutineers, "Not I, my chief, not I—
I'll take my old place by your side, though all be sure to die."

Before his chief could bid him back, he is standing at his
    side;

No word from any lip came forth, their strain'd eyes steadily
    glare
At the vacant gloom, where late the ship had left them to
    despair.
On the dark waters long was seen a line of foamy light—
It pass'd, like the hem of an angel's robe, away from their
    eager sight.
Then each man grasp'd his fellow's hand, some sigh'd, but
    none could speak,
While on, through pallid gloom, their boat drifts moaningly
    and weak.

Seven sick men, dying, in a skiff five hundred leagues from
    shore !
Oh! never was such a crew afloat on this world's waves be-
    fore;
Seven stricken forms, seven sinking hearts of seven short-
    breathing men,
Drifting over the sharks' abodes, along to the white bear's
    den.
Oh! 'twas not there they could be nursed in homeliness and
    ease !
One short day heard seven bodies sink, whose souls God
    rest in peace !
The one who first expired had most to note the foam he
    made,
And no one pray'd to be the last, though each the blow
    delay'd.

Three still remain. "My son! my son! hold up your head,
    my son !
Alas! alas! my faithful mate, I fear his life is gone."
So spoke the trembling father—two cold hands in his breast,
Breathing upon his dead boy's face, all too soft to break his
    rest.

The roar of battle could not wake that sleeper from his sleep;
The trusty sailor softly lets him down to the yawning deep;
The fated father hid his face while this was being done,
Still murmuring mournfully and low, " My son, my only son."

Another night; uncheerily, beneath that heartless sky,
The iceberg sheds its livid light upon them passing by,
And each beholds the other's face, all spectre-like and wan,
And even in that dread solitude man fear'd the eye of man!
Afar they hear the beating surge sound from the banks of
        frost,
Many a hoar cape round about looms like a giant ghost,
And, fast or slow, as they float on, they hear the bears on
        shore
Trooping down to the icy strand, watching them evermore.

The morning dawns; unto their eyes the light hath lost its
        cheer;
Nor distant sail, nor drifting spar within their ken appear.
Embay'd in ice the coffin-like boat sleeps on the waveless tide,
Where rays of deathly-cold, cold light converge from every side.
Slow crept the blood into their hearts, each manly pulse
        stood still,
Huge haggard bears kept watch above on every dazzling hill.
Anon the doom'd men were entranced, by the potent frigid air,
And they dream, as drowning men have dreamt, of fields far
        off and fair.

What phantoms fill'd each cheated brain, no mortal ever
        knew;
What ancient storms they weather'd o'er, what seas explored
        anew;
What vast designs for future days—what home hope, or
        what fear—
There was no one 'mid the ice-lands to chronicle or hear.

So still they sat, the weird faced seals bethought them they
  were dead,
And each raised from the waters up his cautious wizard head.
Then circled round the arrested boat, like vampires round a
  grave,
Till frighted at their own resolve—they plunged beneath the
  wave.

Evening closed round the moveless boat, still sat entranced
  the twain,
When lo! the ice unlocks its arms, the tide pours in amain!
Away upon the streaming brine the feeble skiff is borne,
The shaggy monsters howl behind their farewells all forlorn.
The crashing ice, the current's roar, broke Hudson's fairy
  spell,
But never more shall this world wake his comrade tried so
  well!
His brave heart's blood is chill'd for aye, yet shall its truth
  be told,
When the memories of kings are worn from marble and from
  gold.

Onward, onward, the helpless chief—the dead man for his
  mate!
The shark far down in ocean's depth feels the passing of that
  freight,
And bounding from his dread abyss, he snuffs the upper air,
Then follows on the path it took, like lion from his lair.
O God! it was a fearful voyage and fearful company,
Nor wonder that the stout sea-chief quiver'd from brow to
  knee.
Oh! who would blame his manly heart, if e'en *it* quaked for

The shark hath found a readier prey, and turn'd him from
    the chase;
The boat hath *made* another bay—a drearier pausing place—
O'er arching piles of blue-vein'd ice admitted to its still,
White, fathomless waters, palsied like the doom'd man's fet-
    ter'd will.
Powerless he sat—that chief escaped so oft by sea and land—
Death breathing o'er him—all so weak he could not lift a
    hand.
Even his bloodless lips refused a last short prayer to speak,
But angels listen at the heart when the voice of man is
    weak.

His heart and eye were suppliant turn'd to the ocean's Lord
    on high,
The Borealis lustres were gathering in the sky;
From South and North, from East and West, they cluster'd
    o'er the spot
Where breathed his last the gallant chief whose grave man
    seeth not;
They mark'd him die with steadfast gaze, as though in heaven
    there were
A passion to behold how he the fearful fate would bear;
They watch'd him through the livelong night—these couriers
    of the sky,
Then fled to tell the listening stars how 'twas they saw him
    die.

He sleepeth where old Winter's realm no genial air invades,
His spirit burneth bright in heaven among the glorious
    shades,
Whose God-like doom on earth it was creation to unfold,
Spanning this mighty orb of ours as through the spheres it

His name is written on the deep, the rivers as they run
Will bear it timeward o'er the world, telling what he hath
    done;
The story of his voyage to Death, amid the Arctic frosts,
Will be told by mourning mariners on earth's most distant
    coasts.

THE LAUNCH OF THE GRIFFIN.

I.

Within Cayuga's forest shade
The stocks were set—the keel was laid—
Wet with the nightly forest dew,
The frame of that first vessel grew.'"
Strange was the sight upon the brim
Of the swift river, even to him
   The builder of the bark;
To see its artificial lines
Festoon'd with summer's sudden vines,
   Another New World's ark.

II.

As rounds to ripeness manhood's schemes
Out of youth's fond, disjointed dreams,
So ripen'd in her kindred wood
That traveller of the untried flood.
And often as the evening sun
Gleam'd on the group, their labor done—
   The Indian prowling out of sight
   Of corded friar and belted knight—
And smiled upon them as they smiled,
The builders on the bark—their child !

III.

The hour has come: upon the stocks
The masted hull already rocks—
The mallet in the master's hand
Is poised to launch her from the land.
Beside him, partner of his quest
For the great river of the West,
Stands the adventurous *Recollet*
Whose page records that anxious day.[12]
To him the master would defer
The final act—he will not bear
That any else than him who plann'd,
Should launch " the Griffin " from the land.
In courteous conflict they contend,
The knight and priest, as friend with friend—
  In that strange savage scene
The swift blue river glides before,
And still Niagara's awful roar
  Booms through the vistas green.

IV.

And now the mallet falls, stroke—stroke—
On prop of pine and wedge of oak
  The vessel feels her way;
The quick mechanics leap aside
As, rushing downward to the tide,
  She dashes them with spray.
The ready warp arrests her course,
And holds her for a while perforce,
While on her deck the merry crew
Man every rope, loose every clew,
  And spread her canvas free.
Away ! 'tis done ! the Griffin floats,
First of Lake Erie's wingèd boats—.

v.

Gun after gun proclaims the hour,
As nature yields to human power;
And now upon the deeper calm
The Indian hears the holy psalm—
Laudamus to the Lord of Hosts!
Whose name unknown on all their coasts,
The inmost wilderness shall know,
Wafted upon yon wings of snow
That, sinking in the waters blue,
Seem but some lake-bird lost to view.

VI.

In old romance and fairy lays
Its wondrous part the Griffin plays—
Grimly it guards the gloomy gate
Seal'd by the strong behest of Fate—
Or, spreading its portentous wings,
Wafts Virgil to the Court of Kings;
And unto scenes as wondrous shall
Thy Griffin bear thee, brave La Salle!
Thy wingèd steed shall stall where grows
On Michigan the sweet wild rose;
Lost in the mazes of St. Clair,
Shall give thee hope amid despair,
And bear thee past those isles of dread
The Huron peoples with the dead,
Where foot of savage never trod
Within the precinct of his god; [134]
And it may be thy lot to trace
The footprints of the unknown race
'Graved on Superior's iron shore,
Which knows their very name no more. [135]

Thy Griffin bear thee, brave La Salle—
True Wizard of the Wild ! whose art,
An eye of power, a knightly heart,
A patient purpose silence-nursed,
A high, enduring, saintly trust—
Are mighty spells—we honor these,
Columbus of the inland seas !

A PLEA FOR SPAIN.

I.

WHEN Asiatic plague and darkness, worse
  Than that which late appall'd the young and old,
A cholera smiting souls, with Ishmael's curse,
  Torrent-like, from the gates of Mecca roll'd;
A deluge from below ! it surged and spread
  O'er Salem, Syria, and the isles of Greece,
Darkening the heavens, save where a symbol dread
  Its crescent rose to rob the West of peace.

II.

From Jesus' death, the fifteen hundredth year,
  Beheld the panic of the Christian world—
Saw, like Death's ominous and fatal shear,
  Mahomet's moon on Stamboul's towers unfurl'd,
Shrines beaten down, a people flying far,
  The Christian banner tremulous and torn,—
Saw, year on year, the Moslems to the war,
  With haugbtier pride and mightier host return.

III.

No more the Red Cross in the West inflamed
  The valiant to the ancient enterprise—
In vain, Jerusalem, all pale and maim'd,

Godfrey and Richard in their armor slept,
  The sword of Tancred rusted in the clay—
Europe still wept, but for herself she wept,
  Her grief but deep'ning as Hope wore away!

IV.

Rome, menaced like Jerusalem of old,
  Kept open ear to every eastern breeze,
None in all Christendom was there so bold
  To seek the Sultan in his new-won seas;
The Adriatic capes by day were dark,
  Sardinian galleys crept in close to shore;
Venice, beneath the Lion of Saint Mark,
  Paid the Turk tribute, thankful 'twas no more!

V.

France gather'd in her limbs, like one benumb'd
  Beneath an icy and destructive sky,
And once before the Crescent she succumb'd,
  And once she begg'd the peace she could not buy;
Albion, as yet disjointed and unbound,
  Slumber'd securely in the watery West,
One only champion Christendom had found,
  One only arm to guard her naked breast.

VI.

Among the troubled Powers swart Spain arose,
  Arm'd and inspired the battle's brunt to bear—
God's foes were Spain's—but even to heathen foes
  Her chivalry would open a career;
Gentle and faithful—constant to her creed—
  Joyful amid the banners of the field,
Wisest in council at the hour of need,
  Ready to act as plan—or sword or shield.

VII.

Such then was Spain to Christendom.   Oh! shame
    That you and I should coldly here debate
The tribute due to her, whose age of fame
    Bears, like a rock aloft, the Christian State!
Fitter the gather'd nations group'd around
    Should lay their annual garlands at her feet,
Than thus and here conspirators be found
    To rob her of her last Atlantic seat.

VIII.

We are but young, and being young, must learn
    The past hath claims even as the present hath—
One eye through all things can a cause discern,
    One hand imperial holds the bolt of Wrath.
A common reckoning through the ages runs,
    And thine, America, to Spain lies due;
Arouse thee, then—restrain thy eager sons,
    Nor let the Old World's story shame the New!

POEMS OF THE AFFECTIONS.

THE PARTING.

I.

Sad the parting scene was, Mary!
   By the yellow-flowing Foyle,
Dark my days have been, and dreary,
   All this long, long while:
Now the hermit of misfortune,
   In my rock I coldly dwell;
In my ears are booming ever,
   "God be with you, love—farewell!"

II.

Such the words your lips last utter'd—
   Mistress of my woful heart;
'Twas the first time you were pleasured,
   Thus in haste with me to part;
For, behind, hot foes were pressing
   After him you loved so well;
Sad and eager was our parting—
   "God be with you, love—farewell!"

III.

Nightly, as through ocean's valleys,
   We held on our silent way,
Memory brought the bitter chalice

In my exile still I drank it,
  Darkest gloom upon me fell—
Like a requiem, still rang round me
  " God be with you, love—farewell !"

IV.

Daily gazing towards the eastward,
  Underneath the blinding sun,
I am seeking for the dear ship
  Which should bring my chosen one;
Daily do I count the white sails
  Looming o'er the long sea-swell—
When among them will my Mary
  Come to end our long farewell ?

THOUGHTS OF IRELAND.

WRITTEN ON THE RIVER HUDSON DURING THE SUMMER OF 1848.

I.

'Tis summer in the green woods closely growing
  In valley and on hill-side's steep,
Their shady awnings fringe the Hudson softly flowing
  O'er its sands to the engulfing deep.

II.

'Tis summer, and the brilliant birds are singing
  Songs of joy under Freedom's feckless sky,
And mirth and plenty round me luxuriantly are springing,
  But they neither glad my heart nor eye.

III.

What more, to me, is the golden summer glowing,
  Without you, than the murkiness of March ?
What, to me, is the Hudson grandly flowing

IV.

Were we two in yon boat upon its current,
    Then, indeed, it had been a stream divine;
Every ripple on its tide would bear an errand,
    Every rock along its shore be a shrine!

V.

Joy dwelleth not for man in the external—
    Pleasure cometh not to us from afar;
True love it is that makes the very desert vernal,
    And lights the deepest darkness like a star.

VI.

In vain the summer spills its spikenard round me,
    Skies brighten and flow'rs bloom for me in vain;
A parting and a memory hath so bound me,
    That I could bid the very birds refrain.

VII.

This surely is the noblest of new nations,
    And happy at their birth are its heirs;
But for me, I still turn to the isle of desolations,
    Where the joys I felt outcounted all the cares.

VIII.

'Tis summer in the woods where we together
    Have gather'd joy and garlands long ago—
The berries on the brier, the blossoms on the heather,
    The Wicklow streams are singing as they flow.

IX.

There Nature worketh wonders less gigantic—
    Man rears himself not there so sublime—
But still I would I were beyond the vast Atlantic,

I.

But God, who decrees our joys and trials,
　　Hath led us to this far new land—
Hath ordain'd for our good these self-denials,
　　Let us bow beneath his Fatherly hand !

ST. KEVIN'S BED.

I.

Dost thou remember the dark lake, dearest,
　　Where the sun never shines at noon ;
Dost thou remember the Saint's bed, dearest,
　　Carved in the hard, cold stone ?

II.

Dost thou remember the history, dearest,
　　Of the Saint of the churches, Kevin ?
Hard was his couch here, and desolate, dearest,
　　But his bed is now made in heaven.

III.

Dost thou remember the waterfall, dearest,
　　Furrowing the rocks so gray ?
So, through this stony scene the sainted one, dearest,
　　Channell'd out his onward way.

IV.

Out of the dark lake, saw ye not, dearest,
　　Issue the light, laughing river ?
So, from his cold couch, his soul went up, dearest,
　　Like a new star, to God's sky, forever.

V.

Oh ! never forget we the dark lake, dearest,
　　And the moral of tales told there ;
So may our souls meet the Saint's soul, dearest,

TO MARY IN IRELAND.

WRITTEN ON MAY EVE.

I.

MARY, Mary, are you straying
　In our olden haunts alone?
In the meadows are you Maying,
　Where the other flowers have blown?
In the green lanes are you roaming,
　Where we chantèd young Love's hymn?
Do you think you see me coming,
　Through the evening shadows dim?

II.

Do you think I'm happy, dearest,
　In the wondrous sights I see?
Ah! when my new friends are nearest,
　Happiness is far from me!
Two things have I loved supremely,—
　Two things that I cannot see—
Mother Ireland, fallen but queenly,
　Mother Ireland, Love, and thee.

III.

Oh, for one June day together,
　By the Ovoca's auburn tide!
Oh, to walk the empurpled heather,
　Mantling royal Lugduff's side!
On the mountain, still to heaven,
　Like its hermit, I could pray,[120]
All my days—if God had given

IV.

In the moonlight, groves that we know,
  Silent stand as sheetèd ghosts;
Where the fairies dance till cockcrow,
  Marshall'd in unbanished hosts.
If you look forth from your lattice,
  At the star that squires the moon,
Know the same star looketh at us,
  And shall see our union soon.

V.

Seas and storms may be between us—
  Anger and neglect are not—
Time, too, rolls his tide between us,
  Vainly to the unforgot.
For your dwelling I have builded
  Here, a home, my heart's delight;
Hope the eaves and panes hath gilded,
  Freedom makes the landscape bright.

VI.

Groves as stately fill the far-sight,
  Walks as silent tempt the feet;
Steering by the polar star-light,
  Night winds bear the fairy fleet;
Fraught with dews, and sweets, and voices,
  Bound for every open heart;
Mine, my love, almost rejoices—
  Would, if you were here for part.

VII.

Courage, never fear the ocean,
  Summer winds and summer skies,
Without clouds or wild commotion,

Love shall be your pilot, dearest,
  Over the charmèd summer sea;
Love, who a new home hath builded,
  In the West, for you and me.

A DEATH-SONG.

I.

Take me to your arms, belovèd,
  Before that I am dead—
Let me feel your warm hand at my heart,
  Your breast beneath my head;
For my very soul is gasping,
  And it fain would be away
In the far land, where the spirits dwell,
  For ever and for aye.

II.

The cold tear on my chilly cheek
  For this world is not shed—
But, to think how lonely you will be
  When I, belovèd, am dead.
I'm thinking of you, sad and lone,
  Here staying joylessly,
When I am cold as the white gravestone,
  Beneath the dripping tree.

III.

I little dream'd, belovèd,
  When you woo'd me long ago
In our own green land, I'd leave you

But, ah! my heart's delight, we'll meet
  Beneath the immortal hills,
Where falleth never snow or sleet,
  Where entereth not earth's ills.

IV.

Oh! hasten, darling, hasten,
  To follow after me,
For in heaven I will be desolate,
  Until rejoin'd by thee.
Now, take me to your arms, love,
  Before that I am dead—
Let me feel your warm hand at my heart,
  And your breast beneath my head;
For my very soul is gasping,
  And fain would be away
In the far land, where the spirits dwell,
  For ever and for aye.

LIVE FOR LOVE.

I.

I LIVE not alone for living—
  I woo not glory's prize,
The world, I hold, worth giving
  For one beam from beauty's eyes;
I never seek to clamber
  My brother men above—
I pay court in a lady's chamber,
  And reign in a lady's love.

II.

Of gold I am not chary,
  In death's dawn it melts away,
Like gifts of the night-trapp'd fairy,
  In the gray, grim break of day;

For power—all power is hollow—
  And like to it are they,
Who, the bloodless phantom follow,
  Turning from love away.

III.

Oh, call it not "idle passion,"
  Or, prostrate poet's dream—
Since Adam 't has been the fashion,
  Since Ossian 't has been the theme;
In this dear girl before me
  The sum of my hope is set—
The Past and the Present o'er me,
  Foes, future, and all, I forget.

IV.

Let others rule in the Senate,
  Let others lead in war;
And if they find pleasure in it,
  May it stand to them like a star;
But give me—a simple dwelling,
  Away from the crowd removed—
A bower by the waters welling,
  And you by my side, beloved.

THE EXILE.

I.

No more to bless my soul, shall rise
  The joys of by-gone years;
No more my unstrung harp replies
  To wordly hopes or fears.
In mirkest night is lost the star,
  Whose light my pathway led;
I am lonely, very lonely,

II.

No more along thy banks, sweet Foyle,
  My evening path shall lie;
No more my Mary's love-lit face
  Shall meet my longing eye.
All that could cheer my wayward soul,
  Like sunset tints hath fled;
I am lonely, very lonely,
  Oh! would that I were dead.

III.

Ah! when the pleasant spring time came,
  Like bride bedeck'd with flowers,
How blest, adown the hawthorn lane,
  We pass'd the twilight hours.
My Mary, Heaven had call'd you then,
  Its light was round you shed;
I am lonely, very lonely,
  Oh! would that I were dead.

IV.

Even then your words of love would blend
  With hopes of freedom's day,
And whisper thus—" No woman's love
  In slavish hearts should stay."
The while, the wild rose in your hair,
  Scarce match'd your cheek's pure red;
I am lonely, very lonely,
  Oh! would that I were dead.

V.

Oh! that my stubborn heart should live
  That dreadful moment through,
When those bleak robes I raised, to give

When there lay all my earthly joy,
  Array'd for death's cold bed;
I am lonely, very lonely,
  Oh! would that I were dead.

VI.

Yes, Mary dear, thy earnest wish
  Is all that wakes me now:
To haste the day, when slavery's blush
  Shall flee our country's brow;
To toil, to strive, till free she'll rise,
  Then lay with thee my head;
For I'm lonely, very lonely,
  And longing to be dead.

TO MARY'S ANGEL.

A VALENTINE.

I.

YE angels, to whom space is not,
  Who span the earth like light,
Keep watch and ward around the spot
  Where dwells my heart's delight;
And when my true love walks abroad,
  Spread roses in her path,
And let the winds, round her abode,
  Subdue their wail and wrath.

II.

Ye angels, ye were made to be
  To one another kind;
And she to whom I charge ye, see,

As gentle as soft strains, as wild
  As zephyrs in their youth,
As artless as a country child,
  The very word of truth.

III.

Ye guard the sailor far at sea,
  The hermit in his cell;
Yet they are less alone than she—
  Good angels, watch her well!
He who should be her guard and guide,
  Alas! is far away;
Ye spirits, leave not Mary's side,
  I charge ye, night or day!

LINES WRITTEN IN A LADY'S ALBUM.

TO MARY D.[*]

My gentle friend, your father's guest
Might not refuse your high behest,
Even though it were a sterner task
Your loveliness was pleased to ask.
If one who once was "reverend" [100] may
For his own special favorites pray,
Then heaven will hoard its blessings up
To pour them in your path and cup.

Daily and hourly on your head
The blessings of both worlds be shed!
May sorrow have no power to stay
Beneath your roof a second day!

[*] The accomplished daughter of an Irish lawyer of Philadelphia, now the estimable wife of a prominent New York physician.

May every weed, and woe, and thorn
Out of your destined path be torn !
May all for whose delight you live
Pay back the bliss you're born to give !

But if, like all earth's other flowers,
You, too, shall have your chilly hours,
May God sow stars thick through your night,
And make your morrow doubly bright !
May Love still wait, a faithful page,
Upon your grace from youth to age—
And may you crown the gifts of Love
With peace that cometh from above !

Oh ! how I wish that I were old,
That seventy years of beads I'd told—
That all my sins were quite forgiven,
So that I might be heard in heaven—
Ah ! then these blessings, one by one,
Should on your path of life be strown,
And neither earth nor fiends should rend
God's favors from you, gentle friend !

PHILADELPHIA, Nov. 26, 1848.

I LOVE THEE, MARY!

INTRODUCED IN AN IRISH LEGEND—THE EVIL GUEST

I.

I MAY reveal it to the night,
   Where lurks around no tattling fairy,
With only stars and streams in sight —

II.

Your smile to me is like the dawn
    New breaking on the trav'ller weary;
My heart is, bird-like, to it drawn—
    I love, I love thee, Mary!

III.

Your voice is like the August wind,
    That of rich perfume is not chary,
But leaves its sweetness long behind,
    As thou dost, lovely Mary!

IV.

Your step is like the sweet, sweet spring
    That treads the flowers with feet so airy,
And makes its green enchanted ring,
    As thou dost, where thou comest, Mary!

MEMENTO MORI.

I.

My darling, in the land of dreams, of wonder and delight,
I see you and sit by you, and woo you all the night,
Under trees that glow like diamonds upon my aching sight,
You are walking by my side in your wedding garments
        white.

II.

My darling, my Mary, through the long Summer's day,
Though many are the scenes I pass and devious be my way,
You follow me forever, and I cannot turn away—
Oh! who could turn from wife like mine in her wedding

III.

My darling girl, it is a year—a year and little more—
Since I took you in my arms from your happy mother's door,
I thought I loved you *then*—that I knew you long before,
But I know you ten times better now, and love you ten times
    more.

IV.

Yet 'tis not what the world calls " love," that for my love I
    feel,
'Tis pure as martyr's memory, and warm as convert's zeal,
'Tis a love that cannot be dispell'd by time, or chance, or
    steel,
'Tis eternal as my soul, and precious as its weal.

V.

Dear Mary, do not grieve if I am long away,
There is an added twilight hour joined to my life's long day,—
To rest with you in peace, may God grant me, I pray,
And to sleep beside you, darling, until the Judgment-day!

MEMORIES.

I LEFT two loves on a distant strand,
One young, and fond, and fair, and bland;
One fair, and old, and sadly grand—
My wedded wife and my native land.

One tarrieth sad and seriously
Beneath the roof that mine should be;
One sitteth sibyl-like by the sea,
Chanting a grave song mournfully.

A little life I have not seen
Lies by the heart that mine hath been;
A cypress wreath darkles now, I ween,

The mother and wife shall pass away,
Her hands be dust, her lips be clay;
But my other love on earth shall stay,
And live in the life of a better day.

Ere we were born my first love was,
My sires were heirs to her holy cause;
And she yet shall sit in the world's applause,
A mother of men and blessèd laws.

I hope and strive the while I sigh,
For I know my first love cannot die;
From the chain of woes that loom so high
Her reign shall reach to eternity.

HOME THOUGHTS.

If will had wings, how fast I'd flee
To the home of my heart o'er the seething sea!
If wishes were power, if words were spells,
I'd be this hour where my own love dwells.

My own love dwells in the storied land,
Where the holy wells sleep in yellow sand;
And the emerald lustre of Paradise beams
Over homes that cluster round singing streams.

I, sighing, alas! exist alone—
My youth is as grass on an unsunn'd stone,
Bright to the eye, but unfelt below—
As sunbeams that lie over Arctic snow.

My heart is a lamp that love must relight,
Or the world's fire-damp will quench it quite;
In the breast of my dear, my life-tide springs—
Oh! I'd tarry none here, if will had wings.

XI

AN INVITATION TO THE COUNTRY.

I.

Oh! come to the flower-fields, Mary,
  Where the trees and grass are green,
And the trace of Spring—the fairy!—
  Is in emerald circles seen.
For the stony-streeted city
  Is not fit for your tiny feet;
Oh! come, in love, or in pity,
  And visit my calm retreat.

II.

Was never so green a glade
  For human heart's desire—
Was never so sweet a shade,
  Since the fall, and the sword of fire.
The birds, of all plumage, here
  Are singing their lovingest song—
Oh! that she stood list'ning near
  For whom my lone heart longs!

III.

Fair Spring is the fond Earth's bride,
  That cometh all wreath'd in flowers;
And he laughs by his lady's side,
  And leads her through endless bowers.
My lady's the Spring to me,
  And her absence wintereth all—·
For others the hours may flee,
  On me like a mist they fall.

IV.

Oh! come to the flower-fields, Mary,
  Where the trees and grass are green,
And the trace of Spring—the fairy!—
  Is in emerald circles seen.
For the stony-streeted city
  Is not fit for your tiny feet;
Oh! come, in love, or in pity,
  And visit my calm retreat!

THE DEATH-BED.

I.

Up amid the Ulster mountains,
    Oh, my brother!
Where the heath-bells fringe the fountains,
    Oh, my brother!
Like a light through darkness beaming,
Like a well, in deserts streaming—
Like relief in dismal dreaming,
    I beheld her, oh, my brother!

II.

Hair like midnight, eyes like morning,
    Oh, my brother!
Breaking on me without warning,
    Oh, my brother!
Shooting forth fire so resistless,
That my heart is low and listless,
And my eyes of Earth are wistless,

III.

Daily, nightly, I've been pining,
    Oh, my brother!
For those eyes like morning shining,
    Oh, my brother!
And that voice! like music sighing
O'er the beds of minstrels dying,
'Twas a voice there is no flying,
    Oh, my brother!

IV.

Say not, hope—oh! rather listen,
    Oh, my brother!
When the evening dew-drops glisten,
    Oh, my brother!
On the grass above me growing,
Strew my grave with blossoms blowing,
Where that haunted fount is flowing,
    Oh, my brother!

V.

Where her feet did print the heather,
    Oh, my brother!
Grace and goodness grow together,
    Oh, my brother!
Even yon wither'd wreath doth move me,
Seems to say, she might have loved me—
Strew no other flowers above me,
    Oh, my brother!

MEMENTO MORI.

[To the memory of Nicholas S. Donnelly, of New York, who died of cholera
when on a visit at St. Louis, Mo., May 18, 1849.]

I.

He sought the South in his early prime,
   Ere half the worth of his heart was known,
While yet we thought—oh, how many a time!—
   By the light of his life to guide our own.

II.

He went where "the Father of Waters" rolls
   His united waves to the gulf of the sea—
Where the Pestilent Spirit was showering souls
   Into the lap of Eternity.

III.

Like a mower, it swept the tropical South
   Of mead, and flower, and fruit, and thorn;
The vested priest, with the prayer in his mouth,
   It took, and the infant newly born;

IV.

The bride at the altar it breathed upon,
   And the white flowers fell from her clammy brow;
And the hand the ring had been just placed on,
   Blacken'd, and fell like a blasted bough.

V.

But of all the pestilence gather'd in,
   The noblest heart and truest hand,
And the soul most free from stain of sin,
   Was thine, young guest of the southern land!

VI.

In him the fullness of manly sense,
  With the Christian's zeal, were finely blent;
While a tender, child-like innocence
  The charm of love to his friendship lent.

VII.

And he is dead, and pass'd away,
  And we have bow'd to the chast'ning rod;
In holy earth we have placed his clay;
  His soul rests on the breast of God.

VIII.

Yet still sometimes we think we hear
  His quick, firm step, and laughter shrill;
So fancy cheats the accustom'd ear,
  While the heart is bent to the Maker's will.

IX.

Rest, brother, rest in your early grave;
  Rest, dutiful son, our dearest, best—
In vain have we pray'd your life to save,
  But not in vain do we pray for your rest !

IN MEMORIAM.

TO THE MEMORY OF THE LATE LAMENTED BISHOP O'REILLY.

WRITTEN FOR THE EXHIBITION OF THE NEW HAVEN CATHOLIC SCHOOLS.

I.

SHALL the soldier who marches to battle require,
From the chief, his own time to advance and retire ?
The choice of the foe, or the choice of the field,

Then, how weak would his trust be, how faint his belief,
Who could barter for favors with Christ for his chief?
How unworthy to follow our Lord would he be
Who could fly from the tempest, or shrink from the sea!

II.

Oh! not such was *his* hope, as we saw him depart
On the work of his Master—not such was his heart—
His spirit was calm as the blue sky above—
For there dwelt the Lord of his life and his love;
No terrors for him whisper'd over the wave,
For he knew that the Master was mighty to save;
The ocean to him was secure as the land,
Since all things obey the Creator's command.

III.

How oft in the eve, o'er the sky-pointing spar,
His eye must have turn'd to the luminous star;
"'Tis the star of the sea!" he would say, as he pray'd
To Mary our Mother for comfort and aid.
In the last fatal hour, when no succor was nigh,
How blest was his lot, with such helper on high!
When the sordid grew lavish, the brave pale with fear,
How happy for him, our dear Mother was near!

IV.

Where the good ship hath perish'd, or how it befell,
No man that beheld it, is living to tell—
All is darkness, all doubt, on the sea, on the shore,
But we know we shall see our dear father no more.
Ye cold capes of Greenland, oh! heard you the sound?
The shout of the swimmer, the shriek of the drown'd?
Ye vapors that curtain Newfoundland's dark coast,
Have you tidings for us, of our father that's lost?

V.

We may question in vain; still respondeth the Power
Almighty,—" Man knows not the day nor the hour,
He was Mine, and I took him—why question ye Me,
On the secrets I hide in My breast, like the sea—
Oh, ye children of faith! why bewail ye the just?
That I have the spirit, and you, *not* the dust!
The dust—what avails where the righteous may sleep,
In the glades of the earth, or the glens of the deep?

VI.

" When the trumpet shall sound, and the angel shall call,
To the place of My presence, the centuries all—
The dust of the war-field shall rise in its might,
Embattled to stand or to fall in My sight,
And the waves shall be hid by the hosts they give forth,
From the sands of the South to the snows of the North,
And ye too shall be there!—there with him you deplore,
To be Mine, if ye will it, when Time is NO MORE!"

CEAD MILLE FAILTHE, O'MEAGHER!

I.

As from dawn in the morning,
    As relief comes through tears,
Beyond hope, beyond warning
    Our lost star appears.
Lo! where it shines out,
    Our long-loved and wept star,
Hark! hark to the shout—
    *Cead mille failthe, O'Meagher !**

II.

In the *melée* of duty
  Your young light was lost,
To the sad eyes of beauty
  What vigils you cost !
On the bronze cheeks of men,
  Where each tear leaves a scar,
There was trace of you then—
  Cead mille failthe, O'Meagher !

III.

The fond spell is broken,
  The bonds are all broke,
As of old, God hath spoken,
  You walk'd from the yoke !
May the guidance that passeth
  All eloquence far,
Be thine through the future,
  Cead mille failthe, O'Meagher !

A MONODY ON THE DEATH OF GERALD GRIFFIN,

Author of " The Collegians," " Gysippus," etc.   Died at Cork, June 12, 1840.

WHEN night surrounds the sun, and the day dies,
Leaving to darkness for its hour the skies,
Nought has the heart of man thence to deplore—
The day lived long, was fruitful, is no more;
But when the hurricane at noon o'erspreads
The orb divine, which life and gladness sheds,
Or some disorder'd planet rolls between
The sun and earth, darkling the verdant green,
Eclipsing ocean, shadowing like a pall
The busy town,—men, discontented all,

By sea and land, anxiously pause and pray
For the returning giver of the day—
So have bright spirits been eclipsed and lost,
Forever dark, if by Death's shadow cross'd.

In Munster's beauteous city died a man
As 'twere but yesterday, whose course began
In clouded and in cheerless morning guise—
Had climb'd the summit of his native skies,
And, as he rose, brighter and fairer grew,
Beneath his influence, every scene he knew.
His country hail'd him as a Saviour, given
To chronicle past times; when 'mid the heaven
Of expectation and achievement, lo!
A monastery's gate,—therein the Bard doth go,
And sees the children of the poor around
Feed on the knowledge elsewhere yet unfound.
The Poet then, his former tasks foreswore,
Vowing himself to charity evermore,—
Folded his wings of light—cast his fresh bays aside—
His friends beloved abjured, abjured his pride,
There lived and labor'd, and there early died.

Short was his day of labor, but its morn
Prolific was of beauty; thoughts were born
In his heart's secret spots, which grew, attended
By a fine sense—instinct and reason blended—
Till, like a spring, they spread his haunts with glory,
O'er-arch'd their streams, upraised their hills in story,
Fixed the broad Shannon in its course forever,
And bade it flow for aye, a genius-haunted river.

Ye men of Munster, guard his sleep serene!

But once in generations.   He was an echo, dwelling
Amid your mountains, all their secrets telling,
Their mem'ries, their traditions, and their wrongs,
The story of their sins—the music of their songs,
Their tempests, and their terrors, and the forms
They bring forth, impregnated by the storms.
He knew the voices of your rivers, knew
Every deep chasm they leap or murmur through,—
Blindfold, at midnight, by their sounds could tell
Their names and their descent o'er cliff and dell.
Oh! men of Munster, since the ancient time,
Ye have not met such loss as in this monk sublime!

The second summer's grass was on his grave,
When to his memory Melpomene gave
A laurel wreath wove from the self-same tree
That shades Boccaccio's dust perennially;
Fair were the smiles her mournful glances met
In woman's lovely eyes, with heart's-dew wet,
And many voices loudly cried, " Well done!"
As the sad goddess crown'd her lifeless son.
Oh, ever thus: Death strikes the gifted, then
Come the worms—inquests—and the award of men!

Low in your grave, young Gerald Griffin, sleep;
You never look'd on him who now doth weep
Above your resting-place—you never heard
The voice that oft has echo'd every word
Dropp'd from your pen of light—sleep on, sleep on—
I would I knew you, yet not now you are gone!

Written during the Author's visit to Ireland, in March, 1855.

CONSOLATION.

I.

MEN seek for treasure in the earth;
 Where I have buried mine,
There never mortal eye shall pierce,
 Nor star nor lamp shall shine!
We know, my love, oh! well we know,
 The secret treasure-spot,
Yet must our tears forever fall,
 Because that *they* are not.

II.

How gladly would we give to light
 The ivory forehead fair—
The eye of heavenly-beaming blue,
 The clust'ring chestnut hair—
Yet look around this mournful scene
 Of daily earthly life,
And could you wish them back to share
 Its sorrow and its strife?

III.

If blessèd angels stray to earth,
 And seek in vain a shrine,
They needs must back return again
 Unto their source divine:
All life obeys the unchanging law
 Of Him who took and gave,
We count a glorious saint in heaven

IV.

Look up, my love, look up, afar,
   And dry each bitter tear,
Behold, three white-robed innocents
   At heaven's high gate appear!
For you and me and those we love,
   They smilingly await—
God grant we may be fit to join
   Those Angels of the Gate.

MARY'S HEART.

I.

I KNOW one spot where springs a tide
   Of feeling pure as ever ran,
The path of destiny beside,
   To bless and soothe the heart of man.
By night and noon, be't dark or bright,
   That fountain plays its blessèd part; .
And heaven looks happy at the sight
   Of Mary's heart! of Mary's heart!

II.

There's wealth, they say, in foreign climes,
   And fame for those who dare aspire,
And who that does not sigh betimes
   For something better, nobler, higher?
But here is all—a golden mine,
   A sea unsail'd, a tempting chart;
These, all these may be, nay, *are* mine—
   The wide, warm world of Mary's heart!

III.

Blow as ye will, ye winds of fate,
   And let life's trials blackly lower;
I know the garden and the gate,
   Ye cannot strip my roseate bower.
That safe retreat I still can keep,
   Despite of envy's venom'd dart;
Despite of all life's storms, can sleep
   Securely lodged in Mary's heart!

IN MEMORIAM.

RICHARD DALTON WILLIAMS.
DIED AT THIBODEAUX, LA., JULY 5, 1862, AGED 40.

I.

THE early mower, heart-deep in the corn,
   Falls suddenly, to rise on earth no more—
The lark he startled carols to the morn,
   The field flowers blossom brightly as before—
Gay laughs the milkmaid to the shouting swain,
Who calls the dead afar, but calls in vain.

II.

Thus in the world's wide harvest-field doth life,
   Unconscious of the stricken heart, rejoice—
Thus through the city's thousand tones of strife
   The true friend misses but the single voice—
Thus, while the tale of death fills every mouth,
For us there is but one, fallen in the South!

III.

One that amid far other scenes and years
   Leal mem'ry still recalls full to our view,
Ere life as yet had reached the time of tears

Blithe was his jest in those fraternal days,
Before we reach'd the parting of the ways.

IV.

They were a band of brethren, richly graced
   With all that most exalts the sons of men—
Youth, courage, honor, genius, wit, well-placed—
   When shall we see their parallels again ?
The very flower and fruitage of their age,
Destined for duty's cross or glory's page.

V.

And he, our latest lost among them all,
   No rival had for strangely-blended powers—
All shapes of beauty waited at his call ;
   Soft Pity wept o'er Misery in showers,
Or honest Laughter, leaping from the heart,
Peal'd her wild note beyond the reach of Art.

VI.

Out of that nature, mingled to the sun,
   Sprang fount and flower, the saving and the sweet ;
The gleesome children to his knee would run,
   The helpless brute would twine about his feet
For he was nature's heir, and all her host
Knew their liege lord in him—our latest lost !

VII.

Meekly o'er all, the rare and priceless crown
   Of gentle, silent Pity he still wore—
Like some fair chapel in the midmost town,
   His busy heart was wholly at the core ;
Deep there his virtues lay—no eye could trace
The Pharisee's prospectus in his face.

VIII.

Sleep well, O Bard! too early from the field
    Of labor and of honor call'd away ;
Sleep, like a hero, on your own good shield,
    Beneath the Shamrock,* wreath'd about the bay.
Not doubtful is thy place among the host
Whom fame and Erin love and mourn the most.

IX.

While leap on high, Ben Heder, the wild waves ;
    While sweep the winds through storied Aherlow ;
While Sidney's victims from their troubled graves
    O'er Mullaghmast, at midnight, come and go ;
While Mercy's sisters kneel by Mercy's bed—
Thou art not dead, O Bard! thou art not dead!

X.

War's ruffian blast for very shame must cease,
    And Nature, pitiful, will clothe its graves—
And then, true lover of God's blessed peace,
    When earth has swallow'd up her vaunting braves,
Thy gentle star shall shine along
The path of ages, solaced by thy song.

WORDS OF WELCOME.

TO MRS. S———, ON REVISITING MONTREAL.

THE leaves of October are wither'd and dead,
All our autumn's brief honors have faded or fled,
But this season the saddest, our brightest shall be,
For there's sunshine and gladness in welcoming thee !
We heed not how darkly the evening may lower,
Round yon mountain, surcharged with the tempest or
    shower,

O'er the light in our breasts there's no shadow of grief,
From the tree of our friendship there falls not a leaf.

Your voice brings the perfume and promise of spring,
And we strive to forget 'tis a voice on the wing,
For never was May-time to poets more dear,
Than these days of October since you have been here ;
If evening falls swiftly it lengthens the night,
While with music and legend we burnish it bright,
The sole pang of sorrow our bosoms can know,
Is how lately you came, and how soon you must go.

Alas ! for this stern life, how far and how few
Are the friends we can honor and cherish like you !
Yet that rivers and realms so cold and so wide,
Such friends from each other long years should divide !
But a truce to reflection, a *congé* to care,
This weather within doors is joyously fair,
Here's a toast ! fill it up ! let us drink it like men :
" May we soon see our dear guest among us again !

MONTREAL, October 25, 1861.

TO A FRIEND IN AUSTRALIA.[*]

OLD friend ! though distant far,
  Your image nightly shines upon my soul ;
I yearn toward it as toward a star
  That points through darkness to the ancient pole.

Out of my heart the longing wishes fly,
  As to some rapt Elias, Enoch, Seth ;
Yours is another earth, another sky,
  And I—I feel that distance is like death.

[*] Charles Gavin Duffy.

Oh ! for one week amid the emerald fields,
    Where the Avoca sings the song of Moore;
Oh ! for the odor the brown heather yields,
    To glad the pilgrim's heart on Glenmalur !

Yet is there still what meeting could not give,
    A joy most suited of all joys to last;
For, ever in fair memory there must live
    The bright, unclouded picture of the past.

Old friend ! the years wear on, and many cares
    And many sorrows both of us have known;
Time for us both a quiet couch prepares—
    A couch like Jacob's, pillow'd with a stone.

And oh ! when thus we sleep may we behold
    The angelic ladder of the Patriarch's dream;
And may my feet upon its rungs of gold
    Yours follow, as of old, by hill and stream !

A DREAM OF YOUTH.

I.

When the summer evening fadeth from golden into gray,
    And night, dark night, sets his watch upon the hill,
A gentle shadow standeth in my secret path alway,
    And whispereth to my heart its fond words still.

II.

When the fleeing of the shadows foretells the coming light,
    And morn, merry morn, winds her horn on the hill,
There glideth by my bed the shadow of the night,
    Whispering to my heart its fond words still.

III.

And dearer far to me is that shadow and that dream,
    Than all the grosser joys our daily life can give;
'Tis a lesson—and a blessing, far more than it doth seem,—
    It will teach me how to die, as it teaches me to live.

IV.

'Tis the memory of my youth, when my soul was free from
        stain,
    The memory of days spent at my mother's knee;
'Tis the language of my youth that thus speaks to me again—
    Dear dream, do not desert me; dear shadow, do not flee

WILLIAM SMITH O'BRIEN.

I.

Thus we repeat the wretched past,
        Thus press to give
Our offerings at the tomb at last,
        Forget—forgive—
All that was warring, erring, lost,
        In those who now
Can lift no more among our host,
        Or voice, or brow!

II.

Two nations in our land are found:
        One lowly laid—
A host, an audience under ground,
        Sons of the shade;
And one a noisy, driftless throng,
        Heroes of the day—
Who chorus still the spendthrift's song,

III.

Now with the dead, the just, the true,
    Let our thoughts be—
To them the tribute long time due
    Give willingly;
And when ye name the names who most
    Deserve our praise,
Was there his peer in Erin's host
    In latter days?

IV.

Behold the man! ye knew him well,
    Erect, austere—
Whose mind was as an hermit's cell,
    Whence purpose clear
Sprang headlong, thoughtless for its source,
    A self-will'd stream,
Embower'd on all its onward course
    By dream on dream!

V.

Pride, cold as in the stiff-ribb'd rock,
    Was in his mould,
And courage, which withstood the shock
    Of trials manifold;
And tenderness unto the few he loved,
    His all in all—
And fortitude in fiery furnace proved
    At honor's call.

VI.

But over these—friend, lover, patriot, seer,
    Let us proclaim,
His name to Erin ever shall be dear,

Justice—o'er all—the saving salt of earth,
    He still pursued—
Justice, the world's regenerate second birth,
    Its holy rood!

VII.

Sleep, pilgrim, sleep, beneath that blessèd sign
    Whose saving shade
Shadows for man the mystic sun divine,
    For whom 'twas made;
Sleep, stainless of a Christian land,
    Whose arts—all just—
Thy witnesses before the judgment stand,
    So let us trust!

THE DEAD ANTIQUARY, O'DONOVAN.

FAR are the Gaelic tribes, and wide
Scatter'd round earth on every side
    For good or ill;
They aim at all things, rise or fall,
Succeed or perish—but through all
    Love Erin still.

Although a righteous Heaven decrees
'Twixt us and Erin stormy seas
    And barriers strong,
Of care, and circumstance, and cost,
Yet count not all your absent lost,
    Oh, land of song!

Above your roofs no star can rise
That does not lighten in our eyes,
    Nor any set

That ever shed a cheering beam
On Irish hillside, street, or stream,
    That we forget.

No artist wins a shining fame,
Lifting aloft his nation's name
    High over all;
No soldier falls, no poet dies,
But underneath all foreign skies
    We mourn his fall!

And thus it comes that even I,
Though weakly and unworthily,
    Am moved by grief
To join the melancholy throng,
And chant the sad entombing song
    Above the chief—

The foremost of the immortal band
Who vow'd their lives to fatherland;
    Whose works remain
To attest how constant, how sublime
The warfare was they waged with time;
    How great the gain!

I would not do the dead such wrong;
If graves could yield a growth of song
    Like flowers of May,
Then Mangan from the tomb might raise
One of his old resurgent lays—
    But, well-a-day,

He, close beside his early friend,
By the stark shepherd safely penn'd,

So his wierd numbers never more
The sorrow of the isle shall pour
    In tones of might!

Tho' haply still by Liffey's side
That mighty master must abide
    Who voiced our grief
O'er Davis lost;* and him who gave
His free frank tribute at the grave
    Of Erin's chief;†

Yet must it not be said that we
Failed in the rites of minstrelsie,
    So dear to souls
Like his whom lately death hath ta'en,
Although the vast Atlantic main
    Between us rolls!

Too few, too few among our great,
In camp or cloister, Church or State,
    Wrought as he wrought;
Too few of all the brave we trace
Among the champions of our race.

His fortress was a nation wreck'd,
His foes were falsehood, hate, neglect,
    His comrades few;
His arsenal was weapon-bare,
His flag-staff splinter'd in the air,
    Where nothing flew!

Had Sarsfield on Saint Mary's Tower
More sense of weakness or of power,
    More cause to fear

* Samuel Ferguson.
† Denis Florence McCarthy, whose poem on the death of O'Connell was one

Weak walls, strong foes, the odds of fate,
Than had our friend, more fortunate,
    The victor here?

Far through the morning mists he saw
Up to what heights of dizzy awe
    His pathway led;
A-bye what false Calypso caves,
Amid what roar of angry waves,
    His sail to spread!

On, on he press'd, from rise of sun
Until his early day was done,
    Strong in the truth;
As dear to friends, as meek with foes
At evening's wearied sudden close
    As in his youth.

He toiled to make our story stand
As from Time's reverent, runic hand
    It came, undeck'd
By fancies false, erect, alone,
The monumental arctic stone
    Of ages wreck'd.

Truth was his solitary test,
His star, his chart, his east, his west;
    Nor is there aught
In text, in ocean, or in mine,
By chemist, seaman, or divine,
    More fondly sought.

Not even our loved Apostle's name
Could stand on ground of fabled fame

But never sceptic more sincere
Labored to dissipate the fear
        That good men feel;

The pious but unfounded fear
That reason, in her high career
        Too much might dare;
Some sacred legend, some renown
Should overturn or trample down
        Beyond repair.

With gentle hand he rectified
The errors of old bardic pride,
        And set aright
The story of our devious past,
And left it, as it now must last,
        Full in the light!

Beneath his hand we saw restored
The tributes of the royal hoard,
        The dues appraised
On every prince, and how repaid;
The order kept, the boundaries made,
        The rites obey'd.*

All tribes and customs, in our view,
He had the art to raise anew
        On their own ground;
But chief, the long Hy Nial line,
We saw ascend, prevail, decline
        O'er Tara's mound.

The throne of Cashel, too, he raised—
High on the rock its glory blazed,
        And, by its light,

The double dynasty we saw
Decreed by Olliol Ollum's law,
        Emerge from night.

Happy the life our scholar led
Among the living and the dead—
        Loving—beloved.—
Mid precious tomes, and gentle looks,
The best of men and best of books,
        He daily moved.

Kings that were dead two thousand years,
Cross-bearing chiefs and pagan seers,
        He knew them all;
And bards, whose very harps were dust,
And saints, whose souls are with the just,
        Came at his call.

For him the school refill'd the glen,
The green rath bore its fort again,
        The Druid fled;
Saint Kieran's *coarb* wrought and wrote,
Saint Brendan launch'd his daring boat,
        And westward sped!

For him around Iona's shore
Cowl'd monks, like sea-birds, by the score,
        Were on the wing,
For North or South, to take their way
Where God's appointed errand lay,
        To clown or king.

He marshall'd Brian on the plain,
Sail'd in the galleys of the Dane—
        Earl Richard, too,

Fell Norman as he was, and fierce—
Of him and his he dared rehearse
        The story true.

O'er all low limits still his mind
Soar'd Catholic and unconfined,
        From malice free;
On Irish soil he only saw
One state, one people, and one law,
        One destiny!

Spirit of Justice!   Thou most dread
Author divine, whose Book hath said—
        The just man's seed
Shall never fail for lack of bread,
Oh, let the flock his labor fed,
        Thy mercy feed!

Inspire, oh Lord! with bounteous hand,
The magnates of the Irish land,
        That, being so moved,
As fathers of the fatherless,
They shield from danger and distress
        His well-beloved.

And teach us, Father, who remain
Filial dependents on that brain
        So deeply wrought;
Teach us to travel day by day
By honest paths, seeking alway
        The ends he sought!

MONTREAL, January, 1862.

SURSUM CORDA.

["Those, however, who are aware of the crushing succession of domestic afflictions and of bodily infirmities with which it has pleased Providence to visit me during the last three years, will, I am sure, look with indulgent eyes on these defects, as well as on those concerning which I have already confessed and asked pardon."—*Mr. O'Curry's Preface to his "Lectures on the MS. Materials of Ancient Irish History."*]

HEALTH and comfort! may thy sorrow
   Pass as lifts the mournful night,
Bringing in the calm to-morrow,
   Thoughtful, dutiful, yet bright—
Though the new-made graves should thicken,
   Though the empty chairs increase—
Still the wakeful soul must quicken,
   Still through labor seek for peace.

If, oh friend! in all our forest,
   Healing grew on herb or tree
For the wound that grieves thee sorest,
   Surely I would send it thee!
But the healing branch hangs nearer,
   By thy seldom-idle hand,
Draws the magic—all the dearer—
   From the core of fatherland.

That which made thy youthful vision,
   That which made thy manhood's goal—
Over coldness, toil, derision,
   Bore thee, heart and fancy whole;
That which was thy first ambition
   In the early, anxious past,
By the Almighty's just provision,
   Is thy stay and strength at last.

Turn for solace to those pages
  Where your hived-up lore we read,
To that company of sages
  Who for you have lived indeed;
Think of him who strove to smother
  In his books a noble's grief;
Think of the poor footsore brother
  Of the Masters Four the chief!

Think what life the *scald* of Lecan
  Led, through evil penal days,
Let his gentle spirit beckon
  Yours to render greater praise.
Sad must be your fireside, only
  Sadder was the wayside inn
Where he perish'd, old and lonely,
  By the Letcher of Dunflin!

All who honor Erin, honor
  You with her, beloved friend!
Blessings we invoke upon her,
  Without limit, without end;
Blessings of all saints in glory,
  We invoke for him who drew
Old Egyptian seeds of story
  From the grave, to bloom anew!

Sursum Corda! with the Masters
  Whom you love, your place must be,
There no changes, no disasters,
  Ever can imperil you!
Happy age! unstain'd, untarnish'd
  By one blot of blame or shame,
Happy age! protected, garnish'd,
  With a patriot-scholar's fame!

EUGENE O'CURRY.

WE listen to each wind that blows
   The white ship to our yearning shore;
We tremble—as if secret foes,
   Or alien plagues, it wafted o'er.
Instinct with fear, we seize upon
   The record of the latest lost,
To find some friend forever gone,
   Some hope we held forever cross'd.

Oh wretched world! who would grow old—
   Outlive the loving, generous, just—
See friendship's fervid heart all cold,
   Laid low and pulseless in the dust!
Who would ordain himself, in age,
   To be of all he loved, the heir,—
To linger on the starless stage,
   With all life's company elsewhere?

Give me again my harp of yew,
   In consecrated soil 'twas grown—
Shut out the day-star from my view,
   And leave me with the night alone!
The children of this modern land
   May deem our ancient custom vain;
But aye responsive to my hand,
   The harp must pour the funeral strain.

It was, of old, a sacred rite,
   A debt of honor freely paid
To champions fallen in the fight,

Alas! that rite should now be claim'd,
　O world! for one we least can spare;
Whose name by us was never named
　Without its meed of praise or prayer!

An *Ollamh* of the elect of old,
　Whose chairs were placed beside the king,
Whose hounds, whose herds, whose gifts of gold,
　The later bards regretful sing;
Ay! there was magic in his speech,
　And in his wand the power to save,[130]
This sole recorder on the beach
　Of all we've lost beneath the wave.

Who are his mourners? by the hearth
　His presence kindled, sad they sit,—
They dwell throughout the living earth,
　In homes his presence never lit;
Where'er a Gaelic brother dwells,
　There heaven has heard for him a prayer—
Where'er an Irish maiden tells
　Her votive beads, his soul has share.

Where, far or near, or west or east,
　Glistens the *soggarth's** sacred stole,
There, from the true, unprompted priest,
　Shall rise a requiem for his soul.
Such orisons like clouds shall rise
　From every realm beneath the sun,
For where are now the shores or skies
　The Irish *soggarth* has not won?

Oh! mortal tears will dry like rain,
　And mortal sighs pass like the breeze,
And earthly prayers are often vain,
　E'en breathed amid the Mysteries;

Happy, alone, we hold the man
  Whose steps so righteously were trod,
That, ere the judgment-act began,
  Had suppliants in the Saints of God.

Arise, ye cloud-borne saints of old,
  In number like the polar flock—
Arise, ye just, whose tale is told
  On Shannon's side and Arran's rock,
In number like the waves of seas,
  In glory like the stars of night—
Arise, ambrosial-laden bees
  That banquet through heaven's fields of light!

This mortal, call'd to join your choir,
  Through every care, and every grief,
Sought, with an antique soul of fire,
  O'er all, God's glory, first and chief.
And next he sought, oh, sacred band!
  Ye disinherited of heaven,
To give you back your native land,
  To give it as it first was given!

No more the widow'd glen repines,
  No more the ruin'd cloister groans,
Back on the tides have come the shrines,
  Lo! we have heard the speech of stones;
In the mid-watch when darkness reign'd,
  And sleepers slept, unseen his toil—
But heaven kept count of all he gain'd
  For ye, lords of the Holy Isle!

Plead for him, oh ye exiled saints!
  Ye outcasts of the iron time!
He heard on earth your mute complaints,

If venial error still attaints
  His spirit wrapt in penal fire,
Plead for him, all ye pitying saints,
  And bear him to your blessèd choir!

Let those who love, and lose him most,
  In their great sorrow comfort find;
Remembering how heaven's mighty host
  Were ever present to his mind;
Descending on his grave at even
  May they the radiant phalanx see—
Such wondrous sight as once was given,
  In vision, to the rapt Culdee![131]

May Angus of the festal lays,
  And Marian of the Apostle's hill,[132]
And Tiernan of the Danish days,[133]
  And Adamnan and Columb-kill,
Befriend his soul in every strait,
  Recite some good 'gainst every sin,
Unfold at last the happy gate,
  And lead their scribe and *Ollamh* in!

WISHES.

ADDRESSED TO MRS. J. S——.

I.

WHAT shall we wish the friends we love,
  To wish them well?
That fortune ever may propitious prove,
  And honor bear the bell?
Or that the chast'ning hand of grief,
  If come it must,
May spare the stem, while scattering the leaf
  Low in the dust!

II.

Then let us wish our lov'd—the youthful zest—
    To wish them well—
That laughs with childhood, gladdens for the guest—
    That loves to tell,
With brow unshamed, the story of its youth,
    Its simple tale—
Proving a life well spent, leads on, in sooth,
    To old age, green and hale !

III.

This life we lead in outward acts, 'tis known
    Is ill contained—
By heart and hand, not equipage alone—
    Our goals are gained ;
Trappings and harness made for passing show,
    Are little worth,
When halts the hearse, where all things human go,
    With earth—to earth !

TO MR. KENNEDY, THE SCOTTISH MINSTREL,

ON HIS REVISITING MONTREAL.

I.

Full often we ponder'd, as distant you wander'd,
  If friends rose around you like light on the lea—
Earth's fragrance unsealing, fair prospects revealing,
  With welcome as loyal as wishes were free.

II.

For the songs you had sung us were never forgotten,
  And your name among all our rejoicings would blend ;
Nor was it the Minstrel alone was remembered,

III.

May the promise of spring, and the fullness of summer,
    The burthen of many an old Scottish song,
Be before you wherever your duty may call you,
    And the fruits of your harvest remain with you long.

IV.

And when for repose in some hour you are sighing—
    For even a Minstrel must pause in his strain—
To one point in the north, like the needle returning,
    May the magnet of friendship here have you remain!

IN MEMORIAM.

[Mary Ann Devaney, a child of twelve years, daughter of the author's
friend, Mr. L. Devaney of Montreal, lost her life while endeavoring to save two
of her playmates who had been skating on the Welland Canal, at St. Catherine's,
C. W., on Thursday, March 3, 1864.]

Lost, lost to us on earth, O daughter dearest!
    Torn, as by a whirlwind, swift away;
Little we know, when morning's skies are clearest,
    What tempests may engulf the closing day!

Who would have dreamt, as, down to that sad water,
    They met thee passing, buoyant as a bird,
They'd see no more thy face, O angel daughter!
    They'd hear no more the gentle voice they heard!

Mary, "a tear" is said to be in Hebrew;
    Ah! many a tear thy death to us hath cost!
But if all little maidens grew as she grew,

No turf enwraps her, and no tomb incloses*
  The mortal frame, but far in other spheres
Our little maiden gathers Heaven's bright roses,
  Whose roots still widen, fed by human tears.

Sorrow is mighty, but a mightier spirit
  Descends upon the household of the just,
Saying—" Pray to God, that dying, you inherit
  Her life of life, beyond the *dust to dust!* "

THE PRIEST OF PERTH.†

* (Requiescat in pace.   Amen.)

A PRAYER FOR THE SOUL OF THE PRIEST OF PERTH.

I.

WE who sat at his cheerful hearth,
Know the wisdom rare, of priceless worth
He bears away from the face of the earth;
    Peace to the soul of the Priest of Perth!

II.

Dead ! and his sun of life so high !
Dead ! with no cloud in all his sky !
Dead ! and it seems but yesterday
When happy and hopeful he sail'd away,
As Priest and Celt, to his double home,
For Westport bay, and Eternal Rome;
    Ashes to ashes ! earth to earth !
    God rest the soul of the Priest of Perth !

* The child's body was not recovered until the ice melted in the spring.
† The Very Reverend JOHN H. MCDONAGH, of Perth, C. W.; Vicar-General of
the Diœcese of Kingston.

III.

Yet there was a sign in his gracious sky,
Up where the Cross he lifted high,
Glow'd in the morn and evening light,
Kiss'd by the reverent moon at night—
Glow'd through the vista'd northern pines,
" That's Perth, where the Cross so brightly shines."
Many will say, as many have said,
Bearing true tribute to the dead—
 Ashes to ashes! earth to earth!
 Rest to the soul of the Priest of Perth !

IV.

And there was the home he loved to make
So dear, for friend and kinsman's sake ;
Oh, many a day, and many a year
Will come for his mourners far and near,
But never a friend more true or dear.
Many a wreath of Canadian snow
Will hide the gardens and gates we know;
And many a spring will deck again
 His trees in all their leafy glory,
But none shall ever bring back for men
 The smile, the song, the sinless story;
The holy zeal that still presided,
Which none encounter'd and derided—
That yielded not one fast or feast,
One right or rubric of the priest;
 Ashes to ashes! earth to earth!
 Peace to the soul of the Priest of Perth !

V.

A golden Priest, of the good old school,
Fearless, and prompt, to lead and rule;

Freed of every taint of pride,
But ready, aye ready, to chide or guide;
Tenderly binding the bruisèd heart,
Sparing no sin its penal smart;
His will was as the granite rock
To the prowler menacing his flock;
But never lichen or wild-flower grew
On rocky ground, more fair to view
Than his charity was to all he knew;
Laying the outlines deep and broad
Of an infant church, he daily trod
His path in the visible sight of God;
  Ashes to ashes! earth to earth!
  Peace to the soul of the Priest of Perth!

VI.

O Saints of God! ye who await
Your beloved by the Beautiful Gate!
Ye Saints who people his native shore—
Beloved Saint John, whose name he bore—
And ye, Apostles! unto whom
He pray'd, a pilgrim, by your tomb—
And thou! O Queen of Heaven and Earth!
Receive—receive—the Priest of Perth!

EDWARD WHELAN.

DIED DECEMBER 10, 1867, AGED 43.

I.

By this dread line of light,
Rises upon my sight,
Borne up the churchyard white,
  The dead!—'mid the bearers:

Sharply the cold clods rung—
Silent for aye that tongue
On which delighted hung
    Myriads of hearers!

II.

Still, still, oh hopeful heart!
Cold as the clod, thou art,
All, save the Saviour's part,
    All that was mortal;
Rest for the teeming brain,
Rest besought not in vain,
When into God's domain
    Open'd life's portal!

III.

Well for thee in this hour,
That in thy mood of power,
    Truth was still nearest;
Better than babbling fame
That clear unspotted name,
Honor's perennial claim,
    Left to thy dearest!

IV.

Long may the island home*
Look for thy like to come—
    Few may she ever
Find more deserving trust,
Freer from thoughts unjust,
Than this heart—in the dust
    At rest—and forever!

* Newfoundland, which island Mr. Whelan represented in an official delegation to Canada only a few months before his lamented death.—ED.

REQUIEM ÆTERNAM.[*]

LAWRENCE DEVANEY, DIED MARCH 3, 1808.

I.

SAINT VICTOR'S DAY, a day of woe,
The bier that bore our dead went slow
And silent, sliding o'er the snow—
    Miserere, Domine !

II.

With Villa Maria's faithful dead,
Among the just we made his bed,
The cross he loved, to shield his head—
    Miserere, Domine !

III.

The skies may lower, wild storms may rave
Above our comrade's mountain grave,
That cross is mighty still to save—
    Miserere, Domine !

IV.

Deaf to the calls of love and care,
He bears no more his mortal share,
Nought can avail him now but prayer—
    Miserere, Domine !

V.

To such a heart who could refuse
Just payment of all burial dues,
Of Holy Church the rite and use ?—
    Miserere, Domine !

[*] Just one month after this poem was written, the author met his de
the assassin's hand.

VI.

Right solemnly the Mass was said,
While burn'd the tapers round the dead,
And manly tears like rain were shed—
Miserere, Domine!

VII.

No more Saint Patrick's aisles prolong
The burden of his funeral song,
His noiseless night must now be long—
Miserere, Domine!

VIII.

Up from the depths we heard arise
A prayer of pity to the skies,
To him who dooms, or justifies—
Miserere, Domine!

IX.

Down from the skies we heard descend
The promises the Psalmist penn'd,
The benedictions without end—
Miserere, Domine!

X.

Mighty our Holy Church's will
To shield her parting souls from ill;
Jealous of Death, she guards them still—
Miserere, Domine!

XI.

The dearest friend will turn away,
And leave the clay to keep the clay;
Ever and ever she will stay—
Miserere, Domine!

XII.

When for us sinners, at our need,
That mother's voice is raised to plead,
The frontier hosts of heaven take heed—
  Miserere, Domine!

XIII.

Mother of Love! Mother of Fear!
And holy Hope, and Wisdom dear,
Behold we bring thy suppliant here—
  Miserere, Domine!

XIV.

His flaming heart is still for aye,
That held fast by thy clemency,
Oh! look on him with loving eye—
  Miserere, Domine!

XV.

His Faith was as the tested gold,
His Hope assured, not overbold,
His Charities past count, untold—
  Miserere, Domine!

XVI.

Well may they grieve who laid him there,
Where shall they find his equal—where?
Nought can avail him now but prayer—
  Miserere, Domine!

XVII.

Friend of my soul, farewell to thee!
Thy truth, thy trust, thy chivalry;
As thine, so may my last end be!
  Miserere, Domine!

SAINT VICTOR'S DAY (March 6).

MISCELLANEOUS POEMS.

I.

KING ARTHUR, at his Table Round, had never knightlier
    guests,
Nor Charles' Paladins such store of love-tales and of jests;
The choicest spirits of the earth cross over land and sea,
And blow their horns at my gate, and stall their steeds with
    me.
Then fail me not, my trusty friend, be sure fail not to come,
And your fellow-guests shall be the best, and boast of Chris-
    tendom.

II.

Sir Sherry, from the Xeres side, here hangs his Spanish
    sword,
And humorous, though grave, he sits, and sparkles at my
    board;
From Malaga of the Moors, and Oporto by the sea,
Two gentlemen of kindred blood came in his company.
Then fail me not, my trusty friend, be sure fail not to come,
And your fellow-guests shall be the best, and boast of Chris-
    tendom.

III.

A glowing Greek from Cypress came by way of Italy,
And brings with him his tender spouse, Signora Lachrymæ;
Oh! thrilling are the tales he tells of far historic lands,
Where once with demi-gods he fought, amid Homeric bands

Then fail me not, my trusty friend, be sure fail not to come,
And your fellow-guests shall be the best, and boast of Chris-
    tendom.

IV.

And here we have, arrived last night, the gold-encased
    Magyar,
Sir Tokay, from the Danube bank, renown'd in love and war.
He telleth of three Rhinegraves, all men of name and fame,
He pass'd chanting a drinking-song as hitherward he came;
Then fail me not, my trusty friend, be sure fail not to come,
And your fellow-guests shall be the best, and boast of Chris-
    tendom.

V.

Our former friends will all be here—the gifted and the good,
The deputies of the Gironde, with nectar in their blood;
The soul of France had ne'er been stain'd with the sins
    of '93,
If Robespierre had caught from them their high humanity.
Then fail me not, my trusty friend, be sure fail not to come,
And your fellow-guests shall be the best, and boast of Chris-
    tendom.

VI.

And she we love the best shall sit in her accustom'd place,
Lending to joy new pinions, to friendship's self new grace;
And our hearts will leap like schoolboys' in the sunshine of
    her smile,
And nought in tale or thought shall stain our sinless mirth
    the while.
Then fail me not, my trusty friend, be sure fail not to come,
And our fellow-guests shall be the best, and boast of Chris-
    tendom.

New Year's Eve, 1848.

THE ROMANCE OF A HAND.

"I see a hand you cannot see."—*Tickle.*

I.

I REMEMBER me a hand that I play'd with long ago—
It was warm as milk, and soft as silk, and white as driven
    snow—
It petted me and fretted me—by times my joy and bane—
The lovely little hand of my lovely cousin Jane.

II.

It beckon'd me to manly deeds over sea and land—
By night and day, I swear it, I was haunted by that hand;
Like the visitor of Priam, in the midwatch of the night,
It drew my curtains open and let in the dreamy light.

III.

Return'd from lands afar, I sought my cousin Jane—
She grasp'd me by the hand that was now indeed my bane,
For on the third-told finger—who'd have thought of such a
    thing ?—
Of the hand that once was mine, coil'd a horrid yellow ring.

IV.

Oh, cousin, cousin Jane ! how alter'd was that hand—
And the form it belong'd to, through that golden circle
    scann'd,
Indicative of orange wreaths, cradles, custards, nurses,
    babies,
The daguerreotype's original, and many other may be's.

THE STUDENT'S LUCKLESS LOVE.

I.

BRAVE was young Hugh, and cheerful,
   When I met him first, in May;
Dim was his eye, and tearful,
   When last he cross'd my way;
And I knew, though no word was spoken,
   Though no tear was seen to fall,
That the young heart of Hugh was broken,
   That he heard Death's distant call.

II.

It was not the toil of study
   That furrow'd his fair white brow,
For when his cheek was ruddy
   He prized books more than now.
'Twas not the chill October,
   With its cloud of wither'd weeds,
That darken'd his spirit over,
   And shook his frame like the reeds.

III.

But when we met at May-day,
   Though earth and heaven were bright,
'Twas the loving look of his lady
   That fill'd his heart with light.
And now Death's clammy charnel
   Houseth that lady dear,
And he sees but dock and darnel,
   And Death alone doth he hear.

IV.

Thick, and soft, and stainless
Falleth the snow abroad,
Where pulseless all and painless,
Lieth the funeral load;
White plumes are nodding fairly
The dark, dim hearse above—
" Whom the gods love die early,"
And, alas! they die of love.

THE MOUNTAIN-LAUREL. [134]

I.

FAR upon the sunny mountain, laurel groves were growing,
Silently adown the river came a hot youth, rowing;
Looking up, afar he spied
The green groves on the mountain side—
Quoth the youth, and fondly sigh'd,—
" I'll pluck your plumes, and sail anon, fair the wind is
blowing!"

II.

Landing, then, he took his way to where the groves were
growing;
Far he travell'd, all the morn, from the calm stream flowing;
In the sultry June noontide,
He reach'd the groves he had espied,
And sat down on the mountain side;
" Sing the snowy, plumy laurels, laurels gaily blowing!"

III.

Sat and slept within the groves of laurels bright and blowing,

Down they fell on lip and brain,
Oh! that odorous, deadly rain!
He never shall return again
To his boat, upon the stream afar, so calm and gently
    flowing!

DARK BLUE EYES.

STRANGE that Nature's loveliness,
Should conceal destructiveness;
Pestilence in Indian bowers,
Serpents 'mid Italian flowers,
Stranger still the woe that lies
In a pair of dark blue eyes!

In my dreams they hover o'er me,
In my walks they go before me,
Read I cannot while there dances
O'er the page, one of those glances;
Musing upward on the skies
There I find those dark blue eyes!

Woe is me! those orbs of ether
Can I win, or banish, neither!
Never to be mine, and never
To be banish'd by endeavor;
Still my peace delusive flies
Before those haunting dark blue eyes!

THE LORD AND THE PEASANT.

AN ALLEGORICAL BALLAD.

I.

A BARON lived in Lombardy,
  Whose granaries might feed a nation,
And fair his castle was to see
  As any monarch's habitation.
But of its chambers there was one
  Whose inside ne'er had seen the light;
Young and old did that chamber shun
  As the dread haunt of crime and night.

II.

At length this lord, more skeptic than
  His long-descended Gothic fathers,
Resolved to test the tale that ran,
  And round him many a wise man gathers.
The priest he pray'd that bolts and locks
  Might fly asunder, and the devil
Respect the ritual orthodox,
  And leave, at once, his stronghold evil.

III.

An alchemist drew forth a vial,
  Containing something which he swore
Would ope it wide on instant trial,
  If mortal hand had made the door.
The prayer was pray'd—the liquid tried—
  The iron door remain'd unmoved;
A clown stepp'd to the baron's side,

IV.

Forth stalks he with an iron lever—
  "Hold!" cries the priest; "rash man, depart!"
"Great heavens!" cries the sage, "was ever
  Such outrage shown to mystic art!"
In vain they talk; his lusty strength,
  Upon the bar the peasant plies,
Burst wide the stubborn door at length,
  And countless treasures greet their eyes!

V.

"By Holy Rood!" the baron said,
  "My prince of clowns, thy bar shall be
Into a golden one transform'd,
  For this great gain thou bringest me!"
"Nay, lord!" replied the brave explorer,
  "I labor not for mortal meeds,
Truth—whose hard task 'tis to discover—
  A truer, rougher lever needs!"

IRISH PROVERBS.

From the mounds, where altars
    In the old time stood,
Where the pilgrim-scholar
    Treads the Druid's wood;
From the mountains holy,
    Crown'd with hermits' homes,
From the far off Erin,
    Wisdom's voice still comes.

Time, beside his hour-glass
    And his scythe, still brings

Proverbs, far more precious
  Than the gift of kings :
Mark the solemn ancient,
  Chanting, as he passes,
Truths as keen as scythe-blades,
  Morals clear as glasses:

" Young men, old men, listen
  To the sage's word,
Still 'tis worth the hearing,
  Though so often heard;
Hear the earliest proverb,
  Time-tried, trusty yet—
' Doors of hope fly open,
  When doors of promise shut.'

" Young men, old men, trust in
  What the sages say—
' When the night looks blackest,
  We are nearest day;'
Take this creed, and keep it,
  Ever firm and fast—
That 'long withheld reckoning
  Surely comes at last.'

" Young men, old men, wisely
  Journeying o'er life's path,
Know that 'soft words ever
  Break the heart in wrath;'
Waste not time in wishing,
  ' Gather tears or gravel
In life's creels, and see which
  Fills, as on you travel.'

" Young men, old men, humbly

Bear up under trials—
   'The back is for the load;'
'Censure others slowly'—
   'Praise them not in haste'—
'Give the bridge due credit,
   When the river's past.' "

From the mounds, where altars
   In the old time stood,
Where the pilgrim-scholar
   Treads the Druid's wood;
From the mountains holy,
   Crown'd with hermits' homes,
From the far off Erin,
   Wisdom's voice still comes.

"*LOUGH DERG.*"

A RECOLLECTION OF DONEGAL.

I.

In a girdle of green, heathy hills,
   In song-famed Donegal,
An islet stands in a lonely lake,
   (A coffin in a pall),
A single stunted chesnut tree
   Is sighing in the breeze,
While to and fro "the Pilgrims" flit,
   Or kneel upon their knees;
Down to the shore, from North and East,
   From Antrim and the Rosses,
Come barefoot pilgrims, men and maids,

And some from Dublin city, far,
  Where sins grow thick as berries,
From Sligo some, and Castlebar,
  Come crossing by the ferries.

II.

Oh! blessed Isle, a weary wight,
  In body and in spirit,
Last year amid your pious ranks
  Deplored his deep demerit;
And though upon his youth had fall'n
  A watchful tyrant's ban,
Though sorrow for the unfought fight,
  And grief for the captive man, *
Peopled his soul, like visions
  That cloud a crystal sleep,
These sorrows there pass'd from him—
  'Twas his sins that made him weep.
And forth he went, confess'd, forgiven,
  Across the heathy hills,
His peace being made in heaven,
  He laugh'd at earthly ills.

III.

Oh! holy Isle, a ransom'd man
  On a far distant shore,
Still in his day-dreams and his sleep
  Sits by the boatman's oar;
And crosses to your stony beach
  And kneels upon his knees,
While overhead the chesnut-tree
  Is sighing in the breeze;

And still he hears his people pray
  In their own old Celtic tongue,
And still he sees the unbroken race
  From Con and Nial sprung;
And from departing voices hears
  The thankful hymn arise—
That hymn will haunt him all his years,
  And soothe him when he dies.

IV.

Oh, would you know the power of faith,
  Go! see it at Lough Dorg;
Oh, would you learn to smile at Death,
  Go! learn it at Lough Derg;
A fragment fallen from ancient Time,
  It floateth there unchanged,
The Island of all Islands,
  If the whole wide world were ranged.
There mourning men and thoughtful girls,
  Sins from their souls unbind;
There thin gray hairs and childish curls
  Are streaming in the wind;
From May till August, night and day,
  There praying pilgrims bide—
Oh, man hath no such refuge left,
  In all the world wide!

THE MAN OF THE NORTH COUNTRIE.

He came from the North, and his words were few,
But his voice was kind and his heart was true,
And I knew by his eyes no guile had he,
So I married the man of the North Countrie.

Oh! Garryowen may be more gay,
Than this quiet street of Ballibay;
And I know the sun shines softly down
On the river that passes my native town.

But there's not—I say it with joy and pride—
Better man than mine in Munster wide;
And Limerick Town has no happier hearth
Than mine has been with my Man of the North.

I wish that in Munster they only knew
The kind, kind neighbors I came unto;
Small hate or scorn would ever be
Between the South and the North Countrie.

GOD BE PRAISED!

I.

I AM young and I love labor,
          God be praised!
I have many a kindly neighbor,
          God be praised!
I've a wife—my whole love bought her,
And a little prattling daughter,
With eyes blue as ocean water,
          God be praised!

II.

Care or guilt have not deform'd me,
          God be praised!
Tasks and trials but inform'd me,

I have been no base self-seeker;
With the mildest I am meeker;
I have made no brother weaker,
   God be praised!

III.

I have dreamt youth's dreams elysian,
   God be praised!
And for many an unreal vision,
   God be praised!
But of manhood's lessons sterner
Long I've been a patient learner,
And now wear with ease life's armor,
   God be praised!

IV.

The world is not all evil,
   God be praised!
It must amend if we will,
   God be praised!
Healing vervain oft we find
With fell hemlock intertwined;
Hate, not Love, was born blind,
   God be praised!

V.

Calm night to-day is neighbor,
   God be praised!
So rest succeeds to labor,
   God be praised!
By deeds, not days, lives number,
Time's conquerors still slumber,
Their own master-pieces under,

YOUTH AND DEATH.

I.

DAILY, nightly, in the offing
  Of my soul, I see a sail
Passing, with a gay troop quaffing
  Rosy wine from goblets pale;
On the wine floats smiling roses,
  Smiling at the joy they give;
Ah! many a sunken leaf discloses
  How fast the years of youth we live.

II.

Daily, nightly, in the offing
  Of my soul's remoter shore,
Rides a sable ship at anchor,
  Waiting for me evermore.
From the poop a ghastly pilot,
  Sceptred with a scythe, loud calls,
It was *theirs*, and must be my lot,
  To glide down Death's darksome falls.

III.

'Twixt the ships I fain would tarry
  For a time in mid-life vale,
There reposing with my Mary,
  Mock Death for an untrue tale;
There reposing unregretting,
  I would sink to sleep at last,
To awake behind the setting
  Of my sun, Death's passage past.

FALSE FEAR OF THE WORLD.
AN IMPROMPTU.

I.

"The World!" "The World! why, plague it, man,
  Why do you shake your world at me?
For all its years, and all your fear,
  The thing I am I still must be.
I see! I see! fine homes on hills,
  With winding pathways smooth and fair;
But let me moil among the mills,
  Rather than creep to riches there.

II.

"A heather bell on Travail's cliffs,
  Smells sweeter than a garden rose;
The lumber-barge outsails the skiffs,
  And saves men's lives when Boreas blows.
'Tis, sure, enough to note the day,
  With morning hail, and night adieu,
Nor squander precious hours away
  With Affectation's empty crew.

III.

"My friend 's my friend, my foe 's my foe;
  I have my hours of joy and gloom;
I do not love all mankind—No!
  The heart I have has not the room.
But there is half-a-score I know,
  And her, and you, and this wee thing,
Who make my World, my all, below—
  Cause, Constitution, Country, King!"

AN EPICUREAN DITTY.

I.

Come, let us sing a merry song,
  My lady gay, my lady gay,
Nor fret and pine for right or wrong,
  By night or day, by night or day.
Of right, the rich man still can have
  His ample share, his ample share,
For wrong, when done unto the slave,
  Why, who need care? why, who need care?

II.

Is it not plain the world was made,
  My lady gay, my lady gay,
To be bamboozled and betray'd,
  By night and day, by night and day?
Then why not let the fat world hold
  Its ancient course, its ancient course?
Why rage against its calf of gold,
  Or consul horse, or consul horse?

III.

Now listen, listen unto me,
  Thou lady gay, thou lady gay,
'Tis moonshine, all this liberty—
  Talk thrown away, talk thrown away.
There is no joy the world can give
  Like wit and wine, like wit and wine,
He only can be said to live
  Who lives to dine, who lives to dine.

THE STUDENTS.

A FRAGMENT.

I.

CLOSE curtain'd was the students' room,
   And four bright faces fenced the hearth,
Abroad the sky was hung with gloom,
   And snow hid all the earth;
The current in the Charles' midst
   Chafed the thin ice overhead,
The wailing wind of night evinced
   A message from the dead.

II.

Four friends around one hearth! oh, need
   I say the four were young?
Four studious men who talk'd and read,
   Not all with eye and tongue;
But one with heart of regicide,
   To level all earth's lore;
And one for love, and one for pride,
   And one for more—far more!

III.

Cyrus breathed but ambition's breath,
   And dreamt but of renown;
One of the souls his was, from Death
   Would, smiling, take its crown.
Alban, to please a lady fair,
   And wise as fair, did toil;
And Eustace, as became an heir,
   Was liberal of his oil.

IV.

But Harry wrestled with the Past,
  And woo'd the old and dim,
And bound the passing spirit fast
  That answer'd unto him.
That in his heart, as in a cup,
  The heroic thoughts of old
Might be transmuted, coffer'd up,
  As misers guard their gold.

V.

Heroic youth! to him it seem'd
  'Twere joyful but to die,
In any breach above which stream'd
  The banner Liberty!
The scaffold-altar, prison-shrine,
  Where Freedom's martyrs bled

*   *   *   *

.

GRAVES IN THE FOREST.

THREE little graves, you can dimly see,
Made in the shade of the tall pine-tree;
The woodman turns his feet aside,
Where the mother's tears hath the flowers supplied,
For there they bloom when no bud elsewhere
Opens its folds to the chill lake air;
A rustic cross stands over all,
And over the cross, the pine-tree tall;
So while the young souls are with the blest,
        On the grave of grief
        Grows the flower, Relief,
In the solemn woods of the West.

The flower, Relief, on the young wife's breast,
Is caught in an infant's soft caress;
And it sheds its perfume round the room,
And lends to the mother's cheek new bloom;
So fair, so constant, its rosy hue,
You would never deem on what soil it grew.
There is no ill but God can cure,
Nor any that man may not endure;
So, while the young souls are with the blest,
    On the grave of grief
    Grows the flower, Relief,
In the solemn woods of the West.

A PLEA FOR THE POOR.

SONNET.

'Tis most true, madam! the poor wretch you turn'd
  Forth from your door was not of aspect fair;
His back was crooked, his eye, boa-like, burn'd,
  Wild and inhuman hung his matted hair;
His wit's unmannerly, uncouth his speech,
  Awkward his gait; but, madam, pray recall
How little Fate hath placed within his reach,
  His lot in life—that may account for all.
His bed hath been the inhospitable stones,
  His canopy the weeping mists of night;
Such savage shifts have warp'd his mind and bones,
  And sent him all unseemly to your sight.
Want is no courtier—Woe neglects all grace;
He hunger'd, and he had it in his face!

LINES WRITTEN ON THE FLY-LEAF OF A BOOK.

I.

A CHILD of Ireland, far from Ireland's shore,
　Inscribes his name beneath, and fondly prays
For this book's little mistress friends *galore*,
　And peaceful nights, and happy, happy days.

II.

And that, when her best friends are by her side,
　And light and gladness are her pages twain,
She still may think with fondness and with pride
　Of her parental island of the main.

III.

Two things alone in life we can call ours—
　The holy cross and love of native land;
Nor all earth's envy, nor the infernal powers,
　Can make us poor, with these on either hand.

DONNA VIOLETTA.

A SPANISH BALLAD, NOT IN LOCKHART'S COLLECTION.

I.

LYTHE and listen ladies gay, and gentle gallants listen:
In Donna Violetta's eyes the pearly tear-drops glisten;
The hour has come—the priest has come—have come the
　　bridemaids three,
The groomsman's there, but ah! the groom, alas! and where
　　is he?
Then sadly sigh'd that mother sage, "It is provoking, really;
What can the good knight mean, or plead to justify his
　　delay?"

And red and pale alternate, turned the bride as wore the
    morning,
And there she stood amid a crowd, half sorrowing, half
    scorning.

II.

At last outspoke the best bridesmaid, as on the timepiece
    glancing,
Her black eyes fired, and her small foot beneath her robe
    kept dancing:
"If I were you, sweet coz," she said, "I'd die before I'd let a
Man put ring, who first put slight, upon me, Violetta!"
And out bespoke the groomsman gay, a dapper little fellow,
Who, though 'twas early in the day, was slightly touch'd, or
    mellow:
"My lands are full as broad as *his*—my name is full as
    noble—
And as true knight I cannot see a lady fair in trouble;
So, lovely mourner, list to me, and cease those sad tears
    shedding,
Accept the hand I offer thee—and let's not mar the wed-
    ding!"

III.

The lady sigh'd, the lady smiled, then placed her fingers
    taper
Upon the gallant groomsman's arm, who forthwith cut a
    caper.
The vows were said, the prayers were read, the wedded
    pair departed
About the time the former swain had from his lodgings
    started.
Don Sluggard entered by one gate as they drove out the
    other

And where he should have found the bride he only found
    her mother.
" His *Costumier* was slow," he said, "his horses needed
    baiting,
And therefore he, unhappily, had kept the ladies waiting."

IV.

Ye ladies fair and gallants gay, true lovers prone to quarrel,
I pray you heed the rhyme you read and meditate the moral;
Full many a hopeful suitor's doom besides this has been
    dated
From that dark hour when first he left his lady fair belated.
All other sins may be forgiven to the repentant lover,
But this alone in vain he may endeavor to recover;
And should you have a youthful friend—a friend that you
    regard, oh!
Oh! teach him, teach him to beware the fate of Don Slug-
    gardo!

A CONTRAST.

IMITATED FROM THE IRISH.

I.

Bebinn is straight as a poplar,
    Queenly and comely to see,
But she seems so fit for a sceptre,
    She never could give it to me.
Aine is lithe as a willow,
    And her eye, whether tearful or gay,
So true to her thought, that in Aine
    I find a new charm every day.

II.

Bebinn calmly and silently sails
    Down life's stream like a snow-breasted swan;

She's so lonesomely grand, that she seems
  To shrink from the presence of man.
Aine basks in the glad summer sun,
  Like a young dove let loose in the air;
Sings, dances, and laughs—but for me
  Her joy does not make her less fair.

III.

Oh! give me the nature that shows
  Its emotions of mirth or of pain,
As the water that glides, and the corn that grows,
  Show shadow and sunlight again.
Oh! give me the brow that can bend,
  Oh! give me the eyes that can weep,
And give me a heart like Lough Neagh,
  As full of emotions and deep.

RICH AND POOR.

A SEASONABLE DITTY.

I.

THE rich man sat by his fire,
  Before him stood the wine,
He had all heart could desire,
  Save love of laws divine;
A daily growth of wealth,
  And the world's good word through all,
Wife, and children, and health,
  And clients in his hall.

II.

The rich man walk'd about
  His large luxurious room,
His steps fell soft as the snows without,
  On the web of a Brussels loom;

Without, the bright icicles had
  Made lustres of all his trees,
And the garden gods look'd cold and sad
  In their snowy draperies.

III.

The rich man look'd abroad
  Under the leaden sky,
And struggling up the gusty road,
  He saw a poor man go by;
He paused and lean'd on the gate,
  To husband his scanty breath,
Then feebly down on the threshold sate,
  The counterfeit of death !

IV.

The rich man turn'd his head
  And close his curtains drew,
And by his warm hearth, gleaming red,
  The wine-fledg'd hours fast flew;
Without, on the cold, cold stone,
  The poor man's head reclined,
A snow-quilt over him blown,
  A body without a mind !

V.

The rich man's sleep that night
  Was vinous, dreamy, and deep,
Till near the dawn, when a spectre white
  He saw, and heard it weep;
He rose, and stepping forth,
  Beheld a sight of woe—
His brother Abel on the earth

VL

The stone received the head
  Rejected by the brother;
'Twas of colder cause he lay there dead
  Than the cold of the winter weather!
His blue lips gaped apart,
  And the snow that lapp'd his frame,
Lay through life on the rich man's heart
  After that night of shame.

THE CHARTER SONG OF THE TOM MOORE CLUB.[*]

Air—"A place in thy memory, dearest."

The Greeks a Pantheon provided
  For their children of genius who died,
Then let not the race be derided
  That remembers its poet with pride.

Chorus.—Then, while gaiety reigns at the board, boys,
    And the wine in each goblet is bright,
    Let a loyal libation be pour'd, boys,
    To the soul of the minstrel to-night.

The warm Irish blood in each bosom
  Once glow'd in the light of his fame,
And though Fate has ordain'd we should lose him,
  We remember with honor his name.
            Chorus.—Then while gaiety, etc.

For, wherever his footsteps may wauder,
  The Irishman's bosom, be sure,
Through time and through change, will still ponder
  On the genius and glory of Moore.
            Chorus.—Then while gaiety, etc.

[*] The author was then President, as he was the founder, of the "Tom Moore Club" in Boston —Ed.

THE TRIP OVER THE MOUNTAIN.

A POPULAR BALLAD OF WEXFORD.

I.

'Twas night, and the moon was just seen in the west,
  When I first took a notion to marry;
I rose and pursued my journey in haste,
  You'd have known that I was in a hurry.
I came to the door, and I rattled the pin,
I lifted the latch and did boldly walk in,
And seeing my sweetheart, I bid her "good e'en,"
      Saying, "Come with me over the mountain!"

II.

" What humor is this you've got in your head,
  I'm glad for to see you so merry;
It's twelve by the clock, and they're all gone to bed:
  Speak low, or my dadda will hear ye!"
"I've spoken my mind, and I never will rue;
I've courted a year, and I think it will do;
But if you refuse me, sweet girl, adieu!
      I must go alone over the mountain!"

III.

" But if from my dadda and mamma I go,
  They never will think of me longer;
The neighbors about them, too, will not be slow
  To say, that no one could do wronger."
"Sweet girl, we're wasting the sweet hours away,
I care not a fig what the whole of them say,
For you will be mine by the dawn of the day,

IV.

She look'd in my face with a tear in her eye,
　　And saw that my mind was still steady,
Then rubb'd out the tear she was going to cry;
　" In God's name, my dear, now get ready!"
" Stop! stop! a few moments, till I get my shoes!"
My heart it rejoiced for to hear the glad news;
She lifted the latch, saying, " I hope you'll excuse
　　My simplicity, over the mountain!"

V.

'Twas night, and the moon had gone down in the west,
　　And the morning star clearly was shining,
As we two pursued our journey in haste,
　　And were join'd at the altar of Hymen!
In peace and contentment we spent the long day,
The anger of parents, it soon wore away,
And oft we sat chatting, when we'd nothing to say,
　　Of the trip we took over the mountain!

LINES,

WRITTEN ON THE EIGHTY-SECOND ANNIVERSARY OF THE BIRTH
OF THOMAS MOORE.

" Oh, blame not the Bard!" was the prayer he put forth
　　To the age and the nation he wished to adorn,
Well he knew that man's life is a warfare on earth,
　　And that peace only comes to the dust in the urn.

Yet who that has paused o'er his magical page,
　　Could couple the bard, e'en in fancy, with blame?
The delight of our youth, and our solace in age,

Who can think of the thoughts, as in torrents they roll'd
   From the spring of his soul, and forget how, at first,
We learn'd to repeat them from lips that are cold,
   And caught them upheaving from hearts that are dust.

He err'd—is that more than to say he was human?
   Yet how nobly he paid for the errors of youth!
Who has taught, as he taught, man's fealty to woman,
   Who has left us such texts of love, freedom, and truth?

Blame the Bard! let the cynic who never relented
   Dwell alone on the page that is soil'd with a stain,
Forgetting how deeply and long he repented—
   Forgetting his purer and holier strain.

For us—while an echo remains on life's mountain,
   While the isle of our youth 'mid her seas shall endure—
We must pray, as we stoop to drink at the fountain
   Of song, for the soul of the Builder—TOM MOORE.

CONTENTMENT.

MEN know not when they are most blest,
     But all—alway—
Pursue the phantom Future's quest,—
     Anxious to stray;
As young birds long to leave the nest
     And fly away.

Blessed is he who learns to bound
     The spirit's range,
Whose joy is neither sought nor found
     In love of change;
A tiller of his own right ground,

He hears, far off, the city's din,
　　　　But loves it not;
He knows what woes and wrecks of sin
　　　　Beneath it rot;
Vainly the tide allures him on—
　　　　He bides his lot.

So would I live, beyond the crowd,
　　　　Where party strife,
And hollow hearts, and laughter loud,
　　　　Embitter life;
Where hangs upon the sun the coal-black cloud
　　　　With sorrow rife.

Fain would I live beneath a rural roof,
　　　　By whose broad porch
Children might play, nor poor men keep aloof—
　　　　Whose artless arch
The ivy should o'ergrow without reproof,
　　　　And cares should march.

The drowsy drip of water falling near
　　　　Should lull the brain;
The rustling leaves should reach the ear;
　　　　The simplest swain
Should sing his simplest song, and never fear
　　　　A censure of his strain.

But why these wishes? does contentment grow,
　　　　Even as the vine,
Only in soil o'er which the south winds blow
　　　　Warm from the Line?
Wherefore, in cities, if I will it so,

Come, dove-eyed Peace! come, ivy-crownèd sprite!
          Come from thy grot,
And make thy home with me by day and night,
          And share my lot;
And I shall have thee ever in my sight,
          Though the world sees thee not.

WOMAN'S PRAISE.

I.

THE myriad harps of Erin oft,
          In other days,
Were by enthusiast minstrels strung
          In woman's praise;
And though they sometimes stoop'd to sing
          The praise of wine,
Still, nightly, did each trembling string
          Resound with thine.

II.

"Oh, who" (these ancient rhymers asked),
          "Would dwell alone,
That could win woman to his side,
          For aye, his own?
Oh! cold would be the household cheer"
          ('Twas so, they said),
But for the light the mistress dear
          O'er all things shed.

III.

And tuneless many a harp would be,
          And many a brain,
If woman, Queen of Minstrelsie,

And many a heavy tear would chill
On misery's cheek,
If woman were not present still
Her word to speak.

IV.

"Ye who have seen her gentle hand
Do gentle deeds,
In haunts where misery made a stand,
And men were reeds;
Ye who have seen the fetter chain
Undone by them,
Find, find for that a fitting name
Ye vaunting men!

V.

"Oh! blessed be the God that dower'd
The earth with these,
Our truest, firmest, noblest friends,
In woe or ease;
Bless'd for the grace that makes the earth
Beneath their feet
A garden, and that fills the air
With music meet.

VI.

"And still, whate'er our fate may be"
(The minstrel saith),
"Let woman but be near, and we
Will smile in death!
Whate'er the scene, where woman's grief
And woman's sigh
Can mingle round, there bard and chief
May fitly die."

AD MISERICORDIAM.

I.

I sought out your shore, all storm-spent and weary,
    For over the sea your name was renown'd,
My footsteps were light and my heart grew right cheery,
    As I trod, though alone, on republican ground.

II.

The sun shone so brightly, the sky so serenely,
    Your men bore their brows so fearlessly high,
Your daughters moved on, so calmly, so queenly,
    That I felt for your laws I could cheerfully die.

III.

If any distraction assail'd my devotion,
    'Twas only my memory wander'd afar,
To the Isle I had left, the saddest of ocean,
    Whose night never knew a republican star.

IV.

But all this is over; this vision has faded;
    This hope in the west has forever gone down,
And worn out with toiling, brain-sick and heart-jaded,
    Where I look'd for a welcome, I meet but a frown.

V.

When cometh the Messenger, friend of the friendless,
    Sweet unto me were the sound of his scythe;
When cometh the long night, starless and endless,

VI.

Welcome! thrice welcome! to overtax'd nature,
　The darkness, the silence, the sleep of the grave!
Oh! dig it down deeply, kind fellow-creature,
　I am weary of living the life of a slave.

GRANDMA ALICE.°

I.

I HAD just now a curious dream,
　While dozing after dinner,
I dreamt I saw above my bed
　(As sure as I'm a sinner)—
In words and figures broad and tall,
　With flourishes a-plenty,
"This is the time that mortals call
　The year Nineteen Hundred Twenty!"

II.

I rubb'd my eyes—in fancy rubb'd—
　To find myself beholder
Of any date so ancient dubb'd,
　And sixty summers older.
I look'd about,—'twas Cornwall town,
　But grown as fine as Florence!
Only the river rolling down
　Look'd like the old St. Lawrence.

III.

Out from a shady garden green
　Came ringing shouts of laughter,
I watch'd the chase, myself unseen,
　The flight, and running after;

* This playful *jeu d'esprit* was written in the album of a very young lady
in 1861.

A group of matronly mamas,
  With scions in abundance,
Who pour'd around their pleased papas
Their spirits wild redundance.

IV.

Hard by a thickly-blooming bower,
  Rosy, and close, and shady,
I saw, beguiling eve's calm hour,
  A venerable lady:
Her eyes were on a well-worn book,
  And, as she turn'd the pages,
There was that meaning in her look
  Which sculptors give to sages.

V.

Sometimes she smiled and sometimes sigh'd,
. As leaf by leaf she ponder'd;
Sometimes there was a touch of pride,
  Sometimes she paused and wonder'd;
Her station seem'd all plain to me—
  A grand-dame hale and hearty—
Happy and proud was she to see
  The gambols of the party.

VI.

I closer drew, and well I knew,
  In Nineteen Hundred Twenty,
The lady's book was old, not new—
  I caught a well-known entry!
The lady's years of life had pass'd
  Unsour'd by care or malice;
The book—this album 'twas, she clasp'd—
  They call'd her GRAND-MA ALICE!

[Of a similar character are the following lines, placed in a little Indian basket given by the author to the young daughter of a friend.]

TO MISS M. S———

In a dream of the night I this casket received,
From the ghost of the late Hiawatha deceased;
And these were the words he spoke in my ear :
" Mr. Darcy *New Era*,* attention and hear !
You know Minnehaha, the young Laughing-Water,
Mr. S———-r of Montreal's dear eldest daughter;
To her bring this trifle, and say that I ask it,
She'll treasure for my sake the light little casket."
This said, in his own solemn Longfellow way,
With a bow of his plumed head, he vanish'd away !
As I hope to be spared all such ghostly commands,
I now place the said Indian toy in your hands !

August 15, 1857.

THE PENITENT RAVEN.

I.

The Raven's house is built with reeds,
　　Sing woe, and alas is me !
And the Raven's couch is spread with weeds,
　　High on the hollow tree;
And the Raven himself, telling his beads
In penance for his past misdeeds,
　　Upon the top I see.

II.

Telling his beads from night till morn,
  Sing alas! and woe is me!
In penance for stealing the Abbot's corn,
  High on the hollow tree.
Sin is a load upon the breast,
And it nightly breaks the Raven's rest,
  High on the hollow tree.

III.

The Raven pray'd the winter through,
  Sing woe and alas is me!
The hail it fell, the winds they blew
  High on the hollow tree,
Until the spring came forth again,
And the Abbot's men to sow their grain
  Around the hollow tree.

IV.

Alas! alas! for earthly vows,
  . Sing alas! and woe is me!
Whether they're made by men, or crows,
  High on the hollow tree!
The Raven swoop'd upon the seed,
And met his death in the very deed,
  Beneath the hollow tree.

V.

So beat we our breasts in shame of sin,
  Alas! and woe is me!
While all is hollowness within,
  Alas! and woe is me.
And when the ancient Tempter smiles
So yield we our souls up to his wiles,

HALLOWE'EN IN CANADA—1868.

[Written for, and read by the author at the annual celebration of Hallowe'en
by the St. Andrew's Society of Montreal.]

I.

The Bard who sleeps in Dumfries' clay,
Were he but to the fore to-day,
What think you would he sing or say
Of our new-found Canadian way
          Of keeping Hallowe'en?

II.

Ah! did we hear upon the stair
The ploughman tread that shook Lord Dair,
The President would yield his chair,
And honor (over Member, Mayor),
          The Bard of Hallowe'en.

III.

Methinks I catch, then, ringing clear,
The accents that knew never fear,
Saying "I joy to see you here,—
And still to Scottish hearts be dear,
          The rites of Hallowe'en.

IV.

"Whene'er they meet, on any shore,
Whatever sky may arch them o'er,
Still may they honor, more and more,
The names their fearless fathers bore,
          And, like them, Hallowe'en.

v.

"I care not for the outward form,
  'Tis in the heart's core, true and warm,
  Abides the glow that mocks the storm,
  And so—God guard you a' from harm
    Till next year's Hallowe'en."

THE FARTHER SHORE.

How fair, when morning dawns and waters glow,
  Shines the far land by night conceal'd no more;
Gladly we feel how blest it were to go
  And dwell forever on that Farther Shore.

Nothing contents us—nothing rich or fair
  Wears the bright, gladsome hue that once it wore;
Sadness is in our sky and in our air
  To that which smiles upon the Farther Shore.

Noon beams aloft! the distant land draws near,
  The way seems narrower to venture o'er,
Yet hourly grows the scene less green and clear,
  More equal seems the near and Farther Shore.

Eve pale and paler fades into the dark;
  We watch the rower resting on his oar,
Unlovely to our eyes is that dim bark,
  A funeral shape lost in the Farther Shore.

Night nestles down! oh, happy sleep and night!
  The winds are hush'd, the waters cease to roar,
Let us depart by the stars' gentle light,
  And wake to-morrow on the Farther Shore.

THE STAR VENUS.

THE beautiful star, Venus,
    Shines into my heart to-night,
With not a cloud between us
    To mar her radiance bright!

Over the snow-roof'd city,
    Over the mountain white,
With a glance of tender pity,
    Looks the Lady of the Night.

And I think of the long-gone ages,
    When, with her sunny smile,
She thrill'd the coldest sages
    Who sail'd by her Cyprus Isle.

O Venus! Alma Venus!
    Thy lustre surprises nought,
But wherefore so serene is
    The ray that drives distraught?

Is it to teach the lover
    To hope, and to persevere
Till all the clouds blow over
    That hide his lady dear?

So my heart takes thy chidings,
    Fair Queen of Love and Light,
And hoping for hopeful tidings,
    It bids thee hail to-night.

THOMAS MOORE AT ST. ANN'S.[126]

I.

On these swift waters borne along,
   A poet from the farther shore,
Framed as he went his solemn song,
   And set it by the boatman's oar.

II.

It was his being's law to sing
   From morning dawn to evening light;
Like nature's chorister's, his wing
   And voice were only still'd at night.

III.

Nor did all nights bring him repose;
   For by the moon's auspicious ray,
Like Philomela on her rose,
   His song eclipsed the songs of day.

IV.

He came a stranger summer-bird,
   And quickly pass'd; but as he flew
Our river's glorious song he heard,
   His tongue was loosed—he warbled too!

V.

And, mark the moral, ye who dream
   To be the poets of the land:
He nowhere found a nobler theme
   Than you, ye favor'd, have at hand.

VI.

Not in the storied Summer Isles,
   Not 'mid the classic Cyclades,
Not where the Persian sun-god smiles,
   Found he more fitting theme than these.

VII.

So, while the boat glides swift along,
   Behold above there looketh forth
The star that lights the path of song—
   The constant star that loves the north!

GOD BLESS THE BRAVE!

[A New Orleans newspaper, the *Southern Pilot*, lately received, informs us that the Irish soldiers of Companies C and K, Eighth New Hampshire Volunteers, finding themselves encamped in the neighborhood of the grave of RICHARD DALTON WILLIAMS, have had the sacred spot inclosed, and erected " a tall and graceful slab of Carrara marble," with this inscription :

Sacred to the memory of RICHARD DALTON WILLIAMS, *the Irish Patriot and Poet, who died July 5, 1862, aged 40 years.*

This stone was erected by his countrymen serving in Companies C and K, Eighth New Hampshire Volunteers, as a slight testimonial of their esteem for his unsullied patriotism and his exalted devotion to the cause of Irish freedom.]

I.

God bless the brave! the brave alone
   Were worthy to have done the deed,
A soldier's hand has raised the stone,
   Another traced the lines men read,
Another set the guardian rail
Above thy minstrel—Innisfail!

II.

A thousand years ago—ah! then
   Had such a harp in Erin ceased,

His cairn had met the eyes of men,
  By every passing hand increased.
God bless the brave! not yet the race
Could coldly pass his resting-place.

III.

True have ye writ, ye fond and leal,
  And, if the lines would stand so long,
Until the archangel's trumpet peal
  Should wake the silent son of song,
Broad on his breast he still might wear
The praises ye have planted there!

IV.

Let it be told to old and young,
  At home, abroad, at fire, at fair,
Let it be written, spoken, sung,
  Let it be sculptured, pictured fair,
How the young braves stood, weeping, round
Their exiled Poet's ransom'd mound!

V.

How lowly knelt, and humbly pray'd,
  The lion-hearted brother band,
Around the monument they made
  For him who sang the Fatherland!
A scene of scenes, where glory's shed
Both on the living and the dead!

VI.

Sing on, ye gifted! never yet
  Has such a spirit sung in vain;
No change can teach us to forget
  The burden of that deathless strain.
Be true, like him, and to your graves
Time yet shall lead his youthful braves!

THE OLD SOLDIER AND THE STUDENT.

I.

THE star of honor on his breast,
　The gray head bow'd with years,
Hush'd every roister student's jest;
　Still ready for his peers,
The aged soldier gazed around,
　His sight was somehow dim;
We saw that it was classic ground
　That had some spell for him.

II.

" Your pardon, gentlemen," he said;
　" I interrupt your game !
But once I trod the courts you tread;
　The place is much the same;
And if you heed a tale to hear,
　A brief, plain tale I'll tell—
There's none here holds this spot more dear,
　Though all may love it well.

III.

" Years, years ago, when that your sires
　Were eager, planning men,
I, stirred by travel's vague desires,
　Forsook my native glen.
I cross'd the seas, and claimed the right
　A kinsman once bequeath'd,
And long in Nature's sore despite,
　This learnèd air I breathed.

IV.

" For not of books, and not of lore,
    My days and dreams were spun;
A banner some brave band before,
    A bold deed to be done,
A rush upon some bristling wall,
    A midnight *camisade*—
These were my study, and my all
    To be of the brigade.

V.

" I took the cassock from my back,
    I flung my *summa* down,
I rush'd away on war's wild track,
    I served the Church and Crown;
And tottering now on life's last brink,
    I come to-day to view
This place, of which I often think,
    And speak my heart to you.

VI.

" There must be soldiers ! yes, and they
    Should have a mission clear,
To lead them on their awful way,
    As any tonsard here.
There must be soldiers, and there must
    Be soldiers of the Cross—
The bravest, firmest, chief in trust,
    Or all our hopes are lost.

VII.

" Young men, forgive an old man's prose,
    Forgive an old man's tale,
You combat with far fiercer foes,
    Than any we assail.

True chivalry of soul lies not
  In panoply or gear;
Your good fight always must be fought,
  Be firm, and persevere."

Nice, Savoy, March 14, 1867.

SUNSET ON THE CORSO AT ROME.

[An impromptu, written on St. Patrick's Day, 1867.]

I.

The sun has set in amber
  Behind St. Peter's dome,
Like some fair-hair'd Sicamber
  Retreating west from Rome;
But he will bring the morrow,
  With all its promise bright,
With its life, its strife, and sorrow,
  And its merciful "Good night!"

II.

We look upon his setting,
  A silken, smiling throng,
We think—life's span forgetting—
  The darkness is not long;
A few short hours over,
  And, all brighter from his rest,
Like a rich returning lover,
  He'll deck the fair world's breast.

III.

Aye! we believe in being
  Created as we are;
Holding that true—for seeing

Yet deny that the All-giver
  To creatures could assign
A cycle of *forever*
  By a tenancy divine.

IV.

Saint Peter's dome at midnight,
  Though the sun be quench'd and gone,
Will stand as high and upright
  As in the day that's done;
And the Keys in Peter's keeping
  Will still be firmly grasp'd,
Till, from their final sleeping,
  All men see day at last !

V.

In Rome, as on Mount Sion,
  Hides Satan from the first;
Now roused, a roaring lion,
  He dares and does his worst;
Now a serpent, smooth, sweet-spoken,
  As when he ambush'd Eve,
Through the angel-guard had broken,
  And, through man, made God to grieve.

VI.

But still the Eternal City,
  Type of eternal power,
Looks down in patient pity
  On the idols of the hour;
As Genoa looks on the waters
  By passing clouds o'ercast,
As Fiesole looks on Florence,
  From the high-ground of the past !

TASSO'S TOMB, AT ROME.[1]

I.

The tepid air bespeaks repose,
 The noonday city sleeps;
No shadow from the cypress groves
 Athwart the Tiber creeps.
This seems the very land of rest
To wondering wanderers from the West,
 Who walk as if in dreams;
English Ambition's onward cry,
To all beneath this opiate sky
 Yet untranslated seems.

II.

Here is the goal; here ended all
 His tragedy of life!
The honors, banishment, recall,
 The love, the hate, the strife!
A weary man, the poet came
To light a funeral-torch's flame
 At yonder chancel light ;
When here he summ'd up all his days,
Heedless of human blame or praise,
 And turn'd him to the Night!

III.

Oh, holy Jerome! at thy shrine,
 Who could hope better meed,
Than he who sang the song divine
 Of crusade and of creed!

Who loved upon Jerusalem,
As thou didst when at Bethlehem,
   The Master's steps to trace!
Who burned to tread the very sod
Imprinted by the feet of God,
   In the first years of grace!

IV.

   Wrapt in the shade of Tasso's Oak,
     I breathe the air of Rome;
     He found his final home
   Where, freed from every patron's yoke,
The Alban and the Sabine range
Down yonder, seeming nothing strange,
     Although first seen by me ;
Firm as those storied highlands stand,
So, deep-laid in Italian land,
     Shall Tasso's glory be.

V.

   Calm here, within his altar-grave,
     The restless takes his rest ;
   Besculptured, as becomes the brave,
     With nodding casque, and crest,
And shield, on which we trace the line,
The key-note of his song divine,
     "*Pro Fide !*" Tasso lies.
So may we find our legend writ,
What time the Crucified shall sit
     For judgment, in the skies!

ICEBERGS.

STEAMER ALBION, LAT. 46.55 N., LONG. 52.30 W.

I.

Parting their arctic anchors
  The bergs came drifting by,
A fearful fleet for a ship to meet
  Under the midnight sky;
Their keels are fathoms under,
  Their prows are sharp as steel,
Their stroke, the crash of thunder,
  All silently on they steal.

II.

In the ruddy glow of daylight,
  When the sea is clear and wide,
When the sun with a clear and gay light
  Gilds the avalanche's side;
Then the sailor-boy sees castles
  And cities fair to view,
With battlements and archways
  And horsemen riding through.

III.

Lonely in nights of summer,
  Beneath the starlight wan,
A way-worn berg is met with,
  Sad-featured as a man;
All softly to the southward
  Trailing its robes of white,
It glides away with the current
  Like a hooded Carmelite.

IV.

To-day—'twas Sunday evening—
  When dimly from the north,
Under the far horizon
  A church-like cloud came forth;
It came, a white reminder
  Of the memories of the day;
As a silent sign, we fancied,
  It paused, and pass'd its way.

Sunday, 19th May, 1867.

IMPROMPTU.

A happy bird that hung on high
In the parlor of the hostelry,
Where daily resorted ladies fair
To breathe the garden-perfumed air,
    And hear the sweet musician;
Removed to the public room at last,
His spirit seem'd quite overcast,
He lost his powers of tune and time,
As I did mine of rhythm and rhyme
    When I turn'd politician.

THE SEA CAPTAIN.[138]

I.

The anchor is up and the broad sails are spread,
  The good ship is adrift from the land,
And the sportive spray sprinkles the fair figure-head,
  As if flung from some sea-spirit's hand.

II.

The wind pipes aloud through cordage and spars,
   The sea-boy sings back to the wind,
The day is all sunshine, the night is all stars—
   Was never old Neptune more kind.

III.

But the master he paceth the deck to and fro,
   (Impatient of fortune, I ween!)
Now his footstep is hurried, now leaden and slow,
   As he mutters his shut lips between.

IV.

And his eye fiercely glares at the blue blessed sky,
   As if all his tormenting lay there;
Now he smiteth his breast as to stifle a sigh—
   A sigh that resounds of despair.

V.

'Tis the midwatch of night—still unwearied he stalks
   To and fro in the moonlight so dim;
And unto himself or some phantom he talks,
   While the phantom seems talking to him.

VI.

Afar o'er the waters, an index of light,
   Points the eye to the darkness intense;
Say, whence comes the skiff that entrances his sight—
   What destiny carries it hence?

VII.

There standeth a form where the mist might have stood,
   As a sail her scarf catches the breeze—
And the 'kerchief she waves has the color of blood,
   While her girdle hangs loose to her knees.

VIII.

There is sin, there is shame, there is shipwreck of fame
　In the eye, on the brow of the maid;
No need unto him that she should name her name,
　At a glance the whole story is said.

IX.

To the ship's side she drew in her ghostly canoe,
　For a moment has waited her prey :
In vain shout the crew, to the phantom he flew—
　In the darkness they vanish away.

X.

When the Priest heard the tale by the gossips told o'er,
　" Of a truth," so he said, " it may be;
For the sins men imagine they leave upon shore,
　Do follow them often to sea."

PEACE HATH HER VICTORIES.

I.

To people wastes, to supplement the sun,
　To plant the olive where the wild-brier grew,
To bid rash rivers in safe channels run,
　The youth of aged cities to renew,
To shut the temple of the two-faced god—
　Grand triumphs these, worthy a conqueror's car;
They need no herald's horn, no lictor's rod;
　Peace hath her victories, no less than War.

II.

To raise the drooping artist's head, to breathe
　The word despairing genius thirsts to hear,
To crown all service with its earnèd wreath,

This is to stretch a sceptre over Time,
  This is to give our darkling earth a star,
And belt it with the emerald scroll sublime;
  Peace hath her victories, no less than War.

III.

To stand amidst the passions of the hour
  Storm-lash'd, resounding fierce from shore to shore;
To watch the human whirlwind waste its power,
  Till drownèd Reason lifts her head once more;
To build on hatred nothing; to be just,
  Judging of men and nations as they are,
Too strong to share the councils of mistrust;
  Peace hath her victories, no less than War.

IV.

To draw the nations in a silken bond,
  On to their highest exercise of good;
To show the better land above, beyond
  The sea of Egypt, all whose waves are blood;
These, leader of the age! these arts be thine,
  All vulgar victories surpassing far!
On these all heaven's benignant planets shine;
  Peace hath her victories, no less than War.

Paris, April, 1867.

THE SUNLESS LAND.

I.

Know you the sunless land, where throng'd together
The silent hosts stand out, unheeding whether
'Tis summer heat, or bleak December weather—

II.

Mark well the tents that multitude that cover,
On each the crusade-standard flying over,
Where sleeps the blameless maiden by her lover—
Know you that sunless land?

III.

Its fields have never flash'd to share or sabre,
There reigns the night in which no man can labor,
There neighbor knoweth not his nearest neighbor—
Know you that sunless land?

IV.

There Folly wears all year the same tame Fashion;
There Wit the crowd around has ceased to flash on;
There Age feels no regret, and Youth no passion—
Know you that sunless land?

V.

Thence let us go, and slow its pathways measure;
Leaving far off all scenes of sensual pleasure,
There let us dig the cave to store our treasure,
Safe in that sunless land.

THE MINSTREL'S CURSE.

I.

"My malison," the minstrel said,
"I give to man or youth,
Who slights a loyal lady's love,
Or trusts a wanton's truth.

II.

"And on his traitor head shall fall
Not only curse of mine,
But cited down, at Nature's call,

III.

" We've borne our Lady to the grave
    This weary, weary day,
  While our young earl, a wanton's slave,
    Is false, and far away.

IV.

" He riots in his leman's bower,
    He quaffs her philter'd wine,—
  False knight ! false love ! this very hour,
    Where is that wife of thine ?

V.

" He wed her on midsummer eve,
    With taper and with ring;
  His passion wither'd with the leaf,
    But came not with the spring.

VI.

" She marked the change, poor heart ! poor heart !
    She missed him from her side;
  She strove to play the stoic's part,
    She sicken'd, and she died!

VII.

" She lies outstretch'd in churchyard clay,
    She drinks the deadly dew,
  He leads the revels far away,
    The noisiest of the crew.

VIII.

" But on his traitor head shall fall
    Not only curse of mine,
  But cited down, at Nature's call,
    God's malison divine."

THE LADY MO-BRIDE.[139]

I.

WHEN I was a boy, and delighted to dream,
Where the sycamores shadow the bright Banna's stream,
I remember, 'twixt waking and sleeping, I saw
The first sight of the village-saint walking the shaw—
The Lady Mo-Bride!

II.

Her eye was as black as the summer-ripe sloe,
Her brow was as fair as the New-Year's day snow ;
Have you seen the red berry that grows on the yew?
So shone her soft lips and so gleaming with dew,
Oh! Lady Mo-Bride!

III.

In our poor little chapel, next Sunday again,
'Mid the sun-brownèd maidens and toil-weary men,
On the hard-sanded floor, as I live, she did kneel,
While the light of her grace like a glory did veil
The Lady Mo-Bride!

IV.

In summer the fever spread round through the poor,
As a wild-fire devouring a desolate moor ;
Ah! then, through its raging how calmly she trod,
The pure saint that she was—on earth walking with God—
The Lady Mo-Bride!

V.

The grave-yard green crowded, the village forlorn,

Then came that high lady, with comforts and wealth,
Her smile giving joy, and her hand leaving health—
                The Lady Mo-Bride!

VI.

But now she is wedded, and carried away
By some lord of the English, who loved her, they say;
And sad is our village, and valley, and all,
For the lady we pray for, but cannot recall!
                Dear Lady Mo-Bride!

INDEPENDENCE.

I.

LET Fortune frown and foes increase,
And life's long battle know no peace;
Give me to wear upon my breast
The object of my early quest,
Undimm'd, unbroken, and unchanged,
The talisman I sought and gain'd,
                The jewel, Independence!

II.

It feeds with fire my flagging heart
To act by all a fearless part;
It irrigates like summer rain
The thirsty furrows of my brain;
Through years and cares my sun and star,
A present help, a hope afar—
                The jewel, Independence!

III.

Rob me of all the joys of sense;
Curse me with all but impotence:

Fling me upon an ocean oar;
  Cast me upon a savage shore;
  Slay me! but own above my bier,
" The man now gone still held, while here,
          The jewel, Independence!"

AUTUMN AND WINTER.

AN ANTIQUE.

I.

AUTUMN, the squire of Winter, is abroad,
Making much dust upon the breezy road;
His Joseph coat with every hue is gay,
But seems as if 't had known a sunnier day;
His master from the North is drawing nigh,
Fur-clad, and little favor'd to mine eye.

II.

And yet this piebald courier doth him wrong;
He loves a friend, a bottle, and a song;
His memory's a mine, whereof the ore
Is ever-wrought and never-ending lore.
His white locks hide a head full of rare dreams,
Which by a friendly fire with gladness streams,
While Christmas shrives the perishing Old year
He leads the New out from behind the bier.

III.

Oh! motley Autumn, prithee mend thy pace,
I do not like thy costume nor thy face;
Thy hollow laugh and stage proprieties
Tell of a bungling actor, ill at ease,—
To live such life as thine is shame, is sin;

A SMALL CATECHISM.

I.

WHY are children's eyes so bright?
    Tell me why?
'Tis because the infinite
Which they've left, is still in sight,
And they know no earthly blight—
    Therefore 'tis their eyes are bright.

II.

Why do children laugh so gay?
    Tell me why?
'Tis because their hearts have play
In their bosoms, every day,
Free from sin and sorrow's sway—
    Therefore 'tis they laugh so gay.

III.

Why do children speak so free?
    Tell me why?
'Tis because from fallacy,
Cant, and seeming, they are free,
Hearts, not lips, their organs be—
    Therefore 'tis they speak so free.

IV.

Why do children love so true?
    Tell me why?
'Tis because they cleave unto
A familiar, favorite few,
Without art or self in view—

PRIMA VISTA.

"Land! land!" how welcome is the word
  To all—or landsmen bred or seamen!
Deep in their lairs the sick are stirr'd—
  The decks are throng'd with smiling women.
The face that had gone down in tears
  Ten days since in the British Channel,
Now, like Aurora, reappears—
  Aurora wrapp'd in furs and flannel.

"Where?" "Yonder, on the right, dost see
  A firm dark line, and close thereunder
A white line drawn along the sea,
  A flashing line whose voice is thunder?"
"It seems to be a fearsome coast—
  No trees, no hospitable whiffs—
God help the crew whose ship is lost
  On yonder homicidal cliffs!"

"Amen! say I, to that sweet prayer;
  The land, indeed, looks sad and stern,
No female *savans'* field-day there,
  Collecting butterflies and fern.
An iron land it seems from far,
  On which no shepherd's flock reposes;
Lash'd by the elemental war,
  The land is not a land of roses."

Proudly, oh *Prima Vista!* still,
  Where sweeps the sea-hawk's fearless pinion,
Do thou unfurl from every hill
  The banner of the New Dominion!

Proudly to all who sail the sea,
  Bear then, advanced, the Union standard,
And friendly may its welcome be
  To all men, seaward bound or landward!

All hail! old *Prima Vista!* long
  As break the billows on thy boulders,
Will seamen hail thy lights with song,
  And home-hopes quicken all beholders.
Long as thy headlands point the way
  Between man's old and new creation,
Evil fall from thee like the spray,
  And hope illumine every station!

Long may thy hardy sons count o'er
  The spoils of ocean, won by labor;
Long may the free, unbolted door
  Be open to each trusty neighbor!
Long, long may blossom on thy rocks
  Thy sea-pinks, fragrant as the heather;
Thy maidens of the flowing locks
  Safe shelter'd from life's stormy weather!

Yes! this is *Prima Vista!* this
  The very landmark we have prayed for;
Darkly they wander who have miss'd
  The guidance yon stern land was made for.
Call it not homicidal, then,
  The New World's outwork, grim its beauty;
This guardian of the lives of men,
  Clad in the garb that does its duty!

Less gaily trills the lover lark
  Above the singing swain at morning,
Than rings through sea-mists chill and dark
  This name of welcome and of warning.

Not happier to his cell may go
    The saint, triumphant o'er temptation,
Than the worn captain turns below,
    Relieved as by a revelation.

How blest, when Cabot ventured o'er
    This northern sea, yon rocks rose gleaming!
A promised land seem'd Labrador
    (Nor was the promise all in seeming);
Strong sea-wall, still it stands to guard
    An island fertile, fair as any,
The rich, but the unreap'd reward
    Of Cabot and of Verrazzani!

RELIGIOUS POEMS.

RELIGIOUS POEMS.

ETERNITY.

I.

ALL men are marshall'd in array,
And order'd for the Judgment Day !
The grave is but a gate whereby
They pass into eternity.

II.

More fearful will that hour be
When every wave of every sea
Will find a voice, and all shall cry—
" Behold, behold, eternity !"

III.

The metals which the mountains hold,
Like tears adown them shall be roll'd ;
The blinded earth, the shining sun,
To the dread end will stagger on !

IV.

Nought shall endure from pole to pole,
Nought, save th' imperishable soul ;
The sea shall pass, the stars decay,
Souls only can survive that day !

V.

O God of justice! God of love!
Rain down Thy mercies from above,
And make our sinful souls to be
Worthy to dwell for aye with Thee!

VI.

Teach us to live our little time,
By thy deliver'd law sublime;
Teach us to die, so that we may
Endure, in faith, Thy Judgment Day!

THE SAINTS OF ERIN.

A FRAGMENT.

How shall I sing the heavenly host
That burn'd of old en Ireland's coast,
When their joint lustre shone afar,
The Gothic world's morning star?
Their pious arts, their sacred names
Live still in honor'd ancient fanes,
Gray guardians of the isle or lake,
Frequented for the founder's sake.

Sad is the change, and sad the time,
When into hands unmeet as mine,
Descends the white and purple thread
Of what they suffer'd, what they said.
Breathes there no more a soul of fire
To wake to praise the Irish lyre?
To chant in high, enduring song
A lay to be remember'd long?

Has green Momonia lost the art
Through the ear to reach the heart?
Gushes there from no northern mount
Of sacred song the crystal fount?
Has Shannon's tide no magic spring,
Where he who drinks perforce must sing?
Lies Leinster voiceless as the clod
Before the theme—the Saints of God?

Not so! not so!   *   *   *.

HYMN TO SAINT PATRICK.

I.

Oh thou! Apostle of our race,
Look down from thy bright dwelling-place
On us thy suppliant sons, and hear
The prayer we offer to thine ear.

II.

Enthroned upon the eternal hills
Where spring salvation's crystal rills,
Dear Father! from thy chalice grant
That saving draught for which we pant!

III.

Standing hard by the awful throne
Where rules the mystic Three in One,
Beseech, oh Father! for thy race
The entail of God's precious grace!

IV.

By the bright brotherhood of Saints,
By weak humanity's complaints,
By all our wants and all your bliss,
Saint Patrick, hear our prayer in this!

THE CELT'S PRAYER.

L

Oh, King of Heaven! who dwelleth throned afar
Beyond the hills, the skylark, and the star,
Whose ear was never shut to our complaints,
·Look down and hear the children of thy Saints!

IL

We ask no strength of arm, or heart, O Lord!
We still can hoist the sail and ply the sword,
We ask no gifts of grain—our soil still bears
Abundant harvests to the fruitful years!

III.

The gift, O Lord, we need, to David's son
You gave, for asking, once in Gabaon;
The gift of Wisdom, which, of all your powers,
Most needful is, dread Lord! to us and ours!

IV.

Our race was mighty once, when at their head
Wise men, like steadfast torches, burn'd and led;
When Ollamh's lore and royal Cormac's spell
Guided the Gael, all things with them went well.

V.

Finn, famed for courage, was more famed for art,
For frequent meditations made apart;
Dathi and Nial, valorous both and sage,
Were slow in anger, seldom stirr'd to rage.

VI.

Look down on us, oh Sire, and hear our cries !
  Grant to our chiefs the courage to be wise,
Endow them with a wisdom from Thy throne,
  That they may yet restore to us our own !

THE PRAYER TO ST. BRENDAN.

I.

Upon this sea a thousand dolphins swam,
  Tossing their nostrils up to breathe awhile;
And here the lumbering leviathan,
  Lay heap'd and long like some half-founder'd isle;
When, from the west, a low and antique sail
  Swell'd with soft winds that wafted prayers before,
Bore thy frail bark, Columbus of the Gael,
  Far from thy native Connaught's sheltering shore !

II.

Mo-Brendan ! Saint of Sailors ! list to me,
  And give thy benediction to our bark,
For still, they say, thou savest souls at sea,
  And lightest signal-fires in tempest dark.
Thou sought'st the Promised Land far in the West,
  Earthing the sun, chasing Hesperion on,
But we in our own Ireland had been blest,
  Nor ever sigh'd for land beyond the sun !

III.

Shores of eternal spring might cross in vain,
  For all the odious wealth we counted nought ;
The birds-of-paradise might sing in vain,
  Had not our cup with too much woe been fraught !

Then, sailing in thy legendary wake,
　We lift our hearts and voices unto thee;
Bless the fair realm that for our spirits' sake
　You sought of yore through the untravell'd sea!

IV.

And for us, outcasts for the self-same cause,
　Beseech from Heaven's full granary some store
Of grace to love and fear the equal laws
　Enthroned upon that liberated shore.
Help us to dwell in brotherhood and love,
　In the New Home predestined for our race;
So may our souls to thine, in heaven above,
　Pass glorified, through their great Master's grace!

ST. BRIDGET OF KILDARE.

LINES WRITTEN ON THE FIRST OF FEBRUARY.

I.

How few, on this once famous festival day,
　Remember the Virgin of Erin, whose fame
Oft bow'd down the nations devoutly to pray,
　Of Kildare's holy abbess invoking the name!

II.

On the Alps of the Swiss, on the friths of the Dane,
　When the cross had supplanted idolatry's sign,
How the sons of the Gentiles surrounded thy fame,
　What homage, O Virgin! what conquests were thine!

III.

As a queen of the seas, how resplendently shone,
　'Mid the far Scotic islands the shrines of St. Bride,[141]
But they who once claim'd thee, and call'd thee their own,
　Have gone out—but oh! not to return with the tide!

IV.

To reign in one heart, through the changes of time,
  Is the fond expectation of maiden most fair,
But what myriads have felt an affection sublime
  For thy beauty of goodness, sweet Bride of Kildare !

V.

Even now may be found in the bosoms of men
  Some hearts, like the lamp at thy altar of old,
Whose faith burns as bright and as steadfast as then,
  As warm as its flame, and as pure as its gold.

VI.

Let them roam where they may, they can never forget,
  And never forego, let what fate may betide,
To remember the day, and to render the debt
  They owe to Kildare's holy abbess, St. Bride.

SHRINES ON THE SHORE.

WRITTEN OFF THE COAST OF MUNSTER, ASH-WEDNESDAY, 1855.

I.

Evenings there were when yon dim coast
Was lighted by a hermit-host,
Ere yet the fervid faith was lost
     Our fathers held.
How shall I, in this callous age,
Speak of their choir, demure and sage,
Who fed the lamp and fill'd the page,
     In nights of eld !

II.

A pilgrim then to Erin's shore
Would nowhere find the ruins hoar,
Which echo but the surge's roar,
     That I have seen;

From cape to cape, from isle and bay,
Chancels would light him on his way,
His log would be a litany,
        As it hath been!

III.

How alter'd now! our faith how weak,
Since the old days of which I speak,
When every galliot dropp'd her peak,
        And spread her flag,
As soon as saw the conscious crew
Arran, emerging o'er the blue,
Or the wild cell of Saint Macdugh,
        A sea-wash'd crag!

IV.

Mayhap we may have wiser grown,
Since Saints in Erin last were known,
Since honors from the deep were shown
        To God's elect!
But of all gifts our fathers had,
Yon shrines, by impious hands unclad,
Seem to my soul the loss most sad—
        Religion wreck'd!

V.

Wreck'd! no, not so! the eternal shrine
Secure may stand, unquench'd may shine,
In every breast, in mine and thine,
        Mine early friend!
The baffled tyrant cannot tear
From out the heart, once rooted there,
The Cross, our fathers' pride and care,
        Till time shall end!

THE DYING CELT TO HIS AMERICAN SON.

I.

My son, a darkness falleth,
  Not of night, upon my eyes;
And in my ears there calleth
  A voice as from the skies;
I feel that I am dying,
  I feel my day is done;
Bid the women hush their crying,
  And hear to me, my son!

II.

When Time my garland gathers,
  Oh! my son, I charge you hold
By the standard of your fathers
  In the battle-fields of old!
In blood they wrote their story
  Across its field, my boy;
On earth it was their glory,
  In heaven it is their joy.

III.

By Saint Patrick's hand 'twas planted
  On Erin's sea-beat shore,
And it spread its folds, undaunted,
  Through the drift and the uproar;—
Of all its vain assaulters,—
  Who could ever say he saw
The last of Ireland's altars?
  Or the last of Patrick's law?

IV.

Through the western ocean driven,
   By the tyrant's scorpion whips,
Behold! the hand of Heaven
   Bore our standard o'er the ships!
In the forest's far recesses,
   When the moon shines in at night,
The Celtic cross now blesses
   The weary wanderer's sight!

V.

My son, my son, there falleth
   Deeper darkness on my eyes;
And the Guardian Angel calleth
   Me by name from out the skies.
Dear, my son, I charge thee cherish,
   Christ's holy cross o'er all;
Let whatever else may perish,
   Let whatever else will fall.

THE CROSS IN THE WEST.

I.

Oh, fear not! oh, fear not! though storms may assail
Salvation's old symbol in city or vale;
By the waveless Pacific, by the new Median Sea,
The cross over all shall triumphantly be.

II.

Its merciful shadow shall shelter our halls,
Even they who despise it shall pause where it falls,
The index that stands on the dial of time
And shows man his hour and his errand sublime.

III.

The banner of faction shall fall at its feet,
The flag of the free do it reverence meet;
The wrath-driven host shall grow calm in its shade,
And repent of the vows that they rashly have made.

IV.

'Twas the first of all banners unfurl'd on our shore,
'Twas the banner Columbus in humbleness bore;
The needle might vary, the crew mutineer—
With the cross on his prow he was callous to fear.

V.

On thy shores, Guahania, when white men first stood,
Their speech was the Spanish, their standard the rood;
Upon Oregon's slopes, over Labrador's sands
Still the cross of the Jesuit pioneer stands.

VI.

Then fear not! oh, fear not! though storms may assail
Salvation's old symbol in city or vale;
By the waveless Pacific, by the new Median Sea,
The cross over all shall triumphantly be.

THE HERMIT OF CROAGH PATRICK.

I.

A HERMIT here, in days of old,
    Lived by the fox's lair,
The years of his life by his beads he told,
    The hours of his life by prayer.
No roar of the clamorous plains
    Disturb'd his wild retreat,
His paths, familiar to winds and rains,
    Were unknown to human feet.

II.

Night and morn, when the sky was bright,
  He sat on the mountain's crest,
And sung God's praise with all his might,
  Or kneeling, beat his breast.
And when the sky above him frown'd,
  And the storm rose fierce and loud,
He pray'd to Heaven for the land around,
  Its weak, and wicked, and proud.

III.

And many a tempted levin brand
  From its destin'd aim was turn'd,
And many a sinful ship made land
  The sea would have inurn'd;
And many whose final 'counting hour
  Was come, got Time of Grace;
And many a high and haughty tower
  His prayer kept in its place.

IV.

In all that land these things were known,
  Through all the proverb ran:
"The chosen Friends of God alone
  Are real Friends to Man."
Alas! in our own alter'd day,
  Well may the guilty rue
How few are living now to pray
  For the sins the many do!

V.

When we are stricken with age or ill,
  Or frighten'd with God's fires,
Our trust is still in human skill,
  Or art's electric wires.

Oh! sages, make for me a heart
Of ancient mould and faith,
And then I'll venerate your art,
And honor it in death!

"*WINIFRED OF WALES.*"

[Written in the album of a lady whose Christian name was Winifred.]

ALONG our native glens, of old,
In hut and hall, for young and old,
   When Night brought round her tales,
No purer epic was to tell
Than that which on the list'ner fell,
   Of Winifred of Wales!

The virgin martyr fair and true ;
The tyrant sworn his will to do,
   Whose wrath, wild as the gales
That sweep o'er Snowdon, and whose sword
Cropt that bright lily of our Lord,
   Sweet Winifred of Wales!

Where fell her blood, the conscious earth
To a charmèd spring gave instant birth,
   Whose ministry ne'er fails
To heal the sick, to light the blind,
If sought in fervid frame of mind,
   Amid the hills of Wales!

Auspicious name! so meekly borne,
I thee invoke, this holy morn,
   When all men's prayer prevails,
To bless this roof, and her who bears
Thy name—so honor'd through all years—
   Sweet Winifred of Wales!

QUEBEC, Sunday, April 6, 1862.

THE CHRISTIAN BROTHERS.

VERY RESPECTFULLY DEDICATED TO THE CHRISTIAN BROTHERS
OF NEW YORK.

I.

In the streets of the city, where laughter is loud,
Where Mammon smiles down on his worshipping crowd,
Where the footsteps fall fast as the falling of rain,
The sad and the sinful, the vile and the vain;
In the streets of the city what form do we meet,
With long sable robe flowing free to his feet,
Who is it that moves through the wondering mall?
'Tis our teacher—a son of the sainted La Salle.

II.

He hath left his young home in the land of the vine,
For the vineyard of God—for those tendrils of thine;
He hath heard that dear voice which of old calm'd the sea,
As it whisper'd to him, " Bring the children to me,
For of such are the kingdom of God," ere the soul
Hath a speck of the sin that defileth the whole.
'Tis for this that he liveth—upbraid him who shall,
Who walks in the way of the sainted La Salle !

III.

Oh, city ! that looking forth seaward forever
To the fleet on the bay, through the fleet on the river;
Still laving thy limbs in the parallel tides,
And proud of the strength that disaster derides;
Would you win true renown—'tis a dutiful youth,
An heirloom of honor, devotion, and truth;
Would you have them to pillar the home and the hall,
Oh ! teach them the lore of the sainted La Salle !
NEW YORK, 1856.

LIFE, A MYSTERY TO MAN.

You ask me, comrade, "why I speak with awe,
Harping forever on this Theme of Life,
As if it were the only care of man,
Instead of being a rope of slipp'ry strands,
Full of vile accidents, vexations, dreams;
A taper made but to be burnèd out,
A better sort of shroud, a thistle-down,
The airy carriage of an unsown seed,
The wooden shedding of a lasting structure,
A very flimsy, miserable makeshift,
Neither an art, nor yet a mystery?"

Life *is* a mystery, *might* be an art !
Old men know all its secret sleights and laws,
But when they learn to live, 'tis time to die,
And so their knowledge, age by age, goes with them;
And the young still begin to live, as though
A past were not, and future could not be.

It is Life's noon, and the young soul looks out:
Oh Earth ! how fond and beautiful thou art !
How blue the sky is !   How benign the sun !
How glorified the night !   How joyous Spring
And all the seasons look !   He's told
"Life's but a voyage, a river, and a dream;"
And this he takes as literal, nor thinks
The voyager's port is death; the river's end
Is in the sea, eternity; the dream once over,
The sleeper wakes up face to face with God !
He comprehends life's sacred sense no more
Than the mute trumpet does the word it utters.

Upward he goes, a-gathering shells and toys,
As if God sent him museum-making; or,
Sitting at some siren's feet of clay,
He sings away the hours with wanton airs,
Flinging his reason from him: then for days
He will be searching after it, that he
May squander it once more.
He's heard that amid roses beautiful,
Remorse, even as crocodiles of Nile,
Chooseth his den; he well knows that a poison,
Deadliest to men, has ever been distilled
From the fair blossoms of the laurel tree;
Yet, like some laughing child of Memphis old,
Playing among the sphinxes, never notes
That Good and Evil, from their dateless posts
Regard him with their all-unwearied eyes;
He never thinks, while looking at his watch,
A spirit sits within the works to note
His actions by the hour; he little dreams,
Sleep-walker as he is, that even now
Angels descend from heaven every day,
And might be seen if we had Jacob's grace.
His lawless will he makes his only law,
His god is pleasure, and his devil, pain.

The first great end of life, is to be saved;
And next, to leave the world the better for us.
Both are commanded, both are possible.
No good man's life was ever lived in vain:
Like hidden springs they freshen all around,
And by the lonely verdure of their sphere,
You know where good men dwelt.

But man's true empire is his deathless soul—
How capable of culture and adornment!

His memory, which, from the distant years,
Drives its long camel-cavalcades of lore;
His will, a curb'd steed or a cataract,
Full of directness, loftiness and power,
If it were rightly schooled; his reason,
An armory of Archimedean levers,
Such as, reposing on the Word of God,
Might raise the world!   Will man never know
To rule the empire in himself contained,
Its hosts of passions, tastes, affections, hopes;
Each one a priceless blessing to its lord,
If subject to Religion's holy law?

Ah! were there many rulers among men,
How fragrant in God's nostrils would become
This reeling, riotous, and rotten earth!
Then should we see no more guilt and remorse,
Life's vernal and autumnal equinox,
Shaking down roof-trees on defenceless heads,
Scattering the fairest hopes of dearest friends,
And strewing peaceful places with the wreck
Of lofty expectation; then premature old age,
And gray hairs without honor, could not be;
Nor orphans rankly cumbering the waste,
Like garden-seeds to some far prairie blown;
Then blessed peals would daily fill the air,
And God's house be familiar as our own;
Then Faith, and Truth, and patient Charity,
Returning from their long sojourn in heaven,
With all their glorious arts and gentle kin,
Would colonize this moral wilderness,
Making it something like what God design'd!

Thus would I have my friend consider life,

Open his eyes and see it all reveal'd—
Quicksands, currents, monsters, weeds, and shoals.
Thus would I have him school, in humbleness,
His ear to catch the rhythmic admonitions
Which come, upon the wings of every wind,
From the far shore where the dead ages dwell.
I would have him entertain such thoughts,
That, being with him, they might still preserve
His feet from pitfalls, and his cheek from shame,
His heart from sorrow, and his soul from woe.

THE ARCTIC INDIAN'S FAITH.

I.

WE worship the Spirit that walks, unseen,
  Through our land of ice and snow:
We know not His face, we know not His place,
  But his presence and power we know.

II.

Does the buffalo need the pale-face' word
  To find his pathway far ?
What guide has he to the hidden ford,
  Or where the green pastures are ?
Who teacheth the moose that the hunter's gun
  Is peering out of the shade ?
Who teacheth the doe and the fawn to run
  In the track the moose has made ?

III.

Him do we follow, Him do we fear—
  The spirit of earth and sky;
Who hears with the *Wapiti's** eager ear
  His poor red children's cry.

      * *Wapiti*—the elk.

Whose whisper we note in every breeze
That stirs the birch canoe,
Who hangs the reindeer moss on the trees
For the food of the *Caribou.*

IV.

That Spirit we worship who walks, unseen,
Through our land of ice and snow:
We know not His face, we know not His place,
But His presence and power we know.

A CHRISTMAS PRELUDE.

THE seer-prince, the prophet-child,
Who dwelt in Sennaar undefiled,
Proclaim'd with fire-anointed lips,
The elder law's apocalypse;
Told of earth's powers, their rise and fall,
Messiah's birth, and death, and all;
How, prone by Tigris' shore he saw
A vision fill'd with scenes of awe;
All heaven's designs in earthly things,
The fate of kingdoms and of kings;
The Egyptian's, Persian's, Grecian's fate.
But, saddest sight! saw Zion's state:
The second temple overthrown
From pinnacle to corner-stone;
Th' eternal sacrifice suppress'd
By Gentile legions from the west;
Dense darkness in all Judah's skies
Till Michael, Israel's prince, arise,
And He, the Saint of saints, descend

Round roll'd the times, and Asia knew
What Daniel saw; then Rome outgrew
All other bounds.   War's last wild roar
Lay hush'd on Cantabria's shore;
The idol of the two-fold face*
Look'd ou his temple's empty space;
From the far frontier of the Medes,
To where Day stalls his weary steeds,
All earth adored, at Cæsar's nod,
Or frantic cried, "A god ! a god !"

Then when the day had come, and hour,
Augustus loosed the word of power,
And kings and consuls, east and west,
Echoed their sovereign lord's behest:
"Number the nations who obey,
Throughout the world, the Roman sway !"
Then throng'd to tryst the human tide,
Kindred to kin, from every side;
O'er seas and Alps lost exiles came,
Rivers reversed, their source to claim;
Ganges to Gades, floods of men
Throng'd street, and bridge, and foot-mark'd glen;
The very desert seem'd to be
Peopled by Cæsar's dread decree:
"Number the nations who obey,
Throughout the world, the Roman sway !"

Lo ! from their Galilean home
Where two of Cæsar's subjects come !
Like tender sire and daughter, they
Hold reverent converse on their way;
A-foot and simply clad, yet grace
Abundant shines in either face;

* *Janus*—the god of peace amougst the ancient Romans.

He, Neli's son, a thoughtful man,
Whom every sign speaks artisan;
She, fairest of all Israel's fair,
With godlike goodness in her air,
Conscious of royal David's blood,
And of her holy motherhood,
Turns to her guide with filial ear,
Well pleased his reverent speech to hear.
December's breath falls keen and chill
On Jacob's well from Ebal's hill;
The wintry scene looks pale and dim
On Sichem from Mount Gerazim,
Where, pacing slowly, from the north,
A mother near her baby's birth,
Through scenes Samarian, bleak and wild,
Borne, and not bow'd, by such a child !
For thou *Ephrata* art to be
The Man-God's destined nursery !
For thee alone the star shall rise,
For thee alone the morning skies
Shall brighten with the angel's song;
For thee the angel-aided seers
By Ader's tower shall calm their fears,
And ravish'd by the heavenly strain
Shall seek their Lord beyond the plain !
For thee alone the magi bring
From the far East their offering !
For thee alone shall Herod quiver,
Ephrata ! blest be thou for ever !

Draw we the veil; this mystery
Is all too bright for mortal eye;
How shall it, then, be fitly sung
In earthly strains, by mortal tongue !

In heaven above, by His own choir,
Where shines the strong Divine desire,
Can worthily be raised the psalm
That hail'd on earth the dread I AM!

CHRISTMAS MORN.

I.

Up, Christian! hark! the crowing cock
   Proclaims the break of day!
Up! light the lamp, undo the lock,
   And take the well-known way.
Already through the painted glass
Streams forth the light of early Mass!

II.

Our altar! oh, how fair it shows
   Unto the night-dimm'd eyes!
Oh! surely yonder leaf that glows,
   Was pluck'd in Paradise!
Without, it snows; the wind is loud;
Earth sleeps, wrapp'd in her yearly shroud.

III.

Within, the organ's soaring peal,
   The choir's sweet chant, the bells,
The surging crowd that stands or kneels,
   The glorious errand tells.
Rejoice! rejoice! ye sons of men,
For man may hope for heaven again!

IV.

"Tis but a step, a threshold cross'd,
   Yet such a change we find;

Without, the wand'ring worldling toss'd
  By every gust of wind;
Within, there reigns a holy calm,
  For here abides the dread "I AM"!

THE MIDNIGHT MASS.

I.

Where the mountains gray and weary,
  Watch above the valley pass,
Come the frieze-clad upland people,
  To the Midnight Mass;
Where the red stream rushes hoarsely
  Through the bridge o'ergrown with grass,
Come the whispering troops of neighbors,
  To the Midnight Mass!

II.

No moon walks heaven's high hall as mistress,
  No stars pierce the drifting rocks,
Only wind-gusts try back, whining
  Like dogs on a dubious track.
Hark! there comes a startling echo
  Upward through the central arch!
'Tis the swollen flood that carries,
  Captive off, a raft of larch.

III.

Shines a light; it is the Chapel—
  Softly, 'tis the hour of God;
Poor and small, yet far more lowly
  Was the infant Christ's abode;

Rude and stony is the pavement,
  Plain and bare the altar-stone;
Ruder was the crib of Bethlehem
  Over which the east star shone.

IV.

Confiteor! God of ages,
  Mercy's everlasting source!
I have sinned, oh! do Thou give me
  Strength to stem my passion's force
Mea culpa! mea culpa!
  Saviour of the world and me,
By thy Passion, oh! have mercy,
  Thorn-crown'd of Calvary!

V.

Gloria in excelsis Deo!
  Shout the pæan to the sky!
Eyes of faith, in yon poor stable,
  See disguised Divinity.
Gloria in excelsis Deo!
  Christ, the hope of man, is born!
Shout the anthem! join the angels!
  'Tis our Saviour's natal morn.

VI.

Praise to God, the Eternal Father,
  Who of clay created man!
Praise to Christ, who trod the wine-press
  Till the atonement overran!
Praise to Him, the Holy Spirit,
  Who inform'd our souls with grace!
Alleluia! 'tis the morning
  Of redemption for our race!

THE ROSARY.

I.

"Bring hither to me my rosary!"
  Cried the lovely Lady Anne,
As, by the sick bed where he lay,
  For her dear lord she began
To count her bless'd beads one by one,
As the hours of hope and life sped on.

II.

"Jesus save us!" cried a knight,
  In the pagan forest lost,
No star to lend its guardian light,
  No mereing, track, or post.
"Jesus save us!" and forth he drew
The rosary, salvation's clue.

III.

Brain sore, and feverish with care,
  In Armagh's cloister deep,
The scholar knelt all night in prayer;
  Thought would not let him sleep,
Till the problems, all entangled, he
Unwound them on his rosary.

IV.

When fiercely broke the Atlantic sea
  Around the quivering bark,
And the scowling crew with mutiny
  Made the scowling sky more dark;
Columbus calmly tells his beads,
Nor mutiny nor tempest heeds.

V.

Oh ! scorn not, then, the pious poor,
   Nor the rosary they tell;
Ere Faust was born, or men grew proud
   To read by the light of hell,
In noble and in humble hands
Beads guided souls to heaven in bands.

THE THREE SISTERS.

I.

THERE are three angel sisters
   That haunt the open sea,
Three loving, life-like sisters,
   Though different they be.

II.

One lifts her brow, like morning,
   Above the waters dark,
And the star that brow adorning
   Laves many a beaten bark.

III.

One, by her anchor clinging,
   Walks the waters, like our Lord,
And the song she still is singing
   The dead to life hath stirr'd.

IV.

But of all the angel sisters
   Who haunt the open sea,
The fondest and the fairest,
   Sweet Saint Charity for me.

V.

Her spirit fires the coldest,
   And arms the weakest heart;
When death hath seized the boldest,
   The burial is her part.

VI.

On a thousand giddy headlands
   Her fleeting robe is seen;
By a thousand bays her buried
   Calmly rest beneath the green.

VII.

She hath no star nor anchor,
   Nor lofty look hath she,
But of all the angelic sisters,
   Sweet Saint Charity for me !

A PRAYER FOR THE DEAD.

I.

LET us pray for the dead !
   For sister and mother,
   Father and brother,
For clansman and fosterer,
And all who have loved us here;
   For pastors, for neighbors,
   At rest from their labors;
Let us pray for our own beloved dead !
That their souls may be swiftly sped
Through the valley of purgatorial fire,
To a heavenly home by the gate call'd Desire !

II.

I see them cleave the awful air,
   Their dun wings fringed with flame;
They hear, they hear our helping prayer,
   They call on Jesu's name.

III.

Let us pray for the dead!
   For our foes who have died,
   May they be justified!
   For the stranger whose eyes
   Closed on cold, alien skies;
   For the sailors who perish'd
   By the frail arts they cherish'd;
Let us pray for the unknown dead! etc.

IV.

Father in heaven, to Thee we turn,
   Transfer their debt to us;
Oh! bid their souls no longer burn
   In mediate anguish thus.

V.

Let us pray for the soldiers
   On whatever side slain;
   Whose green bones on the plain
   Lay unclaim'd and unfather'd,
   By the vortex wind gather'd;
Let us pray for the valiant dead! etc.

VI.

Oh! pity the soldier,
   Kind Father in heaven,
Whose body doth moulder
   Where his soul fled self-shriven!

VII.

We have pray'd for the dead ;
   All the faithful departed,
   Who to Christ were true-hearted;
   And our prayers shall be heard,
   For so promised the Lord;
   And their spirits shall go
   Forth from limbo-like woe—
And joyfully swift the justified dead
Shall feel their unbound pinions sped
Through the valley of purgatorial fire,
To their heavenly home by the gate called Desire.

VIII.

By the gate call'd Desire
   In clouds they're ascended;—
Oh, saints ! pray for us,
   Now your sorrows are ended !

SOLDIER! MAKE YOUR SWORD YOUR CROSS!

I.

Soldier ! make your sword your cross,
   Borne as the cross should be ;
So, nor fame, nor honor's loss,
   Ever can o'ershadow thee !
Who were they, the bravest brave,
   In the early days of faith,
When Sebastian died to save
   The Church that glorifies his death ?

II.

The Saints of Rome, the Saints of Gaul,
   Rode arm'd oft o'er tented field,

Who were Maurice, Martin, all
    The legion of the one-lock'd shield?
They, as you, were bred to war,
    Slept in guarded bivouac;
What they were, e'en that you are—
    Follow in their sainted track!

III.

Know that power is from on high,
    Know that duty dwells beside it;
Man's worst fate is not to die,
    If well prepared and well provided!
Soldier! make your sword your cross,
    Borne as the cross should be;
So, nor fame, nor honor's loss,
    Ever can o'ershadow thee!

THE FIRST COMMUNION.

WRITTEN FOR A CONVENT FÊTE.

WERE you bid to the bridal? have you sat at the feast
Of the life-giving bountiful Lord of the East?
Oh! glorious the beauty that shone on His brow,
As the innocent bride made her prayer and her vow.

And who was the maid, in our old cloudy west,
So sought from afar—so chosen—so blest?
Was her lineage as lofty, as old as His own?
Was she born in the purple and nursed on a throne?

Fair Psyche the gentle, no noble was she,
Nor born of lineage of lofty degree,—
A tiller of earth was her father, ordained
To purchase by labor the food that he gained.

Lowly born, lowly nursed, amid trial and tears,
Fair Psyche had passed through her infantile years;
But her heart was her dower, a fathomless mine
Of the graces and virtues that made her divine.

There bloomed all the flowers of a maidenly youth—
Its modesty, purity, piety, truth;
There breathed all the perfumes that halo the air,
From the soul of the saint or the censer of prayer.

Thus it came that the life-giving Lord from His throne
Called the daughter of Earth, his belovèd, His own;
Thus gently He drew that sweet heart to his side,
And thus proudly he crown'd her, a queen and a bride.

Oh, Psyche belovèd! your path now must be   .
With our Lady of Pity, whose image you see;[148]
With the numberless host of those virgins who died,
To be as you are—of Jesus the bride!

With Agnes and Lucy and all the dear saints
That history glories, and poetry paints,
You shall tread in their path, and join in their psalm,
And bear of the same tree, the evergreen palm.

Remember, oh! Psyche,* the day and the hour
When thy Lord in His grace veiled His terrible power—
When under the symbols of bread and of wine
By the lips of His priest, He was offered to thine!

Remember the new robe all spotless and white;
As pure be thy spirit preserved in His sight!
Remember the vow that you breathed at his feast,
Happy bride of the bountiful Lord of the East!

STELLA! STELLA!

I.

WHERE shall we turn, if not to Thee!
  Stella! Stella!
Star of the wilderness-ways of the sea,
  Stella! Stella!
Hope of the ages that were, and shall be,
  Stella! Stella!

II.

'Tis writ on the earth, and 'tis writ on the wave,
  Stella! Stella!
That thou, glorious star, art mighty to save,
  Stella! Stella!
From sin, and from death, and a watery grave,
  Stella! Stella!

III.

Darkness and tempest lie crouch'd in our way,
  Stella! Stella!
Yield us not up to the monsters a prey,
  Stella! Stella!
Shine! and all danger will up and away,
  Stella! Stella!

SUNDAY HYMN AT SEA.

I.

GUIDE thou our ship, Almighty Power!
 Dread Lord of sea and land!
And make us feel, at every hour,
 The helm is in thy hand;
For they alone, by land or sea,
Are guided well, who trust to Thee!

II.

The abyss may yearn beneath our path,
   The angry waves may rise,
The winds rush headlong in their wrath,
   Out of their lowering skies,
But well we know they all obey
The Lord, the Guardian of our way.

III.

When darkness covers all the deep,
   And every star is set,
Serenely we may sink to sleep,
   For Thou art wakeful yet.
How thankful, Lord! we ought to be!
Teach us how thankful—here at sea!

I WILL GO TO THE ALTAR OF GOD.

SUGGESTED BY THE ENTRANCE TO THE HOLY MASS.

I.

In the night-time I groan'd on my bed,
   I felt, O my Father! thy rod ;
     I felt all thy beauty and truth ;
In the morning I rose and I said,
   " I will go to the altar of God—
     To God, who rejoiceth my youth."

II.

I arose, and knelt under the sign
   Of Him who the wine-press hath trod,
     Where it shone like a ruby, in sooth;
And my soul drank the holocaust wine,
   As I knelt at the altar of God—
   " Of God who rejoiceth my youth."

III.

Despair not, O sorrowing friend !
  Down, down on the stone or the sod ;
    To our Father, all mercy and truth,
Cry aloud, " I repent ! I amend !
  I will go to the altar of God—
    To God, who rejoiceth my youth."

THE PEARL OF GREAT PRICE.

I.

THE richest diamond mortal man
  Has ever sought, or ever found,
Lies cover'd up by scarce a span
  Of daily trodden, common ground.

II.

Not far to seek, nor hard to find,
  Oh, jewel of the earth and sky !
Worth all for which the caliphs mined,
  Worth all for which men delve and die !

III.

A tear by Jesus shed, congealed,
  Were not more pure than this poor stone,
That thirty years He bore concealed
  On earth, at first, the only one.

IV.

He taught his twelve to cast the 'net,
  He taught them to believe and trust ;
He show'd them where this pearl was set,
  Its setting cover'd up with dust.

V.

Each gave a jewel unto each,
   And each could find out one for all ;
Ever within the wretch's reach,
   Ever within the poor man's call.

VI.

It bound the risen Saviour's robe ;
   And when above Mount Olivet,
He vanish'd in his own abode,
   The lustre earthward pointed yet.

VII.

It shone a lamp in many a cave
   Beside the Jordan and the Nile ;
It lightened many a stormy wave,
   And brighten'd many a holy isle.

VIII.

It burnèd red on Godfrey's breast,
   What time Mahound was trampled down,
And when in Salem he had rest,
   It graced him better than his crown.

IX.

Its worth is in the wearer's will
   A thousand or ten thousand fold ;
As men may use it, good or ill,
   It fades to dross, or turns to gold.

X.

Would you then know the jewel's name,
   Or where this diamond mine may be?
Never 'twas sought but that it came—
   The jewel is HUMILITY !

JUVENILE POEMS

JUVENILE POEMS

DEDICATED TO THE MEMORY OF A BELOVED MOTHER
AND TWO DEAR SISTERS.*

THE sunbeam falls bright on the emerald tomb,
   And the flow'rets spring gay from the cold bed of death,
Which incloses within it—oh! earth's saddest doom!—
   Perfections too pure for the tenants of earth.

How hallow'd the spot where she rests in the shade,
   A parent unequall'd for virtue and love,
Where the mould'ring remains of two sisters are laid,
   Whose spirits are radiant in glory above!

Sweet spirits, who dwell in the home of the Holy,
   Farewell! a survivor must bid you adieu;
Yet lives with the hope once again to behold you,
   By following the virtues once practiced by you!

BOYHOOD'S DREAMS.

I LOVE the earth, the sea, the air,
A faithful friend and a lady fair;
A cottage half-hid in evergreens,
With a dozen of babies behind the screens,
   Looking out with their arch blue eyes.

I love to roam o'er heath and hill,
Down the dark glen and over the rill,

* Written in 1841, in the author's sixteenth year.

To cool my brow with the mountain gale,
And drink my own health in Adam's ale,
   'Neath the radiant morning skies.

I love to muse on the rocky steep,
Where the old abbey flings its shade o'er the deep,
To watch the bright sail on the sunlit wave,
Like the spirit-land beaming behind the grave,
   Afar, from earth that lies.

I love the lovely land of the west,
Where my sires and their sorrows calmly rest;
An idol her story hath been to me,
And I love her the more that she is not free,
   For she shall and must arise!

BOSTON, August 13, 1842.

TO WEXFORD IN THE DISTANCE.

WRITTEN ON BOARD THE SHIP "LEO," ON THE AUTHOR'S FIRST
VOYAGE TO AMERICA, IN HIS SEVENTEENTH YEAR.

OH, city! o'er the still and silent sea,
   Farewell! my heart is overrun with sorrow,
I am not what I would be, gay and free,
   Farewell! the ocean is my home to-morrow!
Friend of my early days, my happiest hours,
   No more among the rocky wilds we'll stray,
Or in the sunny meadows cull the flow'rs,
   Or while with wondrous tales, the time away;
With riper years come care and sorrow's sense,
Yet meet we may again, please Providence!

APRIL 8, 1842.

CANTICLE OF THE IRISH CHRISTIAN.
ON BOARD THE "LEO," MAY, 1842.

I.

Lord God of our progenitors,
  The mighty and the just,
Of sages, chiefs, and senators,
  Now mingled with the dust ;
Who through the night of ages
  For thee have wept in chains,
Upon whose hist'ry's pages
  Thy foes have scatter'd stains !

II.

Oh, by the love you bore them,
  Look on their suffering sons ;
Cast Thy soft shadows o'er them,
  Guard well their little ones !
Once Thou didst plant Thy fountains
  Of mercy and of grace,
Mid Erin's holy mountains,
  And love her loyal race.

III.

Who rear'd these sacred ruins ?
  Who strew'd them o'er the land ?
Thy wise ones and Thy true ones,
  Who felt Thy guiding hand.
Lord, by Thy love her children
  Have rear'd Thy Cross afar,
Mid rude and untaught wild men,
  Who worshipp'd godless war !

IV.

Jehovah! look with kindness
   From Thy empyrean bowers ;
Remove their selfish blindness,
   Prince of ten thousand powers!
Lord! in thy glorious mercy,
   Oh, let this ordeal cease ;
Confound the fierce oppressor,
   Lord God of praise and peace!

LINES TO THE PETREL.

HERALD of the stormy breezes,
   Where dost thou find thy place of rest,
When billows rage, and each blast freezes
   Around thy wild, wild ocean nest ?
When night hath drawn her robe of sables
   O'er the land, and o'er the billow,
What guiding hand 'tis which enables
   Thee to attain thy secret pillow ?
The hand which made ten thousand creatures
   To fill the earth, the sky, the air,
Has given them spheres of life and natures
   Which in that life see nought of care.
Ours is a life of stormy change,
   Yet *wanting* change, a weary waste ;
Boundless your home, as ocean's range,
   It boasts a life of flight and feast.
Ye view the proudest works of man,
   Torn by the fierce tornado's roar,
Yet calmly the wild scenes ye scan,
   Safe lodged on some lake's woody shore.

But, mortal! when the storm runs high,
   Can your frail bark withstand its wrath?
Can you behold the sea and sky,
   And brave the lightning in its path?
Can you, prince of created things!
   Withstand for aye, great Nature's power,
Skim o'er the wave on buoyant wings,
   Or call your own one little hour?

APRIL 25, 1842, on board the Leo.

SEA SONG.

" OH, PILOT, 'TIS A FEARFUL NIGHT !"

I.

" OH! Pilot, 'tis a fearful night,
   There's horror in the sky,
And o'er the wave-crests, sparkling white,
   The troubled petrels cry!"
The hardy tar stood by the wheel,
   And answer'd not a word,
But well I knew his heart could feel
   Each sound his ear had heard.

II.

I saw the sea-boy far aloft,
   Rock'd on the top-sail yard,
Yet, youthful as he was, and soft,
   He wrought, and little cared
If waves ran high that fearful night,
   If eastern tempests roar,
Nor reck'd, nor dream'd, that wayward wight
   Of friends left on the shore!

III.

I turn'd again—the pilot stood
  Still silent at the wheel,
A billow smote the corvette good
  And threw her on her keel;
The pilot's manly arm shook,
  His eye was big and wild,
Some prayer his troubled spirit spoke
  For distant wife or child.

IV.

"Oh! pilot, 'tis a fearful night!
  There's horror in the sky,
And o'er the wave-crests, foaming white,
  The troubled petrels fly!"
The hardy tar stood by the wheel,
  And answer'd not a word;
Full well I knew his heart could feel
  Each sound his ear had heard.

At Sea, May 2, 1842

SONG,

SUPPOSED TO BE SUNG BY ONE OF THE SEAMEN DURING A STORMY NIGHT.

Oh, launch the life-boat out, my boys,
  Oh! launch the life-boat out!
The raging waves are breaking, boys,
  The coral reef about!

The pride of India's golden streams
  Lies scatter'd on the shore,
And fiercely though the sea-bird screams,
  It wakes the brave no more!
        Then launch, etc.

One tatter'd spar above the bark,
　Still braves the furious gale,
And in the lightning-spangled dark,
　One bleach'd and tatter'd sail!
　　　　　　Then launch, etc.

The pale, horn'd moon withdraws her light,
　The tempests louder roar,
Their wrath has slain not few to-night
　Who ne'er shall brave it more!
　　　　　　Then launch, etc.

On Board the " Leo," April 14, 1842.

TO IRELAND.

Land of my fathers! I could weep
　Thy sorrows e'en as they were *mine*,
Did not a fiercer passion creep,
　Into my thoughts of thee and thine,
To feel earth's basest should so long
Sit throned amid thy pauper throng!

Cannot the past beget some hope?
　Doth not its fire your bosoms warm?
Look back; what foe feared *they* to cope?
　Clontarf, Benburb, beam'd through the storm,
As suns obscured by clouds of years,
Their victors little dreamed of fears!

Go! seek Armagh's all-hallow'd pile,
　The tomb of Brian crumbles there;
Seek Tara's Hall, Iona's isle,
　And ask eve's shadows how and where

The men who made those spots sublime
Were nursed—what was their native clime!

Must the grave yawn to answer them,
　"They were of Erin's sons the best?"
Do not your memories, Irishmen,
　Give answer to the humbling quest?
Yes, yes! such were her sons of yore,
And shall she see such sons no more?

Why boast ye of your olden plains,
　Where triumph'd the Milesians' might?
Are Saxons kindlier than Danes?
　More brave than Romans in your sight?
Or discord—which hath gorged its fill—
Say, does the demon haunt ye still?

Will none arise with sword or cross,
　To drive the fiend from out your land,
Where, fattening on the traitor's corpse,
　He sows defeat with tireless hand?
Still must thy soil bring wretches forth,
To suck blood from their parent earth?

Down with the altars faction-reared!
　Blot out the class-badge of a hue;
Still let the shamrock be revered,
　And drink love from its morning dew!
So may Old Ireland bear once more
Such children as she reared of yore!

Each heart is yet a fitting shrine
　For household gods to harbor in;
An essence dearer far than wine;
　An angel's voice forewarning sin,

Is not more true than the love which dwells
In an Irish heart's ten hundred cells.

There is not one who roams the land,
    From Kenbaan's cliffs unto the Lee,
But owns a valiant heart and hand,
    A spirit panting to be free;
And by our sainted fathers' graves,
They shall no longer live like slaves!

Thus from the founders of their kind,
    Courage and truth descend to them;
And who in majesty of mind,
    Outsoars the sons of those ancient men?
My native land, rejoice! once more
Thy sons shall be as their sires of yore!

LINES

ADDRESSED TO MR. A. M'EVOY, OF BOSTON, ONE OF THE AUTHOR'S
FIRST FRIENDS IN AMERICA.

EACH morn that dawns, each closing hour of day,
I'll teach my soul for thee and thine to pray,
That thy kind, generous heart may pass through life
Unvex'd by care, unknowing woe or strife;
That thou may'st know that peace, best boon of Heav'n,
Unto the righteous man in mercy given;
That o'er the setting of thy mortal sun
The angel choirs may join in orison;
And thou, by them, be thron'd amongst the good—
So prays an Irish heart in friendship's mood!

SONG OF THE AMERICAN REPEALERS.

Oh! Erin dear, our fatherland,
   Across the Atlantic's million waves,
We bless thee for thy noble stand,
   And would be sponsors to thy slaves;
For never doubt, the mighty shout
   They raised on Tara's hallow'd hill,
Has reach'd the exile far away,
   And lives in hearts Hibernian still.

Born on thy soil, we've read thy story,
   And burn to see thy wrongs arighted;
Strip! strip the Saxon's tinsel glory,
   And let thy triumph-torch be lighted!
Though Tamworth's knave,* and Wellesley—slave
   Of gilt and gold—may taunt you,
Yet whilst Columbia stands your friend,
   Ne'er let such dastards daunt you.

Though darkness o'er thy cause should come,
   And fearful friends in terror cower,
And Britain beat her brigand drum,
   To waste thy lands in vengeful power;
Let tyrants rant and traitors cant,
   And craven foes belie thee;
For know thy stout Columbian band
   Scorn all that may defy thee!

September 23, 1843.

* Sir Robert Peel. It will be remembered that this is a boyish effusion, the
author being little over 17 when it was written.

TREES.

I.

How glorious are the works of God!
  How speak they unto man,
Whose spirit sleeps not in the clod
  Flung round it for a span!
The morning sky, the gentle breeze,
  A sea becalm'd by night,
Are glorious things—but tall green trees
  Are lovelier in my sight.

II.

E'en in their wintry skeletons,
  The winds that struggle low,
Will bring to us, earth's transient sons,
  A voice from where we go.
'Twas thus at midnight's solemn hour,
  I loved to talk with them,
To glean a knowledge and a power
  Unknown to sensual men.

III.

It has been thus in every time,
  With men of every land;
They've been to pagan priest a shrine
  With richest incense fann'd.
Oh! if such rites our pity claim,
  The Brahmin's sure is first,
Who worships in his fig-tree fane
  The Power his temple nurst.

IV.

To England's king *one* shelter gave,
    When sorely press'd by Brunswick's spies,
And *one* was Rufus William's grave,
    Though not as felons die, he dies.
All lands have theirs : from Naples' shore
    To Erin's oak—more dear to me
Than all the trees earth ever bore,
    Save two—SALVATION'S—FREEDOM'S TREE!

V.

What is the poet's hapless life,
    If reft of one, his high reward?
The lover's truth, the soldier's strife,
    Claim kindred emblems to the bard.
Oh, may this land for many a day
    Bear sons such diadems to claim ;
May Laurel, Myrtle, Olive, Bay,
    Long bloom around the freeman's fame!

VI.

Yet dearer far to Christian hearts
    The trees of old must be !
What boon to earth the wood imparts,
    Upraised on Calvary !
The trees of Eden once were fair ;
    One caused all after time to weep,
Even while the saving voice of prayer
    Through kindred shadows creep.

VI.

Our father Abram, too, hath seen
    The heavenly ministers of grace,
Beneath the spreading evergreen,
    And wisdom heard, lost to this race ;

Then from their everlasting homes
They came upon the evening breeze,
They sought not Canaan's lordly domes,
But holy Hebron's terebinth trees.

Mat 13, 1843.

LINES

SACRED TO THE MEMORY OF JOHN BANIM.

Go preach to those who have no souls—who would not shed
    a tear
O'er beauty's blight or patriot's worth, or virtue on the bier;
Far from the land that bore us, oft did he restore
The memory of our earlier days, our country's matchless
    lore !

Though Lever's power can raise our thoughts from Despond's
    deepest slough,*
And Lover's rare and sparkling wit may kindle pleasure's
    glow,
'Mid our Morgans and our Edgeworths, our novelists and
    bards,
No wreath more bright than that which fame to Banim's
    muse awards.

Who hath not paused with burning brow o'er his immortal
    story
Of Sarsfield, and his Irish hearts, in Limerick's list of glory;
Or sorrowed with the Aged Priest, or McNary's lovely
    daughter,
Or felt the power that genius sheds o'er Boyne's historic
    water ?

Scarce had he to the world given the ancient pastor's worth,
When he whose pen could paint the soul, was torn away from
　　earth;
And many a calm declining eve, upon his tombless grave,
Shall Kilkenny's daughters strew their flowers and sing a
　　requiem stave.

Sᴇᴘᴛᴇᴍʙᴇʀ 10, 1842.

LINES

Wʀɪᴛᴛᴇɴ ᴏɴ ᴛʜᴇ ғʟʏ-ʟᴇᴀғ ᴏғ ᴀ ᴄᴏᴘʏ ᴏғ "ᴛʜᴇ sᴘɪʀɪᴛ

ᴏғ ᴛʜᴇ ɴᴀᴛɪᴏɴ."

Sʜᴀʟʟ Ireland rise o'er chain and woes,
　　And her deep degradation,
To trample on her ancient foes
　　And write her name—a nation?

Yes! she shall rise and be once more,
　　A glory in the ocean,
And be, as she has been before,
　　The land of our devotion!

Our love, it is no weathercock,
　　It knows no change of season,
Through joy and woe, in calm or shock,
　　We give her heart and reason.

Nᴇᴡ Hᴀᴠᴇɴ, July 9, 1850.

NOTES.

Page 67, (¹). *"Hail to the Land."*
The levin—the lightning ; the levin-bolt—the thunder.

Page 75, (²). *"The Dost and his son."*
Dost Mahommed and Akbar Khan, the leaders of the Afghan War of Independence, in 1842 and '43.

Page 93, (³). *" Ode to an Emigrant Ship."*
The ship that brought out the author's wife and child, as indicated in the fifth stanza.

Page 94, (⁴). "Old Kinsale dons its *baraid* gray."
The *baraid* was the loose hanging cap worn by the ancient Irish.

Page 125, (⁵). *"Home Sonnets."*
" When England's chivalry, sore wounded, fled
Before the stormy charge O'Brien led."
At Fontenoy, July 2, 1745.

Page 125, (⁶). "Mother of soldiers ! France was proud to see
Your shamrock, then, twined with her *fleur de lis.*"
When the Irish Brigade were quitting the service of France, in 1792, the King's brother presented them with a banner, on which the shamrock was entwined with the *fleur de lis.* The motto was : " 1692–1792—*Semper et ubique fidelis.*"

Page 125, (⁷). "The Moors in Oran's trench by them were slain."
At the siege of Oran, in 1732, the Irish under General Lacy drove the Moors from the trenches, obliged them to raise the siege, and relieved the Spanish garrison.

Page 125, (⁸). "Carb'ry's, Tyrconnell's, Breffny's exiled lords,
To Spain and glory gave their gallant swords."
The O'Sullivans, O'Donnells, and O'Reillys were particularly distin-

Page 126, (⁹).   " And fallen Limerick gave the chiefs to lead
                    The hosts who triumph'd o'er the famous Swede.''

Marshal Lacy drilled Peter the Great's first army.   It was by his orders
the Russians reserved their fire at Pultowa until the Swedes were close on
them—a device which is said to have turned the battle.

Page 126, (¹⁰).   " And how the ruling skill that led them on
                    To conquer, was supplied by your own son.''

General Brown, of whom it was observed that " whether he endeavored
to take or liberate a king, he was equally successful.''   *Algarotti's Letters,*
page 24.

Page 140, (¹¹).   " The Stone of Empire.''

The *Lia Fail*, still, according to Dr. Petric, to be seen at Tara.

Page 141, (¹²).   " The Iccian wave.''

The old Irish name for the Irish Sea, or Channel.

Page 172, (¹³).   "*Mileadh-Espagne.*''

Milesius the Spaniard, the leader and patriarch of the Scythio-Spanish
colony, from whom the greater proportion of the present population of
Ireland is descended.

Page 174, (¹⁴).   "*Amergin's Anthem on Discovering Innisfail.*''

Amergin, one of the three sons of Milesius, was the poet-seer of the
emigration.   Innisfail—the Isle of Destiny—was one of the ancient names
of Ireland.

Page 176, (¹⁵).   " Their ocean-god was Man-a-nan McLir.''

Man-a-nan was the God of Waters, the Neptune of the ancient Irish.
He was called Mac Lir, that is, Son of the Sea.   The disposal of good or
bad weather was said to be allotted to him, conjointly with the God of the
Winds, and for this cause he was worshipped by mariners.

Page 176, (¹⁶).   " Cromah, their day-god and their thunderer.''

Crom, or Crom-eacha, was the name given by the ancient and pagan
Irish to their Fire-God, the sun—the dispenser of vital heat, and the author
of fecundity and prosperity.   He was their Deus Optimus Maximus, from
whom all other deities descended.   The name is derived from the Egyptian
word Chrom—Ignis, fire—which was the only *visible* object of devotion
permitted, and that only as the symbol of the Supreme.   Consistently,
however, with this view, they deified also the powers of Nature.   The
Irish Crom-Cruith—God the Creator—was the same as that adored by

Zoroaster and the Persians for more than five hundred years before Christ. Cruith is a derivative from Cruitham—to form, to create—and hence the present Irish Cruithior—the Creator.

Page 176, (17).   " Bride was their queen of song."

Bridh, or Bride, was the daughter of the Fire-God, and was Goddess of Wisdom and Song. Her blessing was esteemed the richest and most valued gift which man could receive from above ; she therefore became the goddess of philosophers and poets.

Page 178, (18).   " *The Gobhan Saer.*"

In Petrie's " Round Towers" there is a short account of the "Gobhan Saer," their builder. He is there supposed to have lived in the first Christian age of Ireland—the sixth century ; but his birth, life, and death are involved in great obscurity and many legends. He is, perhaps, after Finn and St. Patrick, the most popular personage in the ancient period of Irish history.

Page 180, (19).   " Seizing on Mona for his ' kitchen-garden.' "

John Hely Hutchinson—Lord Donoughmore—of whom Pitt said, " if he had got the three kingdoms for an estate, he would still ask the Isle of Man for a kitchen-garden."

Page 181, (20).   " Scots of Ireland."

For many centuries Ireland was called Scotia, and even down to the fourteenth century it was used in Latinity as Columbia is used synonymously with America. The Irish settlers in Argyle brought the name of their mother-land with them, and now Caledonia alone is called Scotia.

Page 182, (21).   " The trapper, by the mountain rill."

Ireland was the " Out West" of Europe until America began to be peopled. So late as two centuries ago, she supplied furs and timber to the Mediterranean ports.

Page 182, (22).   " Unto great Crom, the god of day."

Crom was the Jupiter or " thunderer " of our pagan ancestors.

Page 183, (23).   " Their ' Paradise of Youth ' was laid."

Thierna na Oge, the land of Everlasting Youth, in Celtic mythology, was placed under the Atlantic.

Page 184, (24).   " The Shepherd-Saint I dimly see."

The birth-place of St. Patrick is a mooted point in Irish history. We incline to the belief that he was born of French parents, in the Roman

colony of Valentinian, on the Clyde, near the present Kirkpatrick. He
was made captive by Nial "of the Hostages," upon an expedition against
the Romans in North Britain, and fell to the lot of one Milcho, whose
flocks he was sent to watch, among the romantic highlands of Antrim.

Page 185, (²⁵).   "Lo! there the Pontiff, Celestine,
                    Ordains the Apostle of our race."

Pope Celestine, A.D. 425, appointed St. Patrick to the mission of Ireland.
By this pontiff he was called Patricius, which means noble.

Page 185, (²⁶).   "But, rudely spurn'd from Milcho's door."

St. Patrick, after his return from Rome, first attempted to make converts
in his old abiding-place, but failing there, went boldly to Tara, where he
succeeded most miraculously. Princes, chiefs, Druids, and people, in that
neighborhood, were converted in multitudes.

Page 187, (²⁷).   "*St. Patrick's Dream.*"

Patrick, escaped from his long captivity, restored to his parents, happy
in their love, longs to return as a missionary to the people among whom
he had lived as a slave. "I saw in the visions of the night," he said—
and this passage, from a very authentic period of antiquity, strongly sup-
ports the claim of the Irish to an early knowledge of the art of writing—
"a person coming from Ireland with innumerable letters, and he gave me
one of them, and I read in the beginning of the letter, 'The voice of the
people of Ireland;' and I thought at that very moment that I heard the
voice of those who were near the wood of Focluth, which is adjoining to
the Western Sea, and they cried out thus, as it were, with one voice, 'We
entreat thee, holy youth, to come and walk still among us;' and I was
very much pricked to the heart, and could read no further, and so I awoke.
Thanks be to God the Lord, who, after very many years, hath granted to
them according to their cry."—*Ferguson's Ireland before the Conquest*, p. 134.

Page 195, (²⁸).   "*The Legend of Croagh Patrick.*"

The legend from which the version in the text is almost literally taken,
is given in Messingham's "Florilegium," and Colgan's "Acta Sanctorum,"
Vol. I. For some vulgar mis-tradition of this unquestionably ancient legend,
we probably owe the story of the banishment of the venomous animals
from Croagh Patrick and Ireland.

Page 199, (²⁹).   "*St. Brendan and the Strife-Sower.*"

St. Brendan related that, sailing one night on the great ocean, there
came to him the soul of one (who had been an angry monk, and a sower
of strife among his brethren) supplicating his prayers, etc.—*See Usher's
Religion of the Ancient Irish*, p. 20, ed. 1686.

Page 201, (³⁰). "*The Voyage of Eman Oge.*"

The legend of Hy-Brasil is one of the best known of our national traditions. It is an island which used once every seventh year to emerge from the depths of the ocean, far to the west of Arran, and like a very Eden in its beauty ; and, like Eden too, shut against the race of man. Many voyages were undertaken by the adventurous and the visionary in search of this fable-land, with what success is related in O'Flaherty's " West Connaught," and other old books, English as well as Irish.

Page 201, (³¹). "Eman Oge."

Young Edward.

Page 202, (³²). " Lir of Ocean."

Lir was the Neptune of the Celts, and father of several sea-spirits of inferior order.

Page 205, (³³). "*The Wisdom-Sellers before Charlemagne.*"

When the illustrious Charles began to reign alone in the western parts of the world, and literature was everwhere almost forgotten, it happened that two Scots of Ireland came over with some British merchants to the coast of France—men incomparably skilled in human learning and in the Holy Scriptures. As they produced no merchandise for sale, they used to cry out to the crowds that flocked to purchase, " If any one is desirous of wisdom, let him come to us and receive it, for we have it to sell." Their reason for saying that they had it for sale was that, perceiving the people inclined to deal in saleable articles, and not to take anything gratuitously, they might rouse them to the acquisition of knowledge, as well as of objects for which they should give value ; or, as the sequel showed, that by speaking in that manner they might excite their wonder and astonishment. They repeated this declaration so often, that an account of them was conveyed, either by their admirers or by those who thought them insane, to King Charles, who, being a lover and very desirous of, wisdom, had them conducted with all expedition before him, and asked them if they truly possessed wisdom, as had been reported to him. They answered that they did, and were ready, in the name of the Lord, to communicate it to such as would seek for it worthily. On his inquiring of them what compensation they would expect for it, they replied that they required nothing more than convenient situations, ingenious minds, and, as being in a foreign country, to be supplied with " food and raiment." This account was addressed to King Charles the Fat, grandson of Charlemagne, between the years 884 and 888. It was written by the Monk of St. Gall—by some called Monachus Sangallensis—whom Goldastres and Usher suppose to have been Notker Balbulus "the celebrated." But Mabillon and Muratori simply style him the Monk of St. Gall.—*Muratori's Analia d' Italia*, year 781.—*Lanigan's Ecclesiastical History of Ireland*, Vol. III., p. 209.

Page 211, (³⁴). "*Lady Gormley.*"

The Lady Gormley of the ballad was the daughter of Flann Sinna, and had been married successively to Cormac, King of Munster ; to Carroll, King of Leinster, and to Nial Glunduff, Monarch of Ireland. Several poems of considerable merit are attributed to this lady, some of which are still extant. It is probable she was divorced from Carroll, and was only betrothed to Cormac of Munster. She died, after a miserable old age, in which she wandered friendless from place to place, A.D. 946.—*Annals Four Masters*, Vol. II., p. 573.

Page 214, (³⁵). "*How St. Kiernan Protected Clonmacnoise.*"

The reader will find this legend in the "Four Masters," somewhere, if I remember right, in the fifteenth century. Not having the work at hand at the moment, I am unable to give the entry, which is an exceedingly curious one.

Page 219, (³⁶). "*Iona.*"

We were now treading that illustrious island, which was once the luminary of the Caledonian regions, whence savage clans and roving barbarians derived the benefits of knowledge and the blessings of religion. To abstract the mind from all local emotion would be impossible, if it were endeavored, and would be foolish if it were possible. Whatever withdraws us from the power of our senses, whatever makes the past, the distant, or the future predominate over the present, advances us in the dignity of human beings. Far from me and from my friends be such frigid philosophy, as may conduct us, indifferent and unmoved, over any ground which has been dignified by wisdom, bravery, or virtue. The man is little to be envied whose patriotism would not gain force on the plains of Marathon, or whose piety would not grow warmer among the ruins of Iona.—*Johnson's Journey to the Hebrides*, Vol. VII., p. 385.

Page 221, (³⁷). "*St. Columba to his Irish Dove.*"

This is a very ancient legend of the great founder of Iona, and very characteristic of his exalted patriotism and loving tenderness for all creatures, in which he was an antitype of the seraphic St. Francis.

Page 222, (³⁸). "*Bright brooch on Erin's breast you are.*"

It is said that Macha, the queen, traced out the site of the royal rath of Emania, near Armagh, with the pin of her golden brooch. See Mrs. Fer guson's *Ireland before the Conquest*, for this and other interesting Celtic legends.

Page 222, (³⁹).   " In shelter'd vale, on cloudy *ben.*"

Ben is the Gaelic word for mountain, as Ben Nevis, Ben Lomond, etc., in the Scottish highlands, whose inhabitants are of the pure Gaelic stock.

Page 223, (⁴⁰).   "*Cathal's Farewell to the Rye.*"

Cathal Crov-derg (the red-handed) O'Connor, being banished in his infancy from Connaught, was found in exile in Leinster by the Bollscaire (messenger or herald), who brought him the news of his father, Turlough's death, and his own election.   The Bollscaire found him reaping rye in a field with clowns.   On hearing the news, Cathal cast the sickle on the ridge, saying : " Farewell, sickle, now for the sword !"   To this day, " Cathal's farewell to the Rye " has been a proverb among the Sil-Murray whenever they wanted to express a final farewell.   See O'Donovan's *Annals of the Four Masters*, Vol. I., note, p. 212.

Page 225, (⁴¹).   "*The Death of Donnell More.*"

Donnell More O'Brien was one of the most illustrious princes of that royal line.   He is supposed to have been the munificent founder of Holy Cross Abbey, county Tipperary, one of the best endowed and most beautiful of the great monastic houses of Ireland.   In Hayes' *Ballads of Ireland* may be seen a noble poem on Holy Cross Abbey, by B. Simmons, in which allusion is made to " King Donogh (Donnell) the Red " as founder of the abbey.   It is a sad loss that only fragments of this noble historical poem on " The Death of Donnell More" could be found among the author's MS. remains.

Page 228, (⁴²).   "*The Caoine of Donnell More.*"

Only an Irish poet, and an Irish poet of the highest order, could have written this poem, simple as it seems.   Unfortunately, we have only a part of it, but enough to show that the author was truly and indeed the Bard of the Gael, as he has been styled.

Page 229, (⁴³).   " As to the harp the *Cris.*"

One of the Irish chiefs is lamented in the *Four Masters* as leaving his Kinel Connell " a harp without the *Cris,* a ship without a pilot, or a field without shelter."

Page 229, (⁴⁴).   " *A Legend of the Isle of Lewis.*"

One of the first evangelizers of the Western Islands is known in Gaelic story as " St. Cormac, the Navigator."   He was among the first missionaries sent out from Iona.

Page 231, (⁴⁶).   "*St. Columbanus in Italy to St. Comgall in Ireland.*"

St. Columbanus, the Paul of the Apostolic age of the Irish Church, preached the Gospel in Burgundy, and other provinces of France, in the reigns of the Merovingian kings, and in Lombardy against the Arians. He was an accomplished grammarian (which term then included all book-lore) and a good poet. Goldastus and Usher have preserved some of his epistles, which were numerous, and Henry Caussius has published one of his poems, copied from an ancient MS. of Freisengen, in Bavaria. He was educated under St. Comgall, abbot, at Banchor, in the Ards of Down, to whom it is not unlikely he should give some account of his travels and experiences.   He died in his own monastery of Bobbio, in northern Italy, on the 21st of November, 615. A town and many churches in upper Italy still bear his name.

Page 233, (⁴⁶).   "Peter's *Coarbh.*"

That is, successor.

Page 235, (⁴⁷).   "Of the blessed Bishop Arbogast."

See MacGeoghegan's *Ireland*, Vol. I., p. 201, for the account of the death of St. Arbogast.   (Sadlier's New York edition.)

Page 235, (⁴⁸).   "*The Coming of the Danes.*"

The Danes first landed in Ireland A.D. 795 and 798.   The object of their earliest voyages was Leinster, in which the scene of these verses is laid.

Page 235, (⁴⁹).   "The night is holy—'tis blessed Saint Bride's."

Bride—the abbreviation of *Bridget.*

Page 237, (⁵⁰).   "*The Death of King Magnus Barefoot.*"

King Magnus Barefoot became joint King of Norway with Hakon Olafson, in 1093.   But Hakon, in chasing a ptarmigan over the Dofrefield, caught an ague, of which he died, and after this Magnus reigned alone ten years.   In this time he made many voyages into the West, conquering all he attacked, whether in the isles or on the Scottish or English shores.   In 1102, he was slain in Ulster by an Irish force, near the sea-shore.   In Miss Brooke's *Reliques of Irish Poetry* is a translation of an Irish poem on this event, "the author of which," that lady observes, "is said to have belonged to the family of the O'Neills."   This poem agrees with Sturleson's as to the scene of the fight and its result, but differs in the details.   I have followed the latter for the facts of Magnus's previous life, as well as for the immediate cause of his death.   The Ulfrek's-fiord of the ballad was the Danish name of Strangford Lough.   It is scarcely necessary to add that at this period the Danes were nominal, if not practical Christians.

Page 239, ([51]).   "While the ravens in the darkness were lost."
The ravens—the Danish standard.

Page 240, ([52]).   *The Saga of King Olaf, of Norway, and his Dog.*

King Tryggvesson was king over all Norway from about A.D. 995 to A.D. 1000.   His saga is the sixth in Snorro Sturleson's *Humskringla*, and is very curious and suggestive.   Among other incidents, it contains the episode which suggested these stanzas.   It may be here remarked that the chronicles of the North-men, of the several nations, throw much reflected light on our own more statistical annals.   All through the ninth, tenth, and eleventh centuries, that restless race frown along the background of our history, filling us with an awful interest, similar to that which we feel in watching the advance of one thunder-cloud toward another.   They certainly destroyed many native materials for our early history, but in their own accounts of their expeditions into Ireland, they have left us much we should use.   That Davis was conscious of the value of this historical resource, appears strikingly in his essay on the *Sea-Kings.*

Page 243, ([53]).   "He was named Hiort."
"Hiort," literally a deer.

Page 245, ([54]).   *"King Malachy and the poet M'Coisi."*

It was by the unjustifiable ambition of Brian Boroihme, aided, perhaps, by his own incompetency, that Malachy II. was deposed from the chief monarchy of Ireland.

Page 246, ([55]).   *"King Brian's Ambition."*

The ambition of Brian at this late period of his heroic life was no longer that which had dethroned Malachy.   The "ambition" of the aged monarch had become purified and exalted into a purely Christian motive, namely, that of expelling the pagan Danes from Ireland.

Page 258, ([56]).   *"De Courcy's Pilgrimage."*

Sir John De Courcy, under King Henry (the Second,) was the chief conqueror of Ulster—who about the getting of the same had seven battles with the Irish, five of which he won and lost two.   Having at length reduced it to English rule and order, and occupied it for twenty years or more, King John, hearing that De Courcy had boldly declared that the death of the rightful heir to the English crown—Prince Arthur—was effected through his commands, he instructed the brothers, Sir Walter and Sir Hugh De Lacy, to arrest De Courcy, and send him to England to be hanged.   Sir Hugh went with his host from Meath, and did battle with De Courcy in Down, and after many being slain on both sides the victory

was in favor of De Courcy.—(Finglas's *Breviate*, Harris's *Hibernica*, p. 48.)
Among the traditional heroes of Ireland, John De Courcy occupies a
prominent position. The exploits which fame ascribes to him entitle
him to the character of an Irish Cid. The circumstance related in the
ballad is popular in every homestead from Innishowen to Inisherkin.

Page 260, ([57]). "*The Pilgrimage of Sir Ulgarg.*"

A.D. 1231. The *Four Masters* simply record the death of Ulgarg
O'Rourke, of Breffny, as having occurred beside the river Jordan.

Page 262, ([58]). "*A Legend of Lough Derg.*"

Lough Derg, in Donegal, was a place famous for pilgrimage from a very
early period, and was much resorted to out of France, Italy, and the Pen-
insula, during the Middle Ages, and even in the sixteenth and seventeenth
centuries. In Mathew Paris, and Froissart, as well as in our native
annals, and in O'Sullivan Beare, there are many facts of its extraordinary
history.

Page 264, ([59]). "Living on bitter bread and penitential wine."

The brackish water of the lake, boiled, is called wine by the pilgrims.

Page 265, ([60]). "*A Legend of Dunluce Castle.*"

A portion of Dunluce Castle was destroyed by a tempest some centuries
ago, while the inmates were busily engaged in revelry. Many lives were
lost by the accident.

Page 267, ([61]). "*Death of Art M'Murrough.*"

Art M'Murrough died at Ross, in 1416, after having reigned over Leinster for forty years. He was the chief Irish soldier of the age, and the
first, perhaps, that overreached the Normans by tactics and strategy. His
campaigns were against Roger Mortimer, Richard the Second, the Earl of
Ormond, Sir John Stanley, and Sir Stephen Scrope, Lord Thomas of Lan-
caster, and the first Earl of Shrewsbury—the British Achilles. He took
Ross, Carlow, Enniscorthy, and other fortified places, from the English,
and exacted an annual tribute of eighty marks from Dublin.

Page 268, ([62]). "And from the many-gated town pass'd Easchlaghs in
affright."

"Easchlagh"—a courier among the Gadelians, who was often a woman.
The word is pronounced nearly as if it were written *asla*.

Page 268, ([63]). "To the Calvach in his hall."

The Calvach O'Connor Faly was Murrogh O'Connor, a renowned warrior, who beat the English in several battles ; amongst others, that of Killuchain, fought in 1418.

Page 268, ([64]).   "To MacDavid in Riavach."

Contæ Riavach—a name given to Wexford in the fourteenth and fifteenth centuries.

Page 269, ([65]).   "Forth."

In Wexford.

Page 271, ([66]).   "Where hundreds of our gallant dead await
The long-foretold, redeem'd and honor'd fate."

The coming of a historian who shall liberate our illustrious dead from the bondage of neglect and calumny, is foretold in our prophecies. God send him, and soon!

Page 274, ([67]).   "*The Praise of Margaret O'Carroll.*"

Margaret, the daughter of O'Carroll, married, early in the fifteenth century, the Calvach O'Connor, chief of Offaly. She retained, after her marriage (a not unusual custom with our ancestresses), her maiden name, and under that name she became famous. Several traits of her character, given in McFirbiss' *Annals*, prove her to have been a woman of remarkable spirit and capacity. Thus we read of her pilgrimage to Compostella, and how the English of Trim having taken several Irishmen, her neighbors, prisoners, and her lord having in his keeping certain English prisoners, she " went to Beleathatruim, and gave all the English prisoners for Macgeoghegan's son, and for the son's son of Art, and that unadvised to the Calvach, and she brought them home."—MS. Irish Arch. Society, Vol. I., page 212. "It was she," says the same annalist, " that, thrice in one year, proclaimed to, and commonly invited (in the dark days of the year), on the feast day of Da Sinchel in Killaichy, all persons, both Irish and Scottish, or rather Albians, to the general feasts." The numbers who usually attended these feasts are set down as " upward of 2,000," by some as 2,700. It is stated, also—"She was the one woman that has made most of preparing highways and erecting bridges, churches, and mass-books, and of all manner of things profitable to serve God and her soul." Her death, from a cancer in her breast, is very pathetically bemoaned, as well it might be, by the McFirbiss of her time. It took place in 1451, which is called on that account "an ungratious an unglorious yeare to all the learned in Ireland, both philosophers, poets, guests, strangers, religious persons, soldiers, mendicants, or poor Orders, and to all manner and sorts of poor in Ireland." See MSS. Arch. Soc. Vol. I. In these days of exhortation to female patriotism, such a type of an Irishwoman of the middle ages will, I am sure, gain many more admirers than the grotesque fiction which is usually made of Grace O'Malley, who is represented in our "historians" much more like a savage than the high-bred and high-spirited gentlewoman that she was.

Page 274, (⁶⁸).   "Rath Imayn."

Now Rathangan, County Kildare.

Page 275, (⁶⁹).   "Dan."

The art of poetry.

Page 275, (⁷⁰).   A. D., 1414.   "The O'Higgins, on account of Nial, then satirised John Stanley, who only lived for five weeks after the satirizing, having died of the venom of the satire; this was the second instance of the influence of Nial O'Higgins' satires, the first having been the clan Conway turning gray the night they plundered Nial of Claidan."—*Annals of the Four Masters.*

Page 277, (⁷¹).   "Da Sinchel."

The two Sinchels—Saints of the land of Offaly.

Page 277, (⁷²).   "*Margaret O'Carroll.*"

Duald M'Firbis, the last antiquary of Lecan, in his MS. *Annals*, quoted by O'Donovan (*Four Masters*, page 944), gives several details of the great Irish Pilgrimage "towards the Citie of Saint James, in Spain," undertaken in the year 1445, when the "goodlie companie" numbered the chiefs of the name of M'Dermott, M'Geoghegan, O'Driscoll, several of the Munster Geraldines, Eveleen, wife of Pierce D'Alton, and a great number of others, "noble and ignoble."   The admirable Margaret O'Carroll was a principal person in this pilgrimage.

Page 282, (⁷³).   "*The Irish Wife.*"

In 1876 the statute of Kilkenny forbade the English settlers in Ireland to intermarry with the old Irish, under penalty of outlawry.   James, Earl of Desmond, and Almaric, Baron Grace, were the first to violate this law. One married an O'Meagher ; the other a M'Cormack.   Earl Desmond, who was an accomplished poet, may have made the defence for his marriage.

Page 284, (⁷⁴).   "Or how Earl Gerald match'd with kings.'

Gerald, eighth Earl of Kildare, whose splendor almost rivalled that of the King his master at the famous "Field of the Cloth of Gold."

Page 286, (⁷⁵).   "One went out by night to gather
Vervain by the summer star."

Vervain--a healing plant, in great repute among the ancient Irish ; it should be gathered under the dog-star, by night, barefoot, and with the left hand.

Page 289, (76).   "Who loved to set the prisoner free."

In justice to Queen Mary, it must be admitted that she was the only English sovereign who seems to have freely forgiven Irish state prisoners, as we see in this and other instances.   Lingard (A. D. 1554) shows that her clemency was far superior to that of Elizabeth, and of the governments who punished so severely the Jacobite insurrections of 1715 and 1745.

Page 290, (77).   "False Francis Bryan's guest betray'd."

The insurrection, defeat, submission, and betrayal of Bryan O'Connor Faly, in the reigns of Henry VIII. and Edward VI., is carefully narrated in *The Annals of the Four Masters*.   In 1548, with O'More, he contended unsuccessfully with the Lord Justice St. Leger, and was compelled to retreat into Connaught ; the next year they recrossed the Shannon and attempted by arms to recover what they had lost.   The Four Masters thus record the upshot : "1547 : O'Connor (Bryan) and O'More (Gilla Patrick), having been abandoned by the Irish, went over to the English, to make submission to them upon their own terms, under the protection of an English gentleman, *i. e.*, the Lieutenant.   This, however, was a bad protection."   This Lieutenant, O'Donovan adds, was Francis Bryan, who married the Countess Dowager of Ormond, and was made Marshal of Ireland, and Governor of the counties of Kilkenny and Tipperary.   He was Lord Lieutenant in 1549, and died early in 1550.   O'More died soon after his imprisonment in England ; O'Connor, having made an unsuccessful attempt to escape, was sentenced to "constant confinement ever after." (*Four Masters*, A. D. 1551.)   It was not till 1553 he was liberated.

Page 292, (78).   "She most pursued the English speech."

This curious and highly interesting account of the liberation of O'Connor, on his daughter's intercession, is given in the *Annals*, under the year 1563.   (Vol. V., page 1531.)

Page 292, (79).   "At thought of his true Margaret."
Margaret Roper, More's favorite daughter.

Page 293, (80).   "She lightly leapt on Cambria's strand."
The ancient route from Dublin to London was through Anglesea to Coventry and St. Alban's.   The journey by that way was above three hundred miles.

Page 293, (81).   "O'er Stoke's sad field, enrich'd and red
                        With ashes of the Irish dead."

At Stoke, in 1487, was fought the last great battle of the War of the Roses, under the banner of the poor pretender, Lambert Simuel.   Simnel

had been crowned in Dublin, and accompanied by a large Anglo-Irish and
Burgundian force, invaded England.   They were defeated, with great loss,
at Stoke, leaving among the dead Lords Thomas and Maurice Fitzgerald,
the Earl of Lincoln, and Martin Swartz, Commander of the German aux-
iliaries.

Page 293, ([82]).   "Saint Alban's ransom'd abbey made."

The Abbey of St. Alban's was greatly favored by both the Saxon and
Norman Kings of England.   It was, at the spoliation, one of the richest in
England, and its Abbot took precedence of all others in Parliament.—
Alban Butler, under June 22.

Page 294, ([83]).   "No jewel in her turban'd hair."

The turban is stated by several writers to have formed the head-dress of
Irish ladies.   As for their other raiment, we find it thus depicted in the old
Scottish romance of *Squire Meldruyn*:

> " Her kirtill was of scarlot reid,
> Of gold and garland of hir heid,
> Decorit with enamelyne ;
> Belt and brochis of silver fyne ;
> Of yellow taftais wes hir sark,
> Begaryit all with browderit wark,
> Richt craftelie with gold and silk."

Page 296, ([84]).   "Oh, aid me, gracious Prince of Spain."

" He (Philip) obtained from Mary the release of several persons of distinction, whom she had thrown into prison, on suspicion of their disaffection to her government.—*Watson's Philip II.*, *Book I.*

Page 297, ([85]).   "*Feagh M'Hagh.*"

Feagh McHugh O'Byrne, a celebrated Wicklow chieftain of the sixteenth
century.

Page 298, ([86]).   "*Lament of the Irish Children Imprisoned in the Tower.*"

In the reign of Henry VIII., the school of "King's Wards" was projected, and it seems to have been a favorite practice, in that and the succeeding reigns, to demand the children of our chiefs as hostages, to be
educated in London.   Sir Edward Coke's infamous speech in James the
First's Parliament, defending the perpetual imprisonment of the Irish
children in the Tower, is the most striking document we know as to the
fate of these unfortunate young captives.

Page 300, ([87]).   "*The Poet's Prophecy.*"

Hugh O'Niel had a poet, O'Clery, who foretold the victory of the Blackwater. The original of these lines may have been written by the same hand, as I first met with them in an old MS. in the Burgundian library at Brussels, among other fragments left by Friar Michael O'Clery, one of the Four Masters.

Page 301, (⁸⁸).   "They of the prophetic race."
The Tuatha de Danaans.

Page 301, (⁸⁹).   "They of the fierce blood of Thrace."
The Picts, or Cruithmans, who are derived, by ancient traditions, from Thrace.

Page 301, (⁹⁰).   "They who Man and Mona lorded."
Beside their Scottish colony, the Irish had dominion over the isles of Man and Mona (Anglesea). Holyhead was called in Welsh *Lian y Gwyddyl*, or "Irish Church." Golydan, an ancient Welsh writer, divides the Irish of Vortigern's time into those of Ireland, Mona, and North Britain.—See Irish edition of "*Nennius*," published by the Irish Archæological Society, note, p. 191.

Page 301, (⁹¹).   "*The Summons of Ulster*."
The time to which this ballad refers is that when Hugh O'Neil, Prince of Tyr-Owen, was forming his grand confederation against the oppressive power of Elizabeth.

Page 306, (⁹²).   "Irrelagh."
The ancient name of the Abbey of Mucruss, at Killarney.

Page 307, (⁹³).   "*The Outlawed Earl*."
Gerald, the fifteenth and last Earl of Desmond, who lost life and land struggling against religious persecution and foreign tyranny.

Page 309, (⁹⁴).   "*Sir Cahir O'Dogherty's Message*."
In 1608, O'Dogherty, Chief of Innishowen, seized Derry, garrisoned Culmore, and fought a campaign of five months against the troops of James I. with success.   He fell by assassination in the twentieth year of his age.

Page 310, (⁹⁵).   "*The Rapparees*."
This is a logical defence of a most injured class of brave men.   The Rapparees first appeared in the wars for James II., and were the *guerillas* of that and the succeeding generation.   A false Williamite nomenclature has made the name synonymous with assassination and larceny.   This, to be true, would make all that history records of fugitive heroism false.

Page 312, (⁹⁶). "*After the Flight.*"

These lines were written after perusing Rev. C. P. Meehan's "Flight of
the Northern Earls."

Page 314, (⁹⁷). "*Rory Dall's Lamentation.*"

Rory "Dall," or the blind, a celebrated Irish harper at the court of
James V. of Scotland, who was banished that court for declaring he would
rather be the O'Neil than King of Scotland.

Page 315, (⁹⁸). "*The Last O'Sullivan Beare.*"

Philip O'Sullivan Beare, a brave captain, and the author of many works
relating to Ireland, commanded a ship-of-war for Philip IV. of Spain. In
his "*Catholic History*," published at Lisbon in 1609, he has alluded to the
sad story of his family. It is, in brief, thus : "In 1602, his father's castle
of Dunbuidhe being demolished by cannonade, the family—consisting of a
wife, two sons, and two daughters—emigrated to Spain, where his youngest brother, Donald, joined him professionally, but was soon after killed in
an engagement with the Turks. The old chief, at the age of one hundred,
died at Corunna, and was soon followed by his long-wedded wife. One
daughter entered a convent and took the veil ; the other, returning to
Ireland, was lost at sea." In this version, the real names have been preserved.

Page 317, (⁹⁹). "*Brother Michael.*"

Michael O'Clery, the chief of the Four Masters, was merely a lay-
brother of the Order of St. Francis. "Brother Michael" was his sole
name in religion, and by that alone I have presumed to call him.

Page 319, (¹⁰⁰). "Where the gables of Dunbrody
Stand the proof of Hervey's penance."

The Cistercian Abbey of Dunbrody was founded by Hervey de Montema-
risco, A. D. 1182.

Page 324, (¹⁰¹). "*Sonnet—To Kilbarron Castle.*"

Kilbarron Castle, the time-honored dwelling of the O'Clerys, chief bards
of the princely O'Donnells, overlooking Donegal Bay.

Page 325, (¹⁰²). "*In-felix Felix.*"

Sir Phelim (Felix) O'Neill was executed by Cromwell's order, at Dublin,
in 1662, as a punishment for the alleged "Popish Massacre" of 1641. He
was offered his life, on the scaffold, if he would consent to inculpate King
Charles. He "stoutly refused," and was instantly executed.

Page 330, ([103]). "*To the River Boyne.*"

These stanzas, originally written several years ago, and included in Hayes'' collection of *The Ballads of Ireland*, are here inserted (*i. e.*, in *The Canadian Ballads* of Mr. McGee), as an evidence of what the author at the time of writing them considered, and still does consider, the true spirit in which the events referred to in them ought alone to be remembered by natives of Ireland, whether at home or abroad.

Page 331, ([104]). "And banish'd far the bitterness of strife."

An allusion to the Irish Tenant League, which just then (June, 1851) held one of its reunions on the banks of the Boyne.

Page 332, ([105]). "*The Wild Geese.*"

This name was given to those Irish soldiers who, after the capitulation of Limerick, went over to France and formed the celebrated Irish Brigade.

Page 333, ([106]). "*The Death of O'Carolan.*"

Turlogh O'Carolan, born at Nobber, A. D. 1670, became blind at the age of manhood, and then the harp which had been his amusement became his profession. The lady of the Mac Dermott of Aldersford, in Roscommon, equipped him with horse, harp, and *gossoon.* At every house he was a welcome guest, and for half a century he wandered from mansion to mansion, improvising words and airs. Roscommon, the native county of Goldsmith, was his favorite district, where he died in 1731, at the house of his first patroness. One of Goldsmith's most touching essays is on "Carolan the Blind," and his musical influence can certainly be traced not only in Goldsmith's Poems, but also in Sheridan, Moore, and Gerald Griffin.

Page 334, ([107]). "*The Croppies' Grave.*"

On the top of the hill of Tara is " the Croppies' Grave," and the stone at the head is thought by Petrie to be the true *Lia Fail*, or " Stone of Destiny."

Page 336, ([108]). "*Song of 'Moylan's Dragoons.'*"

"Moylan's Dragoons," says Mr. G. W. P. Custis, nephew of Washington, " were in almost every action during the war."

Page 337, ([109]). "Old Ulster."

Ulster County, Pennsylvania.

Page 338, ([110]). "*Charity and Science.*"

Cities infected with pestilence are usually placed in a state of siege. Dr. Corrigan, of Dublin, in his humane pamphlet, *Fever and Famine as Cause and Effect*, has given a sketch of the town of Tullamore, so blockaded by these invisible and almost irresistible enemies, in the year of our Lord 1818; from that passage these stanzas took their rise.

Page 344, ([111]).　" And ye who shelter'd Harold and Bruce."

Harold, the last of the Saxons, and Robert Bruce, both found refuge in
Ireland from defeat, and returned from it to victory.

Page 352, ([112]).　" *The Battle of Ayachucho.*"

This battle, fought the 8th of December, 1825, was the Yorktown of
South America.　The Spanish Viceroy and his entire force surrendered
themselves as prisoners of war to the Patriots under General Sucre.　Col.
O'Connor, mentioned in the poem, was chief of the Patriot staff.

Page 355, ([113]).　" *The Haunted Castle.*"

Donegal Castle, the chief seat of the princely family of the O'Donnells,
stands now in ruins, in the centre of the village of the same name, at the
head of Donegal Bay.　It was built in the fifteenth century, and shows,
even in its decay, royal proportions.　The present owner, Lord Arran, to
his credit be it told, has it well walled and cared for.　The remains of the
abbey, where the Four Masters completed their *Annals*, are within sight of
the castle.

Page 357, ([114]).　" *The Abbey by Lough Key.*"

A famous monastery of Premonstratensians, the Order of St. Norbert,
founded on Lough Key by Clarus McMailen O'Mulconry, A.D. 1215, figures
frequently in our annals.　There are notices of Clarus in the *Four Masters*,
at the years 1235, 1237, 1240, and 1247, which give us interesting glimpses
of the power and benevolence of this Irish representative of the great Archbishop of Magdeburg.

Page 368, ([115]).　" *Hannibal's Vision of the Gods of Carthage.*"

" In his sleep, as he told Silenus, he fancied that the supreme God of
his fathers had called him into the presence of all the gods of Carthage,
who were sitting on their thrones in council.　There he received a solemn
charge to invade Italy."—Arnold's *Rome*, chap. xliii.

Page 381, ([116]).　" *The Virgin Mary's Knight.*"

In the Middle Ages, there were Orders of Knights specially devoted to
our Blessed Lady, as well as many illustrious individuals of knightly rank
and renown.　Thus the Order called "Servites," in France, was known as
L'Esclaves de Marie, and there was also the Order of "Our Lady of Mercy,"
for the redemption of captives; the "Templars," too, before their fall,
were devoutly attached to the service of our Blessed Lady.

Page 385, ([117]).　" *Sebastian Cabot to his Lady.*"

To the reader, whose idea of Sebastian Cabot is associated with the usual
pictures of him, taken when he was nearly four-score, it may be necessary

to remark, that he received his first commission from King Henry VII.,
jointly with his father, John Cabot, and discoved the Labrador coast in his
twenty-first year (A.D. 1497).   The ardent passion attributed to him in the
ballad, would not be inconsistent with his age, in either his first or second
expeditions.

Page 389, (¹¹⁸).   "Of how they brought their sick and maim'd for him to
                   breathe upon,
             And of the wonders wrought for them through the Gos-
                   pel of St. John."

So great was the veneration for the white men, that the chief of the
. town (Hochelaga, now Montreal), and many of the maimed, sick, and
infirm, came to Jacques Cartier, entreating him, by expressive signs, to
cure their ills.   The pious Frenchman disclaimed any supernatural power,
but he read aloud part of the Gospel of St. John, made the sign of the
Cross over the sufferers, and presented them with chaplets and holy symbols ; he then prayed earnestly that the poor savages might be freed from
the night of ignorance and infidelity.   The Indians regarded these acts
and words with deep gratitude and respectful admiration.—Warburton's
Canada, Vol. I., p. 66.

Page 391, (¹¹⁹).   "*Verses in Honor of Margaret Bourgeoys.*"

The saintly foundress of the great Canadian order, "The Congregation
of Our Lady," established by her in the little village of Hochelaga, the
site of the present city of Montreal, toward the middle of the seventeenth
century.   These verses were written for a convent-fête. at Villa Maria, the
principal house of the Order, near Montreal.   They were recited, on that
occasion, by the daughter of Mr. McGee, then a pupil of the house.

Page 393, (¹²⁰).   "*Our Ladye of the Snow.*"

The original church of Notre Dame des Neiges stood upon what is now
the "Priests' Farm," on the southern slope of the Mountain of Montreal.
It was originally surrounded by the habitations of the converted Indians
and their instructors, of the "Mountain Mission."   The wall of defence
and two towers still remain, in good preservation, fronting on Sherbrooke
Street, Montreal.   The present chapel of the same name stands iu the village of Cote des Neiges, behind the Mountain.

Page 399, (¹²¹).   "Such fate as Heindrich Hudson found, in the labyrinths
                   of snow."

The incilent on which this ballad is founded is related in Bancroft's
History of the Colonization of America. Vol. II.   The name of the faithful
sailor, who preferred certain death to abandoning his captain in his last
extremity. was Philip Staafe- -a Hollander, no doubt.

Page 404, (¹²²).   " The frame of that first vessel grew."

The launch of the first sailed vessel that ever navigated the great lakes,
an event in itself so well worthy of commemoration, is made still more
noteworthy by the circumstances which surrounded it, and of which we
have, fortunately, more than one account from the pens of eye-witnesses.
The accuracy of Hennepin's Journal (*Description de la Louisiane*) has been
disputed in detail, and its pretensions and egotisms severely censured by
several recent writers on those times ; but I believe the very full details he
supplies of the beginning of the Sieur de la Salle's expedition, and the
building of the " Griffin" (at Cayuga Creek, a few miles above Niagara
Falls, on what is now " the American side"), have not been questioned.

Page 405, (¹²³).   " Stands the adventurous *Recollet*
                            Whose page records that anxious day."
Father Hennepin.

Page 406, (¹²⁴).   " Within the precinct of his god."

The Manitoulin Isles, in Lake Huron, were supposed by the aborigines
to be the special abode of the great *Manitou*, and were feared and reverenced
accordingly.

Page 406, (¹²⁵).   " And may it be thy lot to trace
                            The footprints of the unknown race
                            'Graved on Superior's iron shore,
                            Which knows their very name no more."

" That this region was resorted to by a barbaric race, for the purpose of
procuring copper, long before it became known to the white man, is evident
from numerous memorials scattered throughout its entire extent.   Whether
these ancient miners belonged to the race who built the mounds found so
abundantly on the Upper Mississippi and its affluents, or were the progenitors of the Indians now inhabiting the country, is a matter of conjecture.
. . . The high antiquity of this rude mining is inferred from the fact that
the existing race of Indians have no tradition by what people, or at what
period, it was done.   The places, even, were unknown to the oldest of the
band, until pointed out by the white man."—Whitney and Foster's *Report
on the Mining Region of Lake Superior*, published by the United States Congress.

Page 417, (¹²⁶).   " On the mountain, still to heaven,
                            Like its hermit, I could pray."

St. Kevin's Bed is in the side of Lugduff Mountain, above the lake of
Glendalough, County Wicklow.

Page 420, (¹²⁷).   " Like gifts of the night-trapp'd fairy."

Of the fairy legends of Ireland, none is more common than that of the
leprachaun, who, caught by some belated mortal, reveals where gold or

Page 424, (128).   " If one who once was "reverend" may
For his own special favorites pray."

When the author escaped to America, in 1848, it was in the disguise of a priest. He was known on board ship as "Father John."

Page 433, (129).   "*In Memoriam*—BISHOP REILLY."

This eminent prelate, it will be remembered, perished in the ill-fated steamer "Pacific."

Page 458, (130).   "And in his wand the power to save."

For the faculties and privileges of our ancient Order of Ollamhs, see Dr. O'Curry's *Lectures on the MS. Materials of Ancient Irish History*, page 2.

Page 460, (131).   "In vision, to the rapt Culdee."

Angus the Culdee.   The cause of writing his *Festalogium* is thus stated in. O'Curry's words: One time that Angus went to the church of Cull Benn-chair he saw, he says, a grave there, and angels from heaven constantly descending and ascending to and from it. Angus asked the priest of the church who the person was that was buried in this grave; the priest answered that it was a poor old man who formerly lived at the place. " What good did he do?" said Angus. "I saw no particular good by him," said the priest, " but that his customary practice was to recount and invoke the saints of the world, as far as he could remember them, at his going to bed and getting up, in accordance with the custom of the old devotees."   "Ah, my God!" said Angus, "he who would make a poetical composition in praise of the Saints should doubtless have a high reward, when so much has been vouchsafed to the efforts of this old devotee." And then Angus commenced his poem on the spot.

Page 460, (132).   "And Marian of the Apostle's hill."

Marianus O'Gorman, Abbot of Cnoc-na-n-Aspel ("the Apostle's hill"), in Oriel, the present County of Louth.   He composed his Martyrology to supply certain omissions of Angus the Culdee, but "in the first place to gain heaven for himself and every one who should sing it."—O'Curry's *Lectures*, page 261.

Page 460, (133).   "And Tiernan of the Danish days."

Tiernan O'Branin, Abbot of Clonmacnoise (*obit* A. D. 1088), author of our earliest remaining chronology.

Page 477, (134).   "*The Mountain-Laurel.*"

Rhododendron Maximus—the mountain-laurel; a deadly poison has been distilled from the beautiful blossoms of this tree of fame.

Page 513, (¹³⁵). "*Thomas Moore at St. Ann's.*"

At St. Ann's, near the junction of the upper branch of the Ottawa with the St. Lawrence, they show a particular spot as the place where Moore composed his well-known "Canadian Boat-Song." As the poet himself is silent on the subject in the note with which he accompanied the song, in his *Poems relating to America*, we may give St. Ann's the benefit of the doubt. It may not be amiss to remark that to this flying visit of Moore's, which occupied him only from the 22d of July, 1804, when he reached Chippewa, till the 10th of October, when he sailed from Halifax for England, we are indebted not only for the "Boat-Song," but the "Woodpecker," and the ballad "Written on passing Dead-man's Island," poems which must certainly be included in any future Canadian Anthology.

Page 516, (¹³⁶). "*The Old Soldier and the Student.*"

In a recent visit to the Irish College at Paris, a printed account of the College was given to the writer, in which it was stated that many of the theological students, in olden times, forsook the breviary and the cassock for the shako and the sword. The statement suggested these lines.

Page 520, (¹³⁷). "*Tasso's Tomb, at Rome.*"

Tasso's Tomb is in one of the chapels of San Onofrio, on the Janiculum, where there is a modern monument by Falerio. The writing-desk, crucifix, inkstand, and some autographs of the poet, are in the adjoining convent, where he died (A. D. 1595); and the tree called Tasso's Oak is shown in the garden.

Page 523, (¹³⁸). "*The Sea Captain.*"

The legend under this title is a favorite among sailors. I heard it related, many years ago, with the greatest gravity, by an "Old Salt," who laid the scene of the ghostly abduction in the Gulf of St. Lawrence.

Page 529, (¹³⁹). "*The Lady Mo-Bride.*"

Mo, or my, an expression of endearment prefixed to the names of saints, to children, and dear friends. Bride is a popular form of Bridget.

Page 543, (¹⁴⁰). "Mo-Brendan! Saint of Sailors, list to me."

Mo-Brendan, that is, "my Brendan," a term by which the ancient Irish usually addressed their patron saints.

Page 544, (¹⁴¹). "'Mid the far Scotic Islands, the shrines of St. Bride."

The Western Islands—Hy-Brides—are said to have been called for her.— See Mrs. Ferguson's *Ireland before the Conquest*, p. 165.

Page 569, (¹⁴²). "Our Lady of Pity, whose image you see."

The "First Communion" took place in the convent chapel of our Lady of Pity, Montreal.

www.ingramcontent.com/pod-product-compliance
Lightning Source LLC
Chambersburg PA
CBHW021932110726
47901CB00003B/808